Sunset on Golden Wings

Barbara Spencer

Copyright © 2021 Barbara Spencer

The moral right of the author has been asserted.

Apart from any fair dealing for the purposes of research or private study, or criticism or review, as permitted under the Copyright, Designs and Patents Act 1988, this publication may only be reproduced, stored or transmitted, in any form or by any means, with the prior permission in writing of the publishers, or in the case of reprographic reproduction in accordance with the terms of licences issued by the Copyright Licensing Agency. Enquiries concerning reproduction outside those terms should be sent to the publishers.

This is a work of fiction. Names, characters, businesses, places, events and incidents are either the products of the author's imagination or used in a fictitious manner. Any resemblance to actual persons, living or dead, or actual events is purely coincidental.

Matador
9 Priory Business Park,
Wistow Road, Kibworth Beauchamp,
Leicestershire. LE8 0RX
Tel: 0116 279 2299
Email: books@troubador.co.uk
Web: www.troubador.co.uk/matador
Twitter: @matadorbooks

ISBN 9781800464032

British Library Cataloguing in Publication Data.
A catalogue record for this book is available from the British Library.

Cover design by Katie Beltrami

Typeset in 12pt Adobe Garamond Pro by Troubador Publishing Ltd, Leicester, UK

Matador is an imprint of Troubador Publishing Ltd

BOOKS BY BARBARA SPENCER

The Year the Swans Came
Children of Zeus:
    Book 1 – The Click of a Pebble
    Book 2 – An Ocean of White Wings
    Book 3 – The Drumming of Heels
Age and the Antique Sideboard
Broken
Deadly Pursuit:
    Book 1 – Running
    Book 2 – Turning Point
Time Breaking
Kidnap

For Children

The Amazing Brain of O C Longbotham
Legend of the Five Javean
The Jack Burnside Adventures:
    Book 1 – A Dangerous Game
    Book 2 – The Bird Children
    Book 3 – The Lions of Trafalgar
Scruffy
A Fishy Tail
A Serious Case of Chicken-itis

"In the old city, there have always been rumours about the swan people, exactly as there were about black cats and coins dropped in the gutter.' The man laughed, dismissing the comment as being of no importance. 'Over time, most rumours die and others take their place. Yet the one about the swans never dies… not for long, anyway.' His expression changed, gravity assuming control once more. 'There's a large fishing community north of the river. They've lived there for centuries and they keep the rumour alive, frightening their children into behaving with stories that the swan people will steal them from their beds at night. I have no children to scare and so it was not something I bothered with. Not until the night I found Jorge, collapsed on the side of the road. His one arm was fine, the other, the one shattered by a bullet, remained covered in feathers.'

"*The Drumming of Heels.*"

STORY SO FAR

The summer is over as are the hopes and dreams of the actors in the tragedy, Maidy has written about. Of the four children who once stormed up and down the staircases of the Bader house playing their games, only Berthe remains untouched by events.

Pieter, on being jilted by Ruth has left with the swans – his dreams of continuing the family tradition, of creating beautiful mirrors for royalty, over. Hans jealous of Pieter and also in love with Ruth, has gone to Strasbourg to complete his apprenticeship with a company designing stained-glass windows – and Ruth – the beautiful Ruth – has buried events of that night on Klüsta Island deep in the locked box of her mind; the knowledge that her waywardness and relentless pursuit of Zande has destroyed Pieter's one chance to marry and return to a normal life… forgotten.

And the swans – only in the dark of night can Maidy reveal that truth, even to herself, that Zande, Jaan, Tristan and Waldger, students at the college she and Ruth attend, possess the same malign gene as Pieter, one that can change them from human to bird. It is Jaan who reveals to Maidy there may be a way to change back and it is to Jaan that Maidy turns, when all about her descends into darkness. For that chance has already been denied to Zande, the most charismatic and yet the most troubled of the four youths.

Boasting he can have any girl he wants, even while

pursuing other girls, he seeks Maidy's friendship. Seemingly dependent on her good opinion and finding solace in her company; it is not until the final scene, when Zande repudiates Ruth for her betrayal of Pieter that Maidy understands the connection between them; he was the black swan she once rescued from schoolboys who were tormenting it.

Sunset on Golden Wings

Sometimes in the hush of night I imagine a filament of silk connecting me to the heavens. I give it a gentle tug to remind the god in whose care I have been placed that I am still here and as yet my story has no end.

1

Far below me, the ocean danced to a rhythm it knew well. My encyclopaedia promised flying fish, dolphins, and whales that jet great columns of water into the air, while my lingering dreams of childhood yearned for a glimpse of pirates in black-painted ships, with tall masts and salt-caked sails, wet with spray from the vigorous pounding of the waves. With their sails trimmed and taut, their guns primed and ready, they would have easily overhauled any ponderous merchantman that lacked both the skill and the firepower to outrun them. Yet, so far, in this rolling, pounding maelstrom of grey water, I had seen nothing apart from a floating piece of driftwood.

Aware the deck of the liner was likely to be busy during the day, that morning, seeking relief from the snoring of my companion, I had dressed and left the cabin as dawn broke, wanting to experience my life-long ambition of running away to sea. Over the years, sailors who knew what it was like to stare death in the face had become a familiar sight on the quayside near our home, and I had long envied the ease with which they manhandled a yacht's canvas wings into place, their feet striding agilely across the deck, their thoughts, as were their movements, equally unconfined. As a child, I had yearned to take their place.

Content with their role in the world's hierarchy, they remain uninvolved in the minutiae of daily life, their gaze seeking nothing apart from a fresh horizon.

Now I had been given that opportunity, what would I make of it...?

From the moment the wedding invitation arrived in the post, my decision to travel to America had undergone more than one sea-change. Each morning in the previous months, when I awoke, I flew to the window of my bedroom vowing this to be the day when I confronted the world head-on and threw away my dreams. Yet, by nightfall, those same reminiscences dragged me down again. It was Pappy who, although unaware of the full import of that summer three years ago, had witnessed first-hand the suffering it brought, and on learning of Ruth's invitation, refused to let me back out.

'Maidy, I realise how unsure you are to leave the nest. Please remember, even the most reluctant of fledglings must eventually take to the air and assume their rightful place in the skies.' He patted my arm. Perhaps in his mind, I had grown too old for hugs and kisses. 'America is not exactly the place I would have chosen for your maiden flight, nevertheless, by all accounts they are a most generous people. Although somewhat noisy and assertive, if the newspapers are to be believed. Which, for you anyway, my child, may prove beneficial. If you stay the full month, which Meneer Endelbaum's letter suggests, hopefully some of that assertiveness will rub off on you.'

As always, I replied in kind, schooling my voice into playfulness.

'Pappy, if I adopt American habits, you won't like me anymore because when you want a cup of tea, no doubt I'll tell you to get it yourself.'

'And a good thing too.' He nodded, grateful for my effort, and patted his paunch. 'It may help others to notice you. With Berthe safely married, you deserve to be noticed.'

Despite the sadness that has overtaken our lives, Pappy hasn't lost his habit of presenting both rebukes and homilies in a jocular fashion although, at first, when Pieter once again vanished, even he forgot how to smile – the lines of love and laughter that, as a tiny child, I had traced with my finger, hardening into severity.

During those endless months, it was Berthe who helped us survive. Absorbed in the details of her forthcoming wedding, she remained unaware of the currents of anger and despair washing through the building. When she was about, Mother's pride came to the rescue, hiding her air of tragedy behind a smoke screen of platitudes, about the number of guests attending and the choice of food for the wedding feast. And with Pappy, Berthe endlessly discussed where she and Yoav were to live after they were married. Not even Pieter's abrupt disappearance managed to disturb her equanimity.

'He's done it before. He might have stayed on for my wedding though; now Yoav will need to choose another best man.'

And Mother? She cooked, the maids cleaned, and if she was forced by the presence of others in the room to speak to me, she did so. It was my fault, no one else's, that Pieter had left. *Ruth said*, were the words she used to whip me with. 'You kept on and on that she was making a mistake.'

Even when Pappy insisted that Pieter was a grown man, old enough to make his own choices in life, it failed to move her.

And why would it?

Only she and I knew the brutal truth, the version she told to Pappy no doubt carefully sanitised. And to neither did I reveal the events of that night on the beachhead of Klüsta Island, silenced by a sense of loss that ripped me in two.

Had Hans returned it may have been easier, although had he picked up on the currents of disquiet circling the house, he would have labelled them as none of his business. He did visit for Berthe's wedding, when he maintained to any who would listen that he had no time for wood, at least not until the fire consuming him had burned itself out.

'I did what you wanted, Pappy. I completed my apprenticeship and you'll have no trouble finding someone new. There must be loads of boys who will actually enjoy learning how to cut glass.'

And Pappy had found a new apprentice, a nephew of Lars, our foreman. Yet it was not until the spring, more than eighteen months later and when I'd almost given up hope, that I heard him call out, 'Enri, that's a fine piece of work.' On my way out of the door to go to college, I had dropped my books and raced downstairs to the atelier to see his smile beam out, conscious that once again he recognised me as a person, not simply one of those disembodied entities that floated around the house.

To be fair to Pappy, no one knew the whole of Ruth's story, not even Ruth herself. She had carefully buried events of that night, together with her pain and bewilderment, deep in some dark corner where they might never be found. Now, I doubted she would even bother to take a duster to them, her name on the lips of every starstruck schoolgirl. And, if news reports were to be believed, on the lips of men and boys, both married and single too.

And me? As compliant as ever, here I was embarking on a voyage that would end in celebration and a promise to love, honour, and obey.

Pappy went with me on the boat train, the steam engine puffing through towns and villages to the northern city, where great liners destined for the Atlantic docked. Bombed in the war and rebuilt, a patina of both newness and efficiency surrounded the dockside buildings, its officials pleasant and matter-of-fact, which helped quash the butterflies roaming around my middle. Last time I visited a railway station, it had been Pappy and Hans who were travelling away from our tiny country and we had all gone to see them off: Pieter and Ruth, Mother, even Lars and Henrik, Pappy's loyal workmen. It had been a festive occasion, our goodbyes ringing the air long after the carriage doors were shut.

Had Pappy and Hans not taken that train, would the juggernaut carrying our hopes have changed track, and rolled into a siding to await a different resolution? Perhaps Pappy's presence may have been sufficient to make Ruth pause her headlong flight and avert the sham of her engagement to Pieter. How many times had I wished for that to have happened, yet next moment found myself reneging on the idea, replacing it with a heartfelt desire for my brother Pieter never to have returned, at least not that summer, the summer of my sixteenth birthday. Yet, if he had never found his way back to our tiny enclave in the north of the city, neither would Zande, and that was something I refused to regret, despite the tragedy of its outcome – an outcome so strange and bizarre I often wonder if I dreamed it.

As that summer continued, first into autumn and then winter and spring, I tried not to retrace my footsteps, with their inevitable postscript ... what if? At first the recollections had brought solace. To be able to say, this time last week or last month or three months ago, I was talking with Jaan in the college library or I was sitting by the lakeside and Zande was with me. Ultimately, the wishful feelings that gave gloss to these happenings fell away and I was left with their stark outline, that the four college students, Waldger, Tristan, Zande and Jaan – Pieter too – were cursed by some malign force. But what or where? How can you learn about something no one has ever heard of or, if they have, refuse to speak about? In the months preceding Ruth's departure for America, she never once referred to that night we rowed across to Klüsta Island and Zande had snubbed her.

Now, Pappy and I were hemmed in by a wall of noise, with goodbyes being lobbed up the gangplank to where stewards were attempting to check tickets, and porters bowed low under the weight of a trunk they were carrying on their shoulders.

I listened intently to his farewell words. In all my nineteen years, apart from his brief sojourn in Strasbourg with Hans, Pappy had been there, as solid and unmoving as our house on the river.

'Promise me, Maidy, your first morning aboard, you will get up before dawn and go up on deck.' I nodded even before his homily was over. 'Then gather all your memories into a bag and drop them over the side.'

'Over the side!' I protested. 'That's too severe a punishment for the best among them.'

'Maidy, in a new country and with new people around you, you will soon create new ones. Especially,' he added with a twinkle, 'if you learn to smile again. Then people will flock to your side. Nevertheless,' his face changed, dithering between pride and sadness, 'becoming a film star is out of the question, however much the Americans love your smile. One in the family is quite enough.'

He meant Ruth of course. Except she wasn't family, was she? She might have been once had she not broken her promise to marry my brother.

With Pappy's words still ringing in my ears, I followed the line of passengers, those already aboard hanging over the rail to shout last-minute instructions. Hearing the excited tones, I wondered if they had packed all their unused confrontations into trunks with faulty catches, and, on reaching the quayside, these had spilled open releasing all their arguments into the air.

The tension was palpable. The liner obviously felt it too, noisily bellowing a sonorous warning of its imminent departure. A moment later, the gangway fell away and all the last-minute instructions were forgotten in the thrill of setting out.

He was right, and after an almost sleepless night, remembering friends both present and past, that's what I had got up early to do – say goodbye to my memories. Only I'd forgotten to wrap them tightly and some, the most precious, stuck to my fingers like sticky toffee, refusing to let go no matter how hard I tried to shake them off.

'Would a handkerchief help? I always carry a spare.' Fumbling helplessly in my pocket, I swung round registering the friendly warmth in the voice, although the tall shape standing next to me remained a blur, my eyes full of tears.

'That is kind.' I gulped.

'I am told tears are a mandatory part of your first voyage,' the man added diplomatically, gazing steadfastly out over the rail and ignoring my attempts to hiccup my tears away.

'You aren't crying.' I dredged up a smile, hurriedly searching for an explanation suitably convincing, yet trivial enough not to warrant further enquiry.

'This isn't my first voyage. The ocean and I are old friends.'

'Aren't you lucky.' Recalling Pappy's advice about becoming bolder, I added hesitantly, 'I've always wanted to be a pirate. I'm a writer. At least, I'm hoping to be one day,' I hastily retracted my boast.

He laughed. 'And you are trying your stories out on the ocean for size.'

I was, though in a very different manner from the one he envisaged. The stories I was replaying for the umpteenth time were those for which I had found no ending, at least not the one I hoped for, in which my hero and heroine drifted off into a sunset of happy ever-afters.

I'd not noticed the man when we came aboard yesterday afternoon, although in the hullabaloo of departure, with the train emitting noisy blasts of black steam, and a Tannoy booming instructions to departing passengers, that didn't surprise me. Among the hundreds who were boarding, it had been a lottery of movement, its winners pursuing but a single agenda: to find their cabin and settle in for the five-day voyage across the Atlantic. Within that commotion, the man would have been just another tall, well-suited figure. Although the face smiling down at me was one that demanded attention; his eyes blue-grey in colour. They reminded me of the ocean itself, when smiled upon by both sunshine and cloud, and there was a quirk in the heavy eyebrows that almost spoke aloud their curiosity as to why I should be suffering from heartbreak this early in the day.

He wasn't young, at least not in years. If asked to guess, I would have said perhaps older than thirty, yet his smile remained boyish, despite lines of pain on his face that had left permanent shadows.

'I remember thinking the ocean a cranky old parent who suffered from dyspepsia because you never knew its mood from one day to the next. It was also exceedingly selfish and far too high and mighty ever to be interested in anything, apart from its search for a permanent remedy for chronic indigestion.'

I smiled away my tears as he had intended I should. 'That's a lovely idea. And I suppose when all is peaceful, that is because the ocean has found a new restorative?'

'Of course. Is this trip about you following a similar dream?'

As if mesmerised, he returned his gaze to the water. I did too, its movement truly awesome. Poised as we were high-up in the bow, we might easily have been players in a child's fairy tale, carried on the back of a gigantic serpent that could cross the world from end to end with a flick of its tail.

'To be a writer – no. I've been invited to a wedding. And you?'

'I'm going to listen to music.'

'Music?'

I can only presume my tone was one of astonishment because he laughed, the sound as uninhibited as a teenager who smiles more often than he frowns and thinks the whole world a joke. I blushed. 'I didn't mean … I've never really listened to music, not what you'd call real music. At home, our radio was in the sitting room, and I rarely went in there. I preferred my bedroom two flights up.'

'Ah, so it's you who needs educating. If you will permit me…' He gave a tiny bow, and I noticed his left arm hanging crookedly, 'to know your name.'

'Magrit Bader.'

'Bader?'

His expression changed; I could see the name had awakened memories both dark and painful and I hastened to reassure him. 'It's very common in Holland.'

'Yes, indeed.'

'And you, Meneer?'

'I never quite know how to reply to that question.'

Again, I must have shown surprise because once more his smile emerged. 'Most days I am unable to decide what I am … Spanish, French, or Dutch. As for the who? My identity card says Ricardo de L'île de Saint Pierre; my new passport, Yöst Saint Pierre.' He patted his top pocket. 'In any case, everyone just calls me Yöst.'

'How did that happen?'

'My name?' He shifted against the rail, flexing his left hand to ease it. 'You are too young to remember the war. Then, the possession of papers, any papers, could save your life.' He fell silent and I could almost see his mind tracking back over the past. 'The fishermen who saved mine were Spanish. They didn't speak any other language, so they grabbed hold of any words they did understand. The island of Saint Pierre lies in the Bay of Biscay off the south-western tip of France.'

'You lived there?'

He seemed quite content to talk, his body propped up against the rail, his attention drawn to the bow, the ship's pathway through the ocean hurling sparkling water-jewels into the air. Once or twice I saw him flinch with pain, the fingers on his right hand automatically reaching up to massage his arm.

'Not now. I did – once. No, twice. Now I live way out in the country, in a vineyard.' He smiled at the memory of his home. 'Much more pleasant than the sea or a wind-swept island, especially when I'm not expected to pick the grapes. I came north to visit my sister.' He jerked his head towards the now invisible coastline behind us. 'She grows flowers for the city markets.' He paused. 'The Bader I knew was called Pieter. He lived on the northern fringes of Amsterdam.'

I heard stirrings on the deck behind us, footsteps and people greeting one another and, with a heavy heart, the strident tones of my companion calling me to heel, 'Magrit,' and I knew my freedom was about to be curtailed.

Remembering Pappy's homily, I didn't turn, at least not quickly, reasoning that a college graduate was too old to be treated like some wayward schoolgirl.

Mevrouw Visser hadn't exposed this particular trait of character on first meeting up with Pappy, wanting and, in all fairness, needing the work. Nevertheless, a mere half-day's acquaintance had filled me with dread for the forthcoming journey, and a night of her snoring, with annoyance. Not for the first-time, I wished Mevrouw Kleissler, who had worked in our shop for the past twenty years and suggested her spinster sister as a suitable chaperone, didn't take such a personal interest in the goings-on of her employer's family.

'She was trying to be helpful.' Pappy gently rebuked when I complained about the non-stop monologue that had accompanied our short train journey, confiding if the voyage across the Atlantic took longer than the scheduled five days, I couldn't guarantee my still being on board. 'And she will keep you safe, that's all I want.'

'You'd never think she was Mevrouw Kleissler's sister, they're so very different.'

'They both talk,' he teased.

That was true yet even their manner of talking was not the same. Mevrouw Kleissler was always cheerful, despite the grief she still carried for her husband killed in the war. Her sister was the opposite. She had never married and never lost anyone, yet she still complained about everything. I had gone to bed early the previous night to escape her nagging; the words, in my day, applied to every subject touched on at dinner that first evening, as if they were a grammatical necessity.

Seeing her now, I allowed myself to hope the excitement of actually heading across one of the world's greatest oceans might bring about a change of heart – although judging by her stern expression, I feared it wouldn't.

'Keep the handkerchief,' Yöst said as I dithered, unsure whether to give it back or not. 'We're bound to pass one another perambulating around the deck.'

'Magrit,' Mevrouw Visser lost no time in rebuking me. 'You should not be speaking to strange men, it's not seemly. And one so much older.' For an instant, I felt sympathy. My generation rarely if ever bothered about the war; it was gone, vanished into a past in which we had played no part, yet for women who had lost their chance of marrying, it must have been the origin of all evils both real and imaginary. Then she added, 'In my day, we would have been sent to our room ... without supper,' and I meanly decided most probably she would have remained a spinster, war or no war.

Maybe it was also childish to expect this voyage to be a magic carpet ride, yet as I set foot on the gangway and felt it swaying, impatient to cast off its canvas railings, momentarily, I felt the same sense of burgeoning excitement that the sight of a tall-masted schooner sweeping past my bedroom window once triggered. In the next weeks, anything was possible including that fictional pot of gold at the base of a rainbow.

It didn't survive. On exploring my new home, I discovered it to be little more than a floating steel crate into which tiers and tiers of tiny boxes had been fitted; its many corridors, which the crew called a companion way, mirroring one another so closely, they were given numbers and letters to prevent passengers getting lost. Only the public rooms defied this military style presentation and, even then, the young people Pappy had predicted didn't materialise, apart from a couple of schoolboys with their parents, and it was middle-aged couples who took to the tiny circular dance-floor that evening.

By midnight, the ocean had made its presence felt, washing over the decks, growling and grumbling. It didn't particularly trouble me. According to the cabin staff who attended Mevrouw Visser's first bout of sea-sickness, it was quite normal for the North Sea to become boisterous. 'It'll have blown itself out by morning.'

He was wrong. If anything, it was worse, and the following two days the skies joined in the conspiracy, spreading a blanket of dense cloud over an equally hostile expanse of water. With Mevrouw Visser clinging to her berth, I had very little time to myself and, whenever she dozed, I joined other hardy souls lapping the deck. It was a pantomime of attitudes, and a ludicrous one at that, yet the greatest of fun watching the wind snatch at hats and scarves, a sudden blast forcing the unwary into a run or scuttling them into reverse and preventing them from making way.

With the seas still raging, on neither night was the dining room full, although by the third the noise level had grown substantially, with outbursts of cheerful banter vying with an orchestra playing a medley of popular dance tunes. In between courses, perhaps emboldened by a greater familiarity with their surroundings, more couples took to the floor. As they twirled and skipped, their dresses became a glittering sideshow of changing styles and colour. I'd not spoken with any of the women apart from a fleeting good morning to those I encountered on deck; it was their frocks I recognised, the majority wearing the identical outfit the night before.

Berthe had overseen my wardrobe, insisting, when Pappy demurred, I would need a different dress for each night.

'People always wear their best clothes on holiday, especially on-board ship.' She waved a catalogue under his nose. 'And it doesn't end there. Maidy will need something special for the wedding as well.'

Pappy had laughed, comically pulling out his pocket linings.

I remembered Hans doing that.

'And what will we do, Berthe, when my pockets are empty?' She had frowned.

Dear Berthe, motherhood has changed her.

But then none of us are the same.

I was so lucky. For many of those now twirling light-heartedly, to pay for a ticket to the promised land every penny would have been squirrelled away. Little different from the original pilgrims. Only the mode of transport had changed, a rickety old sailing vessel replaced with the comforts of an ocean-going liner.

My mind, as always restless, sped on and I asked myself what price I might have been willing to pay for a chance of a new life? To be free of the guilt and dark thoughts I carried around with me? Maybe then, for me too, the possession of a single dress would have felt like riches.

I watched the dancing a while longer and then excusing myself, crept out onto the promenade deck, the roaring of the ocean almost soporific after the noisy dancehall. Although the wind had subsided slightly, the air was cold, and I debated going below to fetch a coat and my diary. Not yet ready to go to bed, I rejected the idea, aware Mevrouw Visser would insist I shouldn't leave again. Instead, I tucked myself up on a lounger. In the distance, music echoed softly, tugging my drifting thoughts back to the dance floor where couples, as the night drew on, spoke in whispers or not at all.

As for my diary, did it actually matter if I wrote in it today or tomorrow? I had hoped to write a paragraph about the dancing while my thoughts remained fresh, describing the sensuous touch of a woman's hand, her head resting closely on her partner's shoulder, her whisper reaching his ear alone. Again, tonight, I had sensed magic stirring; the previous night too. Wandering about in search of the library, I had caught a glimpse of a glittering ball gown and a pair of satin shoes, its wearer rustling between staircases. With their broad steps covered in deep-piled carpets and overhung with fancy gilt light-fittings, the passenger confused by the gaiety of the music momentarily seemed uncertain which way to go ... up or down.

I wasn't alone on deck; others obviously had the same idea, with dark shapes intermittently strolling past my chair. Mostly couples, perhaps continuing a conversation begun on the dance floor, their gaze and attention fastened on one another, rarely turning to look out into the empty blackness of the ocean.

The safest of all places. Not even seagulls ventured this far out, nothing apart from the lonely albatross. Since Pappy's advice had fallen by the wayside, I could see no harm in allowing Zande to tiptoe from the wings one final time; his presence so strong, for a moment I was convinced if I moved, I would see him standing there, smiling at me.

I thought of Jaan as well, aware, in the past three years, his friendship and solid strength would have proved a great support. He had written. First a postcard, explaining in the letter that followed the postcard had been a mistake. 'Postcards from exotic climes are delusory, and will remind you of what I have become rather than who I am.'

Zande's voice had butted in then, his tone mocking, adding: *one should always envy those who possess sufficient skill to make a need for money obsolete.*

I knew what he was referring to – their beautiful yet soul-destroying capability to change into a great white bird.

2

The following morning, from the moment dawn broke above the horizon, the ocean smiled, seducing onlookers with a glimpse of turquoise and a flash of silver from a leaping fish, embellishing its waves in a flotilla of lace-tipped frills. The rail quickly became crowded, the warm sunshine speeding to the aid of yesterday's victims who, quickly recovering, augmented the babel of noisy conversation with their own voice, determined to make up for lost time.

Unable to find a seat or a space by the rail, I followed the long lines of people walking off their breakfast, and greeted Yöst with pleasure when I saw him strolling towards me.

I had hoped to see him again. Mevrouw Visser's abrupt interruption had left me with the feeling I knew him – that he was someone I had once met. It both intrigued and irked, and I had already trawled painstakingly through my memory of staff and students at college and revisited Berthe's wedding, where many of the male guests had attended at the same accountancy college as Yoav. It was a mystery and with little else to interest me, I was keen to solve it.

Swinging round, he joined me, attracting the attention of two women walking behind, the younger smiling coquettishly.

I wasn't alone in my attention. Women slanted their gaze as they overtook, their feet momentarily hesitating in admiration of his height and sculptured profile, hurrying on when they noticed his deformed arm. I knew what that was, our neighbour, the tobacconist, explained it. 'I keep behind the counter as much as possible,' he told me, 'because people find deformity embarrassing and may well avoid my shop if they see I have a peg leg.'

'I was hoping to catch up with you.' He fitted his stride to mine. 'The last couple of days, you've set too ferocious a pace for me. In this weather, I struggle.'

I grimaced, recalling it was my uncharitable musings about Mevrouw Visser who, in deciding her seasickness warranted twenty-four-hour nursing, was responsible for my furious pace, although having grown up with older brothers I rarely dawdled. 'I'm glad you didn't, I was in a foul mood.'

He laughed. 'Let me guess. Your companion was seasick and blamed you.'

'How did you know?' While he'd been talking, I again examined his face, hoping to place that elusive resemblance, disappointed to find it quite gone – imagination, after all. Inside, I felt disappointment, although why I wasn't sure. Maybe it was nothing to do with a name or a face, perhaps disappointment that the magical voyage I was anticipating hadn't yet materialised.

'That first morning, before Mevrouw Visser interrupted, you were saying about once knowing someone called Bader, and I never got a chance to reply. I had an Uncle Pieter who was killed in the war. My family aren't city folk; we live in the old quarter by the river. Could it have been him?'

He swung round, his gaze intense almost devouring my face. 'What an extraordinary co-incidence. Of course, it's the same man – it has to be. If so, I once visited your house.' His eyes, already shining, sparkled with enthusiasm. 'It's on the south bank of the river, near the swing bridge. That's right, isn't it?' I nodded. 'I also met his father. Your grandfather?'

My voice came alive, matching his for excitement. 'In that

case, have we ever met? After we chatted that first day, I felt convinced we had and have been wracking my brains ever since.'

'Impossible. You…' He stopped, staring down at the deck, searching for something.

I waited.

'No.' He bellowed the words. 'I remember Pieter telling me his brother lived in the south.' His face gleamed with life, his eyebrows creating a triumphant banner across his forehead. 'I lost my memory for a while,' he explained, noticing my concern. 'It's still coming back. Recalling events from the past doesn't happen every day and I get excited when it does.'

I nodded, disappointed at not solving my mystery. 'I was too young to remember living anywhere else. My father joined Grandfather in the business after Uncle Pieter moved away.'

'And your grandfather? Is he still living?'

His excitement had stirred something in me and, all at once, I was happy to talk about my family. All of it … all the way back to that night. For three years, I had searched for something to make it all right. Perhaps this was it. My words rushed out, as eager as children on an outing. 'No. But he did live to see the end of the war.'

Yöst raised his eyebrows, asking the question.

'Pappy said that is what kept old people alive – their determination to see the city liberated.'

'Pappy?'

'My father, Gerard Bader, and the best father in the world.' I hesitated, hoping Yöst wouldn't consider me childish to gush about Pappy. Yet he was, he always had been. Even three years ago, no word of rebuke had ever crossed his lips. 'He was younger than my uncle. He also has two sons, my brothers, Pieter and Hans. I have a sister as well; she's older than me – Berthe.'

'Are they—'

'Going into the business?' I forestalled his question. Dare I talk about Pieter? After all, he wasn't dead. *Nevertheless, it will take a great deal of good fortune to bring him back*, the voice, a frequent intruder into my reflections, sounded out. 'I don't think so. Pieter still has a year of his apprenticeship to complete and, sadly, he no longer lives with us. My other brother, Hans, refused to join the business. Said he loathed mirrors, couldn't see any point in pandering to the vanity of women. He's an artist and is determined to paint.'

'Paint?'

'Pictures.'

Dear Hans, he had completed the final two years of apprenticeship in Strasbourg. 'Waste of time,' he said scowling at me. 'Of all mediums, stained-glass has to be the least interesting. In two years, I created nothing original – everything had to be replaced exactly how it was before the war, saints with vacant faces wearing open-toed sandals.' I remembered smiling at the analogy, his paintings full of life, the finished canvasses filled with great sweeping colour.

Walking side by side, I could only register Yöst's profile. I saw the frown and realised, once again, he was attempting to retrieve a memory. I waited.

'I remember your uncle saying that Meneer Bader had drawn a tree on the workroom wall. He said it represented the city. Is it still there?'

'It was whitewashed over,' I replied.

Mother had always stopped me going into the basement workshop, concerned I would set the place alight or create some life-threatening accident involving Pieter. Nevertheless, I did. Under the pretence of going up to my room, I'd sneak down the backstairs and hide under the table, watching Grandfather paint.

He always ignored the tree until the end of the day; concentrating on the completion of an order. Only after he'd tidied away the paint pots and the tools he used that day, did he stand in front of the tree, head back, and scan its branches. Sometimes, his lips would move and once I recognised words from the prayer we said in church on a Sunday, for those who had died in the conflict. Then, taking a pot of white paint, he would paint out a branch, overwriting it with a name. Sometimes, more than one branch. One time … it was so many branches, the letters making up the names had to be squeezed tightly together. Once or twice, the writing of a particular name made his hand tremble and he'd mop his eyes with a handkerchief. Then, Pappy would take over, finishing the lettering in his precise print.

Next time I hid under the table, I made a game of finding that new name, and memorising its spelling, asking Pieter how it was pronounced. And sometimes, I would add up all the new names since my last visit and write them in my journal with the date.

When Pappy was applying that coat of whitewash to the wall, he had asked Pieter to run to the nearest bookshop and buy me a book on spelling and arithmetic, and I realised all along he had known of my silent visits and said nothing.

At the time, I didn't think of the names as anything special other than a test of my reading skills, occupying long minutes spelling them out – too young to understand that each name represented a life lost, a real person, someone who had once lived in the city and perished there. Years later, when the basement walls were again in receipt of their biennial coating of whitewash, I mentioned it to Pappy and he explained that Grandfather believed, however many deaths the city suffered, and however many branches he deleted, there would always be more and the tree would not die. 'And if the tree didn't die, neither would the city. See.' Pappy had pointed to the grating that ran below the pavement, footsteps in the street outside resounding noisily as people walked across it. 'He was right. The city didn't die.'

'It was through watching Pappy and Grandfather that I learned about the end of the war,' I admitted to Yöst. 'No one said and there were still soldiers in the street.'

He regarded me curiously. 'How...?'

'It was the mirror surrounds. Usually, they were plain mahogany but one day Grandfather opened up the big encyclopaedia and began to draw a woodpecker tapping at the wood surround. I remember it was green, and so striking a colour it was almost iridescent. And the brown wasn't just brown, there was gold in it as well. And so life-like, I was convinced the bird would drill holes in the frame.' I smiled, embarrassed by my nonsensical confession. 'Soon after that, Pappy began decorating the edges of a mirror he was working on with nuts and pinecones.'

Yöst listened attentively to my story, seemingly content to pursue our walk together, although we had slowed to a mere dawdle, allowing those behind to overtake. To walk fast made sense when I was alone; now curiosity about my companion outstripped a desire for exercise. Besides, the usual excuses people fabricated when they sought a way to end a conversation – that they had an urgent appointment or would miss the bus – were irrelevant on-board ship. With the ocean superintending our every move, we weren't heading anywhere except for a different point in time.

Noticing a space at the ship's rail, Yöst pulled me to one side. 'Do you mind if we rest a while? Sometimes I find it difficult to walk and talk.' Seeing my concern, he smiled and shook his head. 'It's an excuse I use, when I wish to continue a conversation. Besides, I'm not alone. The war left behind a lot of damaged people.'

It wasn't an excuse; I'd heard the rasping breath.

'Did you ever live in the city?' I changed the subject.

'Yes, for a short while before the war. It was winter and the canals had frozen and my brother and I often skated to school. Later that year, we moved out to Herrendorp on the lakeside.'

All at once, I didn't want to pursue the subject any further. It was too close. Another moment and names I had hoped to forget might well strike the air. 'I have had your handkerchief laundered. Thank you.'

'And I,' he fished in his pocket, pulling out a white card, 'have for you an introduction to music. It's a crime to remain ignorant. I, too, lacked a proper introduction until I was gone twelve.' He flashed his eyebrows comically. It was done to make me laugh, to draw my thoughts away from people being injured and sick. How understanding he was of the world. Admittedly, there were people such as Mevrouw Visser who still took a ghoulish pleasure in the ills of others, but mostly my generation tried to find the best in people. 'This guy is performing at Carnegie Hall next week. If you present this card to the box office, there will be two tickets waiting.'

I read the name on the card: Ramon Martorell and written on the reverse, 2 seats, First Balcony Row A, and the initials YS-P, written in fountain pen.

Seeing the name meant nothing, he added, 'He's probably the most famous guitarist in the world.'

'And you know him?' I gasped, naïve enough to be overawed at the idea of being friendly with someone famous.

I had forgotten Ruth.

'Yes, he introduced me to music, and I have made it my life's work to introduce others.'

That night, with Mevrouw Visser well again, the early part of our evening was spent listening to her stripping the gloss off our fellow diners, commenting on the oddity of their clothing, their features or their choice of companion. I am not quite sure if she was doing it with the intention of making me feel uncomfortable. I hoped not. By any yardstick it was a charming scene and one I hoped to replicate in a novel someday, although the gulf between those on board for pleasure or business and those in search of a new life had become more pronounced. Women who had a choice were wearing their best frock augmented by a dazzling array of jewellery, purposefully tilting their faces to show off a pair of glittering earrings, and angling their ringed fingers around the stem of a wine glass to catch the light; while those who owned no best frock pressed the dress they had worn the previous night, brushing their hair into a different style and adding lipstick and a pair of cheap earrings.

Recognising the importance of the last night, conversation also made a special effort, both speech and laughter louder and more boisterous and, once again, I toyed with the idea of passengers spilling out their innermost secrets, conscious the law of probability was against their ever meeting up again. Certainly Mevrouw Visser believed that, resolutely ploughing through every dot and comma in her life-story and pouring it into her neighbour's ears. She was a woman of a similar age and I felt so sorry for her; also for her husband staring rigidly ahead, barred by his sex from participating in the conversation.

It was an exciting night and I was glad to have been a part of it, tucking away the experience in a drawer marked, to be revisited often. Less than half full, I was hoping my visit to America would supply memories enough to fill the drawer twice over. I had placed Yöst in there already; his kindness in drying my tears that first day earning him a place, although that sense of déjà vu was fast becoming an irritant. If enlightenment ever came, I hoped it wouldn't warrant a closing of the drawer against his entry.

Earlier, I had sought him out, preparing a little speech in advance, a card with Meneer Endelbaum's address printed on it in my bag, disappointed to find he wasn't in the dining room.

Despite having a two-berth cabin, there was little privacy and while Mevrouw Visser was getting ready for bed, I stole back up on deck. It wasn't dark, the skies a giant display case of starlight. Abruptly, the dance music stopped, the slap of water against the sides of the liner filling the silence. From afar, I caught an echo. Straining my eyes, I picked out the shape of a fin and then a dark body rose above the surface.

Next moment it was gone, leaving me to wonder if I had imagined it. The music started over, and a male singer began crooning the lines of a love song.

I listened to the melody, new to me. I was becoming used to that. Since shutting the front door behind me, most everything was new. It was one of those tunes that are easily remembered and difficult to forget, with a chorus of notes repeated over and over. Listening to the words, I was carried away by its lilting melody. That's what I wanted from life. To be one of those women I'd seen on the dance floor, her head cradled against her partner's shoulder, confident that my heart was in safe-keeping, and I was as loved and cherished as the words of the song promised.

That was the magical pot of gold I was seeking.

With a deep sigh almost of impatience, I tossed my memories overboard as I had promised Pappy I would do.

Land came into sight next day, its first intimation a solitary seagull, rather like a scout for an opposing army or perhaps a zealous customs officer ferreting out possible smugglers. Circling, it landed on the rail of the upper deck, coarsely rebuking passengers lingering nearby.

An announcement at breakfast that we were entering the estuary of the River Hudson sent everyone scurrying up on deck, wanting to be first to espy land. I had found a spot on the port side and was disappointed to discover no trace, apart from the changing colours of the water, the myriad greys of the ocean swept with brown stains that hinted at debris washed down river from the hinterland. And it was not until several hours later, on entering the river proper, that land, mimicking the mouth of some vast mythical beast, began to close in around us.

The effect on passengers was startling and a cheer rose up – albeit tinny and slightly embarrassed from those who, when darkness fell, might well have roared out their appreciation, yet remained too insecure in daylight to do so. For a few, prayer was substituted; those passengers gradually awakening to the realisation that their travels were finally at an end and, any minute now, they would gain the promised land. In the remainder, beaming smiles followed a burgeoning assumption that this land might also offer them a new beginning. It was a heady cocktail, resulting in over-loud conversations and constant laughter.

I felt the same, as if the throwing away of that particular parcel of woes over the ship's rail had left me free to partake of this new world. For once, the negatives, so often the companions of my thoughts, stayed away and I joined in the optimism swirling round the deck. I even managed to spare a thought for my companion, saddened that Mevrouw Visser was more concerned about continuing her journey to her cousin, than registering the uniqueness of this moment. It wouldn't happen again ... it couldn't. If any of us made the journey a second time, the frisson of excitement at encountering the unknown would be missing.

Nevertheless, as the recipient of the passengers' hopes and prayers began to reveal itself, Yöst's idea of the ocean's search for a remedy for indigestion was replaced by one I happily endorsed – that now the waves were hurrying towards a secret tryst with a lover.

As the river gradually narrowed, the welcoming forests of spruce and fir fell away, the north shore overtaken by chimneys that spewed dark smoke into the air, as if the Indian tribes I had read about still communicated their messages that way. Tall redbrick warehouses, the totem poles of industry took their place, and a sprawl of dockland ruled by cranes and gantries, a galaxy of roads and railways crisscrossing a hinterland made up of concrete and scrub.

I caught a whisper, *have we arrived*, hastily shushed as the liner steamed on ignoring the docks. Nevertheless, it was a bustling scene, with a half-dozen trading vessels, their thick ropes mooring them to the dockside, patiently awaiting the attention of the trucks that swarmed around like a posse of ants.

Used to the almost finicky neatness of our riverside, I was reminded of Pappy's homily, that thousands had travelled to America and apart from a few, all had survived the experience. 'Not all of it will be good, Maidy, although much will be both wonderful and unforgettable.'

A bend in the river brought a flotilla of small boats into view. They scurried back and forth between the two banks, a queue of people, as yet only tiny dots, waiting on shore for their turn to cross. Once fully breached, any preconceived ideas about the continent were tossed aside as heads which, until that moment had been tilted downwards exploring the river bank, were drawn up to the skyline where a family of giants, built of glass or steel and stone, were waiting to greet us.

I overheard the woman behind me use the French word, *des gratte-ciels* … skyscrapers.

Tall and narrow, they reminded me of a child's collection of bricks that is easily toppled. I was obviously not alone in thinking their structure might do the same, exclamations breaking out as to how it was possible for such tall structures to remain upright.

'Surely, they will break and fall into the river,' someone commented.

In five days, I had become so used to the ship's engines, I failed at first to notice the change in pitch when they were scaled back, fading away altogether as tugs took over and swung the floating colossus towards the dockside. Momentarily an awed silence swept across the deck, almost immediately replaced by excited chatter as passengers, impatient now to disembark, planned what to do first, with suggestions varying from the reading out loud of an address – followed by an anxious comment, 'we should ask someone how to get there,' – to a demand for a real American hamburger or a taxi ride. Equally excited, I scoured the waiting faces, hoping to spot Meneer Endelbaum who had promised to meet us.

With so many hundreds of passengers, it was afternoon before Mevrouw Visser and I were disembarked, and as I walked down the gangway I heard my name being called.

'Magrit?'

I recognised the intonation; only one person had ever pronounced my name that way.

Barely believing, I swung round, a happy smile already on my lips.

Yöst was still on deck waiting to disembark. Perhaps it was a trick of the light camouflaging the pain lines on his face, perhaps it was eagerness to set foot on dry land but all at once he looked much younger. He raised his arm in a salute, calling out, 'See you at the concert.'

I knew then who he reminded me of ... Zande.

3

Cautiously, with the land leaping and turning somersaults around me, I descended the gangway into a maelstrom of noise, its many different versions bouncing off the concrete flooring of the customs shed: its officers bellowing as if that made them easier to understand; porters trundling trolleys with iron-rimmed wheels that clanked discordantly, and those same porters being loudly cursed by others carrying cases and trunks on their back. Even passengers, who on board had appeared soft-voiced and orderly, pushed and shoved their way through the press of people, desperate to be elsewhere. Above that came the crackling of a loudspeaker, its announcements drowned out by taxi horns, a line of yellow vehicles drawn up against the kerb outside. Counting any delay in terms of coins in their hand, their drivers were loudly exhorting customs officials to hurry and place their chalk mark on a piece of luggage, so they could get moving.

'My dear child, how pleased I am to see you and Miss Visser.' Meneer Endelbaum, waving from the gate, beamed his words. 'You are most welcome.'

I must have responded although I'm not sure how, the sound registering though not its meaning.

Abruptly, the tumult in my head began to lessen and I laughed. 'You're speaking English.'

'Not English, no. American,' he corrected. 'And you must too. As brash and noisy as they are, Americans are the most open-hearted people on Earth, provided you speak their language.'

'Is it very different?'

He beamed at me, an expression I had rarely seen and never after the death of his wife. And changes went deeper than his smile. No longer did he walk with a cane, his gait almost limber. Even his complexion was clearer – the pallor that had clung to him throughout the illness and mourning the death of his wife vanished. Yet it was his clothes that presented the greatest alteration; gone was the sober navy, with its narrow white lines running up and down the cloth, and the black hat that he had worn both inside the house and out. Hatless, with his white hair smelling of pomade, he wore a caramel-coloured jacket over beige trousers, both made from different materials. His shirt also drew my attention; his usual wide starched collar replaced by one with narrow lapels that had tiny buttons on them. His shoes too had suffered a sea change; the mandatory black replaced by brown leather, sparkling with polish.

'A few words. Nothing dramatic.' He waved a hand at the line of yellow vehicles. 'A taxi is called a cab and the boot where I am about to place your suitcase is called the trunk.' He gave a little bow. 'And you, Miss Visser?'

'My knowledge of English is quite sufficient, thank you,' she responded. 'We learned it at school.'

I caught a glimpse of Yöst walking towards the taxis and waved. 'See you Friday?' he called.

'Who's that?' Meneer Endelbaum asked. 'Shipboard romance?'

Mevrouw Visser sniffed. 'I can assure you it was no such thing. Not while Magrit is in my care. Quite unsuitable, that man is far too old for such a young girl.'

'It's not that unusual, Miss Visser,' Meneer Endelbaum replied. I noticed the twinkle in his eye, although I don't think Mevrouw Visser did, ferreting in her handbag for a handkerchief.

'In every society, girls marry older men, especially if they are pretty like Maidy here and the men have money.'

'Mevrouw Visser,' I called out, hearing her sniff with distaste, immediately forgetting I should have addressed her as Miss Visser. 'Please don't worry, I promise I'm not seeking a husband.' I pulled the card out of my pocket, showing it to Meneer Endelbaum. 'His name is Yöst Saint Pierre, and he very kindly invited us to a concert. All very proper. It's at the Carnegie Hall, except I don't know where that is.'

'My dear child ... Carnegie Hall? Only the most famous concert hall in the city. How very exciting. Now come along,' Meneer Endelbaum fussed, his manner of speaking so familiar, a part of my childhood despite the change of language. 'My apartment is quite close, just a few minutes by cab.' He emphasised the last word, obviously wanting us both to remember the translation.

Scarcely knowing why, I swung round for a final glimpse of the water, overwhelmed by a sense of confinement, the steel and concrete shapes we had seen from the river almost within touching distance.

Meneer Endelbaum patted me on the shoulder. 'I did the same when I first landed ... glanced back. Not to worry, you'll soon get used to it. My apartment overlooks Central Park where there is a lake. Living here, you tend to forget we Dutch were born with one foot in a canal.'

Ignoring the milling pedestrians, the driver of our cab pulled out into the traffic. With the arrival of the liner and so many departing passengers, this was fierce, with horns and revving engines competing to be the loudest. Having spent the last five days inured in the silence of the ocean, it proved overwhelming. Resisting the urge to place my hands over my ears, I craned out of the window, taken aback by the shabbiness of the street we were driving through, its dark-stone housing dilapidated and lacking paint, the steps up to the front door chipped and dirty. Some school-age children were using them as a prop for their games, with boys playing marbles, while another group, like gamblers, had cigarette cards fanned out and held tightly against their chest.

At the intersection, where the cab swung left into a stream of traffic, I glanced back over my shoulder, reading the sign on the wall – West 49th Street.

It wasn't until the next day, watching the train pull out of the station with Mevrouw Visser on it, that I actually began to see through the confusion this new language had brought. Until that point, the only images to stay with me were those of a policeman, wearing white gloves on his hands to direct the traffic, and the doorman of the building where Meneer Endelbaum lived, who was dressed in a burgundy-coloured frockcoat. He held the door as we passed through and tipped his hat, his piercing whistle designed to bring a cab speeding to a halt at the roadside. I remember Meneer Endelbaum saying, 'And the lift is called an elevator,' as a gilded cage carried us up to the fourth floor. For the rest, what I saw mostly passed unnoticed, overwhelmed by the noise and bustle of the city in which vehicles controlled by traffic lights revved their engines, pushing forward almost before the walk sign had been extinguished, while pedestrians, waiting to cross that same road, sent their voices leapfrogging to the far side of the intersection, in anticipation of the lights changing.

Meneer Endelbaum had suggested a stroll in the park after dinner, where it was quiet, 'and you can catch your breath,' pointing to the buildings, the pride of ownership marking his voice. No different from the cab driver who, after learning we had travelled across the Atlantic, could scarcely wait to give us his opinion. 'Only the greatest country in the world.' Nevertheless, in Meneer Endelbaum, I found the transformation both startling and baffling. Within a very short space of time, the changes had gone much deeper than his clothes. From being a little man, content to remain within the tiny sphere he called home, he had become almost as ostentatious as the city itself, his gestures expansive rather than restrained.

As for Mevrouw Visser, despite her competence in speaking English, she was lost to an even greater degree than me. Alarmed by both the noise and pace of everything, our stroll through the leafy glades of the park, with its elegant floral displays and rowing boats out on the lake, was marred by fear of the crooks and gangsters she had read about in books, convinced they would be lying-in-wait behind the next tree. She had taken the precaution of removing her watch and signet ring, leaving them behind in the apartment, and as she walked she nervously patted the empty space on her wrist, until Meneer Endelbaum, with an exasperated cry of, 'My dear Miss Visser, allow me to escort you back to the apartment,' elicited a tiny smile of relief. A night's repose made little difference. From the moment I took her a cup of tea, she was fussing about the time of her train to Utica, where her cousin lived, and nervously commentating on every aspect of the apartment.

Unlike the traffic, which she described as 'deafening,' her new surroundings bothered her because of their silence, almost too scared to touch anything in case she dropped or damaged it, and timidly nibbling at the food the maid had prepared for our breakfast.

I had understood from snippets of conversation her sister, Mevrouw Kleissler, conveyed to my parents, that even before the war, her life had been both small and compact, and although mine had been the same, I felt sorry. Growing up, I had accepted both the limitations and the advantages of my surroundings, never questioning the size of our house nor the appearance of food on the table.

In the same way, the lavishness, with which Ruth surrounded herself with its silk wallpaper and hangings, were part and parcel of who she was, and only very occasionally, when she'd been especially mean or flaunted a dress I'd love to have owned, did I envy her. For the rest, I was content to buy scraps of fabric at the market and pin them to the walls of my bedroom, happy to discover, whenever the sun peeped through my window, they glowed with life and colour. And now I was ready to accept this new style of living, from which all reminders of a former existence had been banished.

In this new apartment, what I had already learned to call a *living room*, stretched across the corner of the building, with glass doors that opened out onto a narrow terrace. Decked with gilt-edged mirrors and crystal wall lights, its tables made from toughened glass, even the long cream sofas had been carefully sited so wherever you sat, your eye naturally dropped onto a painting. Two in particular captured my attention. Both were of dancers, gypsies, I think, with great swirling movement and colour. One of the dancers reminded me of Ruth, the colour of her hair, brushed with fire, identical, and I guessed the similarity was the reason for its purchase.

Hans may have been infuriating as a brother – and no doubt Pappy found him equally as irritating as an apprentice, uninterested in anything apart from drawing and beer – yet, in dragging me off to museums and art galleries, shouting his condemnation when I mistakenly approved something he considered lacked skill, a little of his knowledge must have brushed off and in those paintings, I recognised the hand of a true master.

Even so, the choice of something so vibrant and full of life I found confusing in such a quiet, self-effacing individual as Meneer Endelbaum. Despite changes to his dress, his manner hadn't changed, still softly spoken and reticent with his language. I had never once questioned why only Ruth's suite of rooms was lavishly appointed. Now I wondered if their former style of living had been forced on him, with him and his wife always in fear of a knock at the door. And now, although sadly Mevrouw Endelbaum had not lived to see it, that fear was quite gone.

Noticing my interest, he nodded, saying quite simply, 'It's for Ruth when she visits.'

Unsurprising, an altar to Ruth's career was very much in evidence, the walls of the entrance hall crowded with black and white photographs, captioned with the name of the film she was starring in. But not as Ruth Endelbaum, as Grace Manning.

Since there were only the two bedrooms, Mevrouw Visser and I had shared Ruth's although, as yet, she hadn't established her ownership. Almost clinically tidy, there was nothing there to suggest Ruth – not even a perfume bottle or a handkerchief sachet – everything brand-new and unused.

I had slept on the ottoman, which sat below the window. I hadn't expected to sleep well. Even on the fourth floor, street sounds rose up penetrating the thickness of the glass, and although traffic sounds had died away, sirens constantly echoed across the night sky waking me from an uneasy doze. Around four, a loud clanking broke out in the street below. Opening the window, I leaned out to see street cleaners emptying the metal bins, lined up on the pavement edge and, once the vehicle moved away, the street was flooded with water, a fierce stream gushing from a hydrant. Earlier, I had thought the rounded metal posts were used for tying up horses, noticing a number of mounted policemen patrolling the park.

The next morning, by the time the cab deposited us at Grand Central Station, Mevrouw Visser's fussing had reduced me to silence and Meneer Endelbaum to exasperated cries of, 'My dear lady', after she had begged him to return to the apartment to search for her spectacles, certain she had left them on the breakfast table. And what if her train had departed early and they had missed it, how could they alert her cousin who was meeting her?

'If only she was on the telephone,' she fretted, eyeing the banks of machines lined up against the wall.

I found myself sympathising, a vast sea of people, most with newspapers and briefcases descending the ramp from the upper storey, a matching stream on the far side of the hall, washing uphill to take their place. It was chaotic and even if I could have found the words, conversation of any sort proved impossible, apart from my comment that it was warmer than the day before. Impulsively, feeling guilt at my relief, I leant forward kissing her on the cheek and wishing her a safe journey.

'I think we need coffee,' Meneer Endelbaum said, as the gates to the platform closed behind my companion. He tucked his arm through mine. 'And quite possibly, either an early lunch or a second breakfast. My dear child, I know she can't help it, but how on earth are you to survive the return journey?'

I began to giggle, all at once feeling free and very alive. 'I refuse to think about it,' I said firmly, 'and I'd love a coffee.'

The streets were busy, leaving me to wonder how, after the teeming masses at the railway station, it was possible for yet more people to be crammed into the available space. Although, as we strolled north, I began to get an inkling of its size, the narrow side streets replicated over and over, with nothing to separate the Brownstone housing on one street from a dozen others, each one having small windows, with steps up to the front door and down to a basement, the children at play indistinguishable from those we had just passed. Only those streets lined with apartments left no lasting impression, simply a thousand glass eyes overhanging shadowy pavements, along which the lucky few were walking their dogs.

Meneer Endelbaum talked steadily, which surprised me. Always before, he had seemed little given to speech, leaving that to his wife, content to spend the daylight hours in his shop, silently conjuring the sparkling facets of a diamond from a lump of cloudy stone.

And there was plenty for him to say. On almost every block, some treasure was waiting to be revealed: an elegant sky-scraper that curved away like a slice of melon or a private collection of art, bequeathed to the city by a wealthy benefactor and housed in some obscure building that you could easily pass by and not notice. He pointed to a scarlet front door, its windows draped with lengths of material, assuring me it was the workplace of one of the great fashion houses and, in a surprisingly short time, I found the city making sense. Even the noise and bustle of the streets which earlier in the day I had viewed with dismay no longer alarmed me, finding amusement in the loud-voiced exchanges between a careless pedestrian and the cab driver who had so nearly clipped him. Almost a pantomime. Attracting the attention of passers-by with a prolonged burst on the horn, the cab driver would follow it up with a bellowed chastisement, throwing both hands up into the air in a gesture of both despair and innocence. One time, it was a single hand that took part in the theatrical display, snaking out through the driver's window, its five fingers appealing directly to the gods of heaven for preservation from idiots.

'Many of the cab drivers are Italian,' Meneer Endelbaum explained when I asked about the hand gestures. 'Here we are.'

The little restaurant, the name of its proprietor inscribed on the maroon-coloured awning, reminded me of home. Not our shop, those in the city, the neat awning over the chocolate shop window where Berthe had once worked having the same dark colour. It was not alone in awakening memories; almost every street corner boasted a restaurant or a bar and my first impression of it being somewhat down-at-heel vanished with the warmth of our welcome, a glorious aroma of freshly baked bread providing the perfect excuse for pushing open the door.

'Joe! How marvellous. And you must be the visitor he promised?' The proprietor bustled across the restaurant floor, as welcoming as I knew Pappy was of his customers, the man's smile as expansive as his waistline. 'Mama, come and see,' he called over his shoulder. 'Joe promised a guest. Never said nothin' about it being a pretty girl.'

I blushed and greeted the couple, the owner patting my hand in a fatherly manner, his wife at the same time handing me a menu.

'And I will bring coffee while you choose what to eat. Please, I beg you...' At this, the proprietor's expression changed, his hands reaching out comically in a pleading gesture, their palms together. 'Please get Joe here to choose something different. Mama has created a magnificent menu with what...' He swung round questioning, his face plaintive.

'Six!' his wife added.

'Yes, six.' He kissed the tips of his bunched fingers. 'Six dishes and all different, and do you believe, he's eaten the same dish every day for the past two years.'

Meneer Endelbaum laughed, his eyes sparkling at the man's teasing and I guessed him to be a regular customer, people seated at other tables, both men and women, calling out a greeting. It was still early for lunch and apart from a couple of men playing chess, who were drinking beer, most were drinking coffee and reading the newspaper.

'You exaggerate, Fredo, it's three times a week not every day,' he said, adding, as the man hurried away, 'Sometimes I go to Brooklyn or I eat with friends up on 89th street. And on Friday, Maidy, I visit my shop, which is downtown.'

'You still own a shop?'

On first sitting down, I had guessed by his loud intake of breath that Meneer Endelbaum had something particular he wanted to talk about – something that warranted extra courage. 'Yes, although Ruth didn't want me to.' He nodded his thanks to the young boy serving our coffee. 'I bought it soon after our arrival.'

Their leaving Holland had been in the early spring, a little more than three months after Mevrouw Endelbaum died. She hadn't been very old although it was not unexpected. We all knew how fortunate the family had been to survive the war. 'She might have managed another year or two,' Pappy confided, 'had it not been for the death of her child. And they say hearts can't break.' He had wrapped a comforting arm around me, hugging me to him. And then they were gone, Ruth and her father; Ruth's excuse for the haste that she had been offered a screen test. I don't know if that part was true or not, yet barely six months later we heard she had been offered a small part in a film.

'She finds having a shopkeeper for a father an embarrassment,' Meneer Endelbaum continued speaking. 'Only, a colleague from the old country was retiring and it was too good an opportunity to miss. Besides, it pays the bills…' he coughed awkwardly, 'and at my age, it's a difficult habit to break.'

'Working, you mean?'

He smiled. 'That too. No, I meant, *putting something away for a rainy day*.' He reached across the table, patting my hand. 'Americans are very good at that, so I feel right at home here. However, that's not what I wanted to tell you.'

He stirred his coffee round and round, taking out his uncertainty as to the wisdom of his confession on the pottery cup.

I had grown up a lot in three years, aware now how young

and naïve I had been at sixteen and although my knowledge of the world remained second-hand, derived from the many books I had studied, in them I had encountered countless variations of human behaviour. My college professors had remarked on my voracious appetite for knowledge, unaware, as Jaan had trawled through books seeking an explanation for their presence, so I was searching for an answer to Zande – why I should have been attracted to someone so complex our language hadn't yet developed a word subtle enough to describe him.

'About my name. When we first arrived, Ruth suggested we change it. She said it would make doing business easier. And she was right,' he hurried the words out. 'I'm Joe Endersby now, not Joseph Endelbaum. I haven't told your father yet and I confess, I'm almost ashamed to do so.' Seeing the question in my eyes, he hurried on, 'I collect my mail from a post office box, downtown. It's not delivered to the apartment.'

I placed my hand on his. 'It makes sense in a new country. But what about me? You know how clumsy I am, I'm bound to trip up.'

'How about Uncle Joe? I don't have any nieces or any other family apart from your own.'

I didn't either. 'Yes, I'd like that.'

The proprietor bustled over with our food, meticulously rearranging the cutlery and glassware to make room for our plates. Knowing he was anxious to chat proved an easy guess. 'Your first visit to our great city?' he began.

I hid a smile. It was obviously a question asked of all foreigners, both the cab driver at the port and the doorman of the building flinging similar words at me, like a demand to see my passport. Perhaps affirmation of the city's greatness needed daily renewal, no different from the headlines on newsstands that cluttered the pavement outside.

All around, conversations swirled and I recognised several different languages, in which broken English was paramount, even in the proprietor, whom customers called Fredo, his accent both thick and inelegant.

'Yes, and I love it.'

Maybe I didn't yet love New York although what I had seen so far, I found both exciting and challenging. 'Everyone is so welcoming, especially ... er ... Uncle Joe. That's his daughter, isn't it?' I pointed to a collection of photographs on the walls, all of famous people who had eaten there. I could understand why, our meal tempting even my taste buds, the bread freshly baked, and our pork served with red cabbage and tiny wedges of fried potato.

'Of course, and because it is Tuesday, Joe has a date with her.'

While we were eating, people stopped by our table offering their best wishes for her marriage, sometimes adding a sentence or two about business, a request for a recommendation or where to buy a certain item of jewellery. And while a few were smartly dressed, most were working men in overalls, their hands engrained with motor oil or wearing a shabby suit that was both clean and pressed, their shoes, maybe worn down at the heels, but still in receipt of polish. A group of elderly men, after slapping the winner of the chess game on the back, stopped, politely offering me advice to: 'Get out there and enjoy New York; it's the best place on Earth.'

I felt buoyed up, beginning to understand the change in my companion. No longer self-effacing, he was quite the opposite – happy to ride the wave of reflected glory his daughter's film star status brought him.

'What did he mean, a date with Ruth?' I said as we left the restaurant, amused to see that no money exchanged hands – nothing apart from a brief nod. A very different way of living from back home. 'Is she here in New York?'

Without replying, he pointed across the avenue and I saw Ruth, her image extended across the façade of a picture house, her amber-coloured hair streaming down her back, pedestrians walking past not even bothering to lift their heads.

'When did you last see her?' I asked as we crossed the road and entered the glossy vestibule, where photographs of Ruth and her handsome leading man were on display. Meneer Endelbaum didn't reply, concentrating on the buying of tickets. It didn't matter, I knew the answer. He hadn't seen her, not for a long time. If I had to guess, not since he moved into the apartment by the river.

As doors opened up into the darkness of the auditorium, I saw Ruth, her face magnified perhaps as many times as the helter-skelter of painful memories it brought with it. Was I never to be rid of them? Then the magic of cinema took over and although the film had been shot in black and white, Ruth gleamed, her presence washing through the celluloid film so powerful you might be mistaken for thinking she was in the auditorium, and the atmosphere so tense people hissed as we entered, admonishing us to, 'hurry up and sit down.'

She hadn't changed perhaps, if anything, more lovely.

Yet there were changes. And although every nuance and every gesture was familiar, especially her voice – it's honey tones unmistakable – nothing about her was the same. This then was cinema, the movie camera revealing facets of which I, her bosom friend, remained unaware. Not flaws. Even the sharp-eyed lens of the camera was incapable of creating flaws where there were none. It was the assurance she revealed whenever her character spoke her lines, something that had once existed only on the surface, with no depth to it at all.

I can't remember what the film was about. I'm not sure if it mattered to the audience: the women who wished their beauty and elegance mirrored the star's, returning home to practise her limpid gaze in the privacy of their bedroom; the men, of whom there were many, longing to possess her... Not Ruth, no, Grace Manning.

I blinked owlishly as we emerged from the cinema into full daylight, the final scene that reconciled the lovers taking place at night.

'I'd love to visit a film set, to see how they can photograph darkness so you can see through it.'

I tucked my arm through his, joining a flock of people descending on Broadway, where the traffic was at a standstill and a cacophony of horns blared out. The side streets proved equally as busy as the main thoroughfares, with people almost treading on the heels of those walking in front, anxious to get home after a long day at the office. A good place to swap secrets, the noise level from the revving engines making it impossible for anyone to eavesdrop.

Meneer Endelbaum chuckled. 'Ask Ruth. She will arrange it for you. I went, when she made her first film. She needed friends then.'

Those final words were softly spoken and I'm not sure if I was meant to hear them. Being slightly deaf himself, maybe he imagined them to be silent musings rather than words spoken aloud.

I hugged his arm all the tighter, thinking how much of themselves parents give to their children. No different from animals and birds that go to extreme lengths to raise their offspring.

'Is that her fiancé?' I referred to her leading man, Roland de Courcy, older than Ruth although from my perspective equally as beautiful.

'Ruth told me she fell in love with him the moment they met.'

Picking up on the change in tone, 'And you don't approve?'

'Because it cannot last.'

I raised my voice so he could hear, other louder voices raised in dispute, absorbing all the space. 'Why not?'

'You should always marry a person who is opposite in every way. My wife loved to talk; I didn't, so we suited admirably and were happy right up to the very end. In that household they will quarrel over which mirror has the most flattering reflection.'

I laughed, immediately censoring him. 'That's a terrible thing to say about your own daughter.'

'We will see, we will see.' He patted my hand. 'She'll be arriving soon, her secretary phoned, and I will invite them to dinner.'

'Ruth won't stay with you?'

'Oh no!' He seemed almost shocked.

I felt stupid, naively believing my life-long friend might actually have thrilled for a chance to gossip the night away. Of course she wouldn't – she was a film star and ordinary rules didn't apply to film stars.

4

I very soon learned from people who shopped at the delicatessen where we were drinking coffee that New York wasn't a city at all, rather a series of neighbourhoods, each one with its own charm and character. It was a public conversation between customers, all of whom were friends, a few, including a policeman who was leaning up against the counter, adding the criticism that while each of its neighbourhoods possessed character, not all of them had charm. 'And some are downright thuggish,' the policeman provided the postscript.

We had gone by cab into Brooklyn, which lies across the river outside the city proper. A smaller version of New York, and lacking the tall office blocks of its more famous sibling, its streets were peppered with crude billboards and neon signs, like a small child smearing make-up on its face, who clatters about in its mother's jewellery and borrowed high-heels. And there were many children. Better dressed than those I had seen playing in the streets near the docks, they peeped shyly from the safety of a doorway, the curly hair of the boys restrained in a skull cap.

I understood from Meneer Endelbaum that Jews had made America their home since the turn of the century. Nevertheless, it wasn't the American language that met my ears when the cab stopped near a group of women gossiping on the pavement, although the proprietor's wife spoke without any accent.

'I was born here,' she confirmed. She smiled possessively at the tightly packed shelves of the delicatessen, a pair of scales and a till adorning the counter. 'My husband and I have been lucky; my father started with a barrow.'

'And people are lucky to have you.' Meneer Endelbaum complimented the elderly woman. Short, with an overall enveloping her ample frame, her dark hair still retained its gloss despite the wrinkles on her face. 'Both during and after the war,' he explained, 'this family have made it their business to help new immigrants, offering them somewhere to live until they find a job. That's how we met. Ruth and I stayed here until I located a suitable apartment.'

'We have room,' she told me, abruptly switching languages to serve a customer, the bell over the door never silent. 'Once our own children were grown,' she reverted back to English, 'why not use it. Besides, as my husband is so fond of saying, friends are good for business – like Joe here.' She smiled at Meneer Endelbaum. 'And soon our house will again be full up.'

'Is your son returning?' Meneer Endelbaum asked.

In the past few days, I had been introduced to so many different people, I had begun to think of conversation as a dance and performing certain steps with certain people. And although their steps were as different as the tales they told, they most always related to family. Uncle Joe had obviously learned the skill well. For the policeman who patrolled the park, it was an enquiry after his horse that brought a smile to the man's face, welcoming questions about the animal's wellbeing. For the doorman of the building, a sentence or two about his youngest son who was in high school, was enough to elicit a smile and a salute, and with it the man's increased willingness to whistle-up a cab or carry a parcel.

Now it was the turn of the proprietor's eldest son, the same question asked by each new customer on entering the emporium. 'When is he returning?'

'In a month when his current job finishes.' She smiled and clapped her hands. 'Soon, there will be children in the house again. Of course,' she added, barely pausing long enough to take a breath, 'You know, Joe is to be married.' Her inquisitive gaze picked up on my astonishment. 'He hasn't told you?' She swung round as the doorbell rang out.

He hadn't, and I responded with the only phrase my astonishment made possible: 'Does Ruth know?'

I could see the question made him uncomfortable; nevertheless, it was a question that needed asking and already I knew the answer.

According to my invitation, Ruth's wedding was to take place at City Hall on the following Thursday – yet the telephone had not rung, nor had the letterbox in the lobby been clattered by the postman, nothing apart from bills and pamphlets. The single clue to her intended visit, a basket of cream and white flowers, the attached card written in green ink: *We are looking forward to working with you.*

I realised too that the guise Uncle Joe presented to the world, that of a man-about-town, was not his natural one. On arrival in America, he may well have decided it to be a way of life he should adopt if he wanted to belong, nevertheless, I saw Ruth's hand in the manipulation. If she was to become a world-famous star, everything around her must follow suit.

'Not yet. I decided it more appropriate after Ruth's big day.'

My thoughts flew to the contents of my suitcase, wondering if the dresses Berthe had packed would satisfy Ruth's expectations.

'Maidy, you're very quiet?'

'I'm not sure I own a dress smart enough for the wedding,' I admitted.

He made no attempt to misunderstand. 'You must have known how self-centred Ruth always was.'

I was carried back to our school days, to my single conceit, that I could run faster than Ruth, claiming ownership of a bridge, both the smallest and the oldest in our city. Here, I had rested, my legs aching from the effort of outrunning her, gazing down at the canal water in the hope of catching a glimpse of the fairies that lived in its depths. That was all I had; everything else belonged to Ruth. She was taller, older, smarter – even the stories I invented were hers. No matter how much I complained, she insisted on playing the part of the princess who owned a different gown for every day of the year; gowns I longed to wear, made of silk shot through with beams of silver light from the moon and floating sleeves that trailed the ground. It never occurred to her that I might want a turn at being the princess who lives happily ever after with her prince. And that was how she lived her life, until the summer of the swans. And I had let her.

Maybe that was the price you paid for friendship – for never being alone.

'I always think of your patience as the mark of a kind and loyal friend.' Uncle Joe nodded at me from across the table.

I laughed, brushing off the praise – it wasn't deserved. I had long since stopped feeling charitable towards Ruth.

In that case, why was I attending her wedding? Curiosity or in the hope that she had changed?

'Why was she like that? You aren't.'

'Then I've lived many more years than Ruth.' He chuckled at my compliment. 'Her mother was the same as a child – both beautiful and wilful. Life taught us a different way.' He sighed. 'Ruth might have escaped had the war not happened and especially those months we were in hiding. In a way, it was almost a relief when we were discovered. That's when Ruth began to live in her own little world surrounded by beautiful things. Now,' he added sadly, 'that's all she sees and all she values.'

The customer served and gone, the proprietress bustled over again to continue the conversation as if the shop bell had not rung out. 'Lilian is my sister and they met here,' she announced proudly. 'Ah, here she is,' she said, her attention automatically drawn to the opening of the street door.

As a child, I had thought of Pappy and Meneer Endelbaum as old. Recently, dreading the very idea of it ever happening to Pappy, I had redefined them as being middle-aged. Exactly like

Lilian. Both a younger and slimmer version of her sister, although their hands shared a similar familiarity with hard work, she wore her dark hair drawn back into a netted snood rather than a tight bun. Of middle height with an open expression, the eyes that regarded her chosen companion with great fondness, were her best feature.

'We meet every Saturday,' she replied to my question, 'although Joe has made me promise to slow down and take life easy when we are married. There's no hurry.' She returned a smile to my second question. 'Neither of us are in a rush to go anywhere.' And she touched his cheek in a gesture that reminded me of Pappy and brought tears to my eyes.

The conversation became general and I tuned out, not especially interested in people who I'd never heard of, who were friends or friends of friends. The snippets that did permeate sounded like a tally of who was doing well in business. A familiar talking point, no different from the mantra of praise being heaped on the city. 'Top of his class, two years running,' or 'he came from nothing and now look at him, I'm that proud.'

'Magrit, my dear, how rude of us. We've been gossiping quite long enough.'

Meneer Endelbaum got to his feet, easing his knees which I'd noticed gave him pain if he sat too long. 'We are off to the Carnegie Hall later. Magrit met someone on the boat who gave her tickets. Was he a musician, my dear?'

'I don't think so,' I said, remembering Yöst's damaged shoulder. 'It was his friend, a guitarist. I've never listened to guitar music.'

'You don't mean Maestro?' Lilian broke in.

'I'm sorry! Who? The name on the card says Ramon—'

'Yes!' Her voice rose excitedly. 'Ramon, *Ramon Martorell*. They call him Maestro! Oh Magrit, you are so lucky.' She grasped my hands in hers, almost dancing with excitement. 'Those seats have been sold out for months. Promise me you will wear your best dress, because every other woman will be wearing theirs.'

Meneer Endelbaum, having reassured me that New Yorkers did indeed dress for the theatre, I wore the dress Berthe had picked out for Ruth's wedding. Made from a bolt of cream silk, shot through with the palest of pink, it was full-skirted, with a matching short-sleeved jacket in the same shade of pink. I had decided to wear my hair loose – assuring myself it was a compliment to the weather rather than vanity, the air mild and dry, as yet unable to cure my dark tresses of their tendency to curl in damp weather.

Ruth's wardrobe, although empty except for my clothes, proved a biddable audience, its mirrored doors reflecting a dozen different versions of myself. So many images, I idly speculated on which was the real one. Perhaps all of them, maybe none of them. 'Pappy,' I called aloud, 'I hope you approve of Berthe's choice, because it was expensive.'

Of course, he would have approved, it was Mother who disapproved of my lifestyle and dressed me in dowdy colours.

I twirled around, checking the seams of my stockings were straight, remembering how Zande had once said I wasn't as beautiful as Ruth.

I know I had promised myself never to think about him or that tragedy-spawned summer ever again. And mostly I had managed, except in dreams – and over those I had no control. I might as easily have dreamt about the family who were renting the house next door, occasionally going out to the cinema with their son – I know he would have liked me to. Perhaps it was my imminent encounter with Ruth that had broken through my resolve ... but suddenly Zande was standing by my side, his presence so powerful I was certain if I moved I would see his reflection in the mirror, those dark eyes undressing me as they had done the first time we met.

'My dear child, you look ... enchanting,' Meneer Endelbaum exclaimed as the doorman literally bowed us out of the building, pulling the outer doors open wide.

I bit my lip to hide my smile, aware he had meant to say *different* and had stopped himself, gallantry rushing to his aid in time. He would have learned from Ruth that for some women, the use of the word different was tantamount to an insult. I wasn't insulted; he was right. Earlier in the day, with my hair tied up in a ponytail and wearing a plain skirt and top, I had appeared practical rather than pretty.

Yet, since arriving in New York, despite wearing the plainest of outfits I did feel different and in a positive way, like someone riding the crest of a wave. Perhaps everyone crossing an ocean experiences this; maybe it's a natural consequence of being marooned on a ship for days, the sheer volume of empty time providing the perfect opportunity to seek out a new identity for oneself.

'Will you stop at the flower shop near the Hall?' he asked the cabdriver. 'We will walk the rest of the way.'

'It should be a young man presenting you with this,' he said as he pinned a corsage of tiny pink orchids to my jacket.

The streets were busy with theatre-goers, men in smart clothes, clean shaven with their hair slicked back, walking side by side with women wearing silly little hats, designed to draw attention rather than protect the wearer from sun or rain. And although not all the clothes were new, all had been recipients of a special effort, with dresses newly washed and suits pressed, all of the theatre goers wearing shoes recently cleaned and shining.

'People are the same the world over.' Meneer Endelbaum waved a thank you at an irate cab driver, his vehicle's progress stalled by the sheer volume of people drifting across the street. 'They love to dress up; the poorer they are, the more important it becomes to keep something back for a special occasion. And here, the theatre is considered a very special occasion. People save for months to afford a ticket. And if you meet up with them months later, it is almost a guarantee they will still be reminiscing on the evening.'

The crowds ascending the steps up to the first balcony weren't in that category. Monied, most of the men wore dinner jackets, the women flimsily clad in gowns that made me think of a flotilla of tropical butterflies, their excited chatter ranging up and down the carpeted stairs.

I didn't add to the voices, too excited to speak, conscious

of the lingering glances that came my way. Tonight, I was the princess I'd always longed to be, the one who had danced through my stories, and childishly I crossed my fingers, hoping my prince would be waiting at the head of the staircase.

Of course, he wasn't, and I smiled at my own naivety. Instead, we emerged into a buzz of excited chatter, with glances spiralling up to the lights and down to the stalls. Fingers pointed whenever a famous face was recognised, 'See, so and so is here. Isn't he that actor?'

Hoping to spot Yöst, I craned over the balcony.

I did so, almost immediately. He was seated in the front row of the stalls among a group of people. Noticing the excited gestures of those in the seats behind and the stealthy, whispered conversations behind hands, I decided his companions were also well-known. Meneer Endelbaum had already explained it was tradition for famous people to occupy the front row of the stalls.

As if I had called out, Yöst swung round in his seat and stared up at the balcony, his sweeping gaze halting when it reached me. He waved, and the man sitting next to him got to his feet, his sightline following Yöst's pointing finger. Immediately a scattering of applause broke out with programmes fluttering their approval. He flashed a smile in my direction, bowing most eloquently.

I know I blushed, hastily sitting down to avoid the stares.

From the row behind, a finger prodded my shoulder. 'You know him?' a voice breathed.

'Not really.' I swung round to see a girl about my age, her eyes as big as saucers. 'I know the man seated next to him; we came over on the liner together.'

'You're so lucky, I'd die for an introduction. He's the Spanish dancer, Rico. Everyone's talking about him. He's appearing at one of the theatres. Naturally, you can't get a ticket for love nor money; it's been sold out for ever. The woman with him, that's his partner.'

The woman sitting alongside was considerably older, although the hair, resting on her neck, was still abundant and confined in a black beaded snood, as Lilian's had been.

Yöst, exchanging a few words with the dancer, held up his left arm and tapped the face of his wristwatch, the fingers of his other hand tiptoeing through the air.

'My dear Maidy.' Meneer Endelbaum beamed. 'How exciting.'

'What is?'

'Your friend is asking us to go down and join them afterwards.'

I laughed, nodding my thanks, and quickly took my seat; applause greeting the conductor as he strode out onto the stage.

I didn't know about music except for the snatches Berthe occasionally hummed, listening to the radio in the sitting room whilst she was sewing. Apart from that, it was bits and pieces that floated through an open window on a long summer's evening. Feeling abandoned by life, on those nights and too restless for sleep, I rode the distant reaches of the river on my bicycle, as I had once done with Hans and Ruth. On cooler days, I explored the flower-strewn alleys of the old city, where magic had once existed in the dark water of the canal, the reflected glow of a streetlamp fragmented into shards of gold. In a sense, I followed in Hans' footsteps, although it was a musical phrase or a series of notes that drew my attention rather than the shape of a bridge or a broken piece of stone. Sometimes, on hearing something that resonated, I returned again and again to the same spot, hoping to hear it again, sometimes lucky, mostly not.

I listened to the piece the orchestra was playing, diligently reading its title in the programme, drawn to the instruments responsible for the various sounds, especially the massive kettledrum with its polished copper cladding and the dark tube-like cylinders of the wind section with their silver accoutrements. Despite these claiming my attention, I found the mix of sounds baffling, my attempts to discover some sort of pattern unsuccessful. Eventually, I came to the conclusion that the sheets of music on the stands were a road map, decipherable only if you were familiar with the language in which they were written. Although the audience obviously disagreed with my assessment, applauding vigorously at the end.

As members of the orchestra began to leave the stage, they

were replaced by two burly men who, greeted by ironic cheers, quickly cleared the conductor's podium to one side, replacing it with a sense of burgeoning excitement. It swept over the audience in a tidal wave, washing over the tiers of seats, with conversation all at once louder and instilled with more energy.

Silence fell and, craning over the balcony, I saw others also leaning eagerly forward, their hands gripped tightly, the appearance of a wheelchair pushed onto the stage by a helper prompting an outburst of rapturous applause.

Lilian had said nothing about the musician being in a wheelchair although it wasn't age that had brought him to that place, his face unlined despite a thick thatch of snow-white hair. Assisting him onto a stool, set down in the middle of the stage, the helper went off, pushing the chair.

Slowly, as the lights dimmed, the spontaneous applause was replaced by the silence of expectation.

And into the silence, came music.

It made no sense, not at first, merely a series of disconnected sounds. Disappointed and bored, I shuffled in my seat, listening half-heartedly and smoothing the nap on my dress. Abruptly, a note sounded out that rang through my head. A second note joined it and in a rippling succession, all at once I wasn't pretending to listen, nor was I listening half-heartedly, every one of my senses wide awake. Now the music created pictures in my head, each picture matched by the relevant sound – even the scent I associated with it. There was a waterfall in springtime, joyous and unconfined, with sunlit fields and baked earth, forests rich with lichen – and bird song, the rippling notes jubilant. A moment later and jarring chords obliterated the peaceful scene in an outpouring of rage. It spread its cloak over the countryside, polluting the streams and levelling the great trees in the forest. There came a passage which reminded me of footsteps and I imagined lines of people trudging through countryside devastated and barren, and I heard children crying, and knew the music was telling a story of a peaceful land overtaken by the brutality of war.

The end equally abrupt was greeted by a collective silence. I sneaked a glance at the elderly woman sat next to me, one hand clutched in her husband's, using a handkerchief to mop her tears. Her sleeve had creased and fallen back, exposing a line of blue numbers on her arm. Then applause broke out, with smiles and laughter resuming their proper place.

A second piece, and again I had to wait for the pictures to flow. This time I was patient, listening intently to the syllables of music emerging from the fingers of the musician in the same way sentences penned by a poet evolve into verse. I noticed too how the position of his fingers on the guitar produced the different sounds, picking up on a simple trill that hopped in and out of the piece he was playing, like a child jumping over a skipping rope held by friends. Afterwards, inspecting the eager faces around me, I guessed this second piece had brought to life a collective memory, one of childhood in which they had experienced both laughter and happiness.

'It's not over, is it?' I asked equally childlike as the wheelchair returned to the stage.

'No, it's the interval.'

As the interval drew to an end, some members of the orchestra filed back in, mostly the string section, the conductor waiting for the guitarist to take his place again before entering the stage. He then introduced a concerto with the orchestra duplicating notes and themes first played by the soloist, each section in the music creating a different picture. In the first, sprightly with patches of gaiety, like sunlight and shadow on water. A change of pace produced an erratic tempo, modulating into an intermittent series of high notes reminding me of the moorhens pecking at the crumbs Zande was feeding them. In the softer middle section, water drifted lazily and I pictured myself sat by the canal with Zande's hand resting on my shoulder, waiting for the mirage of light to take place whenever the sun broke through. I sneaked a glance at the people around me, staring damp-eyed into space, each of them reliving their most precious memories with pictures different from mine.

I can't remember the third movement, nor the pictures it created; I only know it left me feeling happy and full of conviction that the music I'd discovered was not over ... it was just beginning.

5

No one seemed in a hurry to leave the theatre, the couple next to me lingering in their seats still lost in the beauty of the music, and now that the commissionaires had deserted their post at the entrance doors, it was easy enough to slip down the stairs and into the stalls.

A wall of noisy conversation greeted us, amplified by the low ceiling of the balcony above. At least half the audience hadn't yet left, friends gathered into groups chatting, others aimlessly standing around, glancing enviously at the many famous faces and drinking in their every gesture. Nearby, a line of girls and young women, programme in hand, waited to get the autographs of the dancers, Rico and his partner.

It was a daunting scene even for someone with confidence, people curiously swinging round to follow us with their eyes as we made our way against the flow towards the stage. Instantly, what little poise I had acquired from the occasional admiring glance fled, nervous of meeting up with someone so obviously well-known and so very glamorous. No longer young, with her hair dressed to accentuate her high cheekbones and patrician Roman nose, the woman signing autographs was handsome rather than beautiful, yet she greeted each supplicant with a smile that bowled them over. With my corsage and fluffy hair, I was a mere non-entity by comparison.

Noticing us, Yöst waved. 'Come and meet the family.' He held out his hand to Meneer Endelbaum. 'And you must be—'

'Joe Endersby.'

Yöst's gaze sought mine. I remembered mentioning Meneer Endelbaum by name and was relieved when he didn't comment.

'Magrit is my adopted daughter. Our families lived next door.'

'In Holland?'

'Yes, I emigrated more than two years ago.'

Rico glanced up smiling. Signing the last of the autographs, he stepped away, calling out, 'So you're the princess in the tower.'

Every eye focussed on him swivelled in my direction. Feeling exposed and vulnerable, I hastily tucked my hands behind my back. 'Princess in the tower?' I echoed.

Rico raised his eyebrows at me.

'Oh!' I laughed and my courage returned. 'Yöst told you about Miss Visser? She really wasn't that bad.'

'A dragon no less, or so I heard. And with a name like Visser...'

'It's Dutch.' I apologised returning his smile, his laughter infectious, its obvious happiness uplifting.

'Allow me to introduce you.' He swung back to Yöst. 'Yöst you know. We grew up together and have known one another forever.' Rico nudged him with his elbow and they shared a smile. 'The only time we ever squabbled was over Maestro.' He pointed over his shoulder at the stage, now empty except for a couple of violinists who were casually chatting, the one beating time with his bow against a page of manuscript on a music stand. 'When Yöst first arrived at the farm, he was both an ignoramus and a Philistine.'

Yöst laughed, reminding him casually, 'and who taught you the word ignoramus?'

'You did.' Instantly, I sensed a bond between them. 'Continuing the family introductions.' Rico swirled, his one arm extended and mimicking the proud stance of a bullfighter side-stepping a bull. 'This is Katarina. Officially she is my aunt and her age remains a

State Secret. And my cousin Emilee, who is two years younger than me. She also dances. And my cousin Ernestina – who doesn't.' He exchanged smiles with the young woman sitting next to a dark-haired young man, the two girls obviously twins. 'She has preferred to marry and raise children. What about you, do you dance?'

'I don't know, perhaps in the privacy of my bedroom.'

I had instantly picked up on the flamboyance of Rico's character, dramatizing his every movement. A born showman, he obviously revelled in his fame. Once again, he bowed low. 'In that case, let us find out. Wearing the most beautiful of dresses, Magrit, you should be in a ballroom, not some stuffy old theatre.'

'Oh, please call me Maidy,' I said impetuously, drawn in by the exhilaration of the evening. 'Only strangers call me Magrit.'

The air froze and broke apart into movement again – everything in slow motion. I saw Rico ask a silent question of Yöst and heard his reply. 'It must be – what an odd coincidence.'

'A small world.' With barely a hesitation, Rico held out his hand to me. 'Come.'

Between the front row of the stalls and the stage lay a wide space. Taking my hand, he whirled me into a waltz, my skirts billowing out in a drift of rose-pink silk. He was extraordinary, his feet – his whole body – lighter than air. I felt pressure from the arm clasping my waist and responded, skipping up the steps that led to the stage and down again.

People happy to delay their departure swung round applauding. And before I knew it, Katarina had taken Meneer Endelbaum – Uncle Joe – by the hand and they, too, were dancing. Yöst and Emilee joined in, his good arm lightly encircling her waist. Next minute, their attention drawn by laughter and applause, the two violins struck up with a waltz. There'd been no time for consultation. One minute they were deep in conversation, paying no attention to the departing throng; the next they were timing the melody to Rico's cavalcade of steps, a lilting song pouring out from the strings of their instruments. In the background, I heard someone humming and realised where I had heard the tune before. It spoke of a time long-since past when women wore long dresses with satin slippers on their feet, and whirled around a ballroom sparkling with chandeliers, looping the hem of their flounced skirts over their arms to keep them from tripping.

Hearing music echoing out where none should be, backstage helpers wandered onto the stage, the guitarist in his wheelchair among them, while people lingering in the balcony above craned over the rail. By this time, those sitting in the stalls had joined in, the aisles filled with couples whirling in a glittering pageant of grace and colour.

Abruptly, the manager bustled onto the stage, waving his hands in the air. 'Stop, stop! Gentlemen ... and ladies.' He bowed in Katarina's direction. 'Please! This is not a ballroom. As nice as it is, there is furniture and...' His voice faded away lost amongst an outpouring of ironic cheers and laughter.

'Spoilsport,' a woman called out. 'We were having such a great time.'

'And we will continue having a great time,' Rico shouted, sounding as excited as a schoolboy. 'Come! Maestro, you're needed.' Keeping fast-hold on my hand, he grabbed the lead violinist by the arm and frog-marched him up the aisle, pushing open the fire-exit door that led out into a side street.

A wall of excited chatter broke out as the audience, aware something extraordinary was about to take place, flocked after him, the second violinist among them, their noisy chatter reminiscent of a flight of eager starlings.

'Now play,' he commanded the violinist. Ignoring the line of parked taxicabs waiting for the Hall's audience to emerge, Rico once again whirled me into a spin, our steps blending seamlessly with the dance music. Anxious not to miss out on a second of this extraordinary conclusion to their evening, and ignoring handbags and shoes unsuitable for a street party, the audience raced into the middle of the street, spinning joyfully to the strains of an old-fashioned waltz.

Sufficiently confident of following Rico's steps, I watched over his shoulder, seeing musicians not yet left hastening from the theatre also anxious to take part, one clumsily fitting a new reed to his clarinet as he walked, a second looping the belt of his saxophone around his neck with one hand, his fingers already reaching for the keys, anxious to add harmony to the ad hoc orchestra. Emerging from one fast spin, I saw Maestro take up the position of conductor.

A policeman on his horse, attracted by the noise, turned into the street, surprised to find cars parked with their engines switched off, as cab drivers, leaving the driver's door open, deserted their vehicles, the vivid yellow bodies of their vehicles, standing nose to tail, like the yellowing ivories of an old piano.

Rico spun off into the crowd of dancers which was increasing moment by moment, partnering both Katarina and Ernestina before offering his arm to a member of the audience.

'I see you have been deserted,' Meneer Endelbaum said, the two of us performing a stately version of the waltz.

No one seemed at all concerned by the hiatus, neither car owners who had inadvertently got trapped in the melee and were craning forward against the steering-wheel to watch the swirling movement, nor the mounted policeman, leaning back in his saddle to enjoy the fun.

''Scuse me, Miss.'

A middle-aged cab driver tapped me politely on the arm. 'Would you mind? I've always wanted to dance with the prettiest girl in the room. That is, if you don't object, Miss.'

'And I have always wanted to dance with a cab driver,' I replied, scarcely able to believe what was happening. And to me! Any second my eyes would open and I'd be back where I belonged, plain Magrit Bader. Except, I decided as the cab driver whirled me into the throng, this wasn't my imagination; this was real and tonight the clock had no intention of striking twelve.

'Does this happen often?'

He laughed. 'More often than you could believe, Miss. New Yorkers love to party. Look at them.' He pointed to a white-haired couple contentedly moving to the music. 'Eighty if they're a day.'

Abruptly, the music changed, as professional dancers emerged from a theatre on the opposite site of the street and began a fast-paced jive. Then the saxophone took control, a double bass thumping out the rhythm and a drummer, who had wandered out to enjoy the fun, keeping time and beating his drumsticks against the iron bars of the fire escape. Swinging one another about, the dancers quickly took command of the makeshift stage, the audience from the Hall moving aside.

If I had expected the cab driver to do the same, I was wrong. Taking up the rhythm he whirled me round in a spin, while his uplifted arm formed an arch for me to duck under. I was startled at how light he was on his feet, although, if I had to guess, I would think him even older than Pappy.

After a moment or two Rico appeared. 'My dance now, I think.'

'For you, Mister, anything.' The cab driver stepped away. 'Thank you, Miss; fulfilled a dream you have. She your girl?'

'No.' Rico smiled at Yöst who was standing nearby, his eyes gleaming with mischief. 'A friend of a friend; I only met her tonight. But can she dance. Watch!'

'*Guys, hold up!*' the cab driver bellowed, his voice up close a fog horn of sound. 'Rico, he's going to dance.'

Abruptly, the music changed again and the jiving dancers fell away, automatically clearing a space and watching from the sidelines, their arms still wrapped around one another's waist.

Rico raised his voice to a shout. 'Maestro play. Emilee, Katarina ... you ready?'

Obligingly the musician, the one I had watched earlier paint pictures in the sky, began to play, one of the violinists keeping time, beating his fingers against the wooden frame of his violin.

The two women began circling, their arms sweeping through the air in a series of elegant shapes accompanied by their clicking fingers, their feet intermittently breaking into movement, beating out the rhythm.

'Copy them,' he commanded.

I was wearing heels, with flimsy soles that made little sound against the hard surface of the roadway, nevertheless, I did my utmost to strike the ground cleanly, arching my back, describing figures in the air as the women had done. By my side, Rico glided from one movement to the next, each move designed to create a series of elegant tableaux, his gestures spell-binding and extravagant, the watching crowd silenced by the sheer beauty of his silhouette. Flash bulbs popped as press photographers recorded the scene, and at a gesture from Katarina, I moved away leaving Rico to dance alone. Perhaps it was no longer than a few seconds, a minute at the most, the guitar signalling the finale with increasing sound and speed, Rico's feet never missing a beat.

I don't know how much a theatre ticket would have cost to see him perform. The audience silently watching may have, drinking it in, already working out sentences and descriptions with which to regale friends and family who had missed out on this once in a lifetime celebration.

Silence, until his audience, lost in their own fantasy world, abruptly returned to the present and broke into rapturous applause: dancers, cab drivers, even the policeman beating his baton against the palm of his open hand. And then, as if the clock had defied my wishes and decided to strike twelve anyway, it was over. The audience faded away, cab drivers climbing back into the driving seat, hustling up a fare, the ordinary everyday need to make a living reinstated.

Yöst moved to my side, taking my arm. 'He's impossible.'

'He's wonderful.'

He laughed and I thought I'd never seen anyone as happy and wished that might be me one day. 'Yes, he is. We were arguing earlier because he is determined to stay in New York while I am in hospital and their booking at the theatre finishes tomorrow. After this...' He pointed towards the slowly vanishing crowd, a few glancing back over their shoulders, hopeful of there being an encore and not wanting to miss it. 'The theatre will ask them to stay on, aware they will be offering standing room only for the next two weeks.'

Rico wandered up, having once again signed a host of autographs. 'We must go. I have two shows tomorrow and the day after Yöst is heading into hospital to get his shoulder finally fixed.' His eyes gleamed with mischief. 'And we will be by his bedside.'

Yöst laughed. 'I wondered how you'd get your own way. I never imagined you'd hijack the entire population of New York to do it.'

'Enjoy the rest of your stay.' Rico bowed over my hand, momentarily retreating into formality. 'I meant what I said. You should be a dancer. If you ever want a job, come and see me. And please keep in touch with Yöst, I have asked him to give you his address at the vineyard. Tells me he's always in need of friends.' He punched his friend lightly on the arm.

After the final handshake goodbye, we strolled down the street making for Sixth Avenue, where Meneer Endelbaum thought we had a better chance of finding a cab, those driving across the city with their for-hire signs turned off. I had tucked my arm through his, my feet still in the mood for dancing. 'And what generous people. Even the manager of the Hall waited until the photographers had left before chasing us out.'

He laughed. 'Yes, it's a good country.'

As we crossed over the avenue, I glanced up at the skyline, the silhouette of the three skyscrapers and their slightly shorter siblings visible from most parts of the city. At night, their topmost stories were left lit, as a warning to aircraft, so Meneer Endelbaum had explained when I asked, while their closest neighbour, in the process of being built, had lit its cranes similarly.

'Uncle Joe,' I said using his pet name. 'Do you think Rico meant it, about my becoming a dancer?'

'Yöst obviously thought so.'

Yöst had walked to the corner of the street with us and I had wished him luck for his forthcoming operation. He had returned an easy smile. 'I admit, it's been with me so long I shall miss the pain when it's gone.' He fished in his pocket, pulling out a card. 'This has my address. We will be back there in the summer, please come and visit. You will be most welcome and maybe by then you will have made your decision.'

'What decision? You mean about becoming a dancer?'

'Oh no! This one hasn't happened yet,' he returned lightly, 'yet before long it will need to be made.'

6

It was not until very late that we returned from the theatre and I saw the telegram, hastily delivered by the doorman before going off duty and shoved under the door. It was not from Ruth, rather her secretary, announcing that Miss Manning would call on us the following day.

I guessed Meneer Endelbaum wouldn't sleep much; sufficiently agitated by the imminent arrival of his daughter to phone his maid straight away, despite the lateness of the hour.

'Would you please come over early to clean the apartment and bring a chicken.'

Perhaps a little selfishly, considering Meneer Endelbaum's unfettered generosity towards me, I wasn't worried about Ruth's opinion of the apartment, still reliving each joyous moment of the evening. Presumably she would find some fault although I hoped not, for his sake. In any event, she'd be gone again shortly to embark on a new life with her husband, and I hadn't the slightest doubt Lilian, when eventually Meneer Endelbaum plucked up the courage to tell his daughter he was planning to re-marry, would love the place.

The walls in the apartment were thin, and his restless attempts to sleep kept me awake also. I hoped it was worry about the maid not arriving early enough to clean, rather than Ruth's lack of filial attention that was bothering him. How often in the past had I experienced an identical emotion, needing to make sense of some heedless word or gesture? If I was correct, he was searching for words of solace that might silence the doubt he was experiencing ... that the organisation of a celebrity wedding, on top of the demands of a busy film career, must fill at least twenty-five hours in every twenty-four, and only as a last resort would Ruth have asked her secretary to send a telegram.

I recognised the ploy, because I had done the same ... made excuses for Ruth. I wasn't responsible for the tragedy that had befallen Pieter. That had been down to Ruth's own double-dealing. Perhaps I should have spoken out at the time, although with Mevrouw Endelbaum so ill and Ruth so obviously distraught, it was kinder to stay silent. Besides, which version of the truth dare I have used?

That Ruth had led Pieter on and, as a final act, after promising to marry him, she had jilted him?

Or, that Pieter, in love with Ruth, and broken-hearted by her refusal of his marriage proposal, had left because he couldn't bear the idea of her marrying someone else?

Both would have been duplicitous. A teaspoon of truth stirred with a tablespoon of falsehood.

Perhaps it was as well Mevrouw Endelbaum's illness prevented further enquiry and the single account of events was the one according to Ruth ... *that I hadn't wanted her to marry Pieter.* Despite casting me in the role of villain, it was the most palatable of the lies being bandied about.

And the real truth ... the one I dreamt about and awoke to find tears on my face and my pillow damp with grief?

That was unbelievable, no matter how often you heard it told. Only if you had witnessed the fight on the lake between Zande and Tristan might the truth be believed or, later that same fateful day, eavesdropped on the conversation between Mother and me. The most heartrending of all confidences we shared that night, that Pieter was not Pappy's son and was the son of someone else, the man my mother had first loved and doubtless loved still. Someone I had met one time, who carried the rogue gene of the carinatae, and who carelessly left the son my mother bore him to pay the price for his misdeeds.

I did finally sleep and was awakened by the sound of the key turning in the outer door, the maid calling out as she closed the door behind her. My English had improved quickly with daily use although hers, despite her many years in America, remained broken, her conversation a pantomime of arm actions and speech. Still, I liked her, relishing the challenge posed by our two languages, the Germanic and at opposite ends of the spectrum, the Romance. That day she was more excited than usual, carrying several bags and clutching an armful of newspapers which she dumped on the kitchen table.

'Mr Endersby, you must see your daughter,' she called out, 'also the young lady.'

Opening the first of the full-size double sheets to page three, she pointed to a photograph of Ruth arriving at the airport with her fiancé; an article about the films they had appeared in, with details of the wedding arrangements to take place at City Hall printed below. Closing the newspaper, she pointed to the front page, and I spotted the headlines and Rico's name. Spread over the top half of the page was a black and white photograph of the street, the commanding outline of Carnegie Hall with its metal fire escape in the background, and up-close Rico and me, dancing, the silk of my skirt flying up to expose my legs.

'And very pretty legs they are, too,' Meneer Endelbaum laughed at my red face. 'Perhaps it's a good job newspaper reporters have no idea who you are.'

Eagerly, I flipped over the pages, discovering a dozen pictures in which photographers had focussed their cameras on the crowd, highlighting an interesting face or a dance step. In one, two cabdrivers were dancing together; in another, it was the orchestra of five they featured. The musicians, rising to the occasion, had gathered under the first-floor platform of the fire escape. Flanked by rails and a flight of steps, the stone face of the building created a stark and unusual background. The cameras had also singled out the saxophonist. Wanting to be heard more clearly above the noisy crowd, he had shinned up onto the platform, pointing the brass instrument at the actors and dancers from the neighbouring theatre, with their legs and arms akimbo performing their jive. But the majority of the images were the Flamenco poses of Rico, with me, a most acceptable facsimile, at his side, and in the background Katarina and Emilee.

I came down to earth with a bump as Ruth drove into the street. Apart from her secretary who was driving the pale blue limousine, she was alone, her arrival bolstered by the waiting battery of newspaper reporters and photographers, their cameras creating sporadic flashes of white light across the front of the building. I don't know how it came about – certainly neither her father nor I had any foreknowledge of her arrival time, although it was obvious residents in the street did, most hanging out of their windows. Someone had delivered a bunch of flags and the women and children were waving these vigorously, shouting out, much to the delight of the reporters and their flash bulbs.

I had been about to ask what time Ruth was arriving and whether I should call her Grace or Ruth, when the noise broke out. I ran out onto the balcony to find reporters jogging up the street either side of the slowly moving vehicle, and raced down to the lobby, beating the elevator that carried Meneer Endelbaum and the maid.

'Where's your husband?' the reporters chanted once the vehicle had stopped.

'Darlings!' Posing in the back of the open limousine, Ruth blew them a kiss. 'I have five days of freedom; do let me enjoy it. Oh wait!' She flung out her arm in my direction. 'Everyone, this is my dearest friend, Magrit Bader. I have her to thank. Ages ago now, she said I belonged in Hollywood. And she was right.'

Flinging open the car door, she stepped out, blowing kisses at the street's residents who blew them back. A photographer flashed his camera as Ruth twirled, one hand stretched to me. 'Can you believe she's come all the way from Holland to see me married? Aren't I the luckiest of girls?'

I noticed a couple of the reporters, notebooks at the ready, step in my direction.

Ruth saw it too. 'Guys didn't you hear me? Magrit's over from Holland and there they speak a different language. Give her a break, I doubt she's got the hang of American yet.'

Laughing and wishing her well, one by one the reporters disappeared into cabs and cars. I felt a sense of reluctance on Ruth's part, staring round at the fast-emptying street, bemused by the steady slamming of windows as one by one residents, now the show was over, resumed their daily lives.

I still hadn't managed a word, my mind revolving at speed trying to assimilate all the changes. Most obvious of these was her nonchalant wave in the direction of her secretary. 'Pick me up after lunch,' she said, 'unless Emmanuel calls. Then come running.'

'Who's Emmanuel?' Meneer Endelbaum commented as the elevator ascended to the fourth floor.

'A French producer. Papa, I'm sure I wrote you about it. He wants me for his new film. I'm thinking about it. Of course, it will mean moving to Europe for at least six months. Oh, how silly of me. It wasn't you I wrote, it was Hans.'

'My brother, Hans?' I said astonished.

'Of course. He wrote me the sweetest fan letter – actually asked if I remembered him. The cheek. As if I'd let fame change me.'

The lift pulled to a stop. Opening the gates, Meneer Endelbaum unlocked the hall doorway, indicating for Ruth to enter first.

'Oh, how lovely.' She clapped her hands. 'The photographs and they're all of me. How sweet.'

Throwing open the living room door, she waltzed out onto the balcony, peering over the rail in the direction of the park. 'I do miss seeing water. When I get back, I'm planning to buy a house on the edge of the sea. Papa, I'd love a drink. And not coffee.' She kissed him fondly, her expression all at once very familiar ... and very genuine. With the reporters, every gesture had been scripted.

I'd forgotten how lovely she was, the black and white facsimile of the film we had seen, though beautiful, barely doing her justice. Taller than me, as a child I'd envied her height and stature because it kept her out of harm's way in the playground. That's where I had fine-tuned my running skills. Admittedly, both Pieter and Hans were at the same school for part of the time, although they had never associated with me. Pieter always preferred hanging around with boys of his own age, while Hans was part of the little group who followed Ruth about. Then at the age when beauty or a lack of it begins to impinge on girls, I'd also envied her glorious hair, a rich mane of metal, while every aspect of her face and complexion mirrored a spring morning – both fresh and radiant. Once, at college, I overheard two boys actually disputing which was her best feature, unable to agree.

'Why the name *Grace*?'

She relaxed her legs gracefully together, one hand idly smoothing the silken nap on the sofa. As Meneer Endelbaum returned carrying a tray of glasses, filled with something that frothed and bubbled, she reached up and took a glass, closing her eyes with pleasure at the first sip. 'And to think until a year ago I'd only met up with ordinary wine – what was I thinking of?'

'Why Grace?' I repeated.

'Oh, that was the studio. They chose it.'

'You don't get to keep your own name?'

'Don't be so naïve, Maidy. Hollywood exists because people love fantasy and make-believe. Hardly anyone gets to use their own name. Roland's real name is John. When he landed his first starring role, there were so many famous Johns there wasn't room for another.'

'And de Courcy?'

'That's real enough. It's his grandmother's maiden name. She was French.'

'Isn't he also French? That's what the newspapers say.'

'You read the gossip columns?' She laughed. 'How sweet. No,

he was born right here. Well, not exactly right here but pretty close.'

'He should have come with you, at the very least to pay his respects,' her father broke in. 'In the old country...' I hid a smile, amused to think he'd adopted the custom of other immigrants, referring to the land of their birth as if it remained steeped in the middle ages. 'He would have asked my permission.'

Ruth trilled a laugh. 'Oh, Papa, no one does that now. It's so old-fashioned. And you'll meet him at the wedding.' The tiniest of frowns appeared. 'Filming together, we're in each other's company far too much already so we tend to socialise with different people. Who's this?' She picked up the newspaper lying on the sofa, pointing to the photograph on its front page. 'It says he's a famous dancer. He can't possibly be your boyfriend, he's far too old for you. Still, I'd love to meet him.'

I hid a smile. Of course! That was the reason I'd been reduced to the ranks of a foreigner, unable to speak or understand English; she had already seen the newspapers and recognised the unknown girl dancing with Rico.

'He's appearing at one of the theatres.' I'm no actress, my face always the indicator of my real feelings, and I struggled to maintain an expression of absolute innocence. Inside I was glowing, unable to believe I had finally done something Ruth envied. 'According to the newspapers, the theatre is fully booked, not a seat to be found anywhere.'

Recalling how the simple presentation of the musician's card at the box office had resulted in our being given tickers reserved for special guests, I didn't dare add anything else. Already, I was experiencing a tiny flicker of guilt at my duplicity yet, if I was ever to meet Ruth on equal terms, I needed to fight fire with fire. My being a doormat to her whims belonged in the past.

'Papa,' she held out her glass which was almost empty. 'Top me up, will you?'

Taking her glass, he vanished back into the kitchen, where sounds of preparation for lunch accompanied the delicious aroma of chicken roasting. I wondered how difficult this visit might prove for him. Admittedly, he'd had two years to get used to living somewhere both spacious and modern. Nevertheless, apart from the war years, almost his entire life had been spent in the surroundings of a typical Dutch family. Undoubtedly, that is where his memories still lay, in a house that went up rather than out, in which dishes of food were cooked in a tiny kitchen and loaded onto a hoist that trundled them up to an equally inadequate dining room.

'What's he like?'

'Who, Roland? He can't act for toffee but he's so good-looking – and a divine dancer.'

Her reply was casual, almost absentminded, as if her fiancé was a mere bystander and not the person she was actually thinking of. Her next words confirmed it. 'I wondered; did he return?'

'No.' The words came out harsher than I intended. 'Zande didn't return, nor Pieter.'

'What happened to him? I remember fainting.'

She trailed her fingertips across her forehead in a gesture I recognised from the film. Except, then she'd been acting the part of a wartime heroine who, despite the danger, is eventually reunited with the man she once saved from imminent death. The complete reversal of the scenario on the island. She hadn't loved Pieter, and it was her lack of love that had sent him to his death.

Except he wasn't dead, I reminded myself for the umpteenth time. Although for him, denied the chance to work with Pappy, he might as well have been. I tried not to think about it, telling myself there was still time and hope, aware each time the calendar changed, a fragment of both was lost.

'Do you enjoy living in Hollywood?'

'You meet some fascinating people and already I've been to parties at the homes of the top stars. And soon, if this new film works out, I'll be one of them.'

'And you are happy there?'

Again, she ducked the question. Instead, she reached over, and tapped me on the arm. 'You've no idea how wonderful it all is. At long last, I'm actually good at something.'

'Ruth, you're not serious, you can't be.' I caught the frown. 'Sorry, I mean Grace. You were good at everything as a child.'

'That's not true. You always beat me at running and look at your stories. But I am good at this.'

Meneer Endelbaum called from the kitchen. 'I forgot. A basket of flowers came for you the day before yesterday. They're on the table.'

At once the trace of ennui that had briefly cast a shadow over her expression lifted and, jumping to her feet, she hurried over to the table. Trailing her hand across the flowers, she read the card. 'You see.' She brandished it like a weapon. 'Yet another studio wants me for a film.'

'Oh, Papa,' she called as he emerged once again from the kitchen area, 'you are a darling.' Taking the refilled glass from the tray, she glanced down at her watch. Different from the diamond encrusted one she'd worn for college, a sixteenth birthday present from her parents, this was rectangular with four single diamonds replacing the numbers marking the quarter hours.

With Meneer Endelbaum working in the diamond industry, subsequent birthdays must have seen equally as expensive gifts, her diamond earrings sparkling whenever she moved her head. Although it wasn't the watch that drew my attention, rather its strap which mirrored the shade of turquoise in her trousers and silk blouse exactly, a cardigan in the same shade only darker around her shoulders. To match such different materials, and so perfectly, they had to be expensive.

'Will lunch be long?'

'You're not spending the day with us?'

'Oh no, Papa, I am so, so sorry. It's just not possible. Didn't my secretary warn you? She must have forgotten, careless girl. I have to leave at two – Roland and I are being interviewed for television. It's all the rage these days.'

Mumbling he would hurry lunch up, Meneer Endelbaum retreated into the kitchen, refusing my offer of help. 'You stay and talk to Ruth. You've got years of catching up to do. There will be lots of time for us to chat after you return home.'

Except there wouldn't be. Once Ruth was married, based on today, I just knew she would use her married state as an excuse for a lack of phone calls and visits. It was both wrong and unfair. I stared disapprovingly at her jewellery; Uncle Joe had always given her everything she wanted, why couldn't she repay him with a small slice of her time? Was it too much to ask?

Swallowing down my irritation, I hurried into speech. 'Tell me more about your fiancé. Obviously, you love him.' I put out a tentative feeler, determined to get it all out into the open now to avoid any horrid surprises later.

'Do you want me to love him?'

This was vintage Ruth and I answered sharply. 'Ruth, don't play games; we're too old for that.'

She laughed, the delicate sound equally as artificial as her previous response. 'Of course, I do. Why else would I marry him.'

'So how did you meet, do tell?' I said the words because they were expected of me, although I wasn't much interested in the reply.

'I was in the cafeteria.' There was no inflexion or sparkle in Ruth's voice. What she was saying was the public version of events, fine-tuned by her agent, learned by heart and occasionally embellished with genuine memories. Had I expected anything else? If so, it just proved how unbelievably naive I was. Even Pappy, while encouraging me to accept her invitation, predicted that after three years, we would have become very different people. 'You certainly are, my child,' he had teased. 'You can at least enter into new company without blushing.'

'That's where all the extras go and actors that play bit parts,' she elaborated. 'I used to eat there; I don't now, of course. Filming is so unbelievably tiring, I have my meals served in my dressing room. One day Roland walked up to me. Said he'd been at a party where they were watching movies... Actors do that a lot.' She took a sip of champagne. 'It's so important to keep up to date with everything,' she explained. 'Apparently, the second feature was a film I was in. In that, I was given third billing. Still, it was enough to attract his attention. He'd just been signed for a new movie and bulldozed the producer into offering me the main part, playing opposite him. By the time that film was done, he'd divorced his wife and now we're about to be married.'

'How many times has he been married?'

'Only once before that, when he was very young. He admits to being hopelessly naïve.' She laughed. 'Can you imagine a boy of seventeen marrying? The woman was old too, thirty at least.' She shrugged. 'Of course, she was famous which helped his career.' Picking up on my shocked expression, she snapped out. 'Oh, grow up, Magrit. You can't stay narrow minded for ever. It's a different world out there and people play by different rules. Papa!' Relieved, she welcomed her father back into the room.

At lunch I left them to chat, Meneer Endelbaum listening eagerly to Ruth's descriptions of her new life, delighted at his child's success, and aware it had taken her into a far more elaborate world than the one they had once inhabited.

Certainly, a very different world from the one she and I had shared, although I wasn't convinced about the rest. It wasn't me who had been wedded to her bed; that was Ruth. Weeks of waking up before the sun, even if chauffeured back and forth to the studio, she would find exhausting, despite not being required to do anything else – not even pick up her own clothes from the floor or make her own breakfast. Dressers were employed to do that, and coffee awaited her arrival at the studio. Did she even know how to make it? At home, when she visited, Mother or Berthe made the coffee and the Endelbaums employed a maid.

'My first film playing opposite Roland, I used to be in bed every night for eight,' she boasted to her father, her expression happy and carefree. 'I never went out. But it was so worth it. One film was all it took. By the time my next film came around, again starring opposite Roland, I couldn't walk down the street without being recognised and stopped for autographs, and my salary had quadrupled. By my third film, it had quadrupled again.'

I didn't mind, as happy for her as I knew her father would be. Wasn't that what all parents wanted – for their children to be more successful than they? And while aspiring actresses might jealously regard her success as being too easy, it hadn't been. No one knew, apart from me, the years she had dreamed of fame, focusing on every word she spoke, every gesture, checking her profile, the set of her head and her hair in a mirror.

'Maidy, I wanted to ask.'

Off guard after two glasses of champagne, I answered blithely, 'Anything.'

She giggled. 'Isn't champagne just the most wonderful?' She took a deep breath and despite feeling slightly giddy from the alcohol, I listened cautiously. Before lunch she had called me Magrit. As children, that had never been unintentional.

'If I go to Europe to make this film, will you come and work for me, and be my friend? I need someone by my side, someone I can trust. I know you've finished at college.' Impulsively, she reached out and grasped my hand. 'Dearest Maidy, you have always been my best friend. Do come. I promise I'll be good and let you write. I know that's what you plan to do. Hans told me, so do it with me.'

'Does he write often?'

'Who?'

'Hans.'

'Once or twice. He told me he paints.' Idly she took a nail file from her handbag, filing away an imaginary blemish, each nail delicately covered in pale pink polish. 'Is he any good?'

'Ruth,' I reproached, 'you know he is. You've seen his drawings, they're brilliant. He'll be famous one day, I'm sure of it. Where he lives in France, people are already talking about him.'

Her attention sharpened. 'He lives in France?'

'Didn't you say you had a letter from him?'

'Yes. He never mentioned France. My secretary reads my fan letters, I couldn't possibly read them all. Besides, she would have said.'

'Will you be writing back?'

She shrugged. 'Perhaps, if I have time.'

Her visit, as fleeting as it was, left me drained of emotion and I almost welcomed the buzzing of the intercom, the doorman signalling the arrival of her car. 'And would Miss Manning sign my son's autograph book?' he asked as she left.

Once the luncheon washing up was done and the maid left for the day, noticing how tired Meneer Endelbaum seemed, I made us both a coffee. Extraordinarily, the apartment felt empty, the beautiful paintings and elegant settees reduced to ordinary items of furniture, our conversation flat and uninteresting and I recalled how Ruth had always possessed this gift of adding sparkle to the space she was in, her departure leaving a hole. Now, after her stint in Hollywood, it had become more marked, her gestures expanded into a greater awareness of self. Yet few were spontaneous, except, perhaps, her idle smoothing of the fabric on the sofa. Each one was planned, fitting her new larger-than-life persona capable of drawing and holding the attention of an audience watching on a cinema screen.

'I don't envy Ruth her success, but I do admire it,' I said artlessly, aware that, in my position as guest, I was duty bound to keep conversation flowing. Searching for some agreeable subject, I mentioned her offer of employment. 'To be her companion while she's in Europe. What do you think?'

He replied with an embarrassed cough. 'I wanted to talk to you about that.'

'About working with Ruth?'

'Not exactly, although she did confide in me that she hoped you'd say yes. Your father wrote me about the difficult situation you find yourself in at home.'

'Oh!'

With the naivety of youth, it never occurred to me that Pappy and Meneer Endelbaum might well have been friends as well as neighbours. Even so it was a surprise to learn they had corresponded. Pappy hated letter-writing so very much, nothing apart from the most essential of letters would ever get him to sit down at his desk and pick up a pen. If the subject had come up, I might have expected him to send a politely worded note, appreciating Meneer Endelbaum's offer of hospitality during my stay in America – nothing more.

Now I saw how wrong I'd been. The words were out before I could stop them. 'You mean my mother refuses to speak to me?'

My voice emerged harsh and uncaring. Being conciliatory had made no difference, her antipathy hardening each time I imposed myself on her space.

'Yes, Gerard wrote that she blames you for Pieter leaving.' Meneer Endelbaum patted my hand.

'It's not quite as simple as that,' I said, wishing I might, just once, tell the real story and be believed.

Jaan would understand. Possibly he was the only person who would.

I hadn't thought of him for so long. Yes, he would understand; he had been there and witnessed what happened. Encouraged, I said, 'Ruth wanted to marry Pieter and then discovered she loved someone else – and I got in the middle.'

'Who was that someone else? Do I know him? Was it Hans? Ruth spoke about him several times at lunch.'

'Oh no,' I laughed. 'Hans had left for Strasbourg by then.' Picking up on Meneer Endelbaum's frown, I hastily added, 'I'm not sure I can explain it, it's far too complicated.'

He nodded. 'Men rarely understand when women try to explain, especially their daughters' efforts...' He patted me on the arm. 'And you know I always think of you as a daughter, Maidy. In which case,' he sighed. 'If it wasn't Hans and it wasn't Pieter, no doubt it was some totally unsuitable but very handsome guy that all of you girls were in love with.'

I smiled at his unerring accuracy. Were girls always that predictable? I recalled the spark of jealousy that had reared up among the students that day in the college yard, when Zande first made his appearance. For boys and men, it was all about physical prowess; for girls' perhaps a special walk or the angle of a jaw and a pair of come-hither eyes.

'About Ruth,' he continued. 'It may resolve all our problems if you worked for her. I'd feel more comfortable if you were about and it would solve the problem at home.'

I hadn't supposed Ruth to be serious. Why would anyone need

a companion so soon after marrying? It didn't make sense. That was the job of her husband, to be both a friend and a support. I would be in the way.

Still, it would provide me with a reason to leave home.

Could I?

I stared down at my empty coffee cup, thinking about Mevrouw Visser, how being at the beck and call of others had changed her. I had emerged relatively unscathed from my childhood friendship with Ruth, if you can discount a broken heart and one death. It would be sheer folly to risk the fates being so unsparing a second time.

Before I could give my answer, he broke into speech, a flood of words about a generous salary which he would contribute to, and absolute freedom to do what I wanted. 'I've made sure of that. I talked it over with Ruth. There won't be any formal duties – her maid and secretary will take care of those.'

'Then why?' I asked.

He said the words for me.

'Because I don't think Ruth is very happy.'

7

Only the clowns were missing from Ruth's wedding. As a child I had often seen circus posters, the glossy image pasted onto hoardings to advertise their imminent arrival. Then, I had thought them exciting. By the time I tumbled exhausted into my bed, the word that sprang to mind to describe the day's events was make-believe – in which there was too much of everything, from bonhomie to insincerity.

Blaring car horns accompanied our drive to City Hall, alerting pedestrians to the approaching cavalcade, and while men raised their hats in acknowledgement, girls and women darted to the kerbside to wave, with spontaneous applause breaking out all along the route. Vehicles slowed with long traffic jams forming as policemen gave precedence to the line of limousines and privately-owned vehicles, while cab drivers who were leaning on their horns in anger at the delay, on recognising the celebrities, shouted greetings to Ruth for her future happiness, their horns now resounding joyfully.

Roland and his best man travelled in the first of the limousines and along stretches of Broadway, especially where the throughway bisected the city travelling south and east, large groups of women had gathered. Almost in chorus they were shouting, '*Roland,*

Roland, over here,' and blowing elaborate kisses whenever he turned his head. And it was a beautiful head, every part of him perfectly proportioned and perfectly tailored.

I felt sorry for Ruth, convinced it was a publicity stunt arranged either by her husband or his agent. After all, if Roland had been married before, he knew the game better than her. It wasn't coincidence either, the route of the procession had been kept secret from the newspapers. Even those on display in the foyer of the hotel printing only a glossy reminder that Grace Manning would be 'tying the knot' with Roland de Courcy at City Hall at eleven – nothing else.

Despite having never visited a circus, no other simile came to mind as the six matching limousines lined up on the apron of the hotel on Fifth Avenue. Even the gleaming white pavilion of City Hall, flanked by wings of pure white stone – and teeming with autograph hunters and newsmen – played its part, as did the chauffeurs. Dressed in uniform white to match the paintwork on their vehicles, they lounged nonchalantly across the front seat, using a single hand to steer, like acrobats astride the back of white horses.

I didn't care about the folderol but I did care about Ruth, and Roland made me nervous. On being introduced, I had felt his glance, unpleasantly lingering on my body even while light-heartedly kissing my fingertips, the flamboyant gesture meant to attract the attention of waiting cameramen, hoping for something special for the lunchtime edition. Except there was no friendship in the eyes that smiled briefly into mine, only speculation. He turned back to Ruth, 'Almost as lovely as you are, my darling.'

And she was. Ruth, when I asked, had described her wedding outfit in the vaguest of terms, as something she had stumbled across in a shop. Those familiar with New York shops might well have hazarded a guess as to its cost and correctly identified its colour – I couldn't. Those uninterested in fashion might have said orange. Except it wasn't. It was far more exclusive a colour than orange. Yet it wasn't pink or red or bronze either and whenever she moved, both her coat and dress flickered with light.

The day following her visit, Meneer Endelbaum had sent me shopping with Lilian, his fiancé. 'Nothing orange or pink,' he advised. I didn't give it a moment's thought, the thrill of visiting the shops taking precedence. Only afterwards did I realise that Ruth must have confided in him and instructed him to pass on the advice.

Remembering Kirsten's admonitions, so many years ago now, I was nervous Lilian might insist navy to be the correct colour for weddings as black was for funerals and white for christenings. I needn't have worried. Ignoring dark colours, she selected those that mirrored the spring, and I eventually chose a full-skirted dress and bolero, the colour of the sea. Admittedly, I wasn't seeking attention, after all who did I know at the wedding apart from Ruth and her father? And maybe it was pure vanity to expect to register with those I was introduced to. Yet, where I had expected acknowledgement, I found only disinterest, almost the universal attitude of those at the reception – the chorus of 'darlings' seemingly the only language guests shared in common.

'None of this crowd can be bothered to remember names.'

I glanced up, seeing a fresh faced, brown-haired young man in horn-rimmed spectacles. Several years older than me, he was clutching a plate of *hors d'oeuvres*, a bottle and two glasses.

'How did you guess that's what I was thinking?'

'Dazed is the normal expression for anyone on their first encounter with this madhouse.' He swung round pointing casually with the neck of the bottle.

I didn't want to admit *circus* had been my chosen description.

'By the way, you've stolen my greenery,' he accused with a mock frown. 'That's the corner I usually occupy at weddings.'

'It doesn't have your name on it.' I retorted somewhat shamelessly, quickly adding, 'sorry, that was the champagne talking.'

'How much?'

'Two glasses.'

He laughed. 'You're way behind. Let me give you a top up,' and before I could prevent him, he had filled my glass to overflowing.

'In this company, it's considered bad manners to stand with an empty glass for longer than five seconds. You're Grace's friend, Magrit, aren't you?'

'Yes, we grew up together.' I shifted over, patting the space on the bench next to me. 'And you remembered my name.'

'Don't read anything into that. It's my job. I'm Greg. Roland's brother.' Adding, 'don't bother, we're not alike,' as I swung round to view him more clearly. 'Different mothers.' I didn't comment, relief being my only emotion because I had found Roland's intrusion offensive. 'It's also my job to compliment the bridesmaid on her appearance. You look stunning.'

'Oh.' I blushed. 'Hardly a bridesmaid. I held the bouquet for a minute, no more.'

'I mean it. Celebrity weddings are the perfect excuse for a fashion parade, for both men and women. It's a chance to show-off. That's why the guest list is so vast. That's also why no one is sitting down, clothes present better if the wearer is standing up.'

'Do they?' I smoothed the silk fabric of my dress, wishing I was bold enough to mix with the milling throng and show it off. 'My college friend,' I said, meaning Kirsten, 'once described a catwalk in Paris. I was thinking of that when we entered City Hall in procession.'

He grinned at me. 'You'll do.'

'Do?'

'Yes.'

Even not quite understanding the comment, I guessed it to be complimentary. 'And you work for your brother?'

Nodding, he indicated the plate he was carrying. 'Here, take one, it's going to be a long afternoon. Grace sent me. Says I'm to twist your arm about working for her. It's all the rage.'

'What is?'

'Having your family involved. I always think of it like the security blanket babies are so attached to,' and he flashed his easy smile.

I didn't reply for a moment, munching on a roll of smoked-salmon layered between finely cut brown bread, aware I'd not given Ruth an answer. *I'll think about it,* was the nearest I got. 'Aren't you eating?'

'I'm hurt you didn't notice I've been stuffing my face for the past hour. This crowd don't believe in eating so I was almost the only one at the buffet table.' His tone had changed sounding almost belittling.

'Yet this is the crowd you choose to run with.'

'Ouch! You speak your mind, Magrit.'

I stared at him in surprise. 'It must be the wine; I don't usually.'

'Don't judge my existence by this.' He nodded in the direction of the gossiping guests. 'It can be a good life, provided you keep your feet firmly grounded.'

'How do you manage it?'

He grinned. 'By dredging up all the things I hated about my previous existence.'

'Which was?'

From across the room, I heard someone call. 'Greg?'

'That's me.' He rose to his feet, leaving the plate and bottle behind on the seat, his expression serious again. 'I run with them because my ambition is to become a screen-writer.' He swung away immediately turning back, rocking back and forth on his feet. 'Okay, you seem an upfront sort of girl, so I'm going to come right out and say it.'

'Say what?' I glanced up in alarm.

The disembodied voice called his name again. Greg swung round impatiently. 'If you repeat this, I'll deny I ever said it because I need my job. Grace is lovely but she's a fool to marry Roland. Yes, I know,' he waved my interruption aside, 'she says she's madly in love with him. Maybe she is and maybe she isn't.' He noticed my surprise. 'It's publicity that builds careers and marriage creates publicity. Nevertheless, if she is in love with him, and most of the starlets are, undoubtedly, she will get hurt. Accept her job offer. The marriage can't last and then she will need you more than you think.'

As he walked away, I recalled Ruth's face on seeing the reporters leave, the day of her visit to her father. She had seemed bereft as if the only contact with her world had gone too.

8

A feeling of tremendous optimism accompanied me back to the ship at the end of my holiday, as if I had smuggled a little bit of New York aboard in my suitcase. Even Mevrouw Visser couldn't quash it – not that she wanted to. She'd also been infected and when the ship's Tannoy greeted us with the announcement that a smooth crossing was predicted, she was out of the blocks like a racehorse, recounting to everyone who would listen details of her amazing trip. And if no one lingered long enough, I became her audience. Surprisingly I didn't mind, pleased to find traces of colour in her otherwise dull and uneventful life.

It did serve to make up my own mind. I most definitely was not about to become a Mevrouw Visser. Not now, not after seeing what the outside world had to offer. In a few short weeks, the imposing vastness of the American continent had stolen my imagination, as it had for the hundreds who descended daily on New York's vast edifices of steel and glass. There, the whole world was within one's grasp. All one had to do was reach out.

Buoyed up with dreams of a new life, my feet eventually regained their earth-bound status on the boat train carrying us from the dockside to the city when my eyes flew open, jolting me back to reality. Had I really expected the quiet somnambulance of my country to have changed its coat during my absence? If so, I was wrong. If anything, it was smaller than my memory of it, a Lilliputian landscape with tiny rivers and miniscule pockets of earth, in which equally tiny people were living. As the railtracks wandered through a countryside village, I spotted two women who greeted one another with a neat bob of the head, one immediately turning to curtsey to a customer, a man on a bicycle, who had stopped by the roadside to drink a cup of the milk she was selling.

Even the city's skyline which I had once thought so magical now appeared ossified by comparison to the skyline I had just said goodbye to. Had the train's progress stuttered or was it simply a trick of the light that made its spires and chimneys seem unmoving and frozen in time? Even the tell-tale cupola on the museum roof was without life; the white-jacketed doves missing and smoke curling idly from chimney pots hanging stationary in the air.

Without thinking, I'd asked the taxi to drop me outside the Judas gates that opened into the backyard. I could as easily have used the front door; I had a key. It was habit that took me there, my gaze resting on the steps up to the backdoor where, as children, the four of us sat to recover from a rumbustious game of tag.

Noticing the workroom doors tightly shut, I dropped my suitcase on the steps and wandered back out into the street. It was busy, cars nosing their way across the bridge behind a line of cyclists, their heavy tyres rattling the slats in the wooden planking. I'm not sure what I was seeking, my reluctance to return to the house more like that of a small child than a girl of nineteen summers, who naively determines her future happiness on the throw of a dice or the blowing of a fluffy dandelion seed. I didn't voice the mantra, *if there is one thing different, other things will be different as well*, but that is what I was hoping, searching for the courage to face the obstacles waiting for me at home.

Without thinking of anything much, I leant on the rail watching two drakes argue their ownership of a patch of green weed floating on the surface. The tide was ebbing, exposing mud flats pitted with markings where sandpipers, the busy-bodies of the bird world in their flecked brown jackets, played games of dare, flocking towards the water only to flee back next moment to the safety of the bank.

On the north bank, a string of boats like the black keys of a piano were drawn up out of the water and further upriver, straddling the river path, the houses that had played such a significant role in my life, with as many genuine stories as fictional ones, only given life because of my ineptness or forgetfulness that had earned me a tongue-lashing from Mother.

That was something else my voyage had decided. From now on, I would live in the real world.

Except … what had Yöst meant about my making a decision? What hadn't happened yet?

Did he mean my leaving home or something else entirely?

I stared back at our house, standing four-square on the corner of the street, unmoving and unmoved by events. I must have seen it hundreds if not thousands of times, and passed it by, uncaring of its history or indeed the lives of my many ancestors who had once lived there. Apart from our grandparents whom I had so briefly known, the rest were mere shadows, yet all had shared a very similar passion – the ability to create beautiful objects. One after another, according to the style of the day, they had drawn images of birds and beasts on glass or carved them into a wood surround, silvering the back of the glass to produce a pure image. Now, I wished they might speak to me, and assure me I wasn't alone and others had stood where I was, wondering what to do and how to live the life our kindly deity had awarded.

It was already late afternoon. I'd had to wait for a train, and the awning over the shop window had been put away, leaving its plate-glass like an eye without eyelashes … bold but bare. It had been renewed last year, when the sagging sailcloth of the original finally succumbed to rot. Pappy, protective of his investment, had put Enri in charge, instructing him to close the canopy once the sun had moved on, to highlight the courtyard and rear windows.

I had begged Pappy to choose any colour apart from cream or white, conscious neither would keep their pristine freshness longer than a winter or two. 'Perhaps green with a frilled valance, and our name, Bader, on it. Green will last. The salesman promised it will keep its colour for twenty years.' Pappy had smiled at that and I had smiled back grateful to see a lightening of his sombre expression. 'Did you add the last bit, Maidy, as a bribe?' he asked me, for Baders offer a twenty-year guarantee on all their mirrors.

Enri had taken up Pappy's offer to lodge with us from Monday to Saturday. His family were country people, and although Lars and his wife, who lived in the city, had offered the boy a bed, their apartment was miniscule, and Pappy decided it more sensible if he lived 'over the shop' as he described it. Of course, he didn't charge rent, saying if Enri put his heart and soul into learning that would be payment enough.

I loved Pappy even more when I heard him gently reproach Mother for grumbling about the boy living with us. She failed to understand how much Pappy missed the echo of feet up and down the stairs, and while he had grown used to Hans' absence, the disappearance of Pieter so abruptly afterwards and then Berthe had caused him renewed grief. He had wanted to make over the entire top floor to Berthe and Yoav, and install a second bathroom for them. I could easily have moved down a floor into Hans' room. He wouldn't have cared, his single stipulation not to touch the drawings pinned to the wall. 'You'll only mess the arrangement and it took me days to get it right,' he would have reprimanded me.

His fascination with snails had lasted for months and on summer nights when the three of us, Hans, Ruth and I, rode our bicycles out into the countryside, he would scour the grassy banks of the river for suitable specimens. Taking them back home to copy their intricate patterns and being too lazy to return them to the fields, a night or two later he would place them under a bush in some stranger's garden on his way to the inn.

It was Mother who forbade my moving down a floor, declaring Pappy ought to convert the upper-storey of the stable block for the newlyweds instead. 'If you insist on Enri living here, he can use one of the rooms at the rear of the house; it would be most improper for him to share a landing with Magrit.'

It was at those moments I missed Hans the most. On hearing, he would have snorted with derision, for Enri resembled a puff of wind. 'A good blow and he'll fall over,' I could hear him shouting with laughter.

Shortly after, we emptied Berthe's room, filling it with the summer curtains, suitcases, and old lamps that had originally been stored in the back bedroom … and Mother moved into Pieter's room.

Dear Berthe explained, with all the worldly wisdom of a newly married woman, that mother wanting to sleep separately was something that occasionally happened to women when they reached a certain age.

It wasn't that. She hadn't fallen out with Pappy. She couldn't bear him to love her. In our country, no respectably married woman goes to bed with one man and dreams of another. Like some great millstone around the neck, the guilt was choking her.

I stared up at the house. The window on the third floor was slightly ajar, where either Berthe or our maid, anticipating my return, had opened it. A strange feeling, gazing inward rather than outward. Perhaps those tiny panes of glass in their wood surround were more aware of my thoughts than I wanted to admit – and they already knew that, very shortly, my room also would become as empty as those belonging to both Berthe and Hans.

Flustered, I glanced away to next door, picking up on a square of stone a shade lighter than all the rest that topped the lintel of the doorway, where once a pink awning had hung, with the name Endelbaum inscribed on it in elegant calligraphy. It had never failed to demand my attention, always the first thing I noticed when Ruth and I emerged from the river walk on our way home from school.

Silly, I know; then children are often silly, illogically fixing their affections on the most outlandish of objects – no different from Hans and his snails. That's the wonder of childhood; they are allowed to do that. Now the shop doorway, behind which Meneer Endelbaum had spent his days cutting and polishing the diamonds of his trade, was screened by a curtain, and the room he worked in had become a sitting room for the tenants who rented the property. I glanced up to the top floor where Ruth's bedroom used to be and where, one night, exactly where I was standing now, with his hands resting on the rails of the bridge, Pieter took the decision to ask Ruth to marry him.

I doubted anything much had registered with my brother from that point on; his whole being fixated on a future with Ruth as his wife, in which he would finally achieve his heart's desire to become a master craftsman. He'd never confided that particular dream to anyone, but I knew. From the first stories he'd read to me I had been his shadow, sensitive to his every mood, made happy by his interest in me and his contentment with life.

Lars knew it too. 'His heart wasn't in it,' the foreman once said, describing Hans, 'not like Pieter.'

I frowned down at the stream of water littered with debris from an earlier shower, where a trace of wind had fashioned miniature ruffles on its surface. Among the soggy flower petals and leaves already turning brown was a single daisy. Miraculously, it was still white and undamaged, its fragile stalk snapped by a rogue gust of wind or tossed callously aside at the end of a love affair.

At once I was back – back to that night with Mother hissing at me as hostile as any swan, '*This is what comes of your meddling – I have lost my child and for that I will never forgive you.*'

Back to that night in which the volcano of truth finally erupted – the one in which I tried to prevent Ruth breaking her betrothal to Pieter, aware of the tragic consequences if she did.

Concerned by the shadows under my eyes and my white face, these were the memories Pappy had made me promise to toss overboard. I believed them gone, obediently dropping them over the side of the ship. Perhaps not all at once, little by little, the last and the most precious, my memories of Zande. Washed back across the Atlantic as if by the winds of fate, here they were at my feet, like a dog begging for a bone, calling out that their histories were not yet finished.

Yet how to tell the story of Pieter, the real story? Except, which was the real story? The dark clouds that enveloped the shame of his birth and disappearance, or the years of beautiful life that stood between?

And what about Ruth?

What small child doesn't want to see her dreams become reality and marry her prince charming? Isn't that how authors write their fairy stories, with a happy ending?

'Maidy? Maidy?'

Startled, I glanced up to see Berthe heading along the street towards me, wheeling the pram. 'Oh, how wonderful, you're back. We weren't expecting you until tomorrow. Your room's ready, I did it yesterday.'

9

It was Berthe who suggested we ate dinner with them. 'I've been saving up our celebration of baby Gerard's birthday until our new apartment was quite finished and you had returned. I will telephone my mother-in-law, and ask them too.' I heard the pride in her words: for Berthe marriage was the personification of all her dreams.

Dear Berthe, I remembered all the years I took her for granted, never once singling out her plodding tenacity for special recognition, taking it for granted she would help our maids or Mother in the kitchen. Now, because of that, she had grown into the perfect homemaker, the food she served worthy of a place in the most exacting of restaurants. And thankfully, so engrossed in her preparations, she failed to notice Mother's glacial tone whenever she was forced to address me.

'This way,' my sister continued, smiling fondly at her husband every few minutes. 'Maidy can tell us about her trip.'

I liked Yoav. On one of the pages in my journal I had written a series of words to describe him, eventually deciding steadfast the most appropriate. While not the most exciting of men, unless you happened to be a mathematical figure in need of attention, he was perfectly content with what he had, and wanted nothing more. If he had detected the tension floating up and down the many staircases of our house after Pieter left, his lack of curiosity would consign it to disagreements that arose in every family from time to time.

Hans had undertaken the design of their new apartment, although his return for the wedding almost a month early had been more of a financial consideration. Having completed his apprenticeship, he and his friends promptly drank his savings, leaving him with just enough money for his train fare.

The first we had known of his return was a telegram with his arrival time at the station and the words, 'Will walk, no money.'

'Quite normal.' I greeted him with a hug as the train pulled in. 'Why so early? The wedding's not for a month.'

He pulled away, striking a pose. 'I've been appointed chief designer. Can you believe it?'

'You mean you've appointed yourself chief designer?' I picked up his briefcase which bulged with papers. Drawings – rather than the trappings of business life – Hans never bothered with such things, tossing them aside.

'No! Well, perhaps. Pappy told me how much it would cost and I suggested doing it for a pittance. And Pappy agreed. Still can't believe it. He always thought me such a dunce.'

I looped my arm through his, almost dragging him towards the tram terminus fronting the rail station. 'No. He thought you a lousy apprentice but a wonderful artist. Now you've the chance to prove yourself an equally wonderful architect.'

And he was, although the renovations took fourteen months to complete and by that time baby Gerard had been born.

For almost six months after their wedding, Berthe and Yoav moved from one room to another, as builders and decorators pulled the upstairs storage space apart, the newly married couple moving back into the main house and camping in the spare bedroom on the top floor for two months while the roof was replaced.

'Quite like old times,' Lars commented, hearing Hans shout at Pappy that if he wasn't prepared to put his hand in his pocket for a new roof, he would chuck in the towel and he could damn well pay a real architect to finish the job.

'You can't place my design under a roof that leaks – it's sacrilege,' he yelled, thumping the worktable in the basement atelier. 'You wouldn't put your designs in a shabby surround.'

'It's certainly more peaceful when he's not here.' I sighed. 'But emptier somehow, as if we've lost two members of the family – not just the one,' I added without thinking.

'We all hope Pieter will return one day.' Lars eyed me sympathetically.

I edged a laugh. Pieter wouldn't return until something changed. Yet how could anything change? 'No! I meant Hans is noisy enough for two ordinary people.'

Hans had asked the same question, phrasing it differently. 'What did happen to Pieter to make him leave again so suddenly?'

To him, I offered the only possible answer. 'Ruth decided not to marry him.' It brought light to my brother's eyes, and I read in them speculation, although he didn't say anything, returning a somewhat ambiguous comment that it was a shame. 'I'm still not returning for good. I don't mind a week or so once or twice a year... In any case, the new apprentice seems capable enough.'

Hans had changed, a late growth spurt carrying him up on to a higher plane than the one Pappy inhabited, although Pappy insisted it was because he had shrunk, 'as all men do in middle age.' Still boyish although no longer childish, Hans had acquired experience of the world plus a longer hairstyle. It suited him, although I doubt Mother approved. Knowing Hans, he wouldn't care, only interested in the glances he attracted from girls, grinning mischievously at the disapproving frowns of older and more conventional matrons. In his eyes, I saw a cool acceptance of his place in the world. He was a qualified apprentice and had cast aside the nagging and censure that had once been his lot; that now belonged in the past.

It wasn't the only row he and Pappy had over plans for the stable-block, Pappy calling him a popinjay and upbraiding him for his new-fangled notions. 'These principles have been followed by our family for hundreds of years,' he insisted.

'Which is as good a reason as any to get rid of them. They're old-hat.'

Of course, Hans got his way and it was a triumph, with skylights along the length of the new roof creating space and light throughout. In addition to a modern bathroom and kitchen, he had also fashioned a new staircase that rose up from the yard. Curving around in the shape of a helter-skelter, the upper portion was roofed in acrylic glass, a new material Hans wanted to try, its steps wide enough to negotiate with a pushchair yet shallow enough for a small child to circumnavigate. He also found a corner for a nursery, using a sliding-wall made of the same acrylic to separate it from the main bedroom.

Yoav had added his own compliment to the artist, framing the original drawings and hanging them on the wall, despite Berthe's preference for flower prints. Usually taciturn, I'd been startled to hear him say almost forcefully that when Hans became famous, they would be worth a great deal of money. 'And very useful that will be too.'

'When you retire Pappy,' Berthe added, 'or when our family has grown too large, you and Mother can move in here, and we will take over the big house.'

Mother flinched, her mouth a tight line of disapproval, and I noticed that Berthe was expecting a second child. 'I doubt Pappy will think of retiring until after Enri qualifies,' she said with a sting in her words.

Unearthing a copy of the newspaper Meneer Endelbaum had insisted I brought with me to show off my new-found fame, I passed it around the table. 'I loved my wardrobe, Berthe, and can't thank you enough. Especially that dress, it's quite perfect. After meeting up with Ruth, I bought another one for the wedding.'

'Oh, Maidy.' She smiled at me. 'Fancy having your picture on the front cover of a newspaper. An American newspaper too. Who'd have believed it? I'm so glad I made you buy it.'

Pappy coughed, the sparkle in his eyes belying the seriousness of his expression.

Berthe laughed. She had changed too, her sunny viewpoint

very appealing. 'I'm so glad Pappy made you buy that dress,' she corrected. 'You look quite wonderful. And your partner?'

'That's Rico. He's French, of Spanish descent. He and his troop,' I tapped the newspaper, where Katarina, severe in black, and Emilee, her skirt flying up to her thigh, had also been picked up by cameras as they swirled around, 'they were appearing at one of the theatres. To drum up business, they gave an impromptu performance in the street.' I pointed to the makeshift orchestra, the figure of the guitarist in his wheelchair in the foreground. 'And that's Ramon Martorell, the guitarist. It was his concert we attended earlier. It was magical; I've never spent such an exciting evening.'

It was true. Since Pieter's sixteenth birthday, every celebration, even Berthe's wedding, had been blighted by memories of the one person missing from our family circle.

A sense of determination carried me downstairs early next morning, wanting to catch Pappy on his own. I knew Mother wouldn't be down yet, I could hear her moving about upstairs and, although she no longer occupied the marital bedroom, she still considered it her wifely duty to keep it clean and tidy. But Enri might well appear.

'What Berthe said last night, about our moving into their apartment when I retire. It would make good sense.' Pappy greeted me. 'This house is too big for the three of us.'

I stared around the living room. After the elegance of Meneer Endelbaum's apartment, it appeared both shabby and cluttered, as if in my absence it too had shrunk. L-shaped, with windows looking out onto both the street and the river, a door led into the kitchen at the back of the house. Even the mahogany dining table with its matching sideboard and chairs, passed down through the family from our great grandparents, seemed old-fashioned, belonging to a time when families gathered to celebrate birthdays and feast days. Now, we used the breakfast table for all our meals.

'New surroundings may be all that Margaret needs.' Pappy chatted on, 'I'm sure eventually she'll come back to us.'

He said the words as if his wife had taken a suitcase and gone off on holiday.

'Until then...' He raised his eyebrows, questioning as I placed a cup of coffee in front of him. 'I may finally need to learn how to make coffee, unless I can persuade Enri to get up earlier. Still.' He patted the chair beside him – Pieter's chair. 'He's a good lad and coming on well.'

No doubt it had been an absentminded gesture on Pappy's part, having slipped his mind that Mother hated for any of us to use it, and hiding it away in the study for six long years. Whenever guests came and we used the mahogany dining set, she stood Pieter's chair against the wall, prey to the superstitious belief that a missing person could only return if their chair remained empty. His abrupt departure this time had left that superstition without a home and she no longer bothered, too distraught to hide it away as she had once done. Then, perhaps, it was time.

Even so, I ignored Pappy's invitation to sit next to him, and pulled out my own chair on the opposite side of the table.

Perhaps the only thing Berthe and I shared in common was our insistence on our rightful place at the table. If ever our maids inadvertently swapped chairs around while dusting them, the first of us down would instantly replace them on their own spot. The chair Hans used was easily identifiable, its front legs badly scuffed where he had scraped them with his shoes whilst arguing with Pappy or Pieter, frustrated over something he felt passionate about, and the cushion on Pappy's chair sagged at the front, a slight deafness the only visible outcome of Pieter's continued absence, leaning forward at the table to hear more clearly.

As for my chair... As I had grown up, it had grown with me and I treated it as a cherished friend, brushing off crumbs and straightening its seat cushion before sitting down. As a small child, it had been bolstered with a clutch of cushions. Even then, only the colour of the tablecloth ever met my gaze and it was many months before, if I sat up really straight and stretched my neck, I managed to catch a glimpse of Pappy's hand on the far side of the table reaching for the basket of rolls. When I was seven or eight and my height began to gather pace, his face and his upper torso rocketed into view, often sitting with his coffee cup stationary in the air, reading the newspaper. If that happened, I explored the wall behind, picking up on tiny abrasions in the wallpaper that grew into the faces of goblins or fairies if you stared at them long enough. Above everything else, no matter if the sun was shining or it was raining, with the wind howling loud enough to rouse banshees and werewolves from their beds, I cherished the comforting smile on Pappy's face whenever he glanced at me across the table.

The clock on the landing struck the half-hour and I realised how early we were.

'Life cannot stand still, Maidy,' he replied to my unspoken question. 'Neither can you hold onto the past. If it could, I would have you back as a nine-year-old, reciting your stories to Pieter on the back step.'

'Is that really what you'd remember?' I asked, astonished.

'Not always. If I'm hungry, it's usually Berthe laying breakfast.'

I glanced at his empty plate and despite knowing he was teasing, rushed into the kitchen where Mother had left a tray covered with a cloth.

Sitting down again, I pulled the honey towards me, taking a roll from the basket. Since Hans had left, it was the baker's grandson who delivered our bread along with Pappy's newspaper.

'And when are you leaving?'

'Pappy! Why would you think that?'

'Maidy, I will listen to evasions from others, not from you, my child.'

I reached out across the table and grasped his hand. It was warm, the pulse in his wrist beating strongly as it had all my life – always there – its steady rhythm soothing away the pain of a cut knee or bumped elbow. 'Pappy, Mother will never forgive me, not until Pieter returns.' The words came out hotter than I intended. 'She will always believe I drove him away, and that I broke up his engagement to Ruth out of spite and jealousy.'

'Surely not. No one who knows you could ever think that,'

Pappy replied mildly, picking up his cup and taking a sip of the milky white liquid.

I didn't explain further, there was too much disquiet between my parents without my adding to it. I withdrew my hand and reached for the butter.

'Where will you go?'

The card Yöst had given me lay on my dressing table – my lucky omen. Using a ruler, I had already estimated the distance between our two countries. 'Hans asked me to visit him and I wondered if I might find a job in a shop for the summer. Meneer Endelbaum gave me money for my birthday, wasn't that kind?'

'I'd forgotten,' Pappy admitted ruefully. 'Perhaps I can give you money as well. It's always useful.'

'Oh no, Pappy, you gave me money, lots of it to go to America,' I hastily reassured him, spreading honey on my buttered roll. I had learned to eat a little extra whilst in New York, finding the portions in American restaurants much larger, although it had made little difference to my slight frame. Maybe my face was softer except that might well have been just the result of growing up and becoming nineteen. 'Besides, I had a most wonderful birthday. I walked twenty laps around the deck for luck, which I was told by our steward was customary. And all sorts of people wished me a happy day.' I laughed. 'Then at dinner, the table was presented with champagne and a birthday cake and all the English passengers and crew sang, *A Happy Birthday*. And Mevrouw Visser...'

'Oh dear,' Pappy twinkled at me.

'No! America obviously agreed with her. I had written to her about the Spanish dancing. She must have gone straight out and bought a book on Flamenco dance and she gave it to me. There's a picture of the dancer I met, Rico. Wasn't that kind?' I leaned forward eagerly. 'It's a secret, so you mustn't say anything because she hasn't told Mevrouw Kleissler yet; she's hoping to return and live there permanently.'

I heard footsteps on the stairs.

It was habit to listen and to identify each individual and

their humour by the echo on the wooden treads. Sometimes that game replayed through my dreams and we were all present at the breakfast table – no one absent. Pieter and Hans would be chatting, shouting with laughter at jokes only they were party to; Berthe fielding their boyish humour with her usual unshakable calm, and Pappy beaming at the sight of his family gathered around the table while Mother smiled lovingly.

It was Enri who pushed open the door and came in.

He was a pleasant-enough lad, although, with the new-found maturity travel had given me, light-years younger ... barely sixteen.

Lars had suggested Pappy take him on. 'The lad's always drawing. Not much good at games, and quite possibly has trouble adding two and two, but he's a right one with a pencil.'

I had been amused to find that Enri had taken over the back steps, sketching the builders as they worked on the apartment and catching their likenesses with ease, but even I could see his skill lay in a very different direction from Hans – more focussed and detailed.

'Magrit.'

I'd got up to make fresh coffee. Hearing the unaccustomed name on Pappy's lips, I swung round.

Momentary he seemed old, sending fear as strong as an electric shock racing through me, the eyes regarding me weary. Like a child caught out, he immediately schooled his expression into a grimace. 'How silly' he said, the hint of a smile returning to his voice. 'I haven't called you Magrit for years. Must be getting old. You will stay a few days, won't you? Berthe will enjoy the company while Yoav is at work.'

I didn't wait for Mother to come down to breakfast. I knew nothing between us would have changed and it would seem not for Pappy either. The previous afternoon, noticing Lars had already taken my suitcase upstairs, I went on up, leaving Berthe to follow with Baby Gerard. He had decided he wanted to climb the stairs himself, despite their steepness, his mouth all set to emit a loud wail if he didn't get his own way. I had glanced over my shoulder, smiling to see his face tilted upwards, intent on the challenge he'd set himself. For him, the stairs represented the tallest of tall mountains, even with Berthe patiently guiding both his hands and feet onto each step. At the same time, she was carefully explaining that Yoav had been the same at that age, determined to do things himself, despite her not knowing Yoav as a child.

Pappy had already finished work and was in the kitchen drinking tea, my parents voices comfortable with each other. My immediate reaction was one of hope that in my absence she had decided to return to the marital bed; it was short lived, the door of Pieter's old bedroom closing behind her after wishing us both a stilted goodnight.

I knew what had to be done. Pappy had known it too; he'd read the determination in my face when I came down to breakfast.

It was too early to call on Berthe, and crossing the yard I met up with Lars, who was standing at the workshop door, smoking. I remembered Pappy saying: 'I have only one rule – no smoking in the workshop, there's too many flammable substances.' It had been a good rule, and neither Pieter nor Hans smoked, although for Hans, the decision was based on his finances, not earning enough as an apprentice to both smoke and drink.

Despite the hour, the door to the workroom was wide open; Lars had obviously come in early and I was surprised to find Hendrik there too. Wielding a paintbrush, he was busily white-washing the walls. It was a time-consuming process with so many objects to be moved, and one I know Pappy put off until the walls were almost crying aloud their need for a clean coat.

'The master thinks we should have a fresh look to attract new customers,' Lars confirmed, sending a neat circle of smoke into the air.

'That sounds more like Hans than Pappy. Do you want some help?'

I heard his chuckle, hastily swallowed down.

'Honestly, Lars, I haven't broken anything in ages.'

'In that case, Magrit, you can strip that wall.' He was still smiling, and I was lost in a memory of my childhood, and Pappy's insistence that I stand still with my hands behind my back. 'And you are to keep them there,' I remembered him saying, 'otherwise your fingers will doubtless find their way into a paint pot.'

Handing me a small screwdriver, Lars pointed to the sample surrounds displayed on the wall, each one of the vee-shaped corner pieces painted with a different pattern. 'They will need cleaning.'

He couldn't have chosen a nicer job. Over the years the patterns had come to represent a calendar of my changing taste, little different from the marks Pieter had once scratched on the wall to record my height. At first, with only the lower rows visible from my childhood hiding place under the table, the decision as to which of the patterns was my favourite changed in step with my height. Like the photographs on the wall upstairs, they too represented a history of our family, the oldest samples gilt-edged in the flamboyant style of the previous century, and there was one of birds that Grandfather must have drawn, the style formal, copied from the big encyclopaedia that still lay in the drawer. Pappy rarely used it, love and imagination was all he needed to create the fairies that danced around the frame of the mirror, he'd given me on my thirteenth birthday. Among the pieces in the most recent section were woodland animals that Hans had drawn, the bright eyes of a blackbird regarding me curiously, although his style was not yet as delicate and as detailed as Pappy's; and one section in a hand I knew less well – Pieter's.

Using the stepladder, I began at the top, carefully placing each section on the work table. 'What are those?' I pointed to several finished pieces wrapped in a grey cloth to protect them.

'They're new,' Lars replied and I heard pride in his voice. 'It was my nephew who suggested we try out the patterns.'

I never considered Lars anything other than family – always helpful, always there. Grandfather had taken him on when he left school. 'I was only twelve,' he told me. I remember he had patted his false leg. 'And could I run fast.' Apart from the war years, when both he and Hendrik served in the army, ending up as prisoners, he had been with us forever. 'Enri was tidying the drawer in the work table.' He pointed to the monstrosity of a table that Pappy's father had built. It ran down the centre of the workshop, the drawers on either side wide enough for both plans and diagrams. 'And picked out some of the patterns young Hans had drawn. Said it was what modern people wanted – stripes and zigzags.'

Rubbing his hands down the back of his overall to clean them, Lars untied the string on one of the mirrors and partially removed its cover.

'Does Hans know?' I burst out impetuously, surprised to discover the wooden surround to be of ash rather than the traditional woods, oak, walnut, and mahogany. Double the width, with a geometrical diamond pattern etched into the wood, the mirror itself was quite plain without any embellishment, not even a bevel.

'I doubt it,' Lars smiled. 'If memory serves, it's only when Hans needs money does he get in touch and then by telegram. I hope when you leave home, you will at least write,' he admonished.

'Do you approve, Maidy?'

Hearing Pappy's feet on the spiral stair, I swung round. 'It's wonderful. Did Enri create the template?'

'Why would you ask that?'

'Because that's his style, very precise.'

'What a clever family I have, Lars.'

They exchanged a nod that revealed their many years working together, Lars carefully rewrapping the mirror to protect it from specks of whitewash.

'You are quite correct, Maidy.' Pappy smiled his confirmation. 'Hans did the drawings a few years back, whilst Pieter was still with us. At the time I felt they were too avantgarde. Of course, Hans disagreed.' He beamed at me.

Naturally Hans would have protested, he was impatient for life to happen instantly.

'Even now, the patterns are far too intricate to create freehand. Besides, they need younger fingers than my own.' He held his hands up, the knuckles on his right hand swollen with overuse. 'And, yes, Enri did make the template.'

I waited long enough to compliment Enri who arrived at a run still chewing on a roll, but didn't stay; the atmosphere switching to work, with a discussion of the day's schedule.

Outside, a chill wind had blown in with the river tide and I clutched my jacket around me, hurrying across the street into the shelter of the narrow walkways. College and I had officially parted company at Easter, before I left for America and straight after my final exams, although I would need to return to discover the results and perhaps discuss with my professors what I might do next. Except I already knew, it was to write.

I didn't bother with my bicycle, wanting to call on Meneer Meijer. Nevertheless, despite it not being far, I mostly cycled. The sound of bicycle tyres sweeping through puddles or skimming across the slats of a wooden bridge raised no phantoms, only footsteps did that – an echo crossing the street sufficient to give me hope they belonged to Zande and he had returned. Then I would veer off into a side road away from the sound, fearing the disappointment that would follow if I dared look over my shoulder and saw some other young man.

Reaching my bridge, I trailed my fingers across its ancient balustrade, the ledge brittle and flaking, leaving tiny piles of dust against the base of the wall, like dormice seeking shelter from the wind. The familiar nooks and crannies brought back my childhood years with Ruth, and I didn't want anything to do with those, so I ran on down the steps to the canal bank. Meneer Meijer was in the garden, pottering about, although I was shocked to see the tiny vegetable patch, which in previous years had always grown a neat array of vegetables, both untidy and weed-spotted.

I had kept my promise and visited him regularly, and we had become close friends. He loved to talk about his wife, Marie, and I was happy to listen, the elderly man sometimes narrating the exact same story he had told me the week before. He never mentioned Zande, the child they had brought up. Mostly we discussed my studies, and that first winter he introduced me to French, the language he and Marie had spoken for over thirty years.

'It's the language of love and happiness. Despite being born here, Holland has not proved a kindly place. We left originally because of the influenza brought on by the war. Millions died then. We were lucky; Marie caught it and survived though it always left her with a weak chest. And when we moved back, it was to find war once again on our doorstep.'

I still spoke French badly, thinking first in Dutch and translating, although it was no longer an enigma. Nevertheless, at the periphery of all our conversations lay the suspicion that the lessons were simply a ploy, a way to enjoy one another's company without revisiting the tragedy of that storm-filled night when the swans were driven away from the island.

"What's happened to your garden? Aren't you well?' I called. Leaping the last two, I hugged his arm in greeting. We had dispensed with the formal handshake several years before.

'Maidy, what a delightful surprise. And yes, I am quite well.'

Despite his words, I noticed he was using his cane in the garden. Picking up on the direction of my gaze, he grimaced.

'They tell me pride always comes before a fall,' he quoted, making me laugh, 'and having lived most of my life devoid of pride, I am reluctant to acquire it now.'

During the three years since we first met, he had shrunk further, his back rounding with age. Nevertheless, his cheerful spirit remained undiminished. Perhaps he had become a little more birdlike with his lively gaze, his head tilted slightly to one side, explaining when I asked, 'It's the fault of my spectacles never being in the place where I last used them.'

'If I could have asked for a visitor,' he chatted on, 'your name would be first on my list. I was hoping for someone to visit and stay long enough to accompany me to City Hall ... and then you appear.'

'Why City Hall?' I echoed.

'A long story and one deserving of coffee, and maybe a piece of cake. My neighbour,' he pointed upwards to the houses on the street above, their back gardens angling down to the water. 'She often bakes extra. Go on in.'

So familiar had the house become, I no longer noticed the shabby floor-coverings or the paucity of the cooking utensils in the kitchen, my gaze resting on the lustre on the surface of the little dining table and the black-leaded grate that sparkled in the electric light, a line of plates on the dresser glowing with colour. No one knew its history; perhaps the house had simply appeared one day, like toadstools that push up into the air overnight. Pappy said, when I asked, that in some far-distant century, when people were forced to pay tolls to use a waterway or cross a bridge, it might have been built to house the toll-keeper and his family.

It explained the turreted roof and its position on the bank, tight up against the flight of steps to the street. Even so, I preferred my version, the one I had so frequently used in my stories – that it had been blown there straight from fairyland.

'Why do you need to visit the City Hall?' I repeated my question. I spooned two dessertspoons of coffee into the percolator, adding the boiling water.

'Yesterday, I received an official letter from the burghers who run our tiny enclave. Here!' Plucking it from the back of the clock, he handed me the typewritten envelope.

At first, I didn't understand the official-ease in which points were carefully numbered and bracketed. After reading it twice, I gathered that despite extensive checks, enquiries into the former occupants of the house had drawn a blank, the letter continuing, 'no living relatives have come forward,' and confirming Albert Meijer's ownership.

'So, you see, Maidy, officially it already belongs to me and has done since the end of the war. And if I call at City Hall, I will be presented with the title deeds. That will make it doubly sure.'

I carried the tray into the living room and, placing his cup on the table next to his armchair, sat opposite him on the far side of the fireplace. 'Didn't you always own it?'

'Sadly, no. They confiscated our house on the lakeside in 1940 when the highway was built. It's now part of the college building at Herrendorp. I always think the gods were on our side that day. My wife, if she were alive, wouldn't agree.'

'What do you mean?'

'The man who brought us the bad news was the engineer in charge of building the road. Instead of shunting us into a camp, he gave us this place.' Meneer Meijer paused, lost in the past. I caught the glimpse of a smile and guessed he was thinking about his wife. 'He came to see me a few years back, to apologise.'

I didn't comment, only too aware of the depth of feeling that still echoed up and down the country, from people whose friends and relatives had been snatched up during the occupation and never seen again.

'It was the engineer who suggested I should register for ownership. Za—' He took a sip of coffee to cover up his blunder. Even so, the sound hung on the air in the form of a question. 'I did, and this is the result.' He beamed.

I swallowed, daring myself to ask the question yet fearing the disappointment of its answer, as I had dreaded identifying the footsteps ringing the pavement behind me.

'My second reason for being happy you have called,' he gossiped on, 'is today marks my seventy years on this earth.'

'Your birthday? Of course,' I laughed and pointed to the sponge cake, the piece on my plate layered with raspberry jam. 'You should have candles.'

Seeing his expression change, I asked quickly, 'There is something else?'

'You know how delighted your visits make me, Maidy. These last few years, you have brought much needed colour into my life.' He sighed, adding, 'unfortunately, sometimes you see too much. Tomorrow, if the documents are available, I will be going away.'

The ground under my feet quivered. 'Where to?'

'To France. I always promised Marie we would return once the children were grown.'

'When will you be back?' I stared forlornly, aware I knew the answer to that question.

'My dear child.' He reached out clasping my hand in his. 'My dear child, I have already received twice my quota in years, who knows how many days or years I have left. Is it not sensible to spend them in a place where my wife and I were once so happy?'

Immediately, I forgot my own plans to leave. No! This was impossible. 'Please,' I begged. 'Please, you can't leave without telling me. There's no one else I can ask.'

Removing his hand, he shifted round in his seat. 'It won't alter Zande's future.' He fixed me with his bird-like glance.

'Then make me understand, otherwise it will keep going round and round in my head, tormenting me.'

He laughed. 'Maidy, don't look so mournful. I can promise Zande continues to find life most agreeable.'

'Have you seen him?' The words were out before I could stop them.

'No. He phones regularly.' He pointed to the telephone on the table by his chair. 'I never met your brother, Pieter, so cannot give an opinion as to his feelings.' He raised his cup to his lips and I noticed he hadn't touched his slice of cake. 'Of all the privations we endured during the war, the lack of coffee was the worst.' He took a sip, his expression drifting away as the past once again reached out to claim his attention.

Returning to the present, he gave a heartfelt sigh. 'The night the swans were driven out,' he continued without a pause, 'was only the latest skirmish. No one knows how we came to exist or even where it all started. Descendants of Zeus is how we term ourselves. Whether it was the god or simply an anomaly in the evolution of the human species...' His silence invited me to comment and I smiled a negative, my basic knowledge of mythology ill-equipped for such as story. 'I was brought up near here, as were most of the clan.' Noticing my continued bafflement, 'Our official name is carinatae, which means a bird with a sternum or keel to which the flight feathers are attached. Together we are a clan, individuals are known as cobs. The word means male swan, which is appropriate since this mostly happens to men.'

He chirruped with laughter, the clear green of his eyes peeking out from the lines scoring his cheeks. 'Can you imagine being ruler of all you survey; land, sea and air? It was intoxicating especially for young boys who had never before stirred from the street in which they lived. For me too, until I met Marie. Van Vliet's father tried to stop us marrying, and to tempt me back to the clan. It wasn't until a number of years later when I discovered I could no longer change, I worked out why.'

'And that was?' I asked although I already knew.

'If you want to change back, to become wholly human again, the price must be loyalty to one person, your first love. And for neither to stray. Zande wanted that. Right from a small child, he had his future planned out – to build boats. He also sought the happiness I found with Marie, and was prepared to pay the price. He married his childhood sweetheart … Clara.'

'That night,' I burst out recalling Zande's words, tossed into the air like juggling balls. 'He said, there was only one woman I ever took to my heart. Did he mean Clara?'

'I doubt it very much. Knowing Zande, when under strain, it was Marie, my wife, he was remembering.'

'Oh,' I exclaimed, schooling my face to a careful blank, almost ashamed to recall my dreams in which it was my name he called out.

'How old is your brother?' Picking up his stick, Meneer Meijer shuffled upright.

'Twenty-six next birthday.' I helped him on with his coat.

'Then there is nothing to stop him returning to the family, except youthful pride. It will be a life; maybe not the one he was hoping for. Nevertheless, he can make the years he has left count. Leave the cups,' he added as I carried the tray into the kitchen. 'It will give me a job to do when I get back. Ten or eleven years is still a goodly time to spend with the people you love.'

PART TWO

10

Hans met me at the station in Bordeaux.

I'd had to change in Paris, taking a bus from the northern station to Montparnasse, my language skills not up to the challenge of the metro. It was a good decision. Buoyed by the elegance of the city with its gleaming white avenues, I found the slow pace of the bus, with its habit of stopping every few hundred metres to pick up passengers, invigorating. It gave me a chance to look about me, although my gaze rested far more on the shops and pavement cafés, with their elbow-high counters and tall silver taps for serving beer, than it did on the elegant architecture of museums and churches. And apart from postcard shops that also sold newspapers and tobacco, the rest were devoted to fashion and beauty.

Women stopped and gazed although none, as far as I could see, pushed open the shop doors. Maybe that was down to the heat. Unusually hot for May, on arriving at the station, I had immediately packed away my coat in my suitcase. Kirsten would have loved the experience, her knowledge of couture, as she called it, limited to magazines, and she would have been thrilled to see mannequins dressed in polka dots and zigzags, wearing a large decorative bow in their hair. She'd become a good friend, admitting even her dislike of Ruth wouldn't have prevented her going to America if given the chance. And as good friends should, she had enthused over the dancing figures in the newspaper – I would miss her.

Just as the famous cathedral on the banks of the river Seine came into view, a fractious dispute erupted between our bus driver and a taxi cab, who was using his horn as a rapier to spear pedestrians dawdling across the road with a blast of sound. It had stopped an entire line of traffic and I was able to take my time, my gaze drifting across the cathedral's towers and its magnificent stained glass, thrilled to think I might have something of interest to tell Hans when we met up, before remembering he hated anything second-hand, especially descriptions, and was unlikely to listen.

Recalling our life together as I had done in the quiet of the train, I realised we scarcely knew one another – at least not grown up. While Berthe had rarely hobnobbed, even Hans' month-long visit before the wedding produced few occasions for brotherly confidences. Never once had he knocked at my bedroom door seeking a plaster for imaginary wounds as he had so often done as a boy. And while he had made fleeting visits since, his interest had been exclusively directed towards the bricks and mortar of the alterations, and only that last time, almost as an afterthought, had he acknowledged an awareness of my situation.

'I don't know what happened, no one will say, and I don't much care,' he whispered in my ear as he hugged me goodbye. 'Just get out. Mother will drive you mad if you stay. If Pieter were here, he'd have looked after you – he always did, remember?' He unwrapped his arms and stood back, a broad smile on his face. 'Come and visit me, I've plenty of room and there's a spare couch. You can have that for free provided you keep the place clean. And you'll love France. Hotter than here, anyway. Send a telegram when you decide. You know me, I never read letters.'

At Montparnasse, only the kindness of a ticket collector, who obligingly slowed his speech, enabled me to catch the train for Bordeaux. I felt both triumphant and excited at negotiating Paris successfully, and even the view from the train window failed to dampen my spirits. Maybe there was little enough to see while the engine wound around the outskirts of the city, adding gouts of yellow steam to the thick-grime of industry in which buildings were covered. Nor was the sky worth bothering with, hanging low and depressingly sullen. Nevertheless, despite the miserable scenery, it was exciting. I was travelling through yet another new country and here, in cafes, people sipped wine rather than coffee, smoked evil-smelling Gauloises and spoke a different language. Staring down into the shabby streets lined with swatches of cheap housing, I caught sight of a woman in the highest of high-heels and wearing a leather skirt, leaning against a doorway smoking. I watched her call out to a man on a bicycle, both the machine and the man draped in strings of large brown onions. Intrigued, I craned in my seat, wanting to see if he responded. Then they too were gone, replaced by buildings, their brick faces engrained with dirt from passing trains.

As we left the city behind and speed became a reality, the remaining streets and factories flew past, ousted by a horizon that offered a shimmer of colour suggestive of mountain peaks. Insignificant at a distance, the speeding train began to drag them into the foreground, their narrow silhouette swelling like the billowing sails of a schooner into blocks of ragged stone. Then, after an hour of eager anticipation, wanting to see them in close-up, the train, borrowing the characteristics of a tornado, swept arrogantly past and they were gone, too fast for me to gain any impression at all, replaced at the periphery of my vision by a ripple of water.

I must have made some sound, perhaps an exclamation of surprise or admiration, because the occupant of the corner seat, a nun, glanced up and smiled. Offering the window little other than a cursory glance, she returned to her text. Even the man in the seat opposite who had been asleep opened his eyes. Acknowledging the presence of the river, he closed them again, ignoring the gradual approach of a city on the far side of the tracks.

Soon after, from the dizzy heights of an extensive embankment, I was gazing down onto dusty roads lined with the tallest of trees, sunlight flitting in and out of the branches keeping pace with the speeding wheels of the train. A second river appeared revealing villages, so similar one to another you might well have imagined the train to be looping round in a circle, the narrow streets inevitably opening onto a square dominated by a church. And, always nearby, a café and a strip of dusty ground where elderly men were playing a game of boules.

Intrigued by the scenery, the journey passed quickly, and as the city of Bordeaux overtook the gradually slowing train and discovering it to be almost thirty minutes late, I hastily grabbed my suitcase off the rack. As we pulled in, politely wishing the nun a good afternoon and following my fellow passengers, I stepped down onto the platform. I had sent Hans a telegram with my arrival time and, knowing his impatience, hoped he'd not given up waiting and left.

He was there. But for a moment, the appearance of the bohemian with a beard and long fair hair belonged to a stranger, and I was unable to connect the man standing in front of me with the moody teenager who had eased his heartbreak over Ruth with copious amounts of beer. Then the irrepressible grin appeared, and his arms opened wide for me to step into them. 'The train's late. And so are you; I expected you weeks ago. Still, you made it.' He took my suitcase. 'What happened?'

'Berthe's expecting again,' I said, keeping my tone light.

'With you there's always something,' he grumbled. 'Couldn't believe it when I heard you'd gone to America.'

I took a half-breath, wondering if Pappy had written and told Hans I had gone for Ruth's wedding, or maybe it was Berthe who had told him, before remembering neither was keen on writing letters. 'I'm far too busy.' Berthe had kissed me on the cheek when I left. 'It's likely to be a card at Christmas from now on, if you stay away that long.'

I put it out of my mind, it wasn't important.

He'd changed. I thought him taller again. Maybe that was

because he was thinner and no longer slouched or because he was dressed differently, his trousers and shirt loose and flowing. They suited him.

Just about every woman that walked past obviously agreed with me, eyeing our embrace with suspicion.

Noticing, Hans grinned. 'They're trying to decide if you're my girlfriend or my sister.' I recognised the cocky smile – that hadn't changed. 'On balance, they will decide sister. Not glamorous enough to be my girlfriend.'

Instantly the old urge to kick him came over me and I glared.

He wrapped his spare arm around my waist. 'Definitely sister. Still, you look nice.'

I laughed at the compliment, all at once convinced I'd made the right decision. Earlier that morning, still among the fields of home, I'd felt so miserable, arguing with myself that I should have stayed and overcome the difficulties or, for Pappy's sake, taken no notice.

'Right, greetings over and done with, now you speak French.'

'Oh!' I replied, hoping my exclamation sounded French. 'I'm not very good.'

'You soon will be.' He dismissed my argument and pointed to where the open-mouth of a street beckoned. 'The car's along here.' He nodded at the houses lining both sides of the street, those in shade with their shutters pushed back against the wall, eagerly anticipating the evening breeze.

'Car?'

'I've gone up in the world.'

Among the line of parked vehicles was a battered brown Renault. I didn't need to ask its ownership, the back leg of an easel poking out of the open window. 'However much did it cost?' I inspected the dent in the door, its handle firmly tied with string, noticing one of the tyres was missing its mudguard.

'Nothing. I swapped it for a painting and a bottle of wine.'

'Wine?'

'Yes, and wonderful wine it was too. St Emilion. I'd preferred to have drunk it myself. Tragically, it was the only thing I possessed of any value at the time.' He rounded his finger and thumb and momentarily held them to his mouth, making a kissing sound.

Opening the driver's door, he added my suitcase to the crowded back seat, paints and canvases jumbled together, reaching over to unlatch the passenger door for me. 'You might think I was cheated. I wasn't; goes like a dream. Because of her I have sold two paintings. And because of that, I now have a patron.'

The words, though spoken in French, emerged on a defensive breath, hasty and shallow, and I guessed Hans wasn't quite sure how I would react to the word, patronne.

I didn't, merely asking, 'Where are we heading?'

I saw the flicker of impatience. That hadn't changed either. Obviously, he had wanted to get the subject out of the way before … what?

'Inland. The small town where I live, my patron has a house and is happy to rent you a room.'

'I can't stay with you?'

'Oh, I live there too. It's a big house.'

I shifted in my seat, eyeing the hands relaxed on the steering wheel. He might well have wanted my approbation but he wasn't in knots about it. He had become his own man. I studied his profile, picking up on the assurance, no longer that truculent youth envious of everyone and everything.

He gave a confirmatory wave out of the window, swerving to avoid a truck heading down the slope towards us.

'Hans!' I yelped, bracing my hands on the dashboard.

'We missed it didn't we?' he retorted. 'Anyway, it wasn't me, it was that archway.'

I'd forgotten about his lack of attention on anything that didn't involve art, his gaze shifting right and left and ignoring passing vehicles. 'And you wanted to paint it,' I added in a resigned tone, 'although I'm willing to believe killing me in the process wasn't part of the plan.'

He grinned. 'It wasn't.'

'In that case, I'd better hurry up and learn to drive.' Noticing his mouth open ready to comment, 'And you're not teaching me.'

I don't know where the sarcastic edge to my voice came from. Maybe it had always been there when dealing with Hans – and I had never heard it. Maybe it was new, the result of my recently acquired sophistication.

'I hope you're not growing into a nagging shrew,' he retorted with a grin. 'If so, you can return whence you came. I get enough nagging from my patron.'

Either it was my comment or the closeness of the lorry, nevertheless, for the next few minutes he studiously regarded the road, to the extent of using his arm to indicate our turning into a main road. He was correct about the Renault too. Despite its dilapidated appearance, it purred along, the brakes which he applied with gay abandon most capable, squealing to a halt behind the vehicle in front that had abruptly stopped, and missing their back bumper by a hairsbreadth.

Even so, I was relieved to be out of the city, crossing the river into a country road empty of traffic, our only companion, the river, plus an occasional bicycle or farm cart.

I pointed to the water, meandering along at peace with the world.

'That's the Garonne. The village of Flambeau, where I live, sits on a tributary. About twenty kilometres,' he continued anticipating my next question.

'Doesn't Flambeau mean torch,' I said in Dutch, my brain exhausted with the effort of speaking French.

He grinned at me, 'I thought—'

'I'm tired!' I scowled at him.

'Okay. You'll need to speak French with Justine. She's nice, you'll like her. And yes, it does mean torch. History says it's a place of miracles. Can't see it myself. Still, if it brings business, I'm not about to argue.'

'Miracles?'

'That's what the history books say. Most of the villagers believe it, too. They are convinced it saved them in the war – not losing any of their men. I doubt it myself. I think it's the hill. Anyway, so the story goes, when something bad is about to happen, the rockface lights up and becomes a fiery torch. I've not seen it and, to be honest, so far I've not met up with anyone who has.'

With the river behind us now, the open ridges rose to a crest taking the road with them before sweeping down past newly ploughed fields, almost immediately replaced by vines. Field after field, so lush and expansive, the heavy wire supports were barely visible amongst the sculptured greenery, the fresh colour of the new leaves already darkening into summer.

'Why the notices?' I pointed to the edge of the field where a metal sign had been set into the ground.

'Those?' Hans slowed the car, pointing with one hand. 'They confirm the appellation.'

'What's that?' I said, unfamiliar with the word.

'It gives the geographical location of a particular field, and lists the variety of grape. Which means the wine it produces is protected by law. Even if the sign is stolen, it can't be used elsewhere.'

'Why would you ...' I searched for the word, 'steal a notice?'

'Because it's quite possible for grapes in neighbouring fields to produce two very different vintages – one that is great, commanding a high price, and the other, a few meters away, barely drinkable. See?' Hans pointed to the wide strip of bare earth that separated each of the fields. 'The boundary is also measured and protected by law. In the past, blood has been shed over whether a bush belonged here or there.'

He gave a confirmatory wave out of the window, causing the car to swerve. Noticing my clenched fists, he laughed. 'Stop worrying, I've been driving well over a year – no accidents.'

As the vineyards fell away and the narrow road began to edge upwards, the lush vegetation was replaced by grass and stone; wild goats foraging among sporadic outcrops of thorn and wild cherry that littered the wayside.

'That's a poinciana.' Hans broke the silence. He pointed to a tree, set way back from the roadside. 'It's a bit of a mystery how it got there. By rights, it belongs in a botanical garden because it's relatively tender and hates frost. Not that we get much here.'

I stared out of the window expecting something extraordinary; it had to be if Hans had noticed it and was disappointed to find it quite insignificant, its leaves an uninteresting shade of green.

Reading my mind, he laughed. 'I agree, it doesn't look much, not right now. First time I saw it, it was a mass of flower – deep orange. Except you can't call it orange. To an artist, it was every colour except orange – dozens and dozens of different shades.' I remembered Ruth's wedding dress, and my failing to name its colour. 'No idea how I got to see it and at the perfect moment too. Most likely,' he added ruefully, 'I'd had too much to drink and fallen asleep in the car. It was the tree that persuaded me to stay, that and Justine. Sold the painting right away. There's a couple of prints lying around somewhere, if you're interested. I keep meaning to return when it's in flower and do another one.'

'Is that where we're heading?' I pointed to a great outpouring of rock that dominated the horizon, noticing a glint of water at the base.

'Yes, the town sits right up top. Got an interesting history.'

'You're not interested in history.'

I saw the grin. 'Would you believe, at long last I'm becoming educated? That's Justine's doing. Insists if you're a foreigner, it's only polite to learn something about where you live. Besides, it's useful.'

The cliff vanished behind a grove of trees, immediately springing into view again as we rounded a corner, the glint of water I had seen expanding into a wide flowing river, with a bridge spanning the road. Obviously new with shiny iron railings, the concrete road surface white and raw looking, jarred against the mellow reds of the surrounding rocks.

'Don't you just hate it?' Hans growled. Slowing, he pulled to a stop and got out, ignoring the car speeding towards him. 'It's so ugly. Ugliness should be wiped from the world.'

'But necessary.' Climbing out of the car, I peered over the railing to where a flight of metal steps led down onto a natural rock platform. Here, a group of people had gathered, kept safe from the fury of the river rushing past their feet by a metal barrier. 'How else would you get to see the river?'

'You can walk.' He pointed upstream to the far bank and I caught a glimpse of trees, my view blocked by the massive buttress of rock.

As we watched, a chunk of rock fell from the cliff and was swept away.

'And the miracle?' I said, seeing nothing to demand such a sizable audience.

'People live their lives in hope, I guess.' He glanced up at the overcast skies, the heat and sun I had encountered in Paris diminished by a thick covering of cloud. 'It can be quite beautiful especially when the sun is shining.' As if to confirm his words, a stray beam of light edged from the thinning cloud, momentarily highlighting the dense curtain of mist that reached part way up the crag. 'You don't get that later on in summer, particularly after a dry spell when the river's low. It's at this time of the year, we get the majority of visitors – especially photographers. I've tried to paint it. It's impossible; the light changes so rapidly nothing apart from photographs ever works.'

'And that's where you live?'

'Yes, that's Flambeau.' Hans nodded a response to my finger pointing to the top of the steep rise, where a ribbon of rooftops crowned the summit. 'This is the tributary I told you about. It joins the Garonne downstream. Mostly it's pretty peaceful. Come on. Justine's expecting us.'

Setting off again, the gentle purr of the Renault grew noisier as the gradient bit, forcing Hans to change down. A loop in the road brought the wooded slopes and the upper reaches of the river into view. Broader now, with trees lining its banks, the slow-moving flow was strewn with patches of green weed like steps in a child's game. Swans were circling and I caught my breath, imagining a black swan to be among them, only to see I was mistaken. It was a cygnet, its grey plumage darkened almost to black by pools of deep shadow created by the overhanging tree branches. The road looped again, the tyres on the Renault squealing on the dry sandy surface, to reveal a scattering of rooftops and beyond them traces of once-proud walls that loomed high over the surrounding countryside. Then these too were gone, traded for the buildings I had seen from the road. Up close, they were ugly structures, the stone clumsily mortared together. Noticing the half-a-dozen equally shabby tables and chairs outside, I guessed they'd been erected in a hurry to accommodate visitors who, drawn by the water, would welcome a refreshing drink after their steep climb.

'Not a very good advertisement for the town.' Hans pointed to them. 'If I had my way, I'd knock them down.'

Moments later and boulevards of ochre-coloured housing closed in, the roads already narrow made narrower still by trees and parked cars. Fortunately there was almost no traffic and, surprisingly, no one walking their dog or standing gossiping on the pavement. The little town might well have been deserted, only the shutters, closed all day against the sun and again pushed back, hinted at the existence of people.

'It's dinner time,' Hans picked up on my bemusement. 'Say what you like about the French, they are most particular when it comes to food. But it's proved the devil's own job persuading Justine to eat later. I even threatened to leave. Well,' he puffed out his cheeks in indignation. 'In the olden days, no woman would have dared tell an artist – someone as famous as Koekkoek, anyhow – to stop painting because dinner was on the table.'

I smiled, aware of Hans' youthful fondness for plucking obscure names out of the air in an attempt to boost his fragile ego. 'Koekkoek?'

'Dutch painter. In the museum. Don't you remember that barque on the river?'

'We saw a dozen barques.'

'Oh well.' He excused my lack of knowledge with a grin. 'I can't expect you to remember; you're not an artist.'

The streets weren't particularly impressive, nor especially old despite a signpost pointing to La Vielle Ville, and I was just wondering why Hans had chosen this particular town when he swung the car into a short drive and pulled to a stop under a stone archway. It happened so fast, my only impression was of a wide-set, grey-stone building, bare of both greenery and embellishment, apart from a pair of gargoyles perched on the roof. I had seen similar examples on passing through Paris – not gargoyles, archways, where cars drove through, what appeared to be the building itself, into a courtyard. Deciding the house to be both older and grander than the surrounding streets, I imagined horses pulling carriages and guessed there had once been stables at the rear.

Nervously, I tugged at my brother's sleeve.

'What?' Intuitively for someone usually so obtuse, 'Oh, the house? From what you've told me, Ruth's place in New York is far grander.' Leaning over, he flipped the door catch. 'Go on in. You'll have to manage your suitcase.' Signalling with his chin, Hans indicated the painting he'd taken from the back seat. 'I must get this canvas into the shop and I don't trust you.' I saw a swirl of colour and he was gone, walking quickly through into the courtyard.

'Hans? That you?' A voice called and a woman appeared.

After the passionate infatuation Hans had maintained for Ruth, extolling her beauty and elegance and jealous of her love for Pieter, my first reaction was one of astonishment. In her late twenties and older than Hans by some years, Justine at first glance was quite plain. Tall and slight, with long dark hair coiled neatly against her neck, it was her mouth that demanded attention. I could almost feel it shouting out, *Go on, look at me*, the heavy upper lip drooping down, giving her face a sulky, discontented appearance, her feline gaze accentuating the image. Only then did I notice the rest of her. Tall and elegant with a long and willowy neck, she walked like a dancer, upright and so light on her bare feet she could well have been floating. Her skin too, almost luminous in the porch light.

Fascinating for an artist but not beautiful, I decided.

'I presume Hans did meet you and has been called away?' Her voice rasped low and questioning yet it rang with music, and I guessed instantly why Hans looked so happy and was glad for him. 'When I first met him, he was honest enough to warn me not to expect normal behaviour although I do think, at the very least, he might have escorted his sister into a strange house.' She cocked her head on one side, the downward tilt to her mouth very prominent. 'I presume you are his sister?'

'Yes,' I agreed. 'But it's all right. It's Hans.'

'Yes, it's Hans. And you are Magrit, the sensible one in the family, who prefers to be called Maidy.'

'Yes.'

'So, if neither of us ever expect anything of your brother, we will get along well.'

I caught the barely disguised sarcasm and flinched. 'I hope so. He does possess the most amazing talent,' I added naively, believing I needed to justify his peculiarities.

Her eyebrows shot up and I found myself taking an involuntary step backwards. No doubt the gesture was intended to keep people at a distance. 'My dear girl, why do you think he's living here? I can assure you it wasn't for his ability to keep a house tidy. His work is quite outstanding.' She lowered her voice. 'Only you don't tell Hans that.'

'You talking about me?' Hans appeared.

And Justine smiled; her face no longer plain, so vividly alive I was rocked back on my heels.

I had always considered Ruth beautiful yet, by comparison, hers was a shallow beauty, without depth, a likeness drawn by an artist using cheap materials.

Oh Hans, how lucky can one man be, to have loved one beautiful woman and gained another.

'Have you brought me a new painting? May I see it?'

'It's not finished and you know...' He kept his glance level, determined on his own way.

It struck me how much experience of the world he'd gained, and in such a short time, the age gap between us much wider than it once was. The years since he reached nineteen had been well used.

'In any case, I'm starving. You know me, when I'm painting I forget where my mouth is. And although my sister, Maidy, is far too well brought-up to say so, no doubt she is too.'

'Dinner it is.'

The smile lapsed; her face quite ordinary again.

'May I help?'

'Not tonight. Hans will show you to your room while I lay the table. Warm enough for the courtyard, Hans?'

Nodding, he collected my case and, brushing her cheek in a kiss, beckoned me to follow him inside.

The house proved as intriguing as its owner. Immediately wishing I knew the history of both, I followed Hans through into a large kitchen adjoining the archway. Two, three, four times the size of ours at home, glass-fronted cupboards that had once housed china lined the walls, the centre of the room taken up by a white-wood table, in which decades of scrubbing had left deep ridges. With the windows wide open, the air was tinged with the aromatic fragrance of herbs. I glanced up to see the rack once used to hang game now held a selection of cooking pots and bunches of herbs, recognising both thyme and rosemary.

Various doors led off the kitchen, one partially open. Noticing the outline of a refrigerator peeking around the corner and guessing it to be the pantry, I looked inside discovering, apart from a wine rack, its shelves were practically empty with only a few jars of preserves on them. And although the wood-fired range was modern as was the refrigerator, the rest dated from an earlier century, a large stone sink set under the window furnished with an old-fashioned pump-handle.

Noticing my astonishment, Hans grinned. 'We do have piped water, just not from the mains. The government supply hasn't made it up the hill yet and we still rely on rainfall to keep taps flowing. There's a well in the grounds, and several dozen others scattered across town.'

All of this had scarcely time to register before he was pushing open a second door into a lofty hall, its ceiling lost in the shadows; impossible to tell exactly how high because there was no light, and the glass panes in the front door had been boarded up. Hans was already halfway up the staircase, his plimsolls making little sound on the wood, and I hurried to catch up. Not straight, the flight rose gracefully towards the first-floor mimicking the graceful curves of a cello, the wooden banisters under my hand as smooth as silk.

'We also have lights.' Pointing to a bare bulb hanging off a long cord, he clicked a switch on and off, a weak light momentarily stirring the shadows. 'Justine hates having them on unless forced. She says they lay bare too many dark secrets.' Picking up on my expression of bewilderment, he added with a grin, 'Interesting history, this place. Ask Justine sometime,' adding, 'when you know her better.'

'And this?'

At the top of the stairs I was confronted by a vast open space, its lofty ceiling framed in a deep frieze of acanthus leaves, with an impressive selection of sofas, chairs and tables lining the walls. Several had dustsheets over them, and I guessed those remained in good condition, the rest shabby as was the carpet. Impossible to determine its original colour, in places where footfall had been heaviest only threads remained – the whole thing reminding me of a second-hand furniture emporium.

'Ah!' Hans produced an elegant bow and switched on a standard lamp at the top of the stairs, illuminating the space more clearly. There were no windows and, to the rear, wide corridors branched left and right. 'This,' he emphasised the word, 'is the salon. A receiving room for guests.'

We'd been speaking Dutch, Hans giving up on French as my brain shut down. 'In France, the salon was considered a place for intellectual conversation. Justine usually calls it something else, not quite so polite,' and he grinned at me.

Ignoring him, I pointed to a collection of oil paintings. 'And the pictures?' Most had been taken down and now leaned against the base of the wall, the hooks where they'd once hung left in place. From what I could see in the dim light, only a few were portraits and scenes, the rest were set pieces; game birds lying dead on a table or the interior of a house, subjects Dutch artists of the seventeenth and eighteenth centuries specialised in, and something I had become very familiar with when visiting museums with Hans.

'Oh that.' Hans frowned, the laughter lines wiped away. 'We're selling the least valuable first.'

'Don't you earn any money?' I said aghast. 'I mean, can you really afford to have me here. I won't be able to pay much until I get a job.'

'You've got a job.'

'I have?'

Noticing my astonishment, he added, 'Not now. I'm hungry. I'll explain over dinner.'

He pointed to a door. 'That's your room. It overlooks the front of the house and that...' He indicated the door opposite, to the rear of the landing, 'is Justine's.'

I peered past Justine's bedroom door to find an elegant archway, its crown again rimmed with plaster mouldings, and a second furnished area, smaller than the first. Intrigued, I took a step forward and stopped, unsure what I was seeing. A second staircase, the mirror image of the one I had just walked up, led down into an identical hallway, equally as gloomy, although, here, the original chandeliers had been left in place. Dusty and in need of cleaning, with their sconces mired by wax, a few still held partially burned candles. Even so, judging by the quality of the silk that draped the walls of the landing and staircase, I suspected them to be crystal, probably bought in Paris at the end of the previous century.

Maybe electricity had found the journey up the hill daunting too.

'Why the second staircase?'

'Ah! Long story. That'll keep for another day as well. The double doors,' he indicated the opposing corridor, 'lead into the ballroom, which is now Justine's studio, and opposite is the dining room. Like your bedroom, it overlooks the front of the house. Justine says it seats forty. She sold the table and chairs so no idea if that's true or not. Guest bedrooms, including mine, are in the wing at the far end of that corridor.' He pointed to a second archway, barely visible in the gloom. 'My studio is one floor up. And you're not allowed in it ... ever. No one is, so don't go thinking because you're my sister, you're excused.' He grinned, denying his harsh tone. 'Come down when you're ready, and don't take for ever. Patience is not one of Justine's virtues.'

He hadn't changed, quite content to leave me with a dozen questions. Asking myself how on earth Justine put up with his insensitive nature, I twisted the knob on my bedroom door and went in.

The shutters were still closed, the light sombre, almost as downcast as I was now feeling, the exuberance I'd experienced in Paris quite drained away. Determined not to be put off by Hans' off-hand manner, I hurried across to the windows and, throwing them open, felt the breeze on my face easing my disquiet. It would be all right, I decided, it had to be. I swung round for a better look at my new quarters. In keeping with the rest of the house, the room was huge and, judging by its dark wall-coverings, had once been used as a card room. Crown mouldings circled the high ceiling, with a central rosette of matching plaster flowers where once a chandelier had hung.

Apart from its silken walls, no other trace of its former role existed, everything except for the bed, light and modern. That, stood high off the ground, with enough space to hide several people under its base, and it had a heavily carved mahogany headboard incongruously fitted with modern reading lamps. Still thinking about the second staircase and not quite knowing what to expect, I hastily threw back the coverlet to reveal sheets of the finest Egyptian cotton, with lace-trimmed pillows faintly smelling of lavender. Reassured, I opened the two doors leading off the bedroom, discovering both a dressing room and a bathroom which, judging by the pristine appearance of the bath, had never been used. I turned the tap. Nothing happened for the longest while then, with a gurgle and a snort of steam, hot water flowed out.

It was still warm, and returning to the window, I leaned out, hearing traces of music from a radio, wishing I had thought to pack my journal in my handbag rather than in the bottom of my suitcase. I had hoped to begin writing again on my trip to America and on re-reading the lines I had written, found them both boring and lacklustre. Admittedly, how do you write welcome-welcome-welcome on a page for it not to sound dull? I'm not sure whether the niceties of life can ever be recorded in a way that doesn't leave readers bored and skipping pages, but here... Already, I'd a suspicion that dark secrets were hidden beneath the dust of centuries and, if so, I simply had to write about them. My reaction surprised me, as had the house. Despite the echoing hallways, I didn't feel nervous. Perhaps because the air outside was balmy and softly caressing.

Intrigued, I craned out of the window. It was not yet fully dark, and the long twilight had cast deep shadows across the square which, at first glance, appeared no different from any of the others I had seen that day, with a patch of dry earth and benches set among a grove of pine trees. The house itself sat across one corner with a view both of the road Hans had driven along and the one opposite. Through the trees, I spotted the rotund belfry of a small church that reminded me more of Moorish architecture than it did Christian. Flanked by iron railings like a wall of spears, most likely it predated the square, with the house older again. Pulling into the driveway, I'd noticed some sort of crest on the gates, pushed back on their hinges to allow easy access for the Renault, and decided most likely the house had once been surrounded by parkland of which only a narrow strip, planted with shrubs and railed like the church, remained.

Across the square, the only building of any substance apart from a restaurant, with its traditional red canopy extending out over the pavement, was a fancy brick-built structure with high windows and a bell-shaped roof, a large brass plaque at street level that gleamed in the lamplight, marking it out as something official. I tried to remember the French name – une mairie – or perhaps a solicitor's office – l'avocat.

Voices reverberated from under the restaurant awning, and I saw a series of moving shadows and a chink of light from a glass held up in salutation. It reminded me how hungry I was, and, quickly washing my hands, I ran downstairs.

11

It was the church bell that woke me. I had slept well, despite the many unanswered questions. The previous night, when I went down to dinner, Justine awarded me that wondrous smile, the first in my direction. 'No doubt, as is his wont, Hans has left you with more questions than answers.'

'Now look here, no good you two ganging up on me. I won't put up with it.'

That, too, had been said with a smile invested to my surprise with charm, something I had never connected with Hans. Pieter, yes. Was it possible his childhood angst had finally found a shelf in a cupboard labelled the past?

'Offer your sister some wine and tell her our plans. And while he is talking, Maidy, you eat. I'm a good cook.'

She was, having prepared veal with green beans and a salad of artichoke hearts, our meal under the darkening skies made even more pleasant by the lingering warmth.

It would seem that the job being offered was in a shop.

'Not any shop, Maidy. My shop. Except it's not yet mine, I lease it.' My brother's smile was deprecating, his glance encountering Justine's, almost an automatic reaction. 'Before I moved in here, I used it as a studio. The owner and his family occupy the upper floors. Of course, I was still finding my way back then.' I must have looked mystified, because he added, 'My style, Maidy. Some artists never truly find it. I was lucky. I met Justine. And it was Justine who suggested I should turn it into a shop and also sell art equipment; you know, brushes and paper.'

'Artists come here all year round.' Noticing my continuing confusion, Justine took over the explanation. 'Occasionally, if it's good enough, we buy their work and sell it on.'

'If I approve,' Hans confirmed.

'The buying bit or the selling?' she teased.

'We also plan on stocking a line of postcards. Famous paintings – including mine,' he boasted. 'I wish I'd thought of it before selling my earlier work. I won't make that mistake again. I found a local man who does the printing; and he's going to produce the postcards for us. Tourists love postcards. Just walk around the town, there's shops selling postcards on almost every street. They and the prints should provide a steady income.' He read my question and provided the answer. 'I can't paint more than two masterpieces a week.' He halted his explanation to eat a mouthful of food. 'If that. It's exhausting.'

Justine laughed and he glared at her then grinned. 'A real masterpiece can take weeks, Maidy, which is why artists usually starve to death, waiting for the paint to dry. It won't pay much. Once I'm better known, it will,' he added fiercely. 'Meanwhile, we can provide board and lodging and you'll get one and a half days off a week. Besides, what else are you good for? You're not trained for anything.'

Climbing out of bed, I tip-toed over to the window. Around me, the town was still silently sleeping, a flock of pigeons rooting through the dust of the square in search of breakfast. Hans' words may well have sounded harsh but they were true, I wasn't trained for anything.

Abruptly, an old woman clad from top to toe in black, emerged through the front door of the restaurant, the noise of the slamming door scattering the pigeons into the air, their wings fluttering hysterically. From the street opposite, a second woman joined her, still busily tying a black scarf over her head. Silently nodding, they joined a handful of others, similarly garbed, already walking up the steps into the church. As children, we had gone to church every Sunday. I think Mother and Berthe still did. Perhaps Pappy, too, on Saints' Days. Sadly, like the birthday celebrations that had fallen away as we grew up, so had my faith. With no possibility of Pieter ever returning, I found myself doubting the existence of a god that punished the undeserving.

By the time I finished unpacking and had taken a bath, the water gurgling and spitting through the hot-water tap, both Hans and Justine were already in the kitchen drinking coffee. The atmosphere of last night, mellow and full of fun, was gone. Now I felt it brittle and I sensed tension between them.

'No need for you to bother about the shop today. I've got some work to do and will keep an eye on it. You go and explore the town.' Hans greeted me.

'And I must write some letters, let Pappy know I'm safe.'

I smiled at each in turn hoping to lessen the painful atmosphere, only to discover I'd made it worse.

Justine, who was leaning against the range, raised her eyebrows and glowered, her frown including me. She was wearing the most exquisite black kimono. Made of silk, with a magnolia tree embroidered on the back, its branches were weighed down with voluptuous red and gold flowers that spiralled across the front and the silken panels of the sleeves.

'Talking of letters.'

'For pity's sake, Justine.' I flinched at the anger in Hans' voice. 'It was only a letter. Besides, she's Maidy's friend – she wanted to know her address.' Fishing in his pocket, he tossed an envelope onto the table. 'There, read it, if you don't believe me.' I heard the familiar resentment sweep over him, like a small child caught in the act of pinching a toffee.

'Do help yourself.' Justine, her tone still raw, offered me coffee, studiously ignoring the envelope which sat there, staring up at us reproachfully. I knew who it was from, the ostentation of the embossing gave it away – Ruth.

After a loud and painful silence, it was Justine who relented. 'If it was only a letter, why the secrecy?'

'Because...' He shrugged. 'I know how you are.' Swinging away, he leant down to pick up the canvas bag in which he kept his brushes and palette. 'As I said, she's Magrit's friend. Nothing to do with me at all.'

It was the use of my birth name that betrayed him. Mother always used that to express her disapproval. Now I heard disquiet.

Justine picked up the envelope and tapped it against her fingers.

'Ruth?' I broke in.

I saw his relief at my intervention.

'Yes, she wrote asking if I'd seen you and knew where you were.'

'Ruth was my best friend.' I thrust out my response, hoping it would prove sufficient to reassure but not invite further enquiry. I had enough questions for us both. Why was Hans writing letters to a married woman ... film star or not? 'I went to New York for her wedding in April and I promised to write and send her my new address.'

Justine's frown cleared. Picking up the letter, she handed it back. 'What a good job your sister is here,' and blew Hans a kiss.

A moment later, I heard the Renault start up. Justine's gaze drifted to the door, Hans still a tangible presence in the room. 'What are your plans for the day?'

'I must write to Pappy, tell him I've arrived safely,' I mumbled before remembering I'd already said that.

I, too, felt anger and guilt. Ruth had given me the address of the studio in Paris, and I had promised faithfully to write to her there and reply to her job offer. I could as easily have told her my decision when she first asked me at the apartment and I should have done so. If given time to think, I just knew I would conjure up as many reasons for accepting as declining. And at that moment, in New York, it had most definitely been a refusal. When she mentioned Zande, asking if he had returned, blithely unaware and uncaring of Pieter's fate, I knew I couldn't go back down that pathway.

Yet, within a day or so, doubt had once again taken root. Meneer Endelbaum's words had stayed with me as had Greg's, although not about Ruth, about her husband.

And so, I had done nothing. It was easier. Now, Hans' own predicament was forcing me to write that letter.

'Is there anywhere in the village I can buy stamps?'

Justine checked her watch. 'The Tabac in the main street on the far side of the square.' She pointed vaguely over her shoulder. 'They won't be open yet. How about I show you over the house? Hans told me you want to write. If so, you've come to the perfect place.' She sounded almost gay, 'Especially if you enjoy horror stories.' Taking a bunch of keys from a board on the kitchen wall, she pushed open the outside door. 'Come on, we'll start the far side.'

I glanced down, noticing a smear of oil on the paving where the Renault had parked. Although Justine's surroundings no longer spelled money if the dust and lack of carpeting on the stairs was anything to go by, there had been once and lots of it, both the driveway and courtyard where we had eaten dinner paved with fine amber stone.

'Why are there two sides?'

'The eccentricities of the nobility.' Justine replied in a droll tone, unlocking the door.

I took a step into the room and stopped dead.

We were standing in a kitchen, although with its shutters firmly closed only generalities were immediately evident. Nevertheless, she was right about gothic horror, the room, apart from the addition of a fridge and stove, an exact replica of the one across the archway where we had just drunk our coffee, except here surfaces were buried in the grime of disuse.

'When I first saw it, it gave me nightmares. I suppose that's why I keep it locked. Through here,' Justine led the way across the kitchen floor, unlocking the door at the far end. 'Before these ground floor rooms were converted, the layout of both wings was identical, with a private drawing room downstairs and family bedrooms on the first floor.'

'And what about the central section of the house where my bedroom is located?' I asked.

'The first floor was designed for entertaining. And the ground floor belonged to the servants who made that possible.' Her voice had changed, so had her expression – obviously disapproving of something. 'There are three kitchens, this is the biggest, a scullery where pots were washed, larders, boot cupboards, a gunroom, a library, and a study.' She counted on her fingers. 'Oh, and my sitting room. There aren't any cellars, thank heavens.'

'You don't use these rooms?'

'No, not for years. Hans calls them the vault, although most are now empty of plunder.'

Unlocking and locking the doors again in swift rotation, I saw through the gloom into an extensive bedroom, dominated by a monstrosity of a four-poster bed, its hangings once flamboyant and flowing now lying limp and moth eaten, the closed shutters reducing their colour to shades of fawn and grey. A second bedroom had fared no better. Although smaller, it had a dressing room, with the bulky silhouette of a hip bath in one corner. Tiers of drawers and cupboards lined the walls. Once filled with silk cravats and fine cotton undergarments, a partially open drawer exposed only the domain of silverfish. A short corridor took us into a study, lined with shelves from floor to ceiling, most now empty of books, with double doors opening out into a room at the front of the house.

'The story passed down through the family is that sometime in the early nineteenth century, twins inherited the house.' Bending down, she tugged an oil painting from the pile. Two youths sat side by side, dressed identically, in the lace and frills fashionable in that era. 'These are the twins. Pretty, aren't they? I am certain they were the inspiration for the novel about Dorian Gray; they were certainly equally as debauched. Tragically there isn't an image of them old, so I have no idea how they looked then or if they managed to survive to old age.'

'Why the quarrel?'

'Quarrels! The younger, if indeed he was the younger,

although it could never be proved either way, because the midwife vanished, took the elder to court, citing collusion and blackmail. The one that really set tongues wagging was because they both fell in love with the same boy.'

She saw my astonishment and smiled, although this time her smile didn't reflect amusement, rather distaste, the downturn of her mouth bitter. 'I promise, it gets worse. The young man in question was murdered, stabbed to death, and his body strewn with the gifts the twins had given him. Shortly after, they agreed to cut the house in two. The public rooms were shared, the ballroom, dining room etcetera, and they each laid claim to a wing and a driveway. No longer in existence, thank heavens, a more recent ancestor, although undoubtedly equally as ruinous, sold the land on which the town is now built and promptly gambled away the proceeds.'

'I agree.' Justine nodded, even though I'd not spoken, scarcely knowing how to react. 'And while the twins agreed jointly to host grand balls and dinners, the vendetta must have lasted until this century, with guests entering the house through their host's personal front door. Where we sat last night used to be a terrace and beyond that was a formal garden with a park.' She waved a hand, 'Somewhere about there's a painting of it, unless it's been sold. I'll have a search round if you're interested. Come on.'

'If they didn't...?' I began.

'Oh, they both sired sons.' I heard the sarcasm. 'The eldest died in middle age and left no offspring, that I do know. If the younger one had done the same, their evil might have died with them and what happened later may not have taken place.'

She opened a door into the hallway. Recognising the gold motif pattern on the silk hangings of the staircase I had used last night and again this morning, I felt disorientated, sensing figures dressed in ancient costumes, floating up and down, their footsteps silent. Swallowing, I dragged myself back to the present, following my hostess upstairs.

Sensing my disquiet, she led me back through the archway into the part of the house where my bedroom was.

'You don't use the front door?' I pointed down into the hallway.

'Hans would have a fit if I did. He says the stained glass is priceless. He believes them to be an early Lucien Begule.'

I laughed. Of course. 'Hans finished his apprenticeship with a stained-glass artist in Strasbourg. He would know if it was valuable. Were you brought up in this house?'

'Tiens! No! It belonged to my husband's family.'

'You were married?' I exclaimed, noticing both Justine's hands were bare of rings.

'Of course. He was much older than me and thankfully, he died.'

'Thankfully,' I gasped, bewildered.

'Yes. When they brought the news – I danced.'

Noting my confusion, she pushed open the double doors into the ballroom and I found myself in a universe of light and colour, a galaxy of dust motes trapped by the closed windows swirling about in the rays of sunlight.

'Welcome to my world.'

The room was alive with moving figures, my imagination running riot and creating images of women in long gowns, their gloved hands resting gently in their partners. Then I saw it was just Justine and me, our silhouettes endlessly paraded in lengths of mirrored glass. Between each one, there were long silk panels embroidered with a traditional Japanese scene, the coloured threads as delicate as those in Justine's kimono.

Immediately, I forgot the blood-stained history of the house, entranced by the glorious images. The mirrors didn't particularly interest me, having grown up surrounded by them, except to note that several were badly tarnished with blue shadows miring the pure reflection of the glass. It was the embroidery that grabbed my attention, each panel covered in a layer of clear glass to protect the threads and fine brushwork from damage.

I pointed to her kimono.

'Of course.' Grasping a corner of her gown, she danced around the room her arms outstretched, light glistening off the fine silk. 'I discovered it in a trunk with half-a-dozen ball gowns.'

On the long wall, you might mistakenly have believed yourself to be in a garden, its silken panels a flowing river in which living fish jumped and darted, its banks shaded by maple trees, their leaves equally as glossy and shining as living specimens. In the background there were forests, the trees older and less frivolous than the youthful maples and, behind them a line of mountains, their snow-tipped peaks interrupted by glass doors that opened out onto a balcony.

I swung around to be confronted by the fearsome glare of a soldier and found myself in a street. Busy with people, a platoon of soldiers in conical hats, with tall spears in their hands, marched towards me, their ferocious expression sufficient to thrust the bare-footed peasants out of the way. With their head bowed humbly, and a heavy bamboo yoke across their shoulders, they were ferrying baskets of produce to market. There, townspeople were bargaining for food and vegetables at roadside stalls. Next moment, a palanquin entered the scene. Carried by four stout men, a delicate hand tugged at the curtains, its owner curious to see out.

I took a step back, reclaiming the modern world, everything in the images so realistic one could almost hear the clink of coins being exchanged.

Even the double doors out into the corridor played their part. Painted to resemble the outside of a traditional house, red dragons glared down from the corners of the roof, the open doorway displaying a neat row of men shoes, almost threatening against the single pair of ladies' slippers lined up next to them.

'I was a ballet dancer in Paris.'

For a second or two, the phrase seemed almost a non sequitur, until I followed her line of sight. She was staring at the series of panels adjacent to the door which were explicitly devoted to pleasure – the first of them a Geisha performing her traditional dance. Noticing the subject of the next one, I blinked and stepped away. Far too much to take in, in one visit.

'That's how my husband and I met. He introduced me to the house on our honeymoon. A month, my husband said, the traditional length of a honeymoon. That's all we would be away from Paris. After that month, he refused to let me return to the dance.' She shrugged, a gesture of such meaning I could almost feel myself present at that particular encounter. 'Before our marriage, he had never missed a performance. He gave the excuse his Paris creditors were pressing him for money.'

She swung round, her kimono flaring to reveal long elegant legs, adding almost boastfully, 'Naturally, I married him for his money. After all, I am French. Nevertheless, it was a shock to discover the jewels he had gifted me on our wedding day had to be returned.' She waved a hand. 'You saw the empty shelves in the study – I sold those books to pay his gambling debts. If he had survived, no doubt, I'd have been left with nothing.' She waved her hand at the scenes on the wall. 'Apart from those and I would starve before I sold them.'

'How did he die?' I'm not sure why I asked the question – except it was hovering in the air, waiting.

'In a car crash at the bottom of the hill.' She took a deep breath, her clenched fists burrowing into her chin. 'Hans knows so why not you. He was a horrid man.' Her tone had changed. 'A vile collaborator. When I was going through his letters and papers, I discovered his dirty secret. It wasn't due to some miracle that Flambeau escaped the war. And he wasn't the first. The family survived the Revolution the same way – feeding the innocent to the guillotine and buying their own freedom with money or land.'

Dropping her fists, she glowered as if I was responsible, and I realised she was no longer aware of my presence, deep inside some unhappy place. 'I was young, and youth can always be forgiven its foolishness. Besides, he was so glamorous, it was easy to believe the myth created by flowers and jewels.'

As if casting off her gloom, she twirled round and round, her arms tracing a sequence of ballet positions, her negligee spinning in a lustrous swirl of colour. Halting, she pulled open the balcony doors and leaned out taking deep breaths of air. 'I always tell myself I was lucky not to have children. At least the evil died with him.'

Scarcely knowing what to say, I remained silent, content to let the fragrant air restore my equilibrium.

'Now I'm trying to get back. It's hard for a ballerina; very hard, once you stop.' She glanced over her shoulder. 'You should dance. The way you stand,' she complimented, 'so light on your feet. And your long neck.' She reached out as if wanting to measure it. 'You're a natural.'

12

Taking Justine's words as a dismissal, I made my excuses and returned to my room to collect my writing pad before heading out into the courtyard. Last night I had found it to be an enchanting spot with light from the kitchen window framing our table and chairs like a golden oriel, the lingering scent of roses perfuming the air. In daylight, more traces of its former austere magnificence came to light, the courtyard stretching the full width of the building, framed by an elegant cordon of fruit trees, its borders a mass of voluptuous red tulips which, despite being past their best, created a sweep of brilliant colour. As I watched, a petal broke away, hovering lightly on the breeze, languorously twisting and turning as it slipped towards the ground.

Puzzled by the layout of the house and having found Justine's explanation bewildering, I swung round wanting to view the building as a whole. An open E with short and stubby wings, its size alone contradicted Hans' use of the word house. This was a chateau, with dark grey roof tiles that glistened in the morning light, its first-floor windows framed by a balcony that mirrored the curve of the wooden trellis. I could even put a name to the style of roof – Mansard – only because Hans had dragged me around the city pointing out chimneys and roofs, snapping out a reproof whenever I forgot to use the proper architectural term. 'Mansard roofs,' I remembered him saying, 'are particularly stylish, like sloping troughs filled with wine.'

'Not water,' I teased.

'Oh no,' came the lofty response. 'Mansard roofs are too elegant for water.'

With my letters written, I didn't return to the house. I'd found its history disturbing; although its closed shutters and boarded windows created an air of melancholy rather than fear, and the day was too pleasant to be downcast.

Remembering how, last night, Hans had rushed off saying he needed to leave a canvas at the shop and deciding it had to be close by, I set out to find him. A trompe d'oeil in the centre of the trellis opened onto a long, narrow grass walk bordered by elegant fir trees, like an escort of soldiers in long bonnets. That appeared to be the frontier as far as money and grandeur were concerned, the tree-lined expanse on either side roughly scythed and, further on, a line of saplings that hid the stables from the house. Divided into two cottages, with boxes filled with geraniums and petunias on each of the window ledges, no trace was left of their former role, except perhaps for the verdant patch of earth surrounding each one, in which both vegetables and fruit trees luxuriated.

A broken iron railing separated the cottage gardens from a road which quickly vanished out of sight down an incline. Seeing only countryside beyond, I crossed over onto a cobbled lane, its grass verges a dumping ground for bits and pieces of history no one wanted: a broken staircase that led nowhere, the keystone of an arch with the crest of some nobleman carved on it, even part of a window, out of which no doubt a beautiful woman had once waved to her knightly lover.

This then was the old town as indicated on the road sign. The lane, barely wide enough for a vehicle, curved around on itself as if it once had the intention of growing into a square and had run out of building blocks or money to make that happen, leaving behind a lop-sided shape ringed by alleys like the spokes in a wheel.

Intrigued, I let my feet carry me up and down crooked steps, picking out a bright blue shutter that my brother would have called 'the vandalism of modernity' and a red doorway, newly painted, that was equally as intrusive. Bits and pieces reminded me of our old city, in which the vertical had been rendered obsolete or had never existed in the first place. Nevertheless, it was a pretty picture, accentuated by a riotous display of summer flowers in pots which perched on every available ledge and step. And, despite the old town being a world away from the sun-kissed shores that had filled his dreams as a teenager, I knew Hans would feel very much at home here. Maybe he had found both, although during our drive from Bordeaux, and passing through well-watered lands bathed in myriad shades of green, he had paid them scant attention, seemingly more interested in the wine they produced than setting brush to paper.

Not seeing his shop anywhere, I continued to explore, discovering samplers embroidered with verses from the Bible, the delicate silk faded and difficult to read, and old books with their pages yellowed and curling, and pairs of brass candle holders, the matching snuffers mired with wax or badly dented. As I walked past a parade of tiny shops camouflaged by a tiled overhang, a husband and wife emerged carrying a china jug wearing a hat, that had been hastily wrapped in newspaper, and I guessed small pieces, easy enough to pack in a suitcase, would prove popular with tourists who would consider their visit incomplete without a memento.

It was still relatively early and after the bustle of New York and Paris, remarkably quiet, the only sound to break the silence the rasp of a saw biting into wood and when I came across a long line of shallow steps, intrigued I began to climb them. Flanked by continuous lengths of cream housing, the passage was so narrow people leaning from the upper windows might easily have shaken hands. Part way, the walls broke apart making room for an archway. Gnarled and pitted by grapeshot or some other ordnance, it revealed yet another snapshot into the town's military past, in which even the stoutest of walls might succumb to the firepower of a determined enemy. Behind it lay a tiny courtyard, empty apart from a vast stone horse trough, planted with herbs and small shrubs.

More evidence of conflict awaited me at the top of the steps, where I emerged onto a smooth walkway. Once part of a high tower, sections of its original crenelated wall remained intact, although, here too, time had played its part and where soldiers may well have been bivouacked stood a modern office block, a couple of cars outside parked beneath the dense canopy of a tree that patterned the ground in shade.

By this time, I was regretting my walk, my feet as hot as my face, the little passage basking in full sunlight, although in winter it would have been a bleak spot. Yet, even as I took a step towards the walls wanting to feel the cooling breeze on my face, a charabanc emerged from a roadway at the rear of the square, disgorging a battalion of day trippers. They flocked to the ramparts, eager to view the countryside through the lens of a camera, and I was left to imagine the lines of archers who, when called upon, bent their bows, releasing arrows into the hordes of leather-jacketed foot soldiers besieging the walls far below.

I didn't stay. Skipping back down the steps, to my surprise I immediately stumbled on the little art shop. Partially obscured by wooden props that had been used to buttress a wall in danger of collapse, the name Hans Bader, neatly inscribed on the fascia, reproached me for ignoring its presence first-time round. There was no sign of him and, finding the shop door locked and the word fermé on its sign, I tapped on the glass. It made a hollow sound, as if the place had been empty a while and my knocking had disturbed the dust. Instantly I panicked, half believing Hans to be lying dead or injured on the far side, unable to cry out, and leaving me a stranger in a strange land.

Remembering the letter to Yöst in my bag, I hastily pulled it out, re-reading the address. How silly of me. It might be a foreign country but I had money in my pocket and I knew someone who lived not far away. How could I be alone? A more likely explanation was that I had simply misunderstood Hans –

undoubtedly something I should expect to happen on a regular basis until I was able to separate strings of mostly unintelligible noise into speech.

Laughing away my fright, I retraced my steps to the road, and hearing voices chanting followed the sound, a few minutes' walk bringing me back to the square with the church on my right. The heavily studded door had been propped open, maybe as a reminder that God's door was always open, although, a more obvious explanation was the weather, both the buildings and pavements bristling with heat.

Deciding to leave the modern town for another day and, having posted my letters, I cut through the narrow streets in the direction of the trees I had seen on my arrival. Here the air was cooler, a thickly woven canopy blocking the sun except where branches had died back, leaving hopscotch patterns of light and shade trailing across the earthen floor. I wasn't alone, conversation like distant bird song filtered through the trees, which suited my mood perfectly. After the challenge of New York and the crowds on the liner, my exuberance at the thought of a new adventure had taken fright on encountering the rigid face of the shop doorway closed against me.

And closed against hope?

No, not against hope.

In three years, many things can change. Like a child that goes to bed one night with his clothes fitting and wakes next morning to find them too short, at nineteen I found the world a very different place and I with it … except for one thing, the pain around my heart whenever I thought of Zande and the likelihood of never seeing him again.

He was the great showman, with pizazz and charisma intent on controlling the action. Yet beneath the surface, he demonstrated a frailty that drew both love and sorrow.

Why else had I continued my education, trawling through book after book if not to find an explanation, as Jaan had once done, only to find them empty of comforting words.

And Jaan? I had never before encountered anyone who paid

me attention; it was Ruth who influenced their thoughts and demanded their attention – even that of my brothers. At college I had been known as Ruth's friend. It was Jaan who showed me I mattered. More than that, he possessed that common sense attitude I so loved in Pappy – not yet whimsical humour, though I doubt Pappy had ever been anything but proper when he was a young man. Humour and whimsy are the qualities of those who have already found contentment with their place in the world, unknown to someone still scaling the ladder.

Yet, you can't direct your heart. If you could Jaan's name would have been the first spoken. What I felt for him was a warm friendship; only when Zande was about did my heart flutter and stop for a moment or two.

Abruptly the hillside fell away, the ground angling steeply downwards, and in places where felling had taken place, I caught a glimpse of the river where the swans I had noticed the day before were circling. Of course, it couldn't be, I knew that. In the light of day, as with dreams and nightmares, belief faded. Now after more than a thousand days, I had persuaded myself the tragedy of Pieter, his transference from human to swan, had been a lapse, a mere trick of the light.

And yet, despite every common-sense argument to the contrary I had seen it. Or had I? Perhaps after all it had been nothing more than a magic show, in which sleight of hand masquerades as truth before an audience of children. They would accept without question a magician's ability to make a member of the audience disappear from the empty interior of a cabinet or produce a rabbit from an empty hat. If it was possible to believe that why not for my brother to become a bird? Except it hadn't been a show in front of an audience of children. Real and desperate emotions had swirled on every side that night, and there'd been no enchantment only a storm of anger and grief.

I was busily questioning the wisdom of leaving the cool shade to follow the path down to the river, when I caught the sound of voices. Seated on the river bank with their feet in the water, and their voices raised in a heated argument, were two boys and two girls. I don't know why I was reminded of the four of us playing our games, unless it was the fair hair of the eldest. Even not being able to make out the exact words, the subject of their argument was an easy guess. It was about the yacht and the decision by the eldest to be first to sail it, the string that proclaimed his authority already attached to his wrist. The words, *droit du Seigneur*, came to mind, something Hans had fiercely disputed, resentful that an accident of birth deprived him of the privileges assumed by his older brother. Ignoring his siblings, the eldest boy set the yacht adrift. Bearing a full complement of sails, the ship with its white gallants and topsails glided out into the stream, carried by the current.

I began to cry, hastily dabbing away my tears with a handkerchief.

That was how Berthe lived her life, sailing elegantly onwards; and now Hans had joined her. Becoming independent, he was finally able to pursue the career he'd always wanted. But not Pieter and not me. However much I tried to persuade myself otherwise, unless something changed, Pieter could never be part of our lives. And me? My place in the world? So far that had shown itself to be little more than an ineffectual stream of dots and dashes. Grandmother was right. I would never be a fit candidate for life or marriage while Zande's voice still rang in my head.

Turning away, I returned to the house, conscious my brother's offer of employment was most likely the best I could do.

13

I spent the afternoon reading, after a lunch which I helped Justine prepare. 'I can manage cheese and fruit,' I excused my incompetence.

She had laughed, admitting her experience of the culinary arts had taken place after her marriage. 'And apart from learning how to cook, I can assure you, my marriage didn't live up to any of my expectations.'

She didn't explain further and although her words sounded frivolous, I guessed the living of them had been anything but that, her mouth twisting bitterly at the end of the sentence. It did nothing to encourage conversation between us and lunch was mostly eaten in silence, into which I tried to invest my gratitude at the end of our meal with a heartfelt, 'thank you, that was delicious.'

It wasn't just her tight-lipped stance that held me in thrall, more a realisation of the gap between us, far wider than our eight or nine years might suggest. And the few sentences we did speak over lunch about the town's origins did nothing to reduce that gap, my grasp of the French language superficial, stuttering out badly accented phrases, while her responses displayed all the skill of a sword fencer and following up my enquiry about the history of the town with an obtusely phrased question, was Ruth really my friend?

Thankfully she didn't refer to the letter I was supposed to write; perhaps dignity had won out over curiosity, and I wasn't about to reintroduce the subject. I was more interested to learn how she and Hans had got together, for two dissimilar individuals it was impossible to find. Apart from her speech, which on occasions, Hans said, was more suited to the backstreets of Paris, Justine was all elegance, whereas my brother was the opposite – clumsy in just about everything apart from his art. Even that had proved an uphill struggle, an unceasing effort, the requirements of his apprenticeship intolerable at times. Being forced to pay scrupulous attention to the smallest of details was foreign to his nature and in the early years the cause of many a row. Looking back, perhaps Pappy's concern was not about the loss of the Bader reputation, after all, had it been, he might easily have completed the work himself, but about ambition. Not for him, for his apprentice, wanting Hans to develop into a master craftsman.

By evening, the silence, so calm and orderly in the sunshine, had been replaced by a gathering tension, Justine's nails tapping a relentless tattoo on the cover of the novel she was struggling to read, silence returning only when she topped up her wine glass, while her mouth was fixed in a moue of disgruntlement at, or so I thought, being left to entertain an unwanted guest.

In desperation I came out with, 'Justine, will you tell me about your work?' I slapped at a mosquito that had landed on my bare arm.

'Maidy, please don't feel obliged to make conversation.' Justine batted the smoke from her cigarette in my direction. 'My being out of sorts has very little to do with Hans. I'm used to his disappearing. I admit it drove me mad at first, until he explained that artists cannot be considered in the same way as ordinary people.'

'You're an artist.'

'And I'm not like any one I know,' she laughed and the tension between us eased. 'When I get back to the theatre, doubtless you will discover that for yourself. My life is ...' she used the word bouleversé, which I assumed meant topsy-turvy. 'Sometimes, I am awake all night and sleep all day. Sometimes, after a bad performance, I cannot speak until I have re-danced the entire sequence of steps in my mind.' She stood up. 'We'd better go in. Mosquitoes seem to have developed a taste for visitors,' she remarked laconically, 'especially those who don't smoke. Such a shame.' She twisted on her heel, staring out over the courtyard, the gathering dusk accentuating the shape of the various bushes, the scent of their flowers fragrancing the night air. 'For lovers of romantic tales, this courtyard is the most perfect place. Dappled shade the early part of the day, soft moonlight at night. What more can you ask?'

'No mosquitoes.' We spoke together and her mouth softened into an amused smile. Gathering her wine glass and packet of cigarettes, she moved indoors, and still scratching at my arm, I followed her in.

Passing through the kitchen, she led the way through the hallway, opening the door to their living room at the front of the house.

On our brief tour, Hans hadn't bothered with this room and I was astonished to find it almost welcoming. On entering, Justine pushed open the shutters, light from the street lamp on the corner bright enough to read by. Here too, every picture apart from one had been removed, leaving its walls bare except for a trail of picture hooks. The life-size portrait of a modern man hung over the fireplace, his striking elegance deserving of its opulent gilt frame.

'My husband.' Justine seated herself on the chaise longue and raised her glass in mock salute. 'And before you ask, the frame is screwed to the wall. I did suggest dynamite, only Hans said the explosion might shatter the glass in the front door ...' Her voice rose mockingly. 'Why do I leave it?' She stretched elegantly, arranging the cushions behind her shoulders. 'Because it reminds me that part of my life is done with and I survived.'

In the distance I heard the faint growl of a car. Not the

Renault, the engine noise of a higher frequency. Even so Justine jumped, her body tense, disappointment paramount as lights from the vehicle swept past the window.

Her nervousness continued and we sat in silence, until with relief I recognised the tuneless rumbling of the Renault, although it was another moment before Justine reacted. Dropping her book, she raced into the kitchen. I followed almost reluctantly, anticipating harsh words at the lateness of the hour despite her earlier denial, her mouth once again reduced to a tight line.

'Sorry.'

Shutting the car door with his foot, Hans staggered into the kitchen burdened by a canvas in one hand, his canvas bag slung over his shoulder. He looked tired but elated, his eyes glistening, and I realised he'd been drinking. Yet, that was not it; there was hidden excitement there too.

'I was working and lost track of time. It was worth it, look at this.'

Leaving the partially finished canvas on the kitchen table, he unstrapped his bag, pulling out a small pencil sketch.

Giving the canvas a single cursory glance, Justine focussed her attention on the sketch. 'Chéri!' She blew him a kiss. 'Come home with that and I'll forgive you anything. What would you like to eat, anything, anything?' Taking the sketch in both hands, she waltzed it around the kitchen, her full-skirted dress swirling around with her, partnering her in the dance.

'I've eaten. I stopped off on the way to save you bothering.'

Becoming aware of my presence, he mumbled, 'Enjoyed your first day, Maidy? What did you do? It's a pretty town, isn't it?' almost immediately turning his attention to Justine again.

I wasn't needed and, saying goodnight, I flew upstairs, my thoughts as restless as my feet. I couldn't have stayed, my face, always the harbinger of my moods, would have given me away. Justine may well have become accepting of Hans' casual attitude, but I had picked up on the lie. When he collected me from the station, that same drawing had been lying face up on the back seat, and I wondered what he had really been doing ... and with whom?

It troubled me. I had left home to avoid its secrets, yet, within twenty-four hours, I was being faced with a similar imbroglio, for which, unless I was wrong and had misread the signs, Ruth's letter was to blame.

Unable to settle, I pushed open the window and perched on the windowsill, the pleasant aroma of grilling meat still hanging in the air from the restaurant. Above the dark canopy of pine leaves, the night sky shone in an unending coverlet of gleaming stars. A charming and peaceful scene. Reluctantly, I fastened the wooden shutters and turning away from the window left it open.

'What happened to you yesterday?' I challenged Hans next morning as we walked together through the grounds, the music from Justine's studio gradually fading as we crossed the terrace.

Hans hesitated. 'Why?'

'Because I came down to find you and the shop was closed and your car wasn't parked nearby, I'd have noticed.'

'I went to meet Ruth.'

'How was that even possible?' I said, wishing now I had paid Ruth's letter more attention. 'Isn't she in Paris?'

'No, not until the autumn. She's filming in Bordeaux. That's why she got in touch, wondered if I'd be interested in visiting the set. I couldn't say no.'

I swallowed, overcome by a raft of conflicting emotions, most of them anger. 'Hans! How could you?'

He bristled, all at once on the defensive. 'You don't know. You've never been in love. I've loved Ruth all of my life.'

I couldn't believe what I was hearing. Only the day before I'd decided he was safely on the path to maturity and here he was, back to sounding defensive. 'Not all your life, Hans.' My tone sounded sharp even to my ears. 'You're still at the beginning of life.' I meant with Justine.

'You've changed,' he accused. 'I thought you'd understand.'

I could easily have disabused him and related a catalogue of Ruth's misdeeds. 'I'm older,' I snapped back. 'I've grown up.'

He stopped walking. 'Age has nothing to do with falling in love.'

It hadn't; of course, it hadn't. 'Have you forgotten she's married?'

'What's that got to do with it. There's no law against talking to married women.'

There was bleakness in his tone and I wondered if, on the drive back to Flambeau, he had spent the time trawling through every conversation he had ever had with Ruth in the hope of discovering something warmer than friendship – as I had once done, sifting through my conversations with Zande.

'After filming was over for the day, I took her to dinner. That's all. She wanted to know why you haven't written.'

'Ruth came all this way to ask why I hadn't written?'

'No, of course not. The management have rented an apartment for her.'

'And Justine?'

'What about Justine?' He glared at the ground. 'I didn't mention it because she wouldn't understand. She thinks she owns me.'

'And does she?'

He flushed and kicked at a stray pebble which rattled across the hard surface of the lane. 'No one owns me.'

Not even Ruth? I didn't say the words aloud, they wouldn't have helped.

Hans lapsed into silence and I gathered from his mulish stance there was no point attempting to reason with him. Maybe the loosening of family ties was the logical outcome of living away from home; nevertheless, I felt real concern about his protestations on behalf of Ruth. Of course, it was entirely possible that having married, she was content, and their meeting was just that – nostalgia. If so, Hans' irritation with my questions was more readily explained.

There were not many people about, although from what Justine said at breakfast, only shops in the main town closed on a Sunday, with shop assistants and their owners taking a well-earned break. For those in the old town, Sunday was the busiest day of the week.

'There's not a lot for you to do apart from the window.' Hans unlocked the shop door pushing it open for me to enter first. 'I'm going to paint out back. If you need help, call me.' Adding almost as an afterthought, 'When you've done the window you might get a letter off, Ruth'd appreciate that.'

I didn't reply, pretending to examine the objects Hans had placed in the window. How could I write to Ruth? Especially not now, not after those final few words, a casual appendix to his earlier comments yet more revealing than all the rest. It wasn't over, not for Hans.

The day before, whilst out walking, I had come across a bench seat, the wood scored with hundreds of names, hearts and flowers joining two sets of initials together with a date, and I wondered how many of those beating hearts were still together. Tracing the hearts with the tip of my finger, it was Ruth who I was thinking of, the embossed letters of her initials, GM, on the front of the envelope addressed to Hans. I am not sure why or even where the thought came from but it was there, like a clarion call – if Ruth ever made an appearance in Flambeau, the names of Hans and Justine would not be among them.

Hans worked until lunchtime, greeting my efforts at dressing the window with a casual, 'That's okay.' He pointed. 'Except for that brand of oil paint; it's not for sale.'

I glared at him. 'You might have told me before I arranged the window. What about the paint you use for watercolours?'

"Not fussy about them; that's Justine's department,' he retorted, obviously uninterested in the minutiae of the trade. 'Only oil paint can add the depth and texture I need.' And leaving me to lock up, he wandered back to the house.

Despite Justine's delight at the sketch, the convivial atmosphere of the previous evening wasn't repeated, her light-hearted jesting replaced by a series of polite remarks – treating me as some unwanted object that had been placed in her way, forcing her to walk around it and stubbing her toe in the process. Admittedly she said little to Hans either, as if words had suddenly become an enemy with whom she wanted no truck. He ignored her silence, occasionally tapping her hand or arm in an affectionate gesture, browsing a book on the local terrain. I felt disheartened, wondering if I had caused some offence, and shortly after dinner I took myself off to my room.

After an entire day had passed when Justine didn't speak, except for a brief nod, her replies to any of my questions monosyllabic, I whispered to Hans, 'are you sure she wants me here?'

He was on his way out, a new canvas under his arm, already deeply involved with the colours and textures to be used that day, and he replied almost impatiently, 'Maidy, how can you possibly conduct a conversation with someone if you don't speak their language? I gave you a dictionary, use it.'

Dumping the canvas on the back seat of the Renault, he came back into the kitchen, a sheepish expression on his face. 'Sorry, I didn't mean that. Besides, you're not doing too badly. Maybe I should have warned you that Justine doesn't much care for women.'

'Doesn't—' I exclaimed, scarcely able to believe what I was hearing. 'That's so typical and so selfish, Hans. Yes, I know, your precious art comes before family, still, you might have warned me. Do you want me to leave?'

'Why on earth would I want that?' he mumbled. 'And what you said, about my art, that's not fair. I love my family and would do anything for them.' He glared. 'I invited you here, didn't I? Just ride it out like I do. Anyway, you don't count, which is why you're not sleeping at the shop.'

I stared, my face blank with astonishment. 'Now you've lost me, sleeping at the shop?'

He shrugged. 'In France, it's not that unusual. While men enjoy men's company, most women can't stand other women … it's rare for them to have a belle amie, which is what they call a good friend, at least, not 'til they're old.' His body relaxed and he leaned back against the wall, his hurry to set out forgotten. 'I asked Justine. She insists men are to blame.' He flicked his hand at a fly that had landed on the kitchen table. 'With Justine, men are to blame for everything, although even I refuse to repeat her actual words. For her, it was the dancers in the corps de ballet. Jealous as hell those girls are if you're singled out as Justine was.' His grin twisted. 'I went with her to Paris one time and she took me backstage. Of course, they were all over me.' His face lit in a sly smile immediately replaced by a doleful expression. 'We had a most terrible row and she stormed off. Couldn't find her anywhere, searched all night. She'd only gone and caught the train back. Eventually, she admitted there'd been a woman in the car, her husband's latest mistress, when it crashed.'

He hesitated, shifting from foot to foot. 'I know it's a lot to ask, but she's really great, never met anyone like her. Just don't expect her to be easy.' He pointed up at the ceiling, strains of music from the studio where Justine was hard at work drifting down the stairs. 'You can always tell her mood by the music. I promise, it's not personal.'

After Hans' timely intervention, once I accepted that Justine's behaviour, however odd, wasn't directed at me, and never doubting that she loved him, I began to settle.

Nevertheless, despite my best efforts, she remained an enigma. After each confidence, she retreated behind her barrier, her smiles kept for Hans alone and rarely displaying the same humour on successive days – although now I recognised the signs, her mouth a thin line, her eyes fastened unseeing on the stove or wall.

Whenever that happened, she shut herself away in her studio and danced, only emerging as the Renault sounded on the road outside. Then, the sparkle came back into her eyes, her smile so full of feeling, it took away my breath. Very occasionally, evidence of her mood filtered down through the music. It flowed out through the walls of the studio and across the landing into my bedroom, the overloud and often discordant harmonies ringing through the entire first floor – even the ceiling vibrating under a series of angry thumps and I imagined her stamping her feet on the images of her dead husband.

Surprisingly though, it was Justine who added her own assurances to those of Hans – that her moods had nothing to do with me. 'It's best to keep well away and never open the studio door, unless you want something shied at your head.' That day her eyes had sparkled with energy despite the gravity of her words. 'Once, I pushed Hans into the river.' Noticing my surprise, she added, 'He was behaving like a beast, telling me to snap out of it and fresh air would do me good.'

'How did you meet?' I asked the question that had been hanging over me since my arrival. I had asked Hans and received a shrug and a mumbled response, 'Oh, well, you know.'

'I wondered if it was the gargoyles?'

The night of my arrival I'd only caught a glimpse. Then they had resembled mere guard dogs and not until the next day viewing them in daylight, did I become aware of the air of menace that emanated from them. No doubt the work of a talented artist, each aspect of their leaden bodies was intricately sculptured, their features almost elegantly exaggerated with their noses longer and more pointed, their mouths leering and their eyes malevolent.

Her eyebrows rose in astonishment. 'The gargoyles?'

'Yes, that first day when I was looking around the town, a group of artists were painting them.'

'Hideous creatures,' she shuddered.

'I agree but had Hans visited Flambeau and caught sight of the figures, he would have knocked at your door and demanded permission to draw them. To him they represent something unique and therefore beautiful.'

'Yes, most likely he would have,' she replied in a thoughtful tone. She smiled wistfully. 'Actually he picked me up.'

'Hans did?' I said astonished, wondering how my clumsy and bumbling sibling could be so forward. Then I remembered his awkward teenage years were long gone and this individual – judging by the come-hither glances of girls he passed in the street – had no doubt experienced several relationships. 'When?'

Justine laughed. It was such a rich sound, encouraging me to join in. 'It was after a performance in Lyons.'

'You were dancing?'

She shrugged. 'I don't call the provinces dancing. For me, dancing is something that happens only in Paris – where I belong. After the performance, I went to a restaurant with a friend and Hans came over. Said he was a pupil of the school of Degas and he had seen my performance... and he would consider it an honour if I would sit for him.' She recited the words and I guessed they were from memory.

'Wasn't Degas that French artist who painted dancers?'

'That French artist,' she rebuked. 'Maidy, how can you say such a thing – it's sacrilege. Degas is the French artist who painted dancers.' She emphasised the definite article. 'And it gets worse. My dinner companion happened to be a man.'

How lovely she looked, her expression vividly alive with happy memories.

'I never eat with women. Except he wasn't a beau; he was my partner for that performance. Naturally, he was quite beautiful looking. In the theatre, it's traditional.'

'What is?' I said confused.

'To eat with your partner after an opening performance. Their looks may be of concern to their lovers, never to me.' She waved her hand, dismissing the word beautiful. 'Their ability to support is far more important, but this boy just happened to be sublimely handsome.'

'Oh!'

'Justement!' She laughed. 'I decided then and there Hans was either mad or serious about wanting to paint me, so I asked him to join us for a drink. What attracts you to men?'

The sudden change of subject fazed me and I stuttered, 'I'm not sure.'

She stared intently. 'You are nineteen? By now you should know.'

Not allowing me time to reply, she continued, 'French women seek two things in a man.' She began counting on her fingers, as long and slim as the rest of her. 'No three – perhaps even four.' She waved her hand nonchalantly. 'Money ... naturally. That is by far the most important. French women will choose money above everything.'

'Only French women?'

'I have no idea about women in other countries.' The lofty tone made me smile. 'I am French ... what else? Next comes beauty...' She used the words *être beau* which I guessed meant handsome. 'That is also of great importance. However, it is not essential. Provided a man dresses well and has the physique to go with it.' She touched her third finger pushing out her lips in an exaggerated gesture, 'Ugliness can also prove an aphrodisiac. Most of all, French women enjoy a challenge. They do not want, how do you say it? A door mat.' She used the word *l'essuie-pieds* which I'd never heard before and had to guess. 'They want excitement which may be is why they so frequently marry badly and are unhappy.'

Her imperious tone made me smile, and I guessed she was referring to herself. I watched her eyes light up in appreciation of my grasping the subtlety.

'Hans fails on three of the four counts; he is penniless, not exactly good-looking, and dresses badly.'

I wanted to object, and she waved her hand at me. 'No, no. What I tell you is quite correct. For residents of Bordeaux, his clothes may be acceptable, but in Paris – the centre of couture? There, his clothes will never be considered *de rigeur.*' I didn't understand the phrase and she hastily substituted the word, suitable. 'For we French, especially the young, dressing well is almost a religion, although washing not so much, even in Flambeau. Peek over a few fences at night, you will see what I mean; their backyards will be full of clothes drying. *Naturellement*, youth is an aphrodisiac, yet youth on its own may not always be sufficient to hold a sophisticated woman after a few weeks or months. Only someone like me, who recognises genius, will find Hans exciting. At the end of the evening, I gave him my telephone number. He phoned later that same night and I invited him for the weekend...' the shrug came again. 'He stayed.'

Surprisingly, despite days when she clung to her room, it was

Justine who taught me how to keep shop, something Berthe would have learned when she first accepted employment in the chocolate shop. How to deal with both money and difficult customers, and to have patience with small children, who considered choosing a chocolate figurine far more important than getting to school on time. Unfortunately, Justine's involvement came about after a row with Hans. Fortunately, I didn't understand the profanity, understanding only the latter part of the phrase, 'She's your sister, you teach her.'

Casually dismissing rolls of art-paper, postcards and brushes, with the words, 'That side of the business you can learn on your own,' she turned her attention to the paintings which lay scattered across both walls and floor.

At once the glare that had greeted me at breakfast vanished, and she called out almost gaily, 'First, you need to study every painting Hans has created – until you know them by heart as I do. And which are good and which are not.'

'Aren't they all good?'

'Better than good, Maidy.' Justine accepted my naïve question with a nod. 'Hans is a gifted artist. His attention to detail is quite extraordinary. You are surprised?'

'Yes. He wasn't like that as a child.'

'Ah! But then he was a child.' She waved her hand, dismissing my objection. 'Naturally, some canvases are finer than others and when his work goes on show, art experts will expect to pay a higher price for those. Take that one, for instance.' She pointed to the canvas Hans had brought back following his day out with Ruth.

He had placed it on an easel at the back of the shop to dry, wagging the proverbial finger when I asked if I might move it. 'Not until I say. Besides, it's not yet finished. And, if and when you do, no sunlight. Remember the palace museum with its artificial light? That's why I chose this place. It's perfect.' He patted the wall, a long uninterrupted stretch of off-white emulsion extending from front to back. 'Even in Paris, you wouldn't get finer.'

Swinging lightly round, Justine pointed to a piece of work

occupying pride of place on the back wall. 'And that one, are they both equally as fine?'

It was of the Garonne, with the city of Bordeaux in the background, an almost identical aspect to the one he was currently working on, except for the time of day – the painting on the wall late afternoon, with shadows lengthening along the river, the water dark and deeply uneasy.

I felt the river water cold on my arm as if I had plunged my hand into the painting.

'I'm not sure,' I began and hesitated.

'Go on,' she prompted.

'In this,' I pointed. 'I can feel the water.'

'And that one?' She indicated the canvas on the easel.

I knew instinctively what she meant. Equally realistic, it felt slightly flat, as if Hans had been thinking of something else. I didn't need to ask; it was his date with Ruth.

Once again, I felt a niggle of unease. If a single meeting had resulted in something Justine considered substandard, what if there was a second encounter? Justine obviously knew his work well, anything not of an equal competence would doubtless raise questions.

'That was excellent,' she said. 'I couldn't have done better. And helpful, is it not, your knowing your brother's earlier work. I won't need to worry about your selling a great piece cheaply.' She picked up another canvas, arranging it on an easel. 'He's a brilliant artist, and an infuriating individual. Is your other brother the same?'

Surprised by the continuing conversation, I realised Hans must have passed on my comment, her usual quick-fire speech slowed sufficiently for me to follow.

'Pieter? No, he was the opposite, both thoughtful and kind. We all loved Pieter.' Without thinking, I used the past tense. I rushed on. 'Both he and Berthe are artists; at least he was before he went travelling.' I spelled out the lie. 'He worked with Pappy, while Berthe puts her talents into making cakes and needlework.'

'She's married, isn't she?'

I nodded, not stopping my task of checking the number of brushes we held in stock.

'And you?'

Carefully banding the brushes together, I replaced them in their allotted pigeonhole. 'I was left with imagination but no skill.'

'Hans says you are the peacemaker – that's quite a skill.'

'You talk about me?'

'We talk about all sorts of things. Your childhood was very different from my own.'

I was glad then because the word talk inferred something ongoing with a suggestion of permanence, except I was certain in none of those conversations would the name Ruth crop up.

I pulled out a fresh batch of brushes and began counting, noticing how they varied from the previous batch, having broader handles and long stiff bristles. 'What are these made of?'

She pointed to a chart showing coloured images of the different types. 'You'll need to learn that off by heart because salesmen call regularly.'

I pulled it out. '*Pourceau*?'

I hadn't heard the word and Justine, noticing my confusion, snorted.

I laughed. 'What are they used for?'

'Background textures. It's a coarse stiff hair, so anything requiring depth. Have you visited the river yet?'

I glanced up, astonished at the abrupt change of subject. 'Yes, my first day here.'

'And?'

Remembering what Hans had suggested, I recited his advice. 'Hans said to go and see it when it's sunny.'

Justine's mouth softened. 'You should. When the sun is out, a decent artist wanting to paint the gorge will take several dozen brushes with him. It's essential for anyone trying to capture the essence of the river, because there's a different aspect for every hour of the day; one moment it's in deepest mourning, the next transformed into a celebration of colour. When I reached the lowest point in my marriage, that's where I went. It helped. I have a feeling you and the river share something in common.'

Her speech had speeded up again and I struggled to understand. 'Like you the river has hidden depths. Hans is convinced one day you will surprise them all. He thinks it'll be a book. If so, I doubt if it will be written in French,' she added, her smile reaching her eyes.

14

Before I thought about it, a month had vanished, and then a second; the days blurred and impossible to remember clearly as were the faces of customers, yet a pleasant enough existence once I'd settled to Justine's moods.

Except it lacked excitement; each day a repetition of the previous one until by the end of the third month the turning of the key, either to lock or unlock the shop door, became so automatic it barely registered, conscious no surprises awaited me on either side.

Perhaps I'd not have noticed had my visit happened before the gaiety of America. After all, during the previous three years, boredom had proved a welcome reprieve from Mother's belittlement. Now, I found myself swaying to music only I heard and although I was not yet able to write a novel in French, I began dreaming in it, waking to the sound of my voice repeating words that had found a home in my unconscious ear. Occasionally, in the shop, frustrated by my lack of the correct response, customers shrugged their shoulders and reached past me with a smile, helping themselves to the item they were seeking, perhaps the correct size and composition of a brush or the exact thickness of art paper, the more patiently disposed repeating their request word for word.

'I bet they were men,' Hans growled when I told him. 'They don't care how you speak, they just like having a pretty girl behind the counter.'

Justine laughed. 'That sounds like brotherly concern! If I remember rightly, Hans, wasn't it you who marked out being pretty as the main prerequisite of a sales assistant?'

Pappy had written almost straight away, although I hadn't heard from Yöst. Jaan had once used the phrase, *ships that pass in the night*. He'd been referring to us ... him and me. We had met up, enjoyed our meeting, and moved on. Was that how Yöst looked back on our brief acquaintance, my dream of dancing vanishing with the striking of the clock that heralded the dawn?

'Pappy says,' I read the passage aloud to Hans, conscious the effort writing a letter would demand of Pappy and cherishing each word as an expression of his love. 'Enri's mirrors are proving popular...'

'Remind me who he is again.'

'Honestly, Hans,' I said exasperated, well aware throughout our entire childhood he had rarely applied more than half his attention when someone else was speaking. 'He's the new apprentice who happens to think your designs incredible.'

Hans shrugged. 'They are. Go on.'

'"*With the war done with, customers no longer want furniture that will last a lifetime. Of course, it won't surprise you to learn, my dear Maidy, I've taken on a second apprentice. Your mother thinks it an unwise move at my time of life, but I thought it over very carefully. Even when retirement beckons, the Bader business will be needed to provide us both with a pension.*"'

I paused, retracing my steps through Pappy's words, aware how deeply he loathed the silence in a house that had once rung with laughter, missing the noisy clatter of feet on the staircase.

'"*Joost is an art student,*' I read on. "*Now you have left us, he too will take up lodgings, and part time will attend the college at Herrendorp, the one you studied at. At present, he is too nervous to do more than pick up a brush. I remember Pieter, his first attempts were equally as tentative.*"'

I didn't bother reading the last line; Pappy's final sentence: *Of all things, it is at mealtimes I miss my children most*, meant for my eyes only. Sadly, I wondered if his gentle teasing, so much a part of our childhood, was also destined to wither and fade like hope and flowers.

'When you write,' Hans instructed, 'be sure and tell him, my designs must be labelled as originals and signed with my name.'

'Tell him yourself,' I retorted, 'he'd love to hear from you.'

His infectious grin flashed out, and momentarily I saw what Justine meant by sweetness, his eyes wide and innocent. As my bullying older brother, I'd only ever noticed the bad bits, skipping over anything else. 'Not going to happen. I not only resemble Pappy, I have inherited his bad habits too. With a brush in my hand all day, outside of work I absolutely refuse to go near anything brush-shaped and that includes both pens and pencils.'

I glanced up, my eyebrows raised in disbelief. 'A good job wine glasses aren't pen-shaped then.'

He laughed. As a boy he'd so often been sullen, resenting his sibling's mockery and concealing his hurt with wildness. I was glad he now felt secure enough to cope with my teasing and gave silent thanks to Justine, who was responsible for the change.

'If Pappy wants to hear from me, tell him to install a telephone.'

Of course, I didn't do that, despite thinking it an excellent suggestion. I also missed the sound of Pappy's voice.

Daily, I questioned my decision to leave Holland. I wasn't unhappy, yet each morning when I awoke, opening my eyes onto beams of sunlight that filtered through the slats in the shutters, I wondered if this might well become the pattern of my life; long dull periods in which nothing happened interspersed with a brief spell of activity such as travelling on a bus through Paris and my heart-stopping visit to America. Occasionally, wanting to relive the excitement of New York, I'd tug the dress I'd worn for the theatre from my wardrobe. Looping the hanger over my head and hugging the fabric to me, I'd hum the tune the musicians played, and I'd dance.

There had to be something else – a challenge, a striving, something to make my heart go pit-a-pat. If only I could find it.

Except I had no idea what it was I wanted or was waiting for.

Justine saw. She'd glance at me, her mouth partly open as if to ask a question and thinking better of it, would take a sip of coffee or wine to mitigate any concern she felt.

Yet what could she ask, did you have a good day?

As much as I loved Hans, I knew that for him, offering me a job was the simplest way out of the problem of my living at home and certainly the one that required least effort on his part. And gradually as the weeks rolled on, especially on days when Justine was overtaken by depression and kept to her room, Hans, forgetful of his role as my mentor, also forgot about me and disappeared off somewhere, throwing himself into work or so he always claimed when he arrived home after dark.

'Presumably painting by starlight has become the latest artistic fad.' Justine's sarcastic tones greeted him, her temper sometimes erupting into overdrive and throwing a plate with his uneaten dinner on it, before storming off to her studio.

Shouting at me to *keep out of it*, he'd race upstairs after her, the noise of their rowing drifting across the landing into my bedroom so that I too slept badly, once again troubled by nightmares of the past. For me, it was always the same one, the fight between Zande and Pieter in the courtyard of the college, my feet buried in quicksand unable to move or, strangely, shout a warning.

Admittedly right from the start I found their quarrels ugly. Even those that ended up in laughter and a bedroom door that closed quietly instead of being slammed. Maybe that was a lesson I also needed to learn ... that love could be portrayed in a thousand different ways, not all of them kindly and nurturing. Yet even that was easier to cope with than the careless sort of interest Hans occasionally bestowed on Justine, undeserving of him or of any man.

Different from a hailstorm in summer that lasts only a few seconds before rain sweeps it away, traces of their changing relationship were everywhere, not only in the spats that became more frequent, also their drinking, neither much interested in the food Justine cooked. On those days, breakfast became a dismal affair, with Justine sulking and Hans not daring to speak, except for platitudes about the weather, in case it reignited the quarrel of the previous night, leaving me to question the wisdom of leaving home and grateful I had work to go to.

How naïve of me to believe their relationship solid and true. When Hans and I met up at the station, the rasp in his voice when he spoke of his patron had been enough to convince me of his interest. And why not: mysterious and intriguing, Justine's character was sufficiently fascinating to pique any man's interest, her face – so often drawn into a world of darkness – capable of erupting into the most bewitching of smiles.

Nevertheless, when Hans and I were alone together, I guarded my tongue, resisting the urge to rail at him, insisting he'd be a fool to throw away something so unique, rehearsing words I wanted to say a dozen times over before leaving them unsaid: *Every single man in Flambeau and most of the married ones would envy what you have. Don't spoil it.*

I suppose I was brooding on that very thought when the shop bell chimed out. Business had been brisk and I was writing an order for postcards, something else Hans should have done, and I didn't pay it any attention. Hans had agreed we needed a telephone, but there was a long waiting list.

'I decided three years quite long enough to stay away. Yöst tells me, you're not married but Ruth is.'

Maybe after all this time, believing there to be no need, I had learned to ignore footsteps ringing the pavement behind me. Once again, they resounded through my head and I crossed my fingers, praying – begging – hoping this time it might be different and I wouldn't discover the sound simply an echo of my own daydreams.

Then I did something I had never done before – I turned around.

It was Zande.

He was standing in the doorway, his head ducked against the low lintel.

In Ruth's film, the one I saw with Meneer Endelbaum in New York, her character came out with the words: 'If I am to die, let it be now, now when I am so wondrously happy.'

At the time, I thought the lines trite, their sentiment pretentious. Now I considered them a perfect example of what I was feeling. I clenched my fist to keep my arm down at my side and stop it moving.

'Yöst?' I said.

I might have added a million words, all of which I'd rehearsed a dozen times before in the silence of my bedroom at home, changing the tone and strength of my rebuke nightly as my mood varied. Now, none came to my rescue. Only joy.

'Do you realise your mouth is gaping open like a codfish? Not a pretty sight.' He used the French word, *une morue*.

Not understanding except to guess the word to be derogatory, I shook my head.

He laughed and repeated the word in Dutch. He had changed, not older but thinner, his face drawn, yet the smile was the same, slightly mocking with that tiny twist in the corner that plucked at the heartstrings.

'Do I really resemble a codfish?'

His eyes with their myriad specs of light locked on mine, examining my face as if there was nothing else in the world worth bothering with. 'Only if codfish are pretty. You look sad.'

As I always had done, I hastily changed the subject, seeking safer ground. 'How do you know Yöst?'

How I got the question out, I've no idea, lost in a mist of overwhelming excitement. Compared to this – to reality – whether he stayed one minute or five, my memories of him hung around in black and white, none with any colour in them.

'He's my brother,' he replied nonchalantly, as if his answer was of as little importance as the state of the weather.

It was Zande – of course it was, every intonation familiar and valued.

Except I didn't care about what he said nor the tone he used, or whether I had heard those same words before, only that he was talking to me and I could actually hear his voice – the low ceiling in the shop resonating and creating a faint echo. It meant he was alive, he still existed, and he was standing there in front of me; it wasn't imagination.

I still blinked once or twice to make sure.

'How...?'

I saw the folly of my question instantly, expecting one of his rapier-like ripostes and was surprised when he answered quite seriously, 'I was an orphan and Yöst took me in and cared for me. And Tatania.' I remembered Yöst saying he had a sister. 'She was orphaned too. He became our lifeline. He's a good guy, one of the best. By the way, he wrote you a letter.'

He pulled the envelope from his pocket, his expression swept by laughter. 'He didn't have a stamp so I said I would deliver it for him.'

It was ridiculous and absurd but from Zande so entirely to be expected, I laughed. His smile joined mine, the muscles in his one cheek softening the corners of his mouth, and I guessed even for Zande it had taken courage to push open the door to the shop.

'And before you ask—' The muscles in his throat constricted and he swallowed. 'Yöst's shoulder was badly damaged in the war when he was shot.' His tone changed, now pleasantly conversational. 'No one knows how he survived. He swears he didn't and was brought back to life by the ocean.'

The memories I'd so carefully tried to bury stormed back into place, instinct picking up on the hesitation in that sentence. A word was missing; a word he couldn't yet bring himself to speak aloud.

I knew what it was – of course I did.

'And you?'

I waited for him to answer.

He moved then, bending forwards to examine each of the paintings in turn, nodding his approval. 'As a child I was always drawing. I might take it up again.'

Realising I wouldn't get an answer, not yet anyway, I went to ask a different question about Pieter, when the shop door opened, the chiming of the bell abruptly returning me to the present.

If I had thought at all, I would have imagined Waldger to have followed him, his sense of timing always inappropriate, and was almost disappointed to see the man entering to be middle-aged and balding.

'Do you sell brushes?'

He spoke in English and I responded automatically, 'Yes, of course.'

It wasn't what I wanted to say. I wanted to scream aloud: *It's not fair*, and to beat my fists on the counter like an irate child. *Zande will leave again in a minute and I will know more about you and your life story than I will ever know about him.*

I felt my face change, the automatic smile of greeting to a customer altered into one of panic. Noticing, the customer intervened, 'I'm in no hurry. Please finish serving this young man.'

Zande took a step back, saying in impeccable English, 'Please continue. I only called in to say hello, I'm not buying.'

I noticed his fists, stuffed into the pockets of his light-weight jacket. He was as nervous as me but he wasn't running away, not this time, not after forcing himself to seek me out. Instead, he'd wait politely until the man had left, and then calmly enquire about my life. Once he had the facts straight to pass on to Yöst and his friends, and with his conscience assuaged and liberated, only then would he leave.

Except that wasn't going to happen, not this time.

Because...

I chased the word round and round hoping I was right and hadn't misread the tension in his voice. Because Zande was as tired of lugging their secret around with him as I was of keeping it.

'What medium are you intending to use? I'm guessing oil.' I asked politely and pulled out a tray.

'Oil, yes. How did...'

'An easy guess.' My voice sounded almost gay.

Of course, I was showing off, hoping to come across as someone worldly, the opposite of that naïve schoolgirl of three years ago. 'My brother's an artist and he told me when the weather is hot and windy, like today, you're better off using oil paint because water colour dries too quickly.'

The man swung on his heel. 'These are his?' I nodded. 'They're good – very good.' He crouched down, peering at a painting set low on the wall.

'Paintings are always a good investment,' Zande reminded. I recognised the tempting tones, ones he'd used to good effect on girls at college.

The man smiled. 'I know and one day…' He pointed to the price, 'I might be in a high-enough wage bracket to afford one of these.'

'You wanted a brush,' I reminded.

Zande's eyes gleamed at my terse tone, and I saw without any actual decision or effort on my part, I had slipped back into that old cut and thrust that had once existed between us.

I blushed, mortified that my pretence at being grown up and worldly had proved so fleeting.

Zande stepped towards the door, the sound of its bell ringing out, mocking me, although the tone of his voice remained dispassionate and measured. 'I'll leave you to make your choice,' he said, and stepped out onto the pavement.

With his hand resting on the open door, he swung around. His eyes sought mine, betraying his mischievous intent. 'Would it inconvenience you…' He addressed the customer, and I recognised the familiar subtle mockery, adding a nod to match his tone levelled out in polite enquiry. 'If I delayed your purchase for another moment, long enough for me to enquire of this young lady…' It was purposefully done, his eyes fastened on mine, quite well aware of the tension his leisurely tone was creating. 'What time she eats lunch?'

'I close for thirty minutes at two.' I smiled an acceptance, excitement flowing over me like a warm stream of water.

'What a polite young man,' the customer commented as the bell announced the closing of the door. 'And how refreshing. So many today are so lacking in manners.'

Through the shop window, I was watching Zande. He'd swung round, his gaze fastened on mine. He was laughing. Hastily, I schooled my face into a frown, aware that my panic at the notion of his leaving so soon hadn't gone unnoticed. Of course it hadn't – this was Zande. Trying to appear casual, I raised my hand in a salute. He smiled and waved back. Then he was gone.

15

Despite my imagination that two o'clock would prove as much a fantasy as Zande's earlier appearance, it was a good sale, the man buying a dozen brushes in assorted sizes, confiding the price was cheaper than in England where he lived. 'It's a small country town, there's not many shops, although we do have an art shop that sells a range of brushes and paints.'

I barely listened, my mind elsewhere, scarcely knowing how to survive the next few hours until lunch, although no doubt had I shown more than a cursory interest, being on holiday and having time to kill, my customer would have launched into a history of his own life.

Justine had warned me about getting friendly with customers. 'Keep it polite and pleasant but unsmiling, otherwise you'll have young men wanting to date you and older men wanting to tell you their life history. And that's terrible.' Justine used the word *épouvantable* and I'd rushed to the dictionary to look up its meaning. Hans told me, when I complained, that she'd grown bored with using baby words. 'After three months, you should be able to string more than two sentences together. In another month or two, if you're good, I'll teach you how to swear.'

'A polite no thank you might suffice to see off the young ones,'

Justine continued, 'whereas older men refuse to be side-tracked and insist on recounting every detail, believing their history as fascinating for the listener as it obviously is for them. And, I can promise you, it isn't.'

'What about women?'

'You're too pretty for them to stay and chat,' she complimented.

'Boyfriend?' the Englishman enquired, picking up on my abstracted expression and generously curtailing the list of countries he had visited since the war.

'No, just a friend.'

He also bought a print, my favourite view of the square. Surprising for someone who originally discovered the sunshine of France in the bottom of a beer glass, the image was a place of shadows in which there was no actual sunlight. Except there was. When I asked Justine, she said that was down to skill. 'If an artist is good, he can create impressions that don't exist except in your imagination.' On first seeing the original, I spent the rest of the day staring out into the square hopeful of replicating the exact moment Hans had taken the snapshot in his mind.

As the Englishman vanished, another customer took his place, the shop gradually filling right up, a woman confiding they had come by charabanc. 'Heavens, didn't we have trouble climbing that hill. I thought we'd have to get out and push.'

They didn't buy much, a few postcards to remember the occasion. I didn't care what they bought – not today. I was too busy glancing at my watch. Besides, as Justine explained, neither postcards nor brushes were important, only the name, Hans Bader. 'They will carry that back home with them and, one day, when they read his name in the newspapers, they will say, *I was there at the beginning before he was famous.* And he will be, Maidy. That I promise.'

The morning dragged and, unable to concentrate, my thoughts drifted into a blaze of joyful tomorrows, with scenarios in which Zande stayed for months that a moment later became years.

'I gave you ten francs,' a customer reminded irritably as my hand wavered, still staring off into space.

'Yes, of course. I'm so sorry.'

I placed the postcards in a paper bag, fastening the top with a gummed seal printed with the name of the shop, its town and district.

That too was Justine's idea. Hans had grumbled when he saw them, calling them an unnecessary extravagance. 'Something we can well do without until we're better established.'

Snatching the wine bottle from the table and holding it high, Justine danced out of reach to the far end of the courtyard, forcing him to chase her and calling out that wine was also an extravagance and she didn't see him complaining about that.

By the time the last customer had been served, it had gone two – almost half-past – and I was in a state of panic. Not seeing Zande anywhere about, I grabbed my shoulder bag and raced out into the street.

He was there, on the far side of the three-cornered square, gazing into a shop window, although at first I didn't see him, the first-floor overhang creating a patch of dark shadow.

'I walked up to the town to find us a restaurant, only to discover in Flambeau people planning to lunch in a restaurant do so at twelve-thirty, not two-thirty.' He glanced at his watch. 'So, I brought us a picnic.' He was grasping a paper carrier and, as if to affirm his words, swung it forwards on its string handles. 'Right, come on, I've had enough of the dusty street and want to breathe fresh air. We can do the river another day. And because you've been standing up all morning, I reserved us a seat.' He pointed to the narrow pathway with its long line of steps up to the ramparts.

I thrilled at the words, 'another day', scarcely able to believe he might mean it. Even so, by now, the overwhelming sense of joy and disbelief with which I'd greeted his appearance in the shop had been replaced by something more cautious. If I dared read anything into his delivery of Yöst's letter, other than he was visiting the area, on becoming aware of his real purpose disillusionment would surely follow – except I couldn't think what his real purpose might be? Not Ruth, he'd already known about her marriage.

And the events of that summer? They were also better forgotten. Only an insensitive fool who delighted in mischief-making would deign to recall them, and Zande was neither.

Part way up the trailing length of steps, Zande reached out and took my hand, cradling it loosely in his. He didn't say anything to accompany his gesture, continuing the climb in silence and I didn't break it, the slope taking my breath and far steeper than my memory of it when I had dawdled, staring into every nook and cranny. Tears pressed against my eyelids, the warmth and solid feel of his fingers against mine creating in me a sense of belonging, as if they were a glove I had misplaced and had found again.

This was the Zande I always hoped existed, no different from any youth rendered speechless by the proximity of the girl walking beside him, a girl he wanted to know better, perhaps more intimately, yet still nervous how to proceed and scared of making a fool of himself.

A woman came out onto the stoop and, bending down, proceeded to shake the dust from the door mat. She made some remark, too quick for me to catch, making Zande laugh.

'What?' I said.

'She told me it was a long way to go for a kiss.'

'Oh!' I blushed.

There was no one about, the bench seat empty of tourists, no doubt enjoying a siesta or, remembering the woman who had travelled to Flambeau on a charabanc, on the bank of the river painting. Surprisingly, Zande also seemed nervous, breaking the silence with a polite enquiry about the art shop and how long I had worked there. I had said all of that in my letter to Yöst but I didn't care, it got us over those awkward few moments when two strangers, setting out on a first date, search for words.

And if a date was what he was seeking, he had chosen the spot well. In the past few months, I'd often visited, mostly after work when the tourists had all left, intrigued by the immensity of the view. Driving from the station with Hans, I'd thought the area relatively flat. It wasn't. Ringed by hills, the shallowness of its slopes and hollows was deceiving and varied as many times in a day as a sun dial. In June, with the sun reaching its zenith, they had become obscured in soft blue shadow, the dips and folds shrinking back until they were little larger than a mole hill. Now, with the sun beginning to angle down, ridges and elevations were once more easing into view. Yet so peaceful a scene, I found myself wishing the tower's broken walls were the result of age and natural withering rather than conflict, the countryside through which the river meandered the epitome of peace.

Placing a crusty baton on a paper tablecloth which he had spread on the bench between us, Zande began to unpack our lunch, revealing a roulette of cheese and a bottle of white wine, its sides still bearing traces of mist from the refrigerator. 'I even brought glasses. Please eat, it's late and you must be hungry.' His words sounded casual enough despite tension in the hand wielding the corkscrew, his glance avoiding mine.

I waited for his first remark with trepidation, which quickly turned to panic when he spoke Ruth's name.

'Who did she marry? Ruth, I mean?'

Angry that an enquiry about Ruth proved of sufficient importance to be asked first, I tore off a chunk of bread, the soft white of its insides still warm from the oven, and plastering it with a thick layer of the cheese, took a bite to stall my reply. I wasn't hungry, not now, the invitation for Ruth to join the feast sufficient to quash my appetite. Why should it matter who Ruth married? She was married – it was done.

'A film star, Roland de Courcy. They were making a film together. That's how they met.'

'Good for Ruth, she was too beautiful to marry an ordinary man. And your brother?'

I felt doubt creep in, hastily dismissing it as an association of ideas. Pieter ... Ruth ... Zande ... Hans. No, it couldn't be – Ruth was long gone from our lives.

'We haven't seen Pieter – not since.'

He reached out as if to touch my hand in a gesture of

sympathy, quickly pulling back as though he'd been stung. 'I didn't know, I'm sorry.'

I understood the gesture, of course, I did. Believing himself responsible for the loss of Pieter, he had ceded the right of comfort to someone else.

An awkward silence fell, the many unanswered questions between us like ridges of dry earth. By my side, Zande flicked scraps of bread to the pigeons swooping down from the sky.

Abruptly, he jumped up, and sped over to the balustrade, leaning over.

'*Zande? No!*' I couldn't help myself.

He swung round, his eyes gleaming. 'That's a word I'm familiar with, although not usually this early in a relationship.'

'I thought,' I stuttered, silently hovering over the word relationship.

'Yes, I know what you thought. I wasn't planning to chuck myself over – that would be far too easy.' His fierce tone was replaced by one of nonchalance. 'Of course, I might have to if you fail to forgive me.'

'For what?'

Zande didn't reply immediately, examining the rooftops belonging to the old town below us, its original walled construction very evident. 'Pieter! When you mentioned him, you looked so sad, I couldn't bear it.' He drove his fist into the stone embrasure. 'How can you stand being near me?' I heard the bitter tones well up. 'A murderer! Or had you forgotten?'

'You weren't responsible for Tristan's death,' I retorted, 'nor for what happened to Pieter. It wasn't anybody's fault – not really.' I repeated the words I'd said that night.

'I told Yöst...'

Instantly forgetting the drama of the moment, I cried out, 'Oh, how is he? I meant to ask before. Has he recovered from his operation?'

Diverted, Zande burst into laughter, his entire body taking part. He took a step back away from the rail. 'I'd forgotten that's what you do.'

'What?' I still hadn't dared move, the bread in my clenched fist reduced to pulp.

'Make it so easy. Every time we meet up, you dig your sharp little claws into the black curtain in which I spend my life and let in a shaft of light. And he's well,' he replied formally, laughter still ringing his voice. 'They managed to remove most of the bone fragments floating around inside his shoulder, which means he's pretty much pain free. Unfortunately, the arm will never fully recover. Fourteen years is a long time, and the muscles have long since atrophied.'

'You said he was shot. How did that happen?'

I spotted his relief at the change of subject, but he didn't return to sit by me, restlessly examining the polished cannon that stood in the centre of the walkway, smoothing his hand across its sleek black casing.

'He was trying to rescue his friends from a prisoner-of-war camp.'

'Did he succeed?'

His smile returned, exuberant and happy. 'You met up with them in New York.'

I relaxed. 'You mean *Maestro*, the guitarist?'

'Yes, and Rico. A lot of good people were killed that night, including another of our friends, Pepe, a gentle giant of a man. Maestro says the gods chose badly and it should have been Pepe who survived, not him.'

'Then we would have lost his music.'

'That's what Yöst says.'

'You said, *that night?*'

'Back in 1940, there was a mass escape of prisoners from Klüsta.' He grimaced, obviously disliking the subject. I remembered chatting with Kirsten about it, the island's blood-stained history a matter for both idle gossip and speculation among the student body.

'Go on about Yöst.'

His tone settled. 'When I confided what had happened that summer, he was furious. Said no matter the hurt, I had no right to take out my pain on others, and hadn't he taught me better than that.' Zande leaned his elbows conversationally on the rail, although he didn't turn, addressing his story to the countryside. Both ignorant and uncaring of the convoluted lives of mankind, it lay quiescent under the afternoon sun, the river gleaming as if in possession of a basketful of jewels. 'From what I'd told him about Ruth, he didn't much care for her, considering her manipulative and devious. He had met you and he wouldn't let me salve my conscience over Tristan and Pieter by loading it on to you.'

'You didn't,' I protested, overjoyed I'd been wrong. He did remember that summer and it wasn't the leading lady he'd come to see … it was her understudy.

'Not then, he meant now. It's taken me three years to pluck up courage enough to look back. My behaviour was caddish. Not only to you.' He raced on, picking up on the movement of my hand, repudiating his words. 'Had I admitted right at the start I was attracted to Ruth, Tristan might still be alive.'

He fell silent waiting, perhaps hoping I might disagree?

Did I?

Tension between us spiked again as I sped back over my memories, aware he was waiting for some sort of a reply. It took no time at all, barely a fleeting moment. Over the years, in the silence of my bedroom, I had learned each one by rote.

I shook my head. No!

However badly he had behaved, Ruth's was the greater fault. She had used Tristan, a young and inexperienced boy, as a plaything … a means to an end. And Pieter? She had condemned him into what he saw as a living death, certainly one devoid of human contact. Exactly the same state Zande now inhabited.

'You said about Pieter, you had no news. Why not? Doesn't he live with your…' I searched for an appropriate word, 'people?'

Relieved by the change of subject, he returned to the bench and poured us both a glass of wine. Handing me a glass, he struggled to meet my gaze. 'I no longer live with the carinatae, at least not permanently. Years ago, I spent six months working for a boatbuilder and we stayed in touch.' He shrugged. 'A telephone call once a year.'

'He did better than me,' I challenged.

'Ouch!' he laughed, and a dancing gleam of excitement filled his eyes. 'I can't recall, do you own a phone?'

I remembered how Zande always did the opposite of what was expected, contrition a rare trait.

'A while back, on learning he'd broken his leg, I returned and have been there ever since – apart from holidays.'

'Where is this boatyard?'

He pointed towards the horizon. 'South of here.'

'And Waldger, what happened to him?'

'He stayed, said he had no place else to go. I saw him earlier in the summer for the solstice, we always meet up then. And Jaan.'

He struggled with the name, pronouncing it with reluctance.

I shrugged. 'Jaan wrote; you didn't.'

'It was easier for him.' The ice was back in his voice. 'He wasn't culpable. Even so, I hope you still prefer me to him?'

The wine on an empty stomach had gone straight to my head, our surroundings exhibiting a rich aura of sparkling colour. 'I'm not answering that.' I kept my tone neutral. I had learnt from past mistakes, disguising my true feelings with a disinterested smile.

'You'll have to one day.'

I glanced down at my watch to mask my lack of composure. 'I must run, I'm late.'

He raised his glass, a sardonic gleam lighting his eyes. 'Your continued good health, Maidy. Heaven knows the world needs it.'

Then he smiled, that precious whimsical softening of one side of his mouth that spoke volumes and, picking up the remains of the baton, broke it into pieces and tossed them over the ramparts into a flurry of grey and white feathers jostling together, eager for a free meal.

It was Justine who noticed my new dress, commenting that in the months I'd been in the house, never once had I bothered to change my clothes after work. 'Now, you're fretting like some adolescent on a first date. You're blushing!' She laughed triumphantly. 'I guessed right. Does Hans know?'

Before I had a chance to reply, she rushed on. 'Of course, Hans doesn't, he's never about. At least we know he's working, poor lamb. He comes home exhausted with yet another drawing. How are sales?'

'I sold two originals this week,' I said, grateful for the change of subject yet uncomfortable with the topic. Justine had just spent a week in Paris. I had been so thrilled for her and said so, sidestepping her enquiries about Hans because, during that time, he'd not been back to the house once.

'Can you believe, Maidy, at last I am again good enough to have my photograph on the advertising boards outside the theatre. Can you imagine what an honour that is? Only a replacement, and for two performances. The prima ballerina who is taking the part of Odette has a wretched cold. God bless her.' She rewarded me with a smile. In the past few weeks, they'd become so rare, I was counting each one.

Admittedly when I first arrived back in May, her smiles had proved even more infrequent, and despite Hans' assurances to the contrary, I knew I was only being tolerated for her lover's sake. She had shown me around the house, relating its history because Hans had asked her to ... no other reason. And while her general opinion of women hadn't changed, describing the ballerinas who made up the *corps de ballet* as *putains*, she had warmed towards me.

Not understanding the French word, I asked Hans for a translation. He hooted with laughter. 'That had to come from Justine. You didn't stay long enough in Paris to learn that expression.'

Now, the sidelong glances she paid me, at first dispassionate, contained both curiosity and acceptance, our morning coffee which we mostly drank in the courtyard, the recipient of both amusement and occasional laughter.

And Hans? I didn't ask. Nevertheless, Ruth's was the first

name that came to mind. For so many years she'd been the *prima donna*, at the forefront of all the action. From there it was a small step to linking her with Hans. I tried to tell myself that was silly and stupid – she had visited this area of France for a few weeks, months ago now. I was jumping at shadows.

Except I knew I wasn't.

'So, who is he?' Justine said, floating around the kitchen in her silk kimono. It made for a beautiful picture, quite natural for her body to fall into an elegant pose.

I didn't really want to say, still influenced by my childhood superstition in which the speaking of a name broke the spell. 'Just someone I once knew,' I reluctantly replied. 'He's taking me to dinner.'

He had asked me; no, he had told me, 'Because you failed to eat at lunchtime, and I refuse to have that on my conscience as well.'

He had been smiling when he said it.

'And...?' Justine added.

'He's not a boyfriend.'

'And you'd like him to be.' It was kindly said, her interest genuine, and I couldn't bring myself to lie.

'Yes.'

She shrugged. 'Well, don't look at me for advice. I'm the last person you should ask.'

'But you're with Hans now.'

'Maidy!' She burst into laughter and pulling out a chair collapsed into it. 'Do you honestly consider your brother good husband material?' Her hand sped across the table and grabbed mine. 'And don't lie,' she threatened.

Our eyes met and we smiled, our minds tracking the same path ... mine from our childhood years, Justine's more recent. Brilliant, but unreliable and far too casual to ever be a good husband – that was Hans.

'I firmly believe you should never go for looks...'

'That's not what you told me when I first arrived,' I objected.

'What was that?' she cut in.

'That French women always choose the handsomest of men...'

She waved a nonchalant hand. 'I always say that when I'm feeling depressed. My husband was rich, elegant, and very handsome, and look what a swine he turned out to be.'

'How long were you married?'

'Four years. After six months he took his first mistress. *Maidy*, your face!'

I found myself lost for words, my knowledge of French failing me.

'If you want happiness, forget looks, for then you will have to contend with their ego as well as all the rest of their failings. This so-called boyfriend, is he good-looking?'

I thought of Zande's tall figure with its smoothly rounded limbs, crowned by a halo of loose curls that would not have seemed amiss on a Greek statue; the long straight nose, and full lips that twisted not only in mockery but also amusement and laughter; the sheen on his skin that invited your fingertips to linger… No, he was not good-looking; he was beautiful.

'Yes.'

She sighed. 'And is he dependable?' I shook my head. 'I suppose there's not a chance in hell that he's domesticated and can cook, since Hans says you're useless in the kitchen.'

I laughed. 'I don't know.'

'Then you'd better find out, my girl, before it's too late.'

I didn't want to admit it was already too late.

The hotel on the southern tip of the old town where Zande was staying had originally been a monastery, and Zande, who admitted an interest in history, had opted for one of the original cells on an upper floor, its window a narrow stone aperture that had been glassed in.

'Very basic. The view's magnificent. I'd show you,' he smiled wickedly, 'except I'd have to sneak you past the concierge who sits knitting in the doorway.'

We'd met up every day since that first morning, which had been dominated by guilt and despair, and not once since had he mentioned Jaan. Nor had I mentioned Ruth.

That was not to say she wasn't in my thoughts. At night,

when I heard the sound of the Renault, its brakes squealing to a halt under the archway, I'd glance covetously at Justine, hoping and praying for the truth to stay hidden. I couldn't bear for it to come out. Selfishly perhaps, because I was beginning to believe I had found a new friend. Even so, I wanted to rail at Hans and shout, how could he, he was with Justine now. I didn't, my silence bought by the quality of his latest work.

A third the size of his usual canvas, the paintings were arranged in threes like a triptych, and they were exquisite. For me, confirmation, if any was needed, of Ruth's departure for Paris. Yet, more than that. They had parted on loving terms, leaving Hans to pour every strand of longing and sexual energy into his paintings. And although none held any particular religious significance, such as a cross or a shrine, that's the impression they gave. Two sets in particular drew my attention, the first of an old man. Clad in dusty black, he was seated on a bench in the town square, backed by a coppice of pines, his chin resting on the handle of his cane. Yet not until you examined the second image was the reason for his interest revealed. A game of boules was taking place between a group of men, all of them wearing black trousers and short-sleeved white shirts. They were standing about in positions that expressed both pleasure and anxiety, except for the man bowling. He had obviously played a good shot, with the ball striking the jack, and his arms were held aloft in triumph. In the third, long shadows revealed the passage of time, the game of boules over and the elderly men returned to their homes. Children were playing among the trees, so life-like you could almost hear them laughing and screaming with excitement.

That was my favourite until I saw the painting of a farmer tilling his field. Possibly the most overdone of all subjects put to canvas apart from sailing vessels, and one you might have thought demeaning for someone of Hans' capabilities – until you studied it closely. The farmer was walking towards the foreground, his horse-drawn plough leaving behind furrows of earth that were dark and glistening with wet. The skies were also dark and ominously so, a single shaft of light lingering on a puddle in which the twin towers of the medieval cathedral were reflected. The perspective was impeccable and so was the style, something I had seen time and time again in our museums, with points of light reflecting off the animal's harness and a touch of red on the farmer's shirt collar standing out against the rich brown of the furrows.

In the second image, brightening skies highlighted the farmer heading up the field away from the cathedral, which now dominated the background, its towers looming over the field under plough. It drew your attention back to a point in history, before the city became built up, picking up on the farmer's old-fashioned clothes and the clumsy design of the plough. In the third, with sunset framing the cathedral and ploughing over for the day, the farmer was leading his horse back to the farm, leaving the plough in the darkening field.

'Which is why I can't promise to be home on time,' Hans explained away his late return on that occasion.

This wealth of depth and detail didn't happen if Ruth was about. Then the reverse was true. It didn't need a genius or a mind reader to figure out she was demanding of both his time and his energy, so that the painting due that week was rushed or didn't materialise. Even his signature spoke volumes as to the fragmentation of his thoughts. The worst was when he lied, saying he had destroyed that day's work or painted over it, 'because it was poor, not up to scratch,' and I knew it now adorned a wall in Ruth's apartment.

Once or twice I considered taking a bus to Bordeaux to beg Ruth not to play her games. I didn't because it would require an explanation and involve not only Justine, possibly Zande too. Instead, I had written her a silly empty letter, full of nothings, and had received a reply – equally silly and empty, saying nothing – not even that she had met up with Hans.

16

It wasn't right. Those first few hours maybe – they were heaven. Not afterwards, not after that first evening. Until that moment, Zande had behaved as he always did, his moods willow-the-wisp, changing from minute to minute, light-hearted, sorrowful, sometimes full of pain – all a part of who he was.

After that night, he looked and spoke, sounding the same. But he wasn't.

Alone in the silence of my bedroom, I sought a reason behind the formal, almost disconnected sentences, the Machiavellian humour that both gloried in who he was and despaired of it no longer there. Eventually, the only conclusion that held any credence was that he had come seeking Magrit Bader, and found someone more worldly in a beautiful frock.

The frock I'd worn for our first dinner together.

I'd bought it with my wages, eager to spend the money I'd earned and stumbling upon it quite by chance. I didn't need it, my usual attire, a cotton skirt and blouse, suited my lifestyle as a shop assistant, conscious the reason behind its purchase was a desire to experience that momentary thrill of buying something … doing something … new. Yet, when I did find the perfect outfit I still dithered, re-visiting the shop day after day for an entire week before setting foot inside. After all, how much use would it be when I never went anywhere?

Amethyst rather than blue, it enhanced the colour of my eyes, its fitted bodice billowing into a full skirt like clouds blown by the wind, a line of gentian flowers decorating both the sleeves and hem. Preening in front of the shop's full-length mirror, even I failed to associate this elegant young woman with the pathetic drab of a child who had hoped to discover the face of her future husband in a mirror's reflection, my once stick-like legs graceful under its mid-calf skirt.

Zande had stared and not said a word – and that's when it went wrong.

Despite our meeting nightly, there remained a distance between us. We spoke all the time and said nothing. He told me of worlds he had seen, yet the words unspoken and needing daylight he held back. Missing too was the teasing amusement, so much a part of his character, that had fleetingly surfaced that first day. To others maybe it was fine, light-heartedly meeting up, chatting about nonsensical things, telling our histories, always a good stopgap when you couldn't think of anything to say.

Really to say...

I sobbed into my pillow at night, distraught at not being allotted more than those few hours after the shop bell first announced his appearance, when hope had existed and I had sent prayerful thanks to the ears of the deity responsible for making it happen. Now, my prayers were the opposite, almost threatening in their desperation. *He will be gone in a few days ... you can't let that happen – you helped before, why not now?*

The possibility of never seeing him again filled me with terror, yet the thought of his staying was worse. Yet, there were moments – too few and far too brief – when his laughter sounded out, mine too. But they were soon gone and we were back to being strangers. I couldn't bear this empty shell who walked by my side, standing up when I entered a room, who pushed my chair neatly into the table at the restaurant or placed my cardigan around my shoulders if we sat outside ... and said nothing except words of polite enquiry as to the day just past.

The intensity of our previous meetings, few as they were, might well have happened to someone else.

Perhaps it would be better if they had.

I didn't venture down that path, rejecting it out of hand, nor did I consider the aeons of empty time that lay ahead if I did send him away, or the countless nights when I would lie awake with bitter regret on my lips. Except, Zande wasn't happy walking by my side and that hurt too much to let it continue.

All to soon it was Saturday, and my afternoon off. I knew he'd be waiting, most probably with a picnic lunch that included wine. Weary of the veil between us, I turned the key in the shop door, leaving hope behind me. The fairy tale image of happy-ever-after and walking off into a glittering sunset was just that, a fairy tale.

'Everywhere I go people talk of the miracle of Flambeau.' He greeted me with a perfunctory kiss on the cheek. 'I'd love to see it before I leave.'

As always, he was impeccably dressed, his freshly laundered shirt worn over beige slacks and sandals on his bare feet.

'I'm not sure if the miracle actually exists.' I kept my voice easy, wishing my face was better able to disguise my feelings, and when Zande took my hand in his, I realised he had noticed the dark circles under my eyes that even face powder failed to conceal. 'Hans doesn't believe in it,' I prattled on.

I hadn't introduced Zande to Hans or Justine. What was the point? He wouldn't be my boyfriend for much longer.

The town was busy, unpleasantly so, especially for residents whose houses adjoined the town square, their driveways blocked by cars and coaches parked on the street. 'The majority of residents flee and head for the coast,' Justine said when I commented how quiet the town was at night. 'They get fed up with having cameras pointed at them. My bolthole has always been Paris. However, no self-respecting Frenchman would ever descend on Paris in summer – it's a hell hole of heat. Families that do stay in Flambeau shop early before the coaches arrive – as do I.'

Justine's description of Paris aptly described the weather. In the streets, people concluded their daily commentary with the words, *he's got stuck*. I had puzzled over the use of the personal pronoun he, until Justine explained they meant the sky – *le ciel* – and pointed towards the pall of cloud pressing down on the hillside. It had left the air unpleasantly humid and the population languid, their freshly laundered clothes wilting like flowers in the municipal gardens. No one, apart from café owners retained their smiles, their tills ringing merrily under a flood of requests for long-cool drinks with ice in them, elderly clientele using their menu as a paper fan and wafting it vigorously to cool their over-heated faces.

We strolled down through the woods, the canopy that usually swept it with light and shade heavy and unresponsive in the moist air. The route was never discussed, never a 'where shall we go today,' our feet falling into a natural rhythm, always in tune. Why then was it so impossible for our conversation to recreate that same easy pattern and not stall?

We weren't alone, the natural silence of the wood mired by bursts of boisterous laughter and loud conversation which hit the air in a wash of syllables, spoken too fast for me to catch more than the gist. Close by, children, ignoring the gradient that elicited a cautionary *faites-attention* from their parents, played leapfrog over the stumps of trees and tag among the branches. By my side, Zande was silent and I felt him to be far away, his thoughts elsewhere, my hand in his an anchor pinning him to the ground.

'I wish it would rain,' I came out with the words, despairing of the silence between us. 'When it rains, you can easily differentiate between tourists and residents. Tourists wear a plastic mac and carry an umbrella, while townspeople walk about with a newspaper over their head, and big smiles.'

He was listening – that was something.

'Justine says the reason we get so little rain is that clouds rise up over the hill and dump their rain further inland, rather than on us.' I pointed vaguely inland. 'To the delight of those who produce the wine of the area.'

His reply shocked, even though I'd been expecting it. 'Have you decided yet why you bother with me? I know you've been thinking about it.'

There was desolation in his tone, and I guessed he had also accepted that the promise of love between us, so brief and so glorious in summer, had faded with the coming of autumn and winter. We had reached the final pages of our story and he was about to close its cover.

I knew then, at that very moment, I couldn't let that happen. In my silent imaginings, I might laud my heroic sacrifice, sending him away to be happy with someone else. Faced with reality?

'You really don't want me to answer that,' I burst out, my voice a pantomime of desperation and resolve, 'it would deal your vanity too great a blow.'

Momentarily, the old Zande appeared, his eyes ablaze with laughter. 'You're quite right.'

Hearing the roar of water immediately below, he sped up, jumping the bank down onto the river walk and catching me in his arms when I stumbled. He hesitated and just for a second, his eyes searched mine. I daren't breathe, holding my breath, praying...

'*Excusez-moi, mademoiselle,*' a woman called imperiously and the moment, whatever it was, had gone, our clasped hands broken apart by the requirement to walk in single file along the narrow path. Even so, had I not felt so utterly bereft, I might well have found the scene charming, any number of women carrying parasols and brightly coloured umbrellas, lofting them high in the air to avoid collision, their richly coloured panels swooping and pirouetting, reminding me of dancers raised high by their partner.

Joining up with the main road at the bottom of the hill, the crush eased as families peeled off to join a queue for ice cream. There were surprisingly few people on the bridge and noticing our approach, they politely shuffled up to make room at the rail and while I received a brief if speculative glance from the men of the party, the women looked once and then a second time at

Zande, lingering over the tall elegant figure, the warm tones of his caramel coloured shirt complementing the brown of his forearm with its delicate wrist; his long fingers lightly grasping the railing.

He saw the admiring glances – expected them even – and light, once so familiar and so very dear, filled his eyes, the twist at the side of his mouth making a welcome return.

He bent over me; his voice unbelievably sexy and purposefully loud. 'Have I told you yet this morning, you look good enough to eat.'

The party moved away, despite the grumbles of the youngest child, heading towards the steep slope up to the town, one of the men calling loudly, 'Let's not bother. I need a drink.'

'I am never certain if it's my brown overcoat that sends them away or my devastating good looks.' Zande laughed, and moving along the now empty rail, made room for me. 'If they knew my history, which bit would prove of greater concern, do you think, that or my ability to change my form?'

'I'm pretty certain Frenchwomen never notice your brown-overcoat, they're too busy swooning,' I retorted, well aware his throw away remarks were intentional and better ignored. A response of any kind would undoubtedly invite something even more outrageous. I kept my tone light, praying he wouldn't repeat the second part of his question because I couldn't answer that. How can you create belief out of something so unbelievable?

'Anyway, I'm glad they've gone. I hate people eavesdropping on my conversations, making a decision based on my skin colour. When we were children, my sister used to say I got pale and interesting in winter. Kids at school sometimes teased me and when I complained to Yöst, he said when I reached sixteen, they'd all want to be me because I would be an emperor.'

Three years ago, that's what I'd thought.

'What happened to your mother?'

Zande glanced down at my hand and arm lying side by side with his on the rail, my arm browned by the sun a different shade.

'She was killed by an angry mob,' he replied not misunderstanding the relevance of my question, 'when I was four.'

Below, the viewing platform was awash with people made restless by the crush of bodies, only the genuine enthusiast arriving early enough to bag a decent spot. Weighed down with camera equipment, the pockets in their knapsack bulging with spare film, they clung tenaciously to their place at the rail, refusing to cede even to a child. Eventually, those unable to see over their shoulders moved away onto the grass of the river bank, grumbling aloud that they hoped they'd be close enough to witness the spectacle, if it actually took place.

'Justine says it's the same every weekend throughout the summer,' I jumped into the silence, 'especially with the weather so humid. That's when the flame erupts if it's going to happen.'

Zande gathered my hand in his. 'It's all right, Maidy,' his tone had gentled. 'It happened a long time ago and to be honest I don't remember much about my mother – except occasionally the sound of her voice. It was Yöst who filled the gap.'

Crossing over to the far side of the bridge, he peered down at the water, the flow beginning to settle after its prolonged tussle with the rocks of the gorge. 'I went to see him last night, after I left you.'

I made to question the announcement with some folderol about trains and buses, before remembering.

I froze.

'Yes,' his mouth twitched. 'My state does have it uses. I told him what I've been struggling with all week.' He strolled back to my side. 'You must have noticed,' he added with a glint of a smile, 'I've been somewhat preoccupied.' It was gone again next moment, his expression carefully blank.

'Oh!' I managed. 'I thought—'

'What did you think?'

'It doesn't matter.'

He frowned. 'For someone who is not given to long conversations, everything you say matters. What was it?'

'Go on. You went to see Yöst, and...'

'He said, either I got on that bus and said nothing or I told you and if you didn't like what you heard, I could catch a later bus for the station.'

'Told me what?'

He leaned on the railing, studying the river water barrelling under the bridge. I stood apart, although close enough to hear what he was saying.

'Since I was a child, I have wanted to build boats. Yöst wanted to be a farmer. Now, neither of us can realise our dream. Yöst will never again be fit enough to work a full day hoeing or ploughing, and me, I am my father's son. One day I will be my father. Did I tell you about Clara, my wife?' His voice had lightened. 'That was my break for freedom. Unfortunately, I chose badly.'

A family walked past, the children racing down the steps to the viewing platform, each wanting to be first. The wife glanced across at me, no doubt wondering if the silence and distance between us was the result of a quarrel.

This was worse than any quarrel; the words *I'm sorry* or *I didn't mean it* had no place here. My future depended on what Zande might say next.

'I don't know how it works or why it should; it seems that when the gods bestowed on us a change of state, they also loaded the dice.' Noticing my bafflement, my fingers moving to question his statement, he went to cover my hand with his own, quickly drawing back. 'No doubt they found it amusing to do so.' The bitter tones stung. 'Our nature is not given to fidelity, Maidy, we find women desirable and we pursue that desire.'

I remembered then what Jaan had said about being given only one chance.

'I'm not sure if Clara and I would have made it. Believe me, Maidy, I was very different then and I tried my best to make her a good husband. She was everything a man could possibly desire, only I didn't get a chance to be that man. Right from the outset, she wanted more than I could offer: travel, excitement, a lavish lifestyle; accepting a ticket from my father to travel to America.'

The silence between us hurt.

'I pretty much gave up after that. I promised my sister I would devote my life to finding a cure. I was eighteen, Maidy. Of course it didn't last. I couldn't have what I really wanted so I would take what I could. It didn't matter if I hurt others in the process. That was before I met you.'

His words cut the air.

'I know I let you down.' He swung around to face me, studying my expression. 'You look tired, and you've bitten your lip – that's my fault too.'

I stayed silent.

'I didn't dream it, did I, Maidy? There was something between us. You felt it too?' I heard the questioning note and ignored it; this was something Zande had to work out for himself. 'Maybe it happened because we had met that one time. I did try to find you. Deep down, I knew meeting you was important but not why or how much.' He snatched a breath, like an athlete making a special effort to reach the winning line first. 'What I said that first day, about three years being long enough to stay away ... it was true. That night, after causing so much damage to so many, I didn't care if I lived or died. Eventually,' his mouth twisted, 'my better nature came to the rescue. I begged my old boss for my job back and threw myself into work. Last spring, I went back hoping to find you...' My hand moved and he covered it with his own. 'More than anyone, I owed you an apology. I asked my guardian...'

'Meneer Meijer?'

'Yes. What is it about you, Maidy? I have known him forever, yet we almost came to blows before he'd admit where you'd gone. No different from Yöst.'

Emboldened, his eyes sought mine, a long smiling glance. I felt the world tilt on its axis and grasped the rail for support.

'When we met up, he happened to mention this girl he'd met on board ship, with eyes the colour of amethysts. He told me she'd been crying, and he had wanted to gather her up and take care of her.' Zande paused. 'By then I knew you'd travelled to America. I guessed the rest. That's when I realised how much I cared for you.'

I held my breath.

'Is caring the same as love, do you know?'

It was lightly said as if the thought had just occurred to him.

I shook my head.

'You know and won't say, or you don't know?' he challenged. He swung on his heel, his frown rebuking me. 'Have you any idea exactly how infuriating your silences are?' He almost shouted the words.

I repeated the gesture, making him laugh.

'Nevertheless, I do care what happens to you and have done so ever since the night you were attacked.' His expression sobered. 'At that moment, if you had died, I wouldn't have wanted to go on living and had you not been in extremis, I would have killed that drunken lout who hurt you.'

He swallowed, all at once no older than a small child standing repentant at his mother's knee. I longed to comfort him. I couldn't, my hands gripping the rail incapable of movement.

'Maidy.' I heard panic in his voice. 'I can't go back to being that callow, innocent youth of eighteen, who believed the world a miracle of goodness, I'm too damaged for that. God knows, this past week, I've tried; I promised Yöst I would.'

The silence blasted my ears.

'I'm not...' I swallowed, searching for my voice. 'I'm not asking you to.' I attempted to sound unconcerned, as if we were chatting about nothing more important than a restaurant menu, discussing the merits of one dish over another; although, for me, it was far more serious than that, my voice cracking under the strain. 'Since I never knew that person, would I even like him?'

'You *do* care.'

'I never said that,' I replied, flushing.

'You didn't need to say it,' he retorted. 'You forget I know you too; it's always been that way between us, neither of us has ever needed to pretend.'

'That's the point,' I said, hoping my voice sounded bolder and more in command on the outside than it did on the inside, my hands gripped together to stop their shaking. 'It's not the same – not anymore. We're different people, we've changed. I don't know who you are any longer.'

My words hurt and he took a step back, swinging away.

I thought that was it, he was leaving – his decision made. He swung round. He was smiling.

'You are quite unbelievable,' I stormed. 'The first conversation between us that's ever been honest and truthful, and you laugh.'

'I wasn't laughing, I was smiling,' he corrected. 'And not at you.' His hands reached for mine and I quickly tucked them behind my back. 'At Yöst. I did warn him.'

'You warned Yöst,' I repeated, now completely at a loss. I felt I was playing some parlour game, perhaps blind man's bluff. 'What about?' I said bewildered.

'He told me I should try to behave more like other men – you know – polite and predictable, especially with sensitive girls like you, and to take things slow and get all the obstacles out of the way first.'

His entire body was alight with laughter. 'I warned him; told him you'd hate that. Still, if he really thought it would help, I'd give it a go.'

In that instant, I saw how he'd been as a child – eagerly embracing every experience the world had to offer and believing it all good – finally understanding the enormity of the wrong done to him by his father.

'Girls like me,' I repeated, schooling my face and voice to hide the overwhelming sense of joy invading my body. Yes, he did know me; I would have hated that sort of individual, pompous and predictable, the character suggested by Yöst alien to us both.

'He meant well brought up.'

'And the obstacles,' I said hoping he was referring to Ruth.

He shrugged. 'Nothing much, just the small matter of who I am. Yost said ... to tell you. I mean, no decent girl could ever love a freak.'

'One or two must have.' I retorted, borrowing a weapon from his armoury. 'Otherwise neither you, nor Jaan or Waldger would be alive now.' He stared at me, shocked, then gave a roar of uninhibited laughter and picking me up, whirled me around. 'Do you know what I had decided to do today?'

I did, of course I did. 'What?'

'Say goodbye, because I believed it wasn't working. It wasn't, was it?'

'No!'

Footsteps sounded, and a fresh batch of sightseers appeared. Chattering and laughing, they crowded the railing, elbowing one another in an effort to focus their cameras.

'And Ruth?'

Her name had to be said; she was one of the obstacles.

He shrugged and restored me to my feet; the laughter gone. 'You have brothers. You have to know that a man's mind and his body are frequently at odds, especially if the mind is advising caution.'

I thought of how Hans had been, so obsessed with Ruth he'd been jealous of his own brother.

'I was intoxicated by Ruth,' Zande continued. 'Still am, if the truth is told. What man wouldn't be. Lust is such a powerful force; it seeps into your brain and destroys all logical thought. It steals your appetite, yet at the same time you feel perpetually hungry, and it instils in you a feeling of such power, you could contest the whole world. How many men in history have declared war for the sake of a woman's smile? But Ruth, after condemning Pieter to the twilight life I live in, she can go to perdition for all I care.'

The final words were laced with such bitterness, I didn't comment further. It no longer mattered anyhow. She wasn't here, she was safely married to someone else.

He leaned forward pulling me into his arms, his fingers drifting through my hair. His mouth moved gently against mine, wanting my response. I gave it. He drew away, laughing at my confusion. 'Now don't go all prissy on me and demand I apologise. I have been wanting to kiss you ever since that first night, when you wore that dress. You took my breath away – you must have noticed I've had trouble concentrating since.'

What should I say, what could I say! That I'd spent an entire week being jealous of Magrit, the girl I used to be?

'Three years ago, you were all thought and understanding.

Now, you've added beauty and, as you know, I can never resist beauty.'

Twisting round, he glanced over the rail meeting up with a wall of faces. 'Oh, hell!' he exclaimed. 'I forgot they were there. Don't men in this part of the world ever kiss their girlfriends outdoors?'

I hadn't paid any attention to the comings and goings of the people on the bridge. Now I sensed a restlessness especially among those on the viewing platform and imagined, as Zande obviously had, that we were the focus of their attention. Yet, apart from one or two sly grins from children, no one had noticed, their gaze fixed on the rapidly thinning cloud.

'*Il arrive!*' Shouts broke out.

As the sun struggled clear of the cloud, the gorge erupted into flame, the humidity combining with the tumultuous force of the water fashioning rainbows of sparkling colour – thousands of them. Like multi-coloured arrows fired from an invisible bow, they darted through the air so fast one might believe them propelled by heavenly hands. A chorus of amazed shouts floated up from the throng below and people applauded.

A roar of noise filled the air as cars raced down the hillside, haphazardly parking anywhere and disgorging their eager occupants, some still in their work clothes – men in heavy boots, women hastily untying their apron – all running to witness the magic before it faded away. Justine had told me of the townspeople's fixation with the rare appearance of the torch. 'Even the sick and those that are childless believe it a miracle sent from heaven.'

No one noticed us standing there, we might not have existed, wrapped in a bubble of silence, the tension between us palpable; the cries of excitement, the running footsteps, the exclamations of praise and thanksgiving far, far away.

'You really care for me?' I shouted, attempting to be heard against the revving engines and the excited blast of horns.

'If that's what I said, I suppose I must do.' His eyes danced. Like the heavy cloud base now lanced through with light and colour, the despair was gone – banished. His gaze sobered. 'Very much.'

I held out my arm, feeling rainbows brush against it, as delicate as newly hatched dragonflies.

'Magrit, please say something?'

'Why do you call me Magrit?'

'Without doubt, you are the most exasperating female I have ever come across.'

Not giving me time to reply, he picked me up again and whirled me around, the colours in my dress making me part of the rainbow display. 'I think of you as Magrit because that's who you were all those years ago, when you saved me on the canal. And you have been saving me ever since. Now, please answer my question.' He set me back on my feet. 'When a man actually admits his feelings,' he stumbled over the word, 'it is customary to reply.' His voice was light and full of energy.

I hesitated. 'You know I care for you.' I carefully repeated his words.

'No-oh' he extended the word into two syllables, very softly and slowly. 'Please play the game.'

'Is it a game, Zande?'

Zande's expression changed, its playful tones once again replaced by that intensity, so much a part of his character. 'I can honestly and most definitely say, it's not. I have never been more serious.'

I knew so little of love only that there was as many different versions as nations of people. Was it love I felt that night, when he vanished out of sight or was it grief? And was it love that kept me awake replaying our every meeting or loneliness? That feeling of excitement that overtakes your body at the sight of someone, was that love? How could you know? An image of Jaan came to mind. I never once doubted he loved me, every glance, every gesture endorsed that message, offering me a patient level-headed sort of love, not given to mood swings.

I love you. Three little words – words I once longed to say and now couldn't. Trying out the many different scenarios in the privacy of your bedroom is very different from the real thing. There, if you are dissatisfied with an inflexion or the tone of your speech, it is easy enough to set it right. In the silence of your thoughts there is only sunlight, shadows don't exist.

Yes, I loved him, but I still felt the shadows.

I took a step back.

He nodded. 'That's what Yöst figured.'

'What?' I said devastated by my own response. Zande had asked me to love him. Only in my dreams had that ever happened. But this wasn't a dream. I had heard him say it and I had rejected him.

'He insisted you needed more experience of the world before making that decision, yet if you were forgiving enough to give me a second chance, to take my time and to court you.' His expression changed and despite the seriousness of his words, he still smiled at me. 'That's what I've tried to do this week.' His smile was winsome. 'And it would seem I made rather a hash of it.'

Aware he was struggling to make light of my rejection, I reached out. 'I'd decided you found me boring.'

'Boring!' He glanced over his shoulder at the noisy crowd, their exclamations of delight drowning out any attempt at serious conversation. 'Come on, let's get out of here.'

'Where to?'

He pointed down at my feet. 'The market to buy you some plimsolls; one of the stalls is bound to sell them.'

'Plimsolls? Why should I need plimsolls?'

'For when we go sailing. I always take my girlfriends sailing.'

I flinched, recalling Elina.

He knew it the same moment I did.

And understood.

'Maidy, I can't wipe out the past,' he begged. 'That's something only you can do. Please give me a chance.'

Always.

Smiling, I linked my hand with his. 'What happens if you overturn the dinghy? I can't swim.'

He frowned, his brow furled thoughtfully. 'In that case, we might find ourselves with a bit of a problem.'

Deep in his eyes, I caught a flicker of mischief – something

I'd never before seen. Usually his emotions were covered by the bitterness that formed the most prominent part of his character.

I burst into laughter, feeling such pleasure it was scarcely bearable. Whatever happened in the future, I knew for a single moment he'd been happy – all the anger and despair that ruled his life stepped aside.

17

'If you're going sailing, for heaven's sake wear something old,' Justine advised. Our paths had crossed on the landing, and I'd asked if I might use the mirrors in the studio. 'Men always exaggerate the charm of boats. No different from cars and something else more personal.'

'*Justine!*' Hans on the way downstairs, rebuked.

'*Chéri*, did I say your name?' she cooed.

Justine, whatever her mood, had this fascinating habit of waving her hand through the air, as if she was spinning air into thread. 'Unfortunately, the majority already consider they are both sleek and powerful.'

'I'm not sure if that helps, Justine. I haven't got anything really old; I threw all the old stuff away before I left for New York.'

'My dear child, what folly. Women should never throw clothes away. Have you sneaked a peek at my wardrobe yet? Since I joined the ballet company,' she continued not giving me a chance to reply, 'I have never thrown anything away. Hans says you can get lost in my wardrobe, and it will take you a week to find your way out.'

Yet again it was said with that charming twist of her hand. I was glad, all too often in the last weeks she had closeted herself in the studio, the dance music strident and discordant, revealing her distress. Of course, it was having Hans here; what else could it be?

'Come, let's look together. Oh, how I've missed that.' I received one of her rare smiles. 'When I was growing up, I had this particular friend. Her family were wealthy and had far better clothes than me. She didn't care; she still swapped. Said her price was a good gossip.'

'I don't gossip,' I said dismayed.

She laughed. 'In our case, that is all to the good because we couldn't swap clothes, except perhaps scarves and handkerchiefs.'

Pushing open the door to my room, she led the way in and pulled open the wardrobe door. '*Mon Dieu!* There's nothing here.' She glanced with dismay at the empty hangers, the evening dresses I had worn in New York packed away in tissue paper. 'When you get paid next week, you will go shopping.'

'There's no point, summer's over.'

'Maybe in your country; not here in the south. Besides, buying clothes at the end of the season is eminently practical; clothes are always reduced in price.'

'And French women are always practical.' I laughed feeling free and as light as air in the September sunshine.

She smiled. 'Of course. Here, wear the button-through.' She unhooked a dress. Green with a square neck, it had big buttons all the way down, with a matching belt. 'Now I need coffee; household chores leave me exhausted.'

It may have been brief but I had found our conversation exhilarating and, for all sorts of reasons, wished it might happen more often; for us to chat as we had done today. When I first arrived, it was something Hans and I had done whenever he came down to the shop to work on a sketch in the yard. Maybe the conversation had been almost entirely focused on Justine, although, once or twice, as a demonstration of impartiality, he brought up our childhood, despite my recollections of events rarely conforming with his. One time, he had followed up with the words, 'you've changed.' It had sounded complimentary and I had wanted to grab hold of those words and dance them around the room, shouting out, 'Yes, yes, I have changed – thank you for noticing.'

Hans had also changed, already assuming the gravitas that fell naturally upon men as they settle into their twenties, no different from the thickening whiskers in his beard or the gaze that met yours and didn't duck away embarrassed, as his so often had done. Once I might have laid the changes at Justine's door. Not now. No longer did softly worded conversations drift across the landing from their bedroom and lull me to sleep as they once had, at least not very often. Nor did I arrive downstairs in the morning to find Hans with his arms around Justine, holding her in a long embrace.

Yet how was it possible for their relationship to have deteriorated so drastically in a few short months?

Hurriedly dressing, I joined them in the courtyard, excited by thoughts of the day ahead. Already warm, although the morning still retained a hint of freshness that dawn brought with it, the newly opened flower buds flaunted their velvety petals while birds rattled around the shrubbery in search of breakfast.

'My dear child, that's no good at all,' she called out.

'I thought…?' Confused I reached up, fingering the bandana I'd used to tie up my hair.

'Oh no, *ma petite* – you misunderstand. You look divine. And if you fall overboard, the dress being green will make it easier for the coast guard to spot you,' she teased. 'However, you are missing the finishing touches and it is those that make the ensemble. Shorts!' I stared and she gurgled. 'Wear them under your dress and leave a few buttons open.'

Hans, who had been reading the newspaper, laughed, drops of coffee spilling over the edges of his cup onto the table. 'This is my little sister you are talking about.'

'Use the word *young*, Hans,' Justine cooed, 'and I will accept the rebuke. Maidy is not little. Height-wise she easily tops the average Frenchwoman although, naturally,' her tone was condescending, yet her eyes still laughed at him. 'I edge her into second place. And while you will undoubtedly be the last person in Flambeau to notice, very attractive, especially to men. And, despite her youth, I hope sensible,' she lowered her voice, her final comment for my ears alone.

Zande had rented a car, placating my nervous question: 'are you sure you can drive,' with a grin, and negotiating the lanes that led to the coast equally as expertly as the small sailing dinghy, when his laughter roared out at my inability to decide which was left and which right.

He didn't ask and I didn't say, that I was still happier in the car with its open top and firm ground beneath its wheels, even driving one handed with his other arm around my shoulders, than a sailing vessel on an ocean that refused to stay still.

'Do you know where you're going?' I said as he swung away from the main road into a series of narrow cuts, barely wide enough for a vehicle. Fronds of feathery grass brushed up against the running board, adding an orchestra of more subtle sounds to the raucous purr of the car's engine.

He pointed ahead where tall hedgerows blocked any brightness from the sky, 'West!'

'And is there a boat waiting at the end of it?'

'Ah, now we have it.' His smile was crooked. 'An admission of nerves.'

'About your driving?'

'No!' His voice quivered. 'You have just remembered some long-forgotten advice given by your maiden aunt, never to put yourself in a situation you can't escape from, because all men are blaggards and suffer from an overwhelming desire to seduce you.'

It was a light-hearted comment. Even so, it was Elina's tear-swept cheeks that came to mind; undoubtedly there were other girls too, ones I had no name for. Before I had time to either confirm or deny his statement, he removed his right arm from my shoulder replacing it on the wheel.

'It's too wonderful a day to be serious but here goes. Maybe I am a blaggard. However, on this occasion, I have no intention of seducing you, much as I'd like to.' His tone changed. 'Last night, I didn't sleep much, too busy thinking about what you said.'

'I didn't say anything,' I protested.

'That's exactly my point. You don't say; you feel – and that feeling broadcasts itself to those who care about your wellbeing as clearly as any words. I know you care for me – and I am quite aware I don't deserve it and am the luckiest man alive. Yesterday, you took a step back and in that step were the feelings of all those I have hurt with my careless behaviour. Am I making sense?'

'Yes.'

'And is it all right?' Removing his arm from the wheel, he held it up in the air. 'I broke this one badly, remember?' and, just as casually, replaced it around my shoulders.

I translated the gesture into words: we would start again right from the very beginning, the day we should have met.

I smiled, wanting to say, *That's perfect*. 'Yes, it's all right.'

That was the last time we mentioned our history that day.

For the rest of the journey, we dipped in and out of different subjects, like a tiller able to change course whenever the wind determined it. Perhaps it was the very lack of walls that made our conversation so free, because for us there were no charts and no route map to follow, our silences simply a resting place for the ongoing thoughts our discussions had triggered. I recalled his boast that he had wasted his education, preferring to go sailing than read a book. It wasn't true, but with Zande, was anything ever exactly as it appeared? He reminded me of the wooden Babushka dolls that nestled one inside another, each doll having a different pattern and colour. Perhaps that was a better description.

That day, though, his childhood was laid out for my inspection.

'Weren't you too young to work for the Resistance?' I said when he spoke about his sister, and how, together, they had helped people escape the war.

'Tania's stock reply to that question was, how old do I have to be? I hope you'll meet up one day; you'd like her.' Adding with a grin, 'Fortunately she doesn't resemble me in the slightest. After Yöst vanished, Hörst, his best friend, who lives at Norland, where they make the cheese and butter, he sort-of adopted Tania. She and my Aunt both loved growing things, and now she runs a market garden, supplying flowers for the city markets, and moving permanently to Norland after Albert left the city.'

Having removed his shirt, he lay prone on the deck, as relaxed and contented as a seal, laughing when I complained that the dinghy possessed a mind of its own, and replying that it didn't matter since the sea like good conversation held no barriers. 'You can say or go where you will.'

'Except we can't.' I retorted, irritated by sails that constantly flapped at me, instead of remaining taught as Zande had demonstrated. 'I didn't bring a change of clothes. Besides, you promised to return the dinghy in a couple of hours.'

He shot up. 'I was just thinking, this is the longest we have ever spent together.'

'You remember?'

'Oh yes.' He smiled and my heart missed a beat. If I hadn't already been in love with him, that would have been the moment.

'Most evenings I have nothing better to do than remember. Unfortunately or fortunately, Maidy, you have become my own personal ghost.'

I should have known. Afterwards I blamed the informality of the day for lulling me into a false sense of security.

'And never has my ghost worn so charming an outfit, nor revealed quite so much leg.'

I glanced down, noticing a button had popped open. He grinned, his eyes sparkling with laughter as I hastily pulled my skirt over my knees.

It was wonderful and exhilarating although not completely easy, not all of the time. With Zande would it ever be? Maybe we had put behind us the polite exchanges of those first days but how could our conversation resemble the sea and have no boundaries, when his life was so full of places neither of us dare set foot? It would take time, I knew that. Even so, the afternoon saw plenty of flirtatious nonsense and verbal sword-play, although there were long silences when one or both ventured too close to storm-laden waters, like the art of tacking when the lightest of touches on the tiller can throw a sailing dinghy off course.

It was already late when we drove back, Zande entering a long technical discussion with the boat's owner, a young fisherman who relied on the craft for his living, completely forgetting about the need to return the car to the garage before seven. When I reminded him, he drove fast and we sat mostly in silence, the light-hearted banter, with its exploratory forays into new and uncharted territories, discarded. When we did speak, there was a subtle difference, the exchanges intended to inch our minds closer now inching our bodies closer as well, a casual touch laden with feeling.

By the time the car was safely back at the garage, we were hungry, yet eating in a restaurant was no longer an option, the noise and bustle denying our eyes and ears the privilege of soft words and whispered glances. It had been a long time since I saw Zande's charm in action, persuading the restaurant manager to pack up a meal for us, the manager's impatience and intolerance fading away under the power of his smile. 'Plus a good tip,' he laughed at me when I complained he was too charming for his own good. 'It's easy if you remember that the French are first and foremost businessmen. They have no truck with sentiment, not where money's concerned.'

With his hand in mine, we strolled back down to the river, our feet languorously in rhythm, dismissing the steep incline.

Was this, I wondered, almost jealously, how it had been for Ruth?

Maybe, I flinched at the idea someone else might have enjoyed a similar moment. Whatever it was, Zande picked up on it.

'Whatever you're thinking, it was never like this.' He lofted our joined hands into the air, my pale skin luminous in the shadow. 'And I'm not yet certain if I can cope with the feeling. With you,' he grunted out, 'I feel unsure, scared of hurting you. It never mattered before, not since Clara. If girls didn't appreciate my behaviour, there were plenty more who would. I taught myself to blot out every feeling apart from my need for revenge.' He kissed my hand. 'Now, I have to unlearn it. And, yes, you're right,' he continued, though I'd said nothing. 'That will take time.'

We sat without talking. Words weren't necessary, not any more. With darkness edging closer, we had done the same – firstly sitting and then lying side by side, Zande on his back, his arm around my shoulders tightening softly. He drew me to him, so we were facing, and he read my expression.

I had wondered, of course I had, on our walk when his thumb caressed my palm making my skin tingle, if the night would end with his making love to me. I wanted him too, yet knew instinctively it wouldn't and couldn't happen because Zande still needed to forgive himself.

The riverbank was deserted, the air silent except for the cut and thrust of the water gusting through the gorge. Upstream, where overhanging branches created a shadowy tunnel of leaves, I caught a gleam of white. It was the swans. The cygnet had acquired its new coat of white feathers, and with the same elegant glide was almost indistinguishable from its parents.

Used to receiving titbits from the many visitors, they floated towards us, undisturbed by the gathering power of the current speeding floating debris into the gorge, their black emotionless gaze stripping me bare.

All at once, I felt cold, my mind racing back to that summer, although it was Jaan's face I saw and his voice I heard, his alarm at the sight of his two friends locked in combat – Tristan and Zande. Far, far away, I heard his compassionate tones explaining the anomaly, intent on soothing my desperate horror and disgust. I hadn't listened then. Now I did, recalling his use of the word curse. In Jaan's view that's what it had been, a curse rather than an anomaly.

An anomaly was little more than an irregularity, a something or nothing that deviates from the norm – like a squint or knock knees or having one eye brown and one green.

'Passed on by our mothers, it is the price they pay for falling in love with the wrong sort. Many children inherit cruel lives from their parents; none can be as cruel as ours, with its loss of the qualities that make us human.'

But how? How could a human body convulse into a different

shape, one with feathers that gave them the ability to fly, unless magic, mischief, and mayhem still existed in our world?

'What is it?' Zande asked.

'Nothing.'

He followed my gaze and sighed. 'No, it's not nothing; you forget I have had three years to remember every change of expression.' Picking up my hand, he kissed the inside of my wrist.

This was a new side to Zande, something I neither expected nor had looked for – understanding.

18

The town clock had finished striking eleven when I arrived back at the chateau. I didn't want to be there. I wanted to be on the far side of the square where Zande still waited, 'To see you safely into the house.' He twined his fingers in mine. 'I wouldn't trust those guys,' he pointed up at the roof, where the gargoyles maintained a sulky yet belligerent silence on top of the rain pipe, 'not to steal you away.'

I laughed, 'They remind me of a bad-tempered dog that hates its owner but hates everyone else worse.'

I had grown used to them, and they suited the building, its broad expanse of stone quite plain apart from the tiers of wooden shutters that resembled a multitude of eyes, although I'd not yet heard our roof-top ornaments in voice. 'You mean fine voice,' Hans corrected. 'When the autumn rains begin, you're in for a treat. You've never heard such a racket. I asked Justine if that's when she learned her decorative vocabulary,' he chuckled. 'Still, despite their noise, I've grown quite fond of them. They sound like my head feels when I've drunk too much wine.'

Justine, who had just walked into the room, laughed and blew him a kiss. 'No, you're far worse.'

One of the gates had swung across the driveway, caught up

on a clump of weeds sprouting between the tiles. I made to push it back, to save Hans the trouble when he arrived home, and hesitated. Once it was back in its rightful place, so would I be, back in the real world my magical day at an end.

'Can you believe? We've wasted an entire week, like hamsters on a wheel going nowhere.' I told Zande as we parted.

'We got there in the end and are all the better for it.'

Too excited to sleep, I wandered through the archway and out into the courtyard. Justine was there. I had become used to her regular vigils and despite deciding it was none of my business, I was surprised at the retrograde step in my brother's behaviour, his casual attitude surprisingly childlike.

At the echo of my footsteps under the archway, she half-turned. Her expression remained unchanged, simply reaching out to pat the chair next to her. In the light from the kitchen, she made for an exquisite picture and, as always, I wished I had been blessed with Hans' gift and was able to draw her. With her feet stretched out and neatly crossed ankles, the long elegant shape of her back and neck bestowed sophistication on any piece of furniture. Even the slapdash arrangement of the table itself, with a basket of freshly picked peaches next to a wine bottle and glasses complimented the image.

The chair was covered in rose petals and leaning over, Justine brushed them away. 'Voluptuous and blousy like the women Titian painted,' her slightly husky tones greeted me. She held out her hand, catching a further shower as I brushed past the line of rose bushes under the kitchen window. I breathed in their perfume, always stronger after sunset when the air became languid and dolorous.

'Roses have always been my favourite flower.' She buried her nose in her cupped hands. 'Although, sadly, they're not at their best in this weather.' Her voice changed, its tones becoming brisk. 'Quite an exciting weekend, by all accounts.'

'It was extraordinary.' I sidestepped the question, hoping she was talking about the river.

'Mmm!' Her mouth twisted, mocking me. 'The gorge was

crowded again today. People flocked in from everywhere in the hope of a repeat performance – by the river, naturally.'

Aware she was teasing, I added in kind, 'I'm sorry Hans missed it.'

'Yet not the most eventful episode of the weekend,' she drawled. 'I'm surprised you found time to notice. Who is he? This young man you have so carefully failed to talk about all week?' Picking up on my sudden flush, her tone changed, sounding anxious. 'I assume it's the same one?'

I hadn't meant to speak out. I never had, preferring to confide my secrets to the houses across the river where my imaginary friends lived. Now my words refused to be silenced, as if saying them out loud would make those last hours more believable. 'Zande, and yes, it is the same one. Someone I met three years ago,' I reported primly. 'He's just a friend.'

'My dear child, not wishing to pry, scarcely a friend. Your neck gives you away.'

I reached up with my hand, blushing, remembering the touch of Zande's lips below my ear and his murmured words, 'Thank you for a perfectly lovely day.'

'We went sailing. I must have caught the sun.'

'How strange. There was no sun here; the day-trippers went home quite disappointed. So, tell me about him.' She raised her eyebrows, a fine line of superiority that matched her eloquently drawling tone. 'Mon Dieu, I must be bored for those words to come from my mouth. From a woman who despises other women, such words are gold dust. I doubt you will ever hear anything similar from me again.' I saw the flicker of her smile, and knew she wasn't being serious. 'And no, if you don't want me to, I'll not tell Hans. I presume you're in love with this boy?'

'No, of course not.' My face flared and she laughed. 'It's not like that,' I hastily justified my confusion. 'We met three years ago,' I repeated, 'in Holland and we were friends ... sort of. There were four of them, students at our college.'

'And you chose the handsomest?'

I thought of Tristan, his profile with all the sculptured

elegance of a marble statue, and Jaan, the eyes hidden behind his glasses reminiscent of autumn skies. And Waldger, with his habit of turning everything into a joke, his mouth curved in a perpetual smile. 'No, the most complex and badly damaged.'

'That doesn't sound good, yet so very typical of us women.' She heaved a sigh. 'You need a mother.'

I ignored her remark. Justine didn't know and I wasn't about to confide that the last thing I needed was a mother, especially my mother. We wouldn't be having this conversation or perhaps any conversation at all had it not been for her. Any wisdom I might acquire in the future would come from Pappy.

'I'm nineteen.'

'And he is…?'

'Twenty-four.'

'Big difference, Maidy. He's very much a man; you're still a child. As I said, you need a mother. And no, I refuse to volunteer. I have enough problems.'

'And yet you love him,' I said, knowing full-well she was talking about Hans.

Reaching out, she poured me a glass of wine, replying almost savagely, 'I promised myself never again. Now Hans … blocking my view of the rest of the world, like a bloody great mountain. He's frustrating and maddening, yet so sweet; he hasn't a single spiteful bone in his body. And, of course, a wonderful lover. Something I hope you still know nothing about,' she added almost as an aside. 'Being French, that goes without saying.'

'Hans is Dutch,' I reminded.

She waved her hand. 'I've been drinking,' she excused her muddle-headedness. 'He's late as usual. And when I remind him that open season on artists ends with the sun setting, he comes up with some feeble excuse about meeting a guy in a café – a fellow artist and they got talking. No idea why I put up with him.' Her mouth drooped. 'You'd think I would have learned by now,' she repeated the sentiment.

Hearing a vehicle in the distance, I hastily drank my wine and made to go upstairs.

'What?'

'I've decided to have an early night; I've not been sleeping.'

'Don't go. Wait for Hans to get back. He said only this morning he sees too little of you. Besides ... I need moral support.'

I hesitated.

'Please. You're very different from Hans; you see the world clearly, warts and all.' She shrugged. 'All those things I said about him, they're all true. No,' she raised her glass saluting the sky, 'They used to be true. He's changed. Always in a hurry these days and that's bad for his work; it's becoming sloppy.'

I didn't dare react, or admit that I'd already become complicit, hiding paintings that even to my inexperienced eye were less than good. Oh, why hadn't Ruth stayed in America?

'Tell him,' I advised. 'Warn him his reputation will suffer. Only, not tonight. If he's hungry, feed him and leave it at that. I know Hans, he'll listen,' I added hoping to be proved right, yet fearing I might not be. 'His reputation is more important—' I hastily stopped.

'Than his mistress?'

I flinched. 'No! She wouldn't, she's married.' I shouted the words, not really believing them myself.

Justine smiled, a little secretive movement of her bottom lip. 'Oh, I think she would. Regrettably, I'm still not sure if Hans would. She's the type who would put her foot through his paintings if they had a fight.'

'Why would you say that?' I said, trying not to laugh at her outrageous suggestion. 'You've never met her.'

Her eyes gleamed.

'You've seen her!' I exclaimed dumbfounded.

Justine growled out a laugh. 'I went to one of her films when I was in Paris. I hated her for being so beautiful – and that figure! However, in an audience almost exclusively masculine, I'm sure no one else shared my dislike. Perhaps I'm prejudiced. She reminded me of the girl who took my place as prima ballerina, a prize bitch.'

Falling silent, she raised her glass, inviting a reply. I ignored it, my loyalty to Hans sufficient to make me refrain from making a comment that, in Justin's present tipsy state, might well be misconstrued.

'You're quite hopeless, Maidy. You should have learned by now that women are placed on this earth to gossip. Look around you. Even the oldest among us, in their black skirts and stockings, have their heads together, criticising every other woman within a ten kilometres radius. Not their menfolk; they play boules.'

'Justine, you hate women.' I recalled Hans' homily about women disliking other women that could only have come from Justine.

'Maybe, though I'm still woman enough to enjoy listening to the occasional spiteful remark. Still, I forgive you,' she waved her glass, the stem brushing against a rose bush sending a waterfall of petals fluttering to the ground. 'I'm just pleased you can stick up for him.' Topping up her glass, she raised it in mock salute and gave a heartfelt sigh. 'I understand the ambition that drives him. I was the same, and for that, I'll happily play second fiddle.'

Despite wanting to remain, to be a referee in what was likely to erupt into a shouting match, I excused myself and ran upstairs. Naively, I once imagined being in love to be the kind and considerate version Pappy demonstrated towards Mother. It was Justine and Hans who had taught me that love can also be about fun and laughter, as well as irritation and impatience. And Zande? He offered passion, hoping in his world of tragedy it might prove a healing balm. Now I saw in Pappy's unfailing courtesy recognition that his love for Mother went far beyond anything she had felt for him.

Despite what I'd said to Justine, I didn't want to sleep. Running over to the window, I pushed it back on its hinges, and sat listening to the night-time noises: the cicadas in the pines, the distant hum of an engine trawling up the hillside, a radio playing dance music, laughter... Yöst's letter, a talisman to good fortune in my hand.

You must meet up with Rico again. He still talks of teaching you to dance, and of course drink a glass of the new vintage when it's ready. There is so much room, you can stay as long as you want. I will enjoy the company.

Had anyone in the entire history of the world ever been this happy?

19

I lost track of time, the night deepening as the hours wandered gently past, immersed in my memories and wanting to re-experience every glance and smile, intent on embroidering each fleeting moment into something more permanent. Yet sleep, when it did finally overtake me, failed to prolong my sense of euphoria; instead, nightmares that drove deep furrows through the enchantment of the day took over. Constantly lifting me back to the surface, I experienced both tears and sorrow, feeling my pillow damp before they carried me back down again, and it was Justine's voice, shrill and persistent, that brought me fully awake.

Full of hurt and anger, it echoed up and down the stairwell, the speed and ferocity of her words leaving me grateful I didn't fully understand the accent of the south-west. Then the deep growl of Hans' response before silence took over once more.

It was early, despite specks of sunshine already easing through the louvred shutters that promised a sunny day. They quickly dissolved the final traces of my dream, recalling that this was our last day together – mine and Zande's.

He had suggested my accompanying him on the bus to Bordeaux. 'And if there is time, we will take in the cathedral.' His eyes had lit up, leaving me with the heartfelt desire to have met up with him years before, when he had known only the joy of being alive. 'And we will lie down on the floor together and inspect the ceiling. And if people object, I will politely inform them, there is no better way to drink in the beauty of rooftops and ceilings.'

My brother's footsteps sounded on the stairs.

I heard the outer door, his feet returning, thumping out their frustration, a sound I had become familiar with whenever he and Justine argued, and something else ... excitement. He banged with his fist on my door and without waiting for a reply, stuck his head around. 'Slight change of plan.'

'Change of plan? What plan?'

'My plan. I'm leaving.'

Astonished, I stared at him. He seemed almost cheerful, his mouth pursed with amusement at the insults Justine was shrieking at him from the studio doorway.

'Leaving?' I echoed.

'You can stay if you want,' he ignored my interjection. 'No doubt Justine will charge you rent.'

Reaching for my robe, I ran across to the door, opening it wide. 'You're not serious, you can't be!'

He called loudly over his shoulder, 'Maidy's asking if I'm serious. That's right isn't it, Justine? You do want me to leave?'

The canvas bag that accompanied him everywhere was on the floor by the door. So full, he had used a belt to fasten it, attaching a bundle of paintbrushes to the strap with a rubber band.

'But why?'

He shrugged, the movement of his shoulders twisting a muscle in his cheek. Emblazoned on it was the imprint of an open hand, where Justine's ring, a gift from Hans – a yellow citrine in an antique silver mount – had grazed the skin, a bead of blood oozing from the cut.

'She hit you?'

He rubbed his cheek, smearing the blood onto his palm. He stared down at it. 'I probably deserved it. I did try to explain it was a mistake; unfortunately, Justine didn't believe me.'

'You were unfaithful?'

He flinched and his light-hearted expression vanished. 'Not you too.' He shifted uncomfortably. 'Why would you think that?'

'Because Justine wouldn't have thrown you out for anything trivial.'

'Fine sister you turn out to be,' he grumbled. 'I thought you'd be pleased.'

'Pleased! Who was it?' I asked, a feeling of dread stealing over me.

'That doesn't matter.' He seemed almost irritated by the question.

'Of course it matters, if it's Ruth.' I felt my anger rising. 'How could you do that to Justine of all people?'

'The way you're carrying on, you'd think I'd planned for it to happen.'

He thumped the wall with his fist.

'Well, didn't you?' I stormed, almost incandescent with rage.

Abruptly, I remembered Ruth's words that day in the apartment in New York. Hans had written her a fan letter. 'Will you be writing back?' I asked and her reply, 'Perhaps, if I have time.' She may have wanted me to call her Grace but this was vintage Ruth, twisting lives to suit her purpose. It ought to have had my hackles up long ago, my alarm bells ringing.

Suddenly in need of fresh air, I ran across the bedroom floor hastily unlatching the shutters. Pushing them apart, I leant out feeling the air warm on my face and took in some deep breaths; the words, *Not Ruth, not again I won't let it*, playing over and over.

I swung round. 'Oh, Hans, why would you go back?'

The fight went out of him. 'I've always loved Ruth, you know that.' He repeated the words he'd said before when I questioned him, sounding almost surprised at the severity of my tone.

'And you were in love with Justine until she came on the scene,' I snapped. I pounded my fists against the window frame, sharing Justine's desire to throw things. 'Don't you see? It's happening again.'

His voice sharpened. 'Happening again? What's happening again? What the devil are you talking about?'

'Pieter.'

'Nonsense. Pieter may have been in love with Ruth, but she never loved him. She told me it was Mother who pushed for them to marry and you didn't help.'

That was the moment I should have spoken and told my brother that the sibling he both loved and hated, yet always admired and depended on, was no longer a man – and it was Ruth's fault. Yet how could I do that? If I had found the courage, it would also have betrayed Mother and I couldn't do that, not to Pappy – it would be like removing the sun from the sky.

I sighed my acceptance. 'Where do you plan to live? In the room behind the shop?'

'No, Ruth has...' He trailed off and I spotted guilt and embarrassment.

'A posh apartment,' I finished for him. 'And her husband?'

'He doesn't come into the picture.' Hans shifted uncomfortably. He bent his head, staring down at the floor, refusing to meet my gaze. 'The thing is Maidy, they don't live together.'

I stayed silent, well aware that whatever he came out with next would be Ruth's words, not his. 'They don't get on; never have. It was an arranged marriage, designed to help their careers. And she's promised to help my career, make me truly international.'

All at once, it made sense.

Pappy once told me that in Hans, ambition soared far beyond anything a woman might offer.

He had also sent Hans away to save him from Ruth.

A rattling of wooden shutters sounded from the opposite side of the street and a face appeared. A young woman, probably about Justine's age, craned out over the sill, her nightdress diaphanous and low cut. She swung round to call a remark to someone in the bedroom behind her and I heard laughter.

I wondered if the occupants of that bedroom had also woken to find their lives as messed up as ours were about to become. I included my own relationship with Zande – wonderful but scarcely straight-forward.

The door to the restaurant opened and the old woman who

daily attended church emerged. I waited expectantly, her ongoing war with the pigeons something I eagerly anticipated each morning, with the furious waving of her arms that sent the scavenging birds spiralling hysterically into the air in a rush of grey feathers.

I had only been in Flambeau a few short months but in that time memories, like a shelf stacked with favourite books that you return to time and time again, had already built up. 'I'll stay, if that's okay with you.'

Loud crashes gusted across the landing from her studio.

Hans grinned. 'Don't worry, she won't destroy my paintings.' He hesitated, once again shifting his weight back and forth. I waited. His expression changed, now full of concern. 'Look after her, Maidy. And please, don't leave her alone, not today.'

I gasped out. 'I can't.'

'Please, Maidy. She might hurt herself.'

A door slammed.

I jumped.

All at once I recalled my dream, every detail distinct rather than hazy as dreams so often are. It was a Saturday the first time we met out of college, and Zande and I were seated on the grass by the canal. *The human condition can be so restrictive*, he had said. At the time I'd not understood him.

Now, after seeing the swans, I did.

'*No!*' a voice inside me implored. '*No, please, no. Not that.*'

'Maidy!' I felt a hand on my arm and opened my eyes. 'You all right? You've gone white.'

'Yes, I'm fine,' I replied automatically. I glanced down. My bare feet were a blur. 'I didn't sleep well, that's all.' The room steadied; objects were once again in focus, with Hans, his hand on my arm, regarding me with concern.

I forced out a smile. 'Yes, of course, I'll keep an eye on Justine,' unsure if it was even me speaking. It didn't resemble my voice; this voice belonged to a stranger. 'Give me a few minutes. Sit outside in the car if you have to. There's someone I need to speak to first.'

No, not someone; Zande could never be just someone.

Hans, with another shrug and a glance almost of longing over his shoulder, swung away and headed downstairs. And hastily throwing on my clothes, I followed.

Outside, the courtyard lay hushed and tranquil, the ground where last night Justine and I had set the world to rights a carpet of wilting rose petals.

I'd never once considered Hans in terms of a family likeness. Visitors only ever commented how alike Pieter and Pappy were. Maybe that was true, Pieter deliberately copying Pappy's gestures, his manner of working, even his way of holding a chisel and a paintbrush. The merry outlook and softly voiced patience, those too he had on loan from Pappy. Now, I realised it was Hans who most naturally resembled him. Justine was right. In the middle of being made homeless, he was more concerned about her safety than anything else.

I still felt angry though and, as I hurried down the lane, I forgot my dream. All I could think was talking it over with Zande. He would understand. I stopped, appalled by my naivety. Is that what happened to girls after a blissful evening of lovemaking, they lost the ability to think straight? How could I tell Zande? Other things maybe, but not this.

The hotel door stood ajar, with rays of sunlight lingering in the doorway, the concierge, Zande had referred to, possibly a figment of his own brand of chivalry – a virtue he would no doubt have denied, volunteering an even more outrageous explanation if pressed.

He was outside in the garden restaurant, the pottery from his breakfast still on the table. At first, he didn't notice me, his attention fastened on a small boy playing hide and seek with his dog. A game played many times before, the animal, a keen participant, sitting docilely while the boy, counting out loud to a hundred, hid. Then, on the bellowed command *come*, the animal raced off snuffling at the ground for traces of its owner's scent.

Once again, I wished I'd inherited the gift Hans shared with Enri, and with a pencil in my hand might bring to life images equally as efficiently as those seen through a camera lens. Maybe the subject being gloriously photogenic would make it easier; perhaps others on seeing Zande for the first time would add the comment, 'he looks good in clothes,' a phrase I had learned meant elegant. Yet, that wasn't the real Zande, that was mere window dressing. The genuine article found fun and laughter in the most absurd of situations such as a child's game, a button undone on a skirt, a sail flapping in the wind. That was the person I'd always believed existed beneath layers of mistrust and bitterness, and the person I finally encountered the day before yesterday – happy and content to be alive.

As if I had called out, he swung round, 'Hello.' He smiled and I felt my breath go. 'I was waiting.' He pointed to his bag on the ground beside him. 'I wondered if you'd be here early although I hoped you wouldn't.'

'How...' I replied bewildered. 'Hans has only just asked...'

Trembling, I examined his face, half-expecting, nevertheless distraught to find the excitement that had filled his eyes the previous day missing, like the glow from a light bulb when the element snaps. Now, it looked bleak and empty.

I burst out, 'Didn't we arrange to meet at ten?'

'Yet, here you are.' In the distance, the town chimed the quarter hour. 'And it's not yet eight.'

Unsure of my ground, I stayed where I was.

'I decided I'd catch the early bus.'

'I was going with you,' I argued. 'It was all arranged. We'd visit the cathedral and have lunch before you caught your train and...'

'Yet here you are, and it's not yet eight,' he repeated and smiled gently. 'I was just thinking, if we had met up when we were supposed to, all those years ago when we were children, we would have had years and years in which to be happy.'

I felt the ready tears, knowing what my dreams had struggled to make plain – that this was something I couldn't have, not with Zande.

He held out his arms and somehow, without noticing I'd moved, my head found his shoulder.

'Sadly, my dearest Maidy, all we got were two very precious days.'

'There'll be other days,' I hung onto the lie.

'Will there?'

I spilled it out. 'It's Justine! Hans has left her and she can't...' I tripped over my falsehood. 'It's so unfair.'

His face changed, the bitter twist that had once personified his character, something I'd hoped never to see again, predominant. 'That's one thing no one can guarantee ... that life will be fair.'

He held me away, his hands resting on my shoulders, his lip twisting. No longer in mockery or disdain. That had gone; now those eyes that had entranced, that had danced and sparkled with life, looked dull and resigned.

'What I am...' His words sounded like his flesh was being torn open. I wanted to comfort him; only I couldn't, not from this. 'All the wishing in the world can't change what happened. Jaan and Waldger, a few of the others, they can still go back. I can't. Maidy...'

Momentarily, the control was gone, his iron-clad will in need of help. Help I no longer was entitled to give because he had read my thoughts and knew my abhorrence at the idea of his bones, his sinews, his muscles, being pounded into a different shape.

'I was going to say, isn't it better to realise it and part before any lasting harm. Except it's too late for that, isn't it? That's already happened.'

'Yes.'

He hesitated. 'Will you be all right?'

We could well have been stone images, our limbs frozen, unmoving – only our eyes had life in them.

I knew what he needed from me. No tears, no pleadings, no promises to do better in future. I wasn't Elina.

'We had two days.'

'If you ever change your mind...'

'Yes?'

'Yöst will find me and I'll ... I'll be waiting.'

I heard the hesitation and identified the missing word; such a little word *fly*, just three letters, far shorter than either *care* or *love*. Both of those had four letters. And for me, those four letters held the whole world. Not *fly*. Those three letters held nothing for either of us except heartache and loss.

Releasing me, he stepped back and picked up his bag. 'Goodbye,' and blew me a kiss.

20

Within a moment he was gone, and I was left to imagine his footsteps tracking back through the narrow lanes, the quaint old buildings leaning forward in greeting and, as his footsteps faded into the distance, waving goodbye.

As I had done.

He had gone and I didn't want to think beyond that; it hurt too much.

Aimlessly I began to retrace my footsteps – back to where I belonged. Except where was that, I wasn't sure any longer. My feet felt heavy and clumping, the pathway that a week ago had been a springboard of hope reduced to heavy clay and lumps of earth.

All around me, shutters were opening and doors closing behind residents already leaving for work. Those with cars directed their steps to the new town where they'd left them; others, not so fortunate, made their way to the bus stop at the top of the town. Reaching the driveway, I stopped to look at my watch, surprised to find scarcely any time had passed at all. Maybe it was pure imagination to think our conversation had lasted a lifetime, as much an illusion as Zande glancing back over his shoulder expecting a different outcome and wanting it as much as I did.

There was time, the bus wouldn't leave until eight. I could still run to the bus stop, promise him I didn't mean it.

Mean what?

'They make a pretty display, don't they, Mademoiselle?'

I jumped, startled, and swung round to see an elderly woman peering at me from the open window of one of the cottages. I hadn't noticed the flowers apart from registering a blaze of colour.

'If you do this every day, they will flower until autumn,' she called out, snipping away with a pair of scissors at the faded blooms in her window box. Her eyes, glittering inquisitively, examined me intently and what she saw she obviously didn't approve of, staring pointedly at my dress. In my hurry, I had snatched up the clothes I'd worn yesterday to go sailing, and there was a grass stain on the skirt.

'You're from the manor,' she commented, her friendly inquisition on hold. 'Hmm! Fine goings on there, I must say.'

Before today, I would have smiled and passed on by. Today, I wasn't me, was I? I was a girl who had just lost her lover. 'Maybe you should repeat your views to the Countess,' I snapped wishing I could leave my pain behind as I had my manners. 'I'm sure she would be interested.'

She sniffed and shut the window with a bang.

Pappy's voice rebuked me. 'Heartbreak doesn't give you the right to be rude, Maidy.'

Once, long ago, I had complained about the women who sat by the canal side. The men always nodded and smiled whenever Ruth and I walked past; not the women. They had stared at us stony-faced, their gimlet eye disapproving. 'When you are old, Maidy,' I remember him saying, 'and dependent on the charity of a son or daughter for your food and lodging, no doubt you will also disapprove of youngsters who are carefree, and object to their manners and clothing.'

How nice that would be, to be old, with heartbreak safely buried in the past.

I glanced towards the courtyard and saw the archway empty – the car gone. Justine!

Hans had asked me to care for her and I had forgotten. However long had I been absent? Minutes, hours, days? In all that time Justine had been alone.

Fearing what I might find, I raced through the allée of conifers and into the courtyard, pushing open the door into the kitchen. Justine was standing by the stove, a long chef's knife in her hand.

'*Justine, put down the knife.*'

She didn't hear, her chest heaving, her gaze fastened on the window.

'Justine,' I ordered. 'Put down the knife.'

'What?'

'The knife.'

As if awakening from a dream, my presence in the kitchen registered. She gave a shaky laugh. 'It's not what you think, Maidy. I was planning to cook bœuf bourguignon for dinner, before remembering Hans won't be here.' She stabbed the knife into the table. 'I so hate men. They're stupid. If only they thought with their heads, not their...' She used a word I'd never heard and had to guess.

Despite my shock, I laughed. No doubt with relief that the knife was no longer pointing at me.

'What the hell are you laughing at?'

As if her use of her vulgarity had percolated the layers of anger, she too broke free and laughed. 'Oh, I'm so sorry. Hans is always rebuking me. I promise I wasn't born in a gutter. That was the theatre. Oh, Maidy, bastard or not, I'll miss him. And I hit him! Will he ever forgive me?'

'He probably deserved it,' I replied, my own anger gone, relieved my lapse hadn't been the cause of yet more tragedy.

'Do you know what he told me?'

'What?' I straightened my shoulders, determinedly clearing my mind of its confusion. At home the best place for that had been my bedroom, talking to my imaginary friends from across the river, who were always on hand to comfort me. Except I was grown-up now and living in the real world. 'Shall I make coffee? I need a cup even if you don't.'

Distracted, Justine grabbed at the kettle, filling it from the pump and leaving the water flowing into the sink.

'Justine.' I rebuked and hastily closed it off.

'He had the damn cheek to tell me *she* could open doors for him.'

Of course. Everything about Ruth had to be bigger and better. It wasn't anything new, even as a child she'd been the same – her clothes, her parties – I'd just been too stupid to see it. And now? I doubted her actions were ruled by love, at least not on her part. Her life was hostage to her reputation as a film star and becoming the wife of a famous artist could only add to it.

'By *she*, I presume you mean Ruth,' I raised my voice.

Justine didn't hear, talking to herself. 'Imbecile, his talent will do that.'

'It won't last,' I tried to comfort her. 'He might think he loves—'

'She's pregnant!'

Justine collapsed down on to a seat, immediately leaping up again.

'And don't tell me that's natural for a married woman. According to Hans, the honeymoon was so successful they have occupied different houses ever since.'

Pregnant, Ruth?

Snatching the whistling kettle from the stove, she grabbed my arm, running me through the hallway and up the stairs. Brushing my protests aside, we continued to the second floor. I didn't resist; my sympathies all with Justine and had Hans shown his face at that moment, I might well have killed him myself.

I'd never explored the upper floors, respecting Hans' wish to keep his studio sacrosanct, remembering how touchy he'd been as a boy if anyone messed with his things. As Justine pulled open the door at the top of the stairs, the gloom disintegrated into a blaze of light and instinctively, I took a step back.

Now the bare spots on the stairwell where pictures had once hung made sense. Where I had expected to find paltry cubicles, dim and dinghy, there was only space – not a wall in sight. Part of the roof had gone too, the elegant blue grey slates replaced by glass windows that opened by means of a ratchet attached to the frame. Hans, in his hurry, had left one open, its long cord swinging slightly in the draft from the stairwell.

I didn't speak for the longest while, overcome by the scale of the modifications.

'I assume you are rendered speechless by the injustices of society?'

She pointed at the brickwork on the outside wall where parallel indentations determined the width of each room; all of them lacking any source of natural light apart from one at the end opposite an opening window. 'And people wonder why we had a revolution.'

She added a brusque laugh to the shrug of her shoulders. 'The day my husband died, I collected up all his jewellery, his watches, cuff links and tie pins, and gave them to the servants. Then I told them to leave because there was no money to pay them—all apart from the elderly woman who does our cleaning. Nevertheless, I refused to let her live in.'

There was furniture, which, before Justine's comment about firing the servants, I imagined to have been left after furnishing the lower floors. It wasn't, it was part of my brother's secret world.

Artist's easels occupied the central section where the light was brightest. All were covered and all had canvases on them, the floorboards below spattered with drops of paint that represented the palette of colours used in that particular painting. In the far corner a long couch with a velvet seat had been pushed tight up against the wall, its carved mahogany frame peeking out from under a pile of fabric, with a couple of padded stools stacked casually on top. A gilt chair stood next to it; part of a matching pair, the other chair was in Justine's sitting room. Also a tiny table with a marble top circled by a bracelet of ormolu. Even not knowing much about antiques, I guessed this to be valuable, its legs the sensual shape of a cello, its tiny clawed feet like those of a pug, the breed a favourite among French royalty. There was a second table too, light from the open roof tinting its surface gold.

Also, one of a matching pair, its fellow stood on the first-floor landing outside my bedroom door.

Remembering the different woods Pappy used in his work, I had asked Justine if it was walnut, 'Hans says its burr walnut,' she corrected. 'He says, you can tell them by the swirls. Louis something or other.' She had waved her hand casually, 'there's another about somewhere if you are interested. Hans will know where it is.'

The walls hadn't escaped Hans' artistry either; a full-length gilt mirror reflected the silken sheen of a curtain, its glistening folds infused with subtle colour. It made me think of rich beauty and of enchantment and power, the cost of the exquisite fabric no doubt warranting the sale of several first editions.

Justine, no longer aware of my presence, strode about the room, running her fingers across a particular item of furniture, lost in reminiscences of the love affair she and Hans had shared, her face softening, a smile fluttering the corners of her mouth.

'This is all Hans?' I called out, grasping the significance of the furniture.

She nodded.

'One night, he was sat on the floor of my bedroom, giving me a lecture about art being a piece of theatre. For some modern artists, it is all about questioning your view of the world. Hans wasn't interested in square heads and keyhole eyes; he wanted to tell a story.'

'Like the triptychs.'

'Yes.'

'If he painted a woman, it wasn't just for her face, it was because she had something to say.'

Crossing the space, she whisked the cover off the painting nearest me.

It was of Justine, the portrait of a ballerina.

I gasped.

'*Regards* – look.' Justine darted round the room, whisking the covers off the rest.

Nothing could have prepared me for the intensity of the

experience, my mind dithering and unsure, almost incapable of settling on one image before flittering off like a wandering dust mote. All were of Justine yet, only if you knew her could you identify the figure with any certainty, her face inclined away or in shadow. And I did, fortunate enough to have witnessed similar poses many times before. Perhaps when she was dancing around the courtyard in a teasing mood, or leaning on the banister chatting with Hans standing in the hallway below, or sitting with one foot up on a chair, painting her toenails. In all but the last picture she was wearing an ankle-length silk robe tied loosely. Diaphanous and falling open, it outlined the planes and angles of her body.

Yet, her body wasn't the focal point of the paintings. That was only part of the narrative. It was the story of a ballerina preparing for a performance, and it was her ballet shoes that were the star. In the first, obviously new, they were being lifted from a box and presented to the ballerina like an offering. Little more than a shadow in the background, she was leaning forward to accept them, a reel of cotton pierced with a needle on her open palm, the long lengths of pink ribbon draped over her wrist. In the second, the shoes were dangling from a peg while, in semi-profile, the ballerina dressed her hair, the alabaster texture of her arms against the background glistening and very real. In the third, she was leaning down to tie the shoe, her foot resting on the gilt chair. A second shoe and the jewelled headpiece she was to wear for her performance on a table. Again mostly in shadow, only the delicately carved front legs embossed with flowers were clearly defined. Against the gloom, the flowers which complemented the pink of the ballet shoe initially stole your attention. Then as my eyes adjusted, I noticed people in the shadows, the shape of a shoulder, a flounce embellishing the sleeve of a costume, an elbow jutting or a pointed toe, and it became clear from their edgy stance, they too were waiting to go on stage.

In the last, despite it not being finished, it took my breath; Hans' intention quite clear as if he had painted every detail in gleaming colour. It was Justine again, waiting for her cue to begin the performance. Gripping the solid edge of the wings, she was bending down to dip the pink-laced ballet shoe into a box of powdered rosin, her right arm and hand lying quiescent on the sparkling bouffant skirt of her costume.

'See?' Justine stormed, the expression on her face as dark as the fabrics Hans had used for backgrounds. 'Why the hell would he need Ruth?'

By lunchtime I was exhausted. It had been a long morning in which I dogged Justine's heels, keeping up some inane conversation, although I'd not the slightest notion what we were talking about.

Eventually she screamed at me, '*Merde*, if I promise not to kill myself and use the knife for cooking, can I at least make pee-pee without you following me into the toilet!'

It cleared the air and we both laughed, hugging one another.

Later, between sips of wine, she cooked the *bœuf bourguignon*. 'We have to eat; you look as if the breeze will blow you away and I can put what is left on ice for another day,' she called, carrying a tray loaded with plates of salad and meat in a rich wine sauce outside into the courtyard. 'And open some wine; you definitely need it, you're as white as a sheet. Not red; Sauvignon Blanc today, you will enjoy that. Wait!' Dumping the tray on the table, she pointed her finger. 'Last night you were going to Bordeaux. What the hell happened?'

'We broke up.' I hurried inside and grabbed glasses and a bottle of white wine from the fridge, scarcely bothering to read the label.

Reaching over, she filled my glass. 'Drink that, before you burst into tears.' Obligingly, I took a sip. 'And another, go on, go on.'

I replaced my glass on the table, unsurprised to see her top it up. 'Justine!' I protested.

Overwhelmed by her generosity, her own grief put aside to comfort me, I felt tears pressing against my eyelids and hurriedly blinked them away. 'Now I know why Hans drinks; it dulls the pain.'

'Eat!' She pointed her knife at my plate. 'Otherwise the wine will go to your head and you will either gabble incoherently or start crying!' She glowered at me. 'I can't stand either. And Hans doesn't drink, at least not more than a glass or two at night to keep me company. I'm the drinker, Maidy. Or was. Hans has pretty much cured me. *Imbécile!* If I do relapse, I shall blame him.'

'He used to drink,' I reminded her.

The wine was cool and slightly astringent, and I recognised the taste of green apples, tart and crisp. It reminded me of my first ever glass of wine, although I was still unsure if it was Pieter's homecoming or my birthday I remembered most. Swallowing, my taste buds absorbed the piquancy of ripe peaches.

'Beer?'

I nodded, 'Yes.'

'Serious drinkers in France almost never drink beer. Besides, Hans only got drunk because he felt so confined.'

'Confined, is that what he told you?'

'Of course. While he was painting, he often talked about your home and your family. How mean he considered Pieter was to leave. Pieter loved the work Baders did. He wanted nothing more. Hans hated it. He thought the seven years of his apprenticeship would never come to an end. Apparently, so Hans said, brothers rarely share secrets.' She pushed her expression into one of mock severity. 'Boys supposedly are more practical and down to earth, except for the sensitive souls, and Hans never plucked up courage to tell Pieter he despised mirrors.'

I thought then of Berthe – we had never once talked about our ambitions. Perhaps four years for a child is too big a gap. Mine had been to become a writer. Everyone knew that, and Berthe? Now, I saw her ambition had never changed. She had always wanted to be a homemaker.

'That's why I allowed you to come here. Hans said you helped him survive.'

'I did? How?'

'You listened and were interested. He said anyone could make a mirror if they had the right tools, but not a painting.'

'He could have painted in his spare time,' I said, surprised at the turn our conversation was taking.

'He drew in his spare time,' she corrected. 'Real artists need days of emptiness, with nothing being asked of them. That's why I don't bother to involve him in anything – he's too damn good for that. Nevertheless, still a fool. *Allez!* Now it is your turn. Why did you break up with—?'

'Zande.'

'Yes, bloody Zande. What did he do?'

'He builds boats.'

'Sounds sensible so far. Go on. Not the marrying type or he wanted everything except marriage? In which case, I think breaking up a sensible move – you are far too young to become someone's paramour.'

'No, it wasn't that!' In a way, I wished it had been – that would have been so easy. I might then have been able to ignore the rest, persuading myself it didn't matter. 'He just wasn't suitable.' I blinked back my tears, unsure if it was her kindness that was making me cry or the deep well of hopelessness at the thought of never seeing Zande again.

'My dear girl; grow up. No man is suitable. They're all swines and totally impossible. What you do...' Momentarily, forgetting what she was about to say, she began drawing a face in the ring of moisture left by her glass and I knew she was thinking of Hans. 'What you do, is pick the least unsuitable.'

'Is that how you chose Hans?'

'Mon Dieu! No!' She seemed surprised. 'If you ignore his irritating habits, your brother is a real sweety. When he first arrived in Flambeau, he was a mere boy, mall… malleable,' she tripped over the word, 'like clay. Tiens, have some more salad.'

I glanced down at my plate, astonished to see I had almost cleared it.

Smiling triumphantly, she saluted me with her glass. 'If you want someone to eat, talk about people's problems. People find the subject fascinating, especially girls. It's a trick I learned at ballet school. At any one time, at least half the girls were suffering from heartache.'

She had also eaten her food, although she had drunk steadily throughout. Nevertheless, anything was better than the terrible emptiness I had witnessed when she was clutching that knife.

'They also believe you to be sweet and kind,' Justine snorted with derision, 'which means they will do anything to remain in your good graces.'

How stupid Hans was. Admittedly Justine was older yet, in her own way, far more captivating than Ruth could ever be, her cheek bones and sculptured eyebrows dominating a face that would prove as fascinating in twenty years as I found it now.

We remained outside, although the early warmth of the morning had faded, replaced by a brisk wind that hinted at the inevitable arrival of autumn and scuttled leaves across the ground, the topmost branches of the fir trees in the little allée swaying back and forth in tandem.

Justine pointed to them remarking casually, 'They remind me of the *corps de ballet*. However strict the maître, there is always one not quite in step.'

It would have been warmer indoors too, yet it occurred to neither of us, the walls of the building accentuating the empty space Hans had filled so easily. Justine had her feet up on the chair Hans usually used, her one hand stretched out, idly picking at a rose, a pile of petals lying discarded in her lap. We didn't speak much, the wine doing its job and blurring the edges of our pain so that the emotion splintering our flow of words became less frequent, even bearable. Eventually recalling how Hans had implored me to look after her, I asked, 'what are you going to do?'

'I'll go back to Paris next month, if they'll have me.'

'Is that what you want?'

'No, I want Hans. But I need money,' she said flatly.

'What about the shop? If you're in Paris... it leaves a difficulty if you want me to leave.'

'No, you can stay and I will charge you rent. I do have some pride. Anyway, it's not worth your leaving. Knowing Hans he'll bring flowers – he's done it before, except he really was innocent that time, he just wanted to draw her.'

I daren't remind Justine that Hans couldn't return, not if he accepted responsibility for Ruth's child. And he would. 'Who do you mean by her?'

'Some girl. She worked in a confectioner's... and yes, she had one of those faces you can't forget.' Justine took a sip of wine. 'I was jealous as hell; she was younger too.'

'You have one of those faces.'

'That's the wine talking.' She pointed to the empty bottle.

'No, well, possibly a bit. Why don't you sell the door?'

'Hans said not to.'

'Hans isn't here,' I pointed out. 'If you want, I'll write to Pappy and ask how much it's worth. My guess is enough to redecorate—'

'Redecorate? Mon Dieu, you're mad.'

'No! It just occurred to me. Renovate the other section of the house and rent it out; then you'll never need money again.'

She looked shocked. 'Our sort of people, we don't do that.'

'For God's sake, Justine.' I swore. 'You aren't *our sort of people*. That was your husband.'

She started upright, surprised by my fierce tone. 'I don't know who that charlatan was and you refuse to say why he was unsuitable, but in the last week you've been more alive than I've ever seen you. Are you sure you are doing the right thing to ditch him? Before today you'd never said boo to a goose. Hans...'

No, I wasn't sure. 'You're always quoting Hans,' I rebuked, my tone gentling. 'I hate that. He was a pain growing up.'

She responded with a wave of her hand. 'When he told me your home was swallowing you alive, I suggested he teach you to drink and swear.' Her hand floated airily, saluting me with her wine glass. 'He replied, over his dead body. Sadly, that didn't come to pass.'

I lapsed into giggles.

'Bravo. It would seem I have succeeded.' She leaned forward, pointing upwards to the gargoyles. 'And you don't think the hounds of hell will come after me, if I redecorate?'

'Remove them, if they bother you that much.'

They bothered me too, unable to understand what possessed the artist to besmirch the glorious elegance of a roof with something so medieval. When I'd asked Hans, he said most probably they'd been a later addition. But why? A warning from the artist to the population as a whole? Recalling Justine's account of her husband's ancestors, I wouldn't have been surprised. They certainly dominated the façade; with its windows shuttered against the sun, it became merely an empty shell in which spirits and wraiths roamed at will. It was such a false impression; Justine filled the space with brilliant life.

'This house belongs to you now. You've never had a chance to put your mark on it. If you redecorate, you can do that.' My words sound loud even to my ears. 'Heavens, I must be drunk, Justine. That's the second time today I've shouted.' She raised her eyebrows in enquiry. 'The old woman who lives in one of the cottages.'

'That old witch, she hates my guts.' Casually lifting one foot off the chair, she rotated the ankle. 'Her son chauffeured my husband about until we sold the cars.'

'Cars?'

'He had four. Including a Rolls Royce. She blames me for the loss of his job.'

'Do you still own the cottages?'

'Not the buildings, no. The land, yes; my husband did have some scruples, pity they didn't extend as far as fidelity.' The hand waving was back.

I laughed. 'If you sell both front doors together, I'm pretty sure there'll be enough money to buy you a flat in Paris.'

In the days that followed, I couldn't decide if it was Justine who propped me up or I her. Neither of us referred to the break-up. I guessed Justine's humour by the tempo and tenor of the music streaming out from the studio and, doubtless, she guessed mine by the silence I carried within me, struggling to add a cheerful word to the conversation. To some extent I must have succeeded.

I opened up the shop each morning, served customers with a smile and only after they were gone, the key turned in the lock, did I allow my feelings their freedom. Justine knew it; she also knew I couldn't talk about it.

Had I been at home, I would have confided my grief to the houses across the river. They were uncaring however much I rattled on, repeating myself and tripping over words, recounting part-truths grudgingly followed by the actual truth. They wouldn't have condemned as folly my falling in love with Zande or my rejecting him. To them, I could admit the obstacle and they would have reassured me that it wasn't abject foolishness to turn my back on love.

But Justine, whose ideas reflected a very different spectrum of life from my own, what would she say? She might well offer advice; she was well-qualified. It wasn't the first time she had met up with heartache either. Yet, if I dared speak out, my words would be dismissed as the quixotic imaginings of a mind run riot. It was better to say nothing.

21

'I need coffee.' Justine wandered into the kitchen. The October morning was too cold for the courtyard, and she had swapped her kimono for a full-length housecoat in fine wool.

'Hangover?' I accused, catching sight of the dark glasses in her pocket. I jumped up, pouring some milk into a saucepan to warm it. 'Justine, you can't let him win.'

'Mon Dieu, you sound like Hans; he was always handing out advice. Pity he didn't follow it himself.'

I stared astonished. 'What did I do?'

'Nothing. That's the point. All this heroism places the rest of us in a terrible position.' She glared at me, her mouth a thin line repudiating any connection between us. 'Hans drove me mad, you to despair. You calmly discuss my hangover, and yes, all right, I've got a bitch of a head, and there's you torn-up inside. Isn't it about time you did something and actually began thinking about yourself? You can't always be a prop for others. I know damn well you were in love with that guy ... what was his name again?'

'Zande.'

'Yes, bloody Zande. How could he? He'll never find anyone half as nice, not if he searches the entire universe.'

I flinched.

'What?'

I couldn't say that was the reason we had broken up, because he could search the entire universe and I couldn't.

'The handle's hot.' Grabbing a cloth, I removed the milk pan from the stove, adding it to her coffee and pouring myself a fresh cup. 'This isn't about *bloody* Zande though, is it?'

She growled a laugh. 'Why didn't you tell me Hans had visited the shop?'

'How did you find out?'

Without replying, Justine took a leisurely sip of her coffee. She was enjoying this – mocking me, although her gaze was no longer hostile. 'The goings-on of the chateau are of great interest to the town.'

'And?' I demanded.

Replacing her cup on the table, 'Someone recognised Hans' car and told the butcher. And yesterday afternoon, the printer called round to tell me his work was ready. It's in the living room.'

'You didn't...?'

'What, destroy it? No, I wanted to but it's good.' She pushed out her lip in protest. '*Merde!* He must be happy.'

I had actually seen Hans several times, always arriving at the shop unannounced, the first-time hesitating in the doorway, debating the wisdom of entering at all. And always asking the same question. 'How is Justine?'

'Well, as always,' was my inevitable response. Usually he ignored it, passing on to other matters, and one time asking my opinion as to why one particular print had sold and not another. On his last visit, he remained in the doorway, asking, 'Is she really?'

'What do you want me to say, Hans?' I retorted, exasperated by the childish game. 'That Justine is fine or that Justine is the opposite of fine, as anyone would be after a break-up?'

'Hell, Maidy, this is awkward. Help me out here. You know I want her to be fine,' he growled out, adding, 'I still care about her.'

I was astonished by my reply. 'Yes, I believe you do.'

Taking courage from my reply, he came all the way in, closing the door behind him. 'I wanted to drop off some new work at the printer's. Not for here, for the new gallery.'

'Where's that?' expecting him to say Bordeaux.

'Paris. We moved and are looking for a gallery there. By the way, Ruth says we need a phone, then I can telephone you about the shop and not be forced to drive down.'

'I didn't mention it, Justine,' I excused myself now, adding with a smile, 'because, you'd probably have thrown something at me.'

It wasn't the real reason. The days Hans visited, there'd been a palpable sense of excitement about him which had prevented me from speaking out.

'God, life's a bitch!' Justine slammed the coffee pot down on the table, following it down to perch on a chair, one knee bent, her chin resting on it.

'He won't always be in love with her.'

'That's not much help,' Justine glowered. Her expression changed, piqued with curiosity about her rival for Hans' affections. 'You sound very certain. Why?'

I recalled a far distant conversation with Pappy, his telling me that, for Hans, art would always be his first love. 'Because Ruth will never be content to take a back seat, not even to his art. She needs to be loved, to come first,' I said, boldly scattering the ashes of our childhood friendship, 'and to matter to someone before everything else.'

'And her husband?' Justine asked curiously.

'He only matters to himself.'

When the phone rang, I recognised Ruth's dulcet tones immediately. 'Count yourself lucky,' said the engineer who came to fit it, 'your landlord agreed to a party line otherwise...' He removed his cap doffing it almost reverently at the new phone box on the wall. 'It would be at least another year.'

I had expected the call to be from Hans. He hadn't visited for three weeks, although recalling how fine the October weather had been, I wasn't surprised. My brother would have wanted to spend every possible moment outside, drinking in views and images to reproduce on canvas and paper throughout the winter.

November was the reverse, with sweeping rain and wind that brought the gargoyles to life. 'Didn't I warn you they sound like souls in torment,' Justine laughed when I complained they kept me awake. 'Buy some earplugs and close the shutters.'

We had taken to using the sitting room for the same reason. With both windows and shutters bolted shut, the dense masonry blocked all apart from a faint screeching. Despite its comfort, I much preferred the informality of the courtyard, although after a week of rain it looked sad and dejected, fallen leaves caught by the wind scuffling aimlessly across the tiles.

'Darling Maidy,' Ruth cooed. 'You never write, so I resorted to phoning. Please come and visit, I really need someone now. You can't imagine how I feel.'

'Where's Hans, isn't he with you?'

'He's always out painting. I never thought...' I caught the peevish tone, the reception faint but quite clear. 'Anyway, men are no good with a baby coming. And I'm so lonely when he's not at home. Can I speak to him?'

'Him, you mean Hans?'

'Yes, he's driving down. He's decided to close the shop and transfer the business to Paris.'

The shop bell sounded. Expecting it to be a customer, their interest piqued by the colourful images in the shop window, I glanced over my shoulder. It was Hans.

Placing my hand over the mouth of the receiver, I mouthed, 'It's Ruth, do you want to speak to her?'

I'm not sure why I made it into a question.

'Not yet.' He shook his head, wagging it from side to side.

Ruth was still chatting away, and I struggled to catch up with her words. 'You want me to come right away?'

'Weren't you listening. Drive back with Hans; there's nothing to keep you there – not now. Hans will have a gallery here. You can run that if you're so desperate to be a shopkeeper.'

I flinched. She was right though, that's all I was good for, my career as a writer once more on hold.

Noticing my gesture, Hans mouthed the word, 'What?' I flipped my hand, telling him quite clearly it was none of his business.

I hastily cast around for an excuse, any excuse. Recalling Justine's words when she showed me around the house, 'I can't come right away. My book is based here, and I want to make a start on that before leaving.'

'Honestly, Maidy, if experience of your writing prowess has taught me anything, the baby will be going to school before you get around to visiting. You can be godmother if you want.'

Her words were bathed in honey and I duly laughed.

'You will come?'

'Yes, all right,' I agreed cautiously, still seeking a get-out clause. 'What does Hans say?'

'He's all for it.' Ruth's tone, despite the crackling on the line, was jubilant. 'When?'

'I'll talk to Hans. You said he's on his way?'

I nearly burst out laughing then, despite the gravity of the situation, Hans furiously signalling with his hands and mouthing words. 'I'll write you the date,' I said, trying not to giggle, reserving my rancour for my brother.

'That's no way to treat anyone,' I rebuked sternly after replacing the receiver, 'including Ruth.'

'I'll make it up to her. I need to see Justine before deciding.'

'Deciding what?'

'Whether to close the shop permanently. Ruth thinks I should.'

Pushing past him into the street, I removed the metal lid on the dustbin. 'In that case, you'll probably need this.'

He stared at it in horror and burst into laughter.

You're far too good for Ruth, I wanted to shout out, watching his face light up.

He was. She would never appreciate that uninhibited outburst; Justine would. And while he wasn't precisely handsome, having found his way in life, all the meanness and surliness that once weighted his looks had gone, now it was a face in which life meant something.

'That bad, eh!'

I nodded. 'She's broken most of the crockery and has moved on to more dangerous weapons,' I exaggerated, remembering the knife.

'Justine has?' his grin flashed. 'I'd better go see. And no,' he held up his hand, when I again offered up the metal lid as protection, 'I won't need that.'

The morning was busy and flew although not fast enough for me, impatiently discounting the price of a squirrel-hair brush in an attempt to speed a customer's choice between that and the more expensive sable, and at two I hastily flipped over the sign and turning the key in the lock, ran back to the house.

An ominous silence rose from the building, the gargoyles fiendishly enjoying my alarm at the lack of movement and closed windows.

Nervously, I peeked round the door to find the kitchen empty.

'We're in here,' Justine's voice rang out. Earlier in the day, she must have gone out into the courtyard and stripped the rosebushes of their last remaining buds, traces of their fragrance washing through the air. I tiptoed down the hall, noticing the door to the living room open and a fire in the grate.

She waved an arm at me. 'Have a drink.'

An empty bottle lay discarded on the floor, with a second, partially empty, on the table next to where Hans was sitting and I realised he had used a far more practical weapon than my suggestion of a dustbin lid.

'Hans is right,' she greeted me. 'You'll be better off moving.'

'What about you?'

'What about me?' She waved a letter. 'Came today – perfect timing. I shall be in Paris. Les Sylphides.'

'When are you leaving?' I said, alarmed. I hated the thought. Despite my own heartache, we had been comfortable together.

She raised her glass, saluting me. 'Not, my faithful friend, until I'm well and truly sober.' She swung round flirtatiously fluttering her fingers at Hans, exaggerating her movements. 'And that will not happen for a while yet.'

She wasn't drunk, I knew her moods too well to be taken in.

What if Zande had a change of heart and came back to Flambeau? A rush of panic left me feeling weak and it took real effort to make my reply enthusiastic. 'That's the most wonderful news. Will you invite me to Paris to see you dance?'

'We'll both go,' Hans broke in, his glance at Justine full of affection.

I wanted to throw the bottle of wine I was holding at him. How could he be so stupid, before recalling I was the same. I had once placed Ruth on a pedestal.

'And you're closing the shop?' I took a sip of wine to camouflage my irritation. I had crossed a continent for this? To once again take up the role of prompter in a play I wanted no part of?

'Yes, the stuff I want, I'll take with me. The rest can be sent on.'

'Not Justine's painting,' I said without thinking.

The air caught and hung suspended and I heard a simultaneous intake of breath. 'Of course you must,' Justine said.

'No.' Hans struggled for words. 'They're yours.'

'They're your best work.' Her protest was at best half-hearted.

'It doesn't matter. Anyway, they're not yet finished.'

Aware I had started a hare running and was no longer needed, I got to my feet, thinking I ought to return to the shop and begin the task of clearing it.

'In that case...' Justine's tone had changed.

I stopped and glanced back over my shoulder, recognising the casualness of her manner. In the past it had always disguised something important.

'In that case, it makes no sense to close the shop permanently...' She emphasised the word *permanently*. Her wrist revolved airily, in the manner of royalty. A sideshow, nevertheless. The duplicity of her gesture was intentional needing to convince Hans the wine had taken hold.

'No Frenchman ever turns his back on a profitable business – which, thanks to Maidy, it is.'

I fought to keep my face straight, wanting to cheer on her counter attack. What an extraordinary actress she would have made, her words just slurred enough to convince. 'People in Flambeau are always stopping me to say how charming she is. And of course, there's the small matter of your name, *Hans Bader...*' It came out on a breath, sounding almost reverent. 'And the seals we had printed...' She hesitated and despite the gravity of the circumstances, I struggled to conceal a smile. 'I'm sure you remember how very expensive they were.' Her eyes gleamed maliciously. 'We can't possibly let them go to waste. How about we reopen next summer?'

Leaving them to argue it out, I ran back to the shop. If Zande ever returned and saw the notice, he would at least know I wasn't gone for good. It was small comfort but it would have to do. And I wanted to return, very much. I had grown fond of the old town, with its curious corners and tumbledown alleys that changed the colour of their coat and hat into something different, depending on the slant of the sun.

Hans followed shortly after. He didn't seem particularly bothered, whistling cheerfully while packing up the pictures he wanted to take with him in the car. 'Justine's right you know,' he confided on his way out. 'I've informed the landlord. He'll keep an eye on the place 'til Justine returns.' His expression changed, his tone almost begging. 'But you will stay with Ruth at least until the baby arrives? She'll really need you then.'

Justine was back at the kitchen table when I returned to the house, preparations for our evening meal spread out on the table.

'He's gone?'

I nodded and sat down at the table. 'And you're surprisingly sober.'

'I might let you see me in pieces but I'm damned if he will.' The airy-fairy attitude of earlier had been replaced by anger, her eyes flashing. 'He forfeited that right by sleeping with another woman and getting her pregnant.'

I remembered asking Hans, 'Why is she often so sad?' Her depression that day so severe he had put her to bed and then sat with her until she slept.

'She lost a child. They were having an argument about money. She wanted him to sell one of their paintings; her husband didn't,' Hans had confided, his expression shuttered and grim. 'He pushed her and she fell downstairs.'

'Besides, it doesn't make sense closing the shop so soon after opening it,' Justine continued, her tone levelling.

'And your reasoning has nothing to do with there being another woman in his life?'

'Not at all,' she snapped, softening her words with a rueful grimace. 'Where money is concerned, the French have no room for sentiment. Besides, why should she have it all her own way,' neatly undoing her own argument. 'Oh, Maidy, why the hell did he have to fall in love with that woman? Most likely because she's beautiful and ten years younger than me,' she replied to her own question.

'Eight!'

'Poof!' Her eyebrows rose. 'Eight or ten, does it matter? She'll never appreciate him, not as I do. *Oh God, I do miss him.*'

'Is he so special?'

'Not to her,' she snarled. Her tone changed, becoming smooth again. 'To me he is, because I am of an age to appreciate someone like Hans.'

'I'm not quite sure I understand.' I breathed a sigh of relief, aware we were once again on solid ground and happy for Justine to talk.

'You're too young, that's why.'

The kettle began to boil and, reaching over, she removed it from the range. 'Will you do the *haricots verts*?'

Pulling the mound of beans within reach, I picked up a knife to top and tail them. 'You make it sound as if youth is a crime.'

She ignored my comment. 'How often do you meet a decent man? I promise, they're very rare.'

It was Jaan I remembered, kind, patient, never pushy. 'My brother Pieter was decent. Other than him, just the one.'

'And did you fall in love with him?' Almost triumphantly, she hopped up on the table swinging her legs. 'No!' She pointed her finger at me, answering the question herself. 'You fell for someone totally unsuitable – unreliable, irresponsible, and dishonest.' She meant her husband.

'I fell for someone magical,' I defended my choice.

'But totally unsuitable.'

I remembered the swan, the mutation that allowed men to change their shape.

'Yes.'

'Come,' she grabbed the knife out of my hand. 'I am hungry and want to eat dinner before midnight. Set the table and while you are doing that, think about what I was saying. Even magic eventually fades.'

Surprisingly, we had several similar conversations in the days before I left. 'Do you even want to leave?' she said, insisting I take my own time and not to hurry because that dratted woman wanted me to – her vocabulary as exotic as the figs she had bought that morning in the market.

I was packing, and Justine had wandered into my room. She'd not done that before, always keeping her distance. Even if she hadn't confessed to missing Hans, this would have been proof enough. And once I left, that chapter in her life might well be over for good. I didn't place great reliance on Ruth not overturning the decision to keep the shop in Flambeau, nor did I have confidence in Hans' promise of a visit to the ballet – both undoubtedly were empty words. Hans couldn't or wouldn't stand up to Ruth and soon the excitement of his first encounter with Justine would be superseded by memories more recently acquired.

'Do I have a choice?'

She was perched on my bed, as always the epitome of elegance, casually circling her finely boned ankles in the air while she talked. I would miss her, I knew that.

'There are always choices in life.'

I'm not sure if her words were addressed to me; she was staring at the ceiling at the time.

I laughed, replying in the same matter-of-fact tone, 'No, I don't want to go.'

'Then stop dancing to the tune of others.'

'You mean Ruth?' I screwed up my nose.

'If Ruth is what you take from that, then yes.' She held her foot up to inspect it. 'You can always tell a ballerina's toes – they're crooked.' Her tone changed. 'What is this hold she has over you? Some dark and dreadful secret from when you were babies?'

I didn't turn round, addressing her reflection in the mirror. 'She was older, stronger and more beautiful than me and...'

'And what?' She pounced on the word.

'That's how children make sense of the world.'

She pointed to my suitcase which was half full. 'Always leave a dress and a pair of shoes behind, then you'll have to return.' She skilfully changed the subject.

'Return?'

'It's the ploy men and women – lovers – have used for ever.' She waved her hand airily at the outrageous suggestion.

'You make it sound as if people spend all their time taking lovers.' I closed the empty drawer, placing my underwear, still faintly smelling of lavender, neatly on the bed.

'They do, at least the sensible ones do. What was I saying?'

'About Hans.'

'Hans said, no one in the family ever understood what went on in your mind. He never had.' Intrigued, I glanced up from my packing, wrapping the shoes I had worn for the theatre in tissue paper. 'He was telling me about all the different flights of stairs in your house, and the games you used to play on them when it was wet outside. I remember distinctly. There were stairs from the front door, from the shop, the workroom, and also from the backdoor up to the kitchen. He said you occupied a step no one else knew existed.' She sighed, her eyes widening. 'It was the most romantic thing he ever said.' She lapsed into giggles.

'Justine!' I admonished, placing the wrapped shoes carefully in my case.

Her eyes gleamed. 'I promise Hans doesn't do romance, at

least not often. He said his paintings were romantic enough.' She groaned dramatically and rolled over burying her face in a pillow. 'Hans blamed the fairy tales your brother told you.' She shot up, punching the pillow back into shape.

'It's possible,' I added thoughtfully. 'Pieter – he called me a changeling.'

'Hans said Pieter and Berthe were alike. He was different and so were you.'

It was an astonishing thing to say, given the reality of Pieter's birth, and yet quite true. Both were entirely practical, wanting nothing except to be part of the family unit that had occupied the Bader house for the past several centuries.

'Why did he leave?'

Without thinking, I trotted out the lie, so established in my mind even I had begun to accept it as truth. 'He fell in love with Ruth.'

She threw the pillow at me. 'Do us all a favour. When you get a chance, push her in front of a bus.'

PART THREE

22

As the bus reached the outskirts of Bordeaux, the magic that had held me in its thrall fell away like dollops of dried mud from the tyres. Maybe, I had experienced something similar on leaving New York, but now because of Zande's visit each nook and cranny had become invested with magic, even the crowded rooftops that flowed up the hillside like the carapace of some vast mythological creature. And when the dusk of November stole the daylight, footsteps passing in front of the shop were transformed into a column of soldiers marching up to the ramparts. And then, almost like an echo, others heading in the opposite direction became those of the retiring squad who, exhausted from watching siege-fires burn throughout the night, were making for their quarters in the old town to sleep. Into this magic, I poured the singing gargoyles and Justine, with her dramatic variations of mood. Hans was there too, making his bow, his paintings of the ballet shoes sublime.

Gradually as the mellow softness of south faded, the countryside became progressively more bleak in the wintry light, the rain lashing at the carriage windows, cold and disagreeable leaving me to mourn the sweetness of my previous visit to Paris.

'They call Paris the city of lovers. That is certainly true. It is also a city that knows how to fight. Not its leaders – they are made of marshmallow. Its people.' Justine's words, spoken at the bus stop, had been accompanied by a warm smile and, unexpectedly, a kiss on the cheek. 'There is a great deal of steel in you, Maidy, it's just a question of locating it. More surprising, I have grown fond of you; I never imagined I would.' She pointed at the oncoming bus, 'Now, go and knock some sense into your brother's head.'

Looking around, I wasn't too sure how I might achieve that; anyone viewing Ruth's surroundings for the first time would be reduced to silence. I was in a filmset in which nothing owed its presence to either nature or chance, its trees and shrubs displayed to supreme advantage as if a fleet of stylists had been engaged to arrange each twig and branch in the spot designed for them.

Of course, Ruth's apartment was large. The first floor of the modern block with views out across the river and, judging by the cars parked outside, it had been expensive. It must have been to warrant a gate across the entrance to the grounds, the driver of the limousine sent to collect me at the station, sweeping past the lodge with a peremptory toot on the horn. The sound dragged me back to the present. Having promised Justine I wouldn't look back, the moment I found myself alone, my thoughts had feloniously taken to their heels chasing back over our summer of sunshine and laughter.

Ruth met me at the door, although, already disorientated by the superiority of the doorman who escorted me upstairs, her first few sentences remained a blur, chattering excitedly, animation colouring her cheeks. Not that she needed it. She looked wonderful, wearing a dress of raw silk with a matching jacket.

'The limousine belongs to the studio,' she confirmed artlessly, although I was certain I hadn't asked that question. My mind felt like a restless fly flitting over the elegant surroundings, stunned to silence by a lustrous gleam of gold and gilt in the heavy brocade of the furnishings, the silk curtains covering the room-high windows gliding effortlessly at the touch of a button. 'Naturally, we don't own the apartment. The studio leased it.'

I remembered those words amidst the flood of information

coming my way, which included details of her secretary quitting and returning to America and a contract for a film in Hollywood the following year. 'We can return to France if we want when it's done. Never mind all that. First things first, Maidy. I don't want you to do anything except keep me company and … oh yes, I forgot … help me choose a nurse for the baby.'

At the best of times I am never garrulous, but rarely silent for days on end. At least, that's how it felt, that several days had elapsed since I'd last spoken, adrift among surroundings so superior my vocabulary proved insufficient for the demands being made on it, other than a repetitive, 'Oh, how beautiful.'

When I did eventually glance at my watch, I was astonished to discover less than thirty minutes had passed, not the hours I had envisaged, and it was barely four.

I blurted out. 'You can't bring a baby up here.'

Ruth laughed. 'Darling Maidy, what a lot you've got to learn about the film world. The furnishings aren't real, even the studio can't afford genuine antiques. In any case, as I told you, we'll be returning to America as soon as this film is done.'

I wanted to ask what had happened to her assurances of a gallery in Paris, changing it to, 'Does Hans know?'

'Of course.' She seemed amused than otherwise. 'He's so sweet. Really excited at the prospect of owning a gallery in New York.'

New York – the fulfilment of so many dreams. Yes, anyone would be thrilled when that particular carrot was dangled, so why was I thinking of the witch who lured Hansel and Gretel into her cottage with sweets?

'Now I'd better tell you the rules of the house.'

Perhaps the silence lasted no more than a second or two, yet to me still battling a sense of unreality, it seemed far longer. This was vintage Ruth playing her games, keeping all about her in suspense, waiting for that one word which, for one, might prove a stepping-stone to paradise.

'There aren't any.' She indicated a bell push on one side of the fireplace. 'Not until the staff leave. You do what you want. I must warn you, when I'm working, I go to bed shortly after eight. You'll need to as well.' She stretched out her arm grazing mine with her fingertips, 'We leave for the studio at five.'

'You're still working?'

She looked genuinely astonished, as if I had asked the one question for which there was no answer. 'Of course. I can't give up work, the film isn't finished. Besides, it needs me.' She smoothed her hand over her middle. 'Luckily, it's a period piece – Louis, something or other. In those clothes, the entire cast look pregnant. I have to turn sideways to get through a door.'

'Which Louis?' I said interested. 'This one?' I pointed to a chair, recognising the curved shape of its legs with tiny clawed feet, almost identical to the piece in Justine's sitting room. 'The fourteenth?'

'No, later than that. The one who was Emperor of Rome.'

'You mean Napoleon's nephew, Charles Louis Bonaparte? Who are you playing, Eugenie de Montijo, his wife?'

She pushed out her lips in a moue. 'And to think I was the clever one at school.'

For the third or fourth time in as many minutes, she glanced at her watch. 'I have to go out – a working dinner, I'm afraid.' She pointed to her outfit, the soft cream of the silk seamlessly complementing the colour of her skin. 'That's why I changed early. I said to Hans if you had arrived the other day when I expected you, we could have spent the evening catching up. We'll have to do that tomorrow now.' Her smiled flashed out. '*I know!* Come with me. You'll be meeting up with these people on a regular basis anyway – you know producers, directors...'

'Not Hans?'

'Goodness no, not Hans.' She gurgled with laughter that sounded surprisingly natural. 'No, he's my wonderful stay-at-home husband.'

'Except he's not your husband.' I reminded her.

'He soon will be. No, sadly business means Roland. You will come, won't you.' She reached out grasping my hands in hers.

'I can't. I've nothing suitable to wear, at least not with me.'

She laughed triumphantly. 'Welcome to my world.' She crossed to the phone. 'Everything is possible, and nothing is too much trouble.' She spoke into the receiver. 'Chloe, I need you to go down to wardrobe and pick out a dress.'

For a moment her words baffled me then my brain worked it out; she was speaking English. Without noticing, I had slipped effortlessly back into Dutch, obviously the language of the house since Hans didn't speak any English.

She swung round eyeing me up and down. 'Size four, I expect, and any colour except ecru; I'm wearing that. Nothing wishy-washy like pink – that's for blonds. My friend looks better in dark colours.'

Putting down the receiver, she swivelled on her heels. 'Do you remember the twinset I bought you – the magenta one? What a long time ago that seems. I was a nobody then. Now look at me.'

'Who was that?' We were back to speaking Dutch.

'My secretary.'

'Didn't you say she'd left?'

'That was Margaret, the girl you met in New York who drove my car. This one is new and flew over last week.' She sat down again, almost primly smoothing her skirt with her one hand. Other gestures had also emerged since I'd last seen her, twiddling her engagement ring round and round, and running her fingers down the back of her stockings to straighten the seam. 'I keep a list of girls who write in asking to join my staff; Chloe happens to be one of my most loyal fans and has seen all my films dozens of times. She knows my lines better than me.' Ruth's laugh was a mass-produced effort, like the obligatory full stop at the end of a sentence. 'Can you imagine? Her very first day here, I was signing autographs and she put me right on a line.' Unaware, her mouth tightened. 'Naturally, I rewarded her with a chance of a lifetime and now I take her everywhere with me.'

There came a knock on the door, and a maid appeared carrying a silver tray. Ruth nodded her thanks. 'Coffee?'

'In that case, Ruth,' I pursued my argument, determined not to be diverted. 'Why do you need me?'

She hesitated, the phrase *why do you need me* left hanging. This uncertainty was also new, and I saw clearly what I should have spotted that day in New York; the confidence Ruth always demonstrated had become fragmented. Doubt had crept in. About what? Not her beauty nor her talent. Both were in plain sight.

'Because everyone here is a rival.'

There was no affectation or pretence in her voice, not this time. This was something she knew and believed implicitly and she could share it with me because she had never once considered me as a rival.

Surprisingly I wasn't hurt or upset. Long ago, I might have been; not now. In three years, I had learned to live my own life. 'What about your husband?' I said intrigued, considering her separation from her husband after two months of marriage worthy of its own film script.

'Roland? He's the worst.' She laughed. 'Would you believe, while we were together, he'd ask Greg to check how many fan letters I got that week, and then ask his pals to write in, so he had more than me. That's why we separated. I am so lucky, having you and Hans. Neither of you want to upstage me. Now, enough about me. What about you? Hans told me you know about paintings,' she hurried on.

'Don't you remember, how on wet weekends, he'd take me with him to the museum?'

'Did he?' Her voice changed, excitement taking over. 'Oh, what fun we're going to have remembering the olden days.'

'What olden days?' A familiar voice broke in.

'Hans!'

He looked changed from when I had last seen him, his flamboyant style consigned to the dustbin of the south. With his hair cut shorter and wearing a smart sports jacket over dark trousers, he reminded me of a caged bird that had had its wings clipped.

He picked her up, whirling her round. 'Happy?'

'Now Maidy's here, I am. Thank you, darling.' She glanced

back over her shoulder. 'I wanted to spend the evening, just the three of us, and we have to go out.'

'Maidy too?'

'Oh, yes,' she breathed. 'I want her to see what I'm up against. It's business which means Roland will be there.'

Hans groaned and placed her back on the ground. 'I wish he'd clear off.'

She kissed him on his cheek. 'Darling, I hate it as much as you do, especially the love scenes. Ugh!' She shuddered dramatically. 'As soon as this film's done, he will be history, I promise.'

I recognised the tone of voice, as familiar as the promises that had always accompanied it.

I hadn't grasped how close the apartment building was to Paris itself. On leaving the railway station at Montparnasse, the traffic had been dense, made worse by a downpour that slowed it to a crawl, and the journey to the river-side complex had taken for ever. Now less than ten minutes brought Ruth and I to the door of the restaurant. So different from the tiny eatery on Sixth Avenue frequented by Uncle Joe and his friends. Here, the royal blue and gold canopy stretched to the kerbside, and it was crowded with fans alerted by the presence of news reporters, their autograph albums clasped in their outstretched hands like begging bowls.

As the car drew to a halt, she tapped me on the hand. 'I was so happy to see you, I forgot earlier, please remember to call me Grace. I don't mind when we're alone in the apartment. Hans calls me Ruthy – that's his pet name.' She glanced up as the chauffeur opened the door, 'And I always get out first.'

Stung by the rebuke, I retorted, 'Who alerted the press, your new secretary or your husband?'

She giggled, the popping flashlights almost drowning her next words. 'I promise it wasn't me. I forgot!'

'Miss Manning, Miss Manning – who is that lady I see you with?'

Recognising the voice, I swung round. 'Greg,' I exclaimed,

both relieved and delighted to see a familiar face, his smile warm and welcoming.

That was the nicest thing about him and I instantly forgot the sting of Ruth's rebuke in the excitement of meeting up again. 'What are you doing here?'

'Singing for my supper. Roland's inside.' Taking my arm, he opened the restaurant door, the *maître d'* obsequiously waiting for reporters to finish asking their questions before ushering Ruth into the restaurant. 'Am I glad to see you.'

'What happened to your glasses.'

He pointed to his breast pocket, a corner of the frame poking out. 'No longer wear them in public, if I can help it. And yes, before you tell me, I am that vain. It's living with beautiful people. Fame is pernicious. It rubs off on you. I can always see to eat and tonight I'm in clover, with both a decent dinner *and* decent conversation.'

'Still into food,' I smiled an acknowledgement of his compliment,

'Absolutely. I live to eat. Still, I'm glad to see you don't. You look really something.' He slowly drew his eye from neck to hem. The blood-red silk of my borrowed dress was off-the shoulder and fitted me like a piece of sculpture and I had worn my hair loose over a matching cape, although that was barely required, the heater in the limousine at full blast. 'Who chose the dress?'

'Chloe, Ruth's new secretary.' I hesitated, wondering if the poor girl would still have her job after tonight. 'I didn't own anything suitable.'

Hans had accompanied us down to the car, Ruth insisting he much preferred spending the evening at the club, and pointing towards a stretch of brightly lit buildings further down the boulevard. As we drove away, he had called out, 'Never seen you look this pretty, Maidy. You should be a film star.' I caught the brotherly mockery, although picking up on Ruth's expression, she hadn't.

'She won't last long, then,' Greg confirmed. 'Someone should have told her never to let anything or anyone outshine the star.

Come on. A word of warning; don't be surprised if Roland makes a play for you.'

'Oh, I do hope not.' I spoke without thinking, recalling his distressing approach at the wedding.

'Sensible girl.' He patted my arm approvingly. 'Still, on this occasion, I refuse to blame him; you have to know how sensational you look. And, although men, if they plan to live to the following day, should never tell a woman she looks older ... you do.' I waited, amused by his hesitant expression. 'Not precisely older,' he hastily backtracked, rushing on, 'Not as light-hearted. It suits you.' He smiled, his gaze resting on my face. 'At least it suits the dress.'

Even our entrance into the restaurant was stage-managed, although not obviously so. Roland was waiting in the lobby, carefully holding the door for Ruth to enter first. Seeing them together, I doubted the reality of what I had been told, the glance they shared that of two people madly in love, Ruth with her hand resting on his jacket sleeve. Then I recalled that these were actors, skilled in the art of misdirection.

Apart from one woman, the rest of the party were men. Seeing Ruth approach, they leapt to their feet, their sycophantic smiles much in evidence, and I was surprised to hear one call out to Greg, 'who is that?' and beating the hovering waiter, slide a chair out from the table for me to sit down.

'Told you,' Greg whispered taking the seat next to mine. 'It's the dress.' He sounded almost triumphant, as if he was personally responsible for its creation.

'It's not mine,' I reminded.

'Doesn't matter. Find out where it came from and buy one like it.'

'I don't want to be a film star.' I argued, wanting to close the door on the subject.

'How can you say such a thing – its sacrilege.' Greg glared fiercely, immediately ruining the effect with a broad smile. 'At least in this company, it is. May I remind you, those girls and lads waiting for autographs, they'd give anything to be in your shoes.

One word to that man...' He nodded surreptitiously at the man who had held my chair, now talking with Roland. Noticing our interest, he lifted his glass, toasting me. 'And you're made.'

Acknowledging the gesture with a smile, I whispered to Greg. 'Who is he?'

'He's the money bags. Makes his millions investing in films. Fortunately for you, that's his wife. The other two are producers.'

'What do they do?'

'They put the project together, make it all happen.'

'And him?' I indicated the man seated next to the movie mogul's wife.

'He's Roland's lawyer.'

'Is he needed?' I said astonished.

'At a business dinner. Absolutely.' He lowered his voice. 'That's why they broke up, although you didn't hear that from me. Roland made his name long before Grace Manning came on the scene. She was plain – except she was never plain – Ruth Endersby then. Now she's a bigger star than him and she's clever. Unfortunately, for dear old Roland, he isn't. The current fight is about their billing. He insists his name has top billing.'

I recalled Ruth's comment. 'Does it matter, if they're no longer making films together?'

'Who told you that?' he gazed at me mystified.

'R ... er ... Grace.'

He laughed. 'I told you she was clever. A magazine recently published an article in which she spoke about the actors she wanted to work with. All the *really* big names. Success depends a great deal on tactics. If it's rumoured Grace is moving on, her price for another film with Roland just got higher. That's what audiences want; Grace and Roland together again.' He counted on his fingers. 'They've made two – and the appetite for another is strong.'

Our conversation lapsed as food arrived, Greg giving the foie gras with strips of toast his full attention, the lobster even more so. And the food was delicious, nevertheless, feeling somewhat like a goldfish in a bowl, on view for all to see, I found it difficult to think about food. The reverse of Roland's lawyer, who positively courted attention, keeping up a monologue, his hectoring tones so loud people at the nearby tables remained silent, their conversations battered into submission.

When I confided in Greg, he laughingly retorted that the 'fish scenario' was quite usual. 'You'll get used to it.'

'And the loud voices?'

'Those? Something lawyers acquire after a lifetime of shouting down warring couples.'

Admittedly, the lawyer wasn't allowed all his own way; the contentious issues of contracts drawing a sharp retort from one of the producers who, equally as loud, made his remarks in Morse Code, his phrasing abrupt and sharp.

'Are they aware…?'

'That other people are present?' Greg idly ran his gaze around the table, watching the spats of conversation; sentences flung out to one and then another, although none of the men bothered about the mogul's wife. He didn't either, other than a casual, 'May I introduce, Rita, my wife.'

'Of course. Why else do they wear Italian suits and silk ties if not to show off. Tomorrow, it will be shirt sleeves and sneakers. Nothing about this business is what it appears on the surface. If you're a natural cynic and accept it's a game that plays by its own rules, you might just escape unscathed.' He pointed to the *maître d'* who, bowing from the waist, welcomed a couple into the restaurant. 'No one bows that way. He knows at the end of the evening, his tip will pay school fees for his son or daughter, or it will provide a family holiday. 'Don't be fooled, Maidy. They call it the film business and that's what it is … pure business.'

Greg pushed his plate away, having already cleared the salad served in the traditional French manner followed by crème brûlée. 'When can we meet up again? Not tomorrow, we're in the studio all day. Thursday and Friday the same. Saturday, a magazine wants to interview Roland which means we'll be out on the water.'

'He sails?'

'Rather. That's the one time he forgets to be Roland. We were born in Brooklyn and Dad used to take us sailing as kids. I'm off Monday. Could we meet up and go somewhere? I know, I'll take you shopping. I'm brilliant. Know all the best shops.'

Unsure if he was joking, I enquired tentatively. 'How is clothes shopping for women something you know about?'

He grinned. 'A lot of women have passed through Roland's bedroom. It's my job to send them a gift next day by way of a thank you.'

'I'm—'

I stared across the table at my fellow diners, snippets of conversation drifting across the flowers and the wine glasses.

'Shocked, surprised. Wondering why I do it?'

'All of those, I suppose. What broke them up?'

'Surprisingly, they weren't bad together.' He nodded at Ruth, her hand gracing the tip of her husband's sleeve. 'They're actually very alike and on the surface get on well.' He hesitated, unsure if he should continue.

'What?'

'Their egos got in the way, leaving them with nothing to talk about.'

I nodded, understanding Ruth's use of the word *rival*. 'So why are you telling me?'

'Because I've got a script and you want to be a writer.'

'Did I tell you that?' I said, before remembering Greg was bound to know more about me than I did about him, it was his job.

He grinned at me. 'Yes, in a roundabout way. You mentioned a couple of books you'd read and said you enjoyed history, and since the subject matter is Grace Manning and you know her better than anyone ... although, not as Grace Manning. To you she's Ruth Endelbaum, the daughter of a diamond cutter.'

I started up. 'You know about that?'

'Yes, I also know Lilian, his fiancé. Their family is well regarded among the immigrant community; our grandparents lived in the same street in Brooklyn.'

Before leaving for New York, I had read up on the history

of the city and its population, so many of them migrants, and it seemed to me astonishing that two people who had never met before, and who lived thousands of miles apart and separated by water, should discover they had acquaintances in common.

'Why her? There are other people far more interesting you could write about.'

'Because people need magic in their lives, and a rags to riches story is pure box office.'

23

Box office! The words repeated themselves over and over next morning as the limousine drove through the almost silent streets, although it was the people we had left behind in the restaurant I was thinking about. A sudden stirring at our table as the lawyers and producers, having completed their business, stood up, alerted not only the staff but also everyone else in the room to their imminent departure. This was followed, if doubt still existed, by loudly voiced compliments and the stealthy rustling of notes pushed into a grateful pocket. Finally, aware of what was required, the two stars, Grace and Roland, swung round for that all-important last glimpse of the restaurant – an even more elaborate charade acted out with a mock grimace and a rueful smile – implying: *why didn't you inform me there were other people present?*

Waving, they led the way out, leaving behind an atmosphere buzzing with excitement, and I guessed even the most insignificant of incidents was being gathered up to pass on to another equally eager audience, wanting to hear every detail: the elegance of a shoe, the sparkling brilliance of a pair of earrings or a tie pin. Even the most trivial of gestures would be enhanced into something long-lasting and majestic, into which superlatives such a *glamorous, marvellous,* and *so exciting* would be scattered.

Was I any different? Before departing, my admirer came over to give me his card. 'If there is anything,' he murmured before accompanying his wife out of the restaurant. I'd no intention of following up on it, nevertheless, I was still thrilled by the compliment. Maybe … if I wanted it?

The excitement of the evening kept me awake, discovering the apartment to be eerily silent; a phenomenon that had its origin in doors that closed tightly over deep-pile carpets and plumbing interred within sound-proofed piping. My bedroom had been decked out in shades of duck-egg blue, its chandeliers and silk wallpaper something Ruth might accept as her due although I doubted if I ever could. Admittedly, it was the identical sensation to the one I experienced that first night in Flambeau, and I had grown to love my bedroom there, with its nightly accompaniment of music that drifted across the square from the bistro, lulling me to sleep. Once or twice in the night, I got up and wandered over to the window. Leaning out, I was greeted by silence – not black but coloured grey where streetlamps had lifted away the darkness.

I must have slept because it was the operator ringing me on the bedside phone that woke me and I swung out of bed, the warm lighting camouflaging the reality that awaited us outside, the darkness infiltrated by flakes of snow and a biting wind.

'We'll eat at the studio.' Ruth, muffled in a scarf and dark glasses, her fur coat wrapped tightly around her, huddled into the corner of the car, reading her day's lines with the aid of a light attached to the side panel of the limousine.

The previous night, I'd asked Hans what to expect. 'Can't help you there. Ruthy and me, we keep our lives separate.' Nevertheless, it was a surprise when we arrived and stepped out of the car in front of what looked like an empty warehouse, to find the darkness instantly blown away by a salvo of cheerful voices and an explosion of light.

Chloe was there, sifting papers from one box to another. She didn't speak, except for an occasional, 'read this,' to Ruth who was being fussed over by several people at once, hairdressers and make-up artists. A knock on the door heralded a disembodied head and hands clutching a clipboard and pencil, as checks were made on the gown and hairstyle to be worn in the first scene of the day. A more intrusive knocking announced the delivery of a tray of jewellery, 'copies of the pieces worn by the Empress,' the stylist said, presenting it to Ruth.

Realising I wasn't either needed or wanted, I took my coffee and croissant into the studio, the working heart of filming, and found myself blinded by lights, raised voices bellowing out instructions that controlled both their appearance and disappearance. Backdrops descended from the gods in regulation; one moment it was the outside of a palace with sunrise over a nearby hillside, the next, a throne room, the white alabaster surface of the pillars almost more natural than the genuine article. Floodlights focused on the interior of a ballroom with a gilded ceiling; moving from segment to segment, they glided slowly across the massive canvas propelled by surreptitious movement. Then as the moon rose up into the sky, doors were thrust open onto a terrace to offset the imaginary heat of the ballroom and that of its participants.

'That's it,' shouted a disembodied voice, followed by a moment of stillness and tranquillity before a second piece of equipment in need of checking was lowered into view.

'It's far less complicated to shoot a modern film than a period piece.' Greg had confided between courses last night at dinner. 'It may take as much as three, four hours, to get it all worked out, the stars dressed and everything checked. By comparison the actual shot takes only a few minutes. I'll say that for her. Grace, she's good,' he had added the praise. 'Usually gets it in one. Was she always an actress?'

Of course she was. She always had been, reality hidden inside the locked box in her mind. 'Yes, she's always loved acting.'

'She's good with Roland too. He knows it and resents it, but even he accepts the arrival of the baby will help their careers.'

'What?' I exclaimed, thinking I'd heard wrong. 'He knows about the baby, what about Hans?'

'Hans who?' Greg replied.

'No, Greg. I can't believe…' My voice rose, shocked.

'That's just it, Maidy. You can't bring belief into this world. Cynicism, maybe. Nevertheless, if you're going to survive in this industry, that's the first of the Ten Commandments. Forget about reality.'

Now, as if I had called to him, he appeared. Nursing a mug of coffee, he made his way across the cable-strewn floor sitting alongside me. 'Recovered from your ordeal by fire?'

I smiled a welcome. 'Ask me that after my second cup of coffee.'

'Thank Roland for the coffee – he chose the blend. Refuses to drink anything else. It's part of his contract.'

'You aren't serious?'

'Oh, I am. That's good,' he exclaimed, taking a sip. 'I don't approve of much Roland does but his taste in both coffee and wine is superb. Things like coffee, the colour of their dressing room and which flowers they prefer, are written into the Appendix – that's the one below the line containing all the noughts.'

I felt I was back in school, set adrift among subjects I found baffling. 'Last night, you mentioned the Ten Commandments? What are they?'

He didn't reply for a moment, watching one of the men shin up a rope to the gantry, and adjust one of the powerful spotlights. 'It's a term lawyers use when writing up a contract. If you accept that nothing is what it appears unless its written-on paper and signed, you'll get by okay.' He pointed to the man standing by a camera, mimicking the shape of the lens with his hands and peering through them. 'Here, truth is what the camera makes of it. Take their lives...' He seemed content to talk and I to listen. 'The weekly fan magazines do a roaring business, and in every one you will find at least a mention, and most weeks a story, about the two of them. I know because I buy them for Roland. And, as far as the fans are concerned, if its printed in a magazine, it has to be true.' I caught the sarcastic undertone. 'Grace and Roland make films together and are married. Of course they're happy, how could it be otherwise? The business of their not living together is never mentioned. Even the press haven't sniffed that one out yet

– nor news of the baby. Roland and Grace enter the apartment building by the same front door,' his tone changed, becoming almost flippant. 'Ergo they live together. Actually, we lease the apartment above yours, and it's my name on the contract.'

By the end of the afternoon, unused to such an early start, all I wanted to do was sleep and I hoped Ruth had nothing planned for later.

'No,' she confirmed, 'We'll have dinner with Hans and then bed. What did you think?'

'About filming?'

'I meant my performance.'

Earlier in the day, I'd noticed a book about the life of Jean Louis Bonaparte on one of the shelves in Ruth's dressing room and asked if I might borrow it to read. Now I pulled it out. 'What an extraordinary life that family must have led. Have you read it?'

'That's my secretary's job, I don't have the time. Margaret read it before she left and gave me her notes.'

'But...'

'Honestly, Maidy, you've not changed one bit.' Her tone hardened. 'You can't come in here and think you know all about the film business in a day. Have you read the script?'

'Not yet.'

She pounced on the lapse. 'Read it; don't bother with the book. The script provides quite sufficient material as to how the character should be played. Have you seen any of my films yet?'

'One – in New York.'

'And the cinema was full?'

I hesitated, thinking back. 'Yes.'

'Exactly.' She sounded triumphant. 'That's all the producer and director ask of us, full cinemas. And I give them that.'

Taking no further notice of me, she closed her eyes. I turned away, staring out through the window to the dark streets beyond, hoping Ruth hadn't picked up on my smile when I recalled Greg and his preoccupation with the Ten Commandments. Tomorrow, when we met up, I would ask if the film playing to full theatres was the second one.

Hans greeted Ruth with a shout of joy, picking her up and swinging her round. 'No, I didn't get out,' he replied to my question. 'Too wet. It had to be for me to stay in. No idea how you people manage being stuck indoors. I most definitely need a studio.' Replacing her on the ground, he helped her off with her coat.

His adoration was so very evident, it was almost embarrassing, wearing it on his sleeve like a silk patch. Growing up, he had concealed his feelings for Ruth from everyone except Pappy's penetrating gaze. Now, there was no need. To him she was like some hard fought-for trophy, something so treasured it was kept on a high shelf where no damage could possibly befall such a precious object, and never taken down except to dust it.

'What do you think of my amazing wife, the actress?'

I hesitated, unsure if that had been a slip of the tongue before realising Hans was old-fashioned enough to believe he and the woman carrying his child must marry.

'It was exciting. You should go and watch.'

The words were out before I realised how tactless they were. Naturally Hans couldn't go to the studio; that was Roland's preserve. What a mess. No good wishing on a star for better tidings. A mess of this magnitude would, undoubtedly, end in an acrimonious divorce and money bartered between greedy lawyers.

Ruth reached up kissing Hans on the cheek. 'He couldn't possibly – he'd hate it. Besides, he's a real artist, not some hack hired to paint scenery.'

It was a strange evening in which I took little part, slipping silently into the role of onlooker that I always assumed in childhood. Ruth lavished smiles on Hans and blew kisses, offering snippets of gossip circulating among cast members, and Hans matched her with remarks made by a jobbing actor he'd met at the club, who was working in various jobs while waiting for his big break. Tending bar seemed the most popular. Despite her long day, Ruth's stories bubbled with spontaneity and laughter, yet there was none of that easy camaraderie Hans had shared with Justine, where both fur and feathers marked the fires of battle or more often laughter. He treated Ruth like some delicate hothouse plant, his adulation of the moon-goddess whom he'd worshipped from afar for so many years on view for all to see. Even now, he couldn't believe she was actually his.

Yet within an hour or two, I felt a burgeoning disquiet, their conversation reverting constantly to nostalgia – what we had done when we were young, either Ruth or Hans or both swinging round in my direction seeking confirmation. There had to be more between them than the memory of our quayside homes and the social triumphs of the families who lived there? What had happened to the man who argued with Justine, roaring with both laughter and irritation at her remarks, yet who, next day, created a piece of such brilliance you couldn't take your eyes off it? In this turgid atmosphere, how was it even possible for his artistic temperament to flourish. From that, it wasn't much of a leap to my guess the real reason for Ruth's invitation had been to infuse a fresh perspective into stories already traded to boredom.

Only when Hans brought up the subject of the gallery did the conversation achieve any sense of value, insisting Paris to be the city for art.

'I was talking about it at the club,' his tone brightened. 'There's a pretty formidable array of talent there: musicians, artists, architects, also writers,' and he had smiled at me. 'It makes sense to site the gallery in Paris since I speak French fluently. I'll sound like a foreigner in New York.'

'Darling, everyone sounds like a foreigner in New York.'

'Not someone trying to get a toe in the artworld, Ruthy. How can I possibly explain why I painted something and what it means, if I don't know the words? I can't say to a prospective purchaser, will you speak slowly please, I don't understand?' He glanced slyly, and I duly laughed, well aware that had been my favourite phrase for months after arriving in France.

'Darling, English is so much easier than French. I learned it in six months. Besides, I've already written to Papa asking him to find us a place.'

'But Ruthy...' She raised her eyebrows at him. 'I promised Maidy she would be manager.'

'Maidy can come with us. I'll ask Greg to keep an eye on her. I could see how smitten he was at dinner last night.'

I couldn't believe Ruth's referring to me in the third person, as if I wasn't in the room. I waited, expecting Hans to challenge the statement. He didn't, silently warning me to let it go.

I was so angry, had the lure of trying my hand at writing a script not been there, like a fat fly on the end of a fishing line, I might well have found some excuse to leave next morning. Admittedly, I knew the cause of her sniping and it wasn't her secretary's choice of a dress. That had irked, but after receiving a barrage of compliments from her dinner companions, her hand kissed repeatedly, and flowers sent to the studio next morning, her error had been overlooked. This was a resurgence of our childhood preoccupation with age, when even a day or two in the calendar signified superiority, something I'd forgotten until Ruth's make-up artist raised the subject.

Gossiping about nothing much while the young woman skilfully applied the correct shade of face powder and rouge to Ruth's skin, she had introduced the subject of women in the film-world, declaring how unfair that they managed so few years at the top. 'Men are lucky; lines are positively *de rigueur* for a male actor. My last film,' she chatted on, 'I was actually asked by the director to add laughter lines. With a woman, it's the reverse. In our instructions, words are often underlined – must look eighteen. I've nothing but sympathy for those still trying to make it at twenty-four. They should be sensible and do what I did – find a job.'

And Ruth who would be twenty in a couple of months and already ultra-sensitive about her burgeoning shape had, in her own mind, already crossed that milestone, while I, several months her junior, hadn't.

As Christmas came and went, I got used to saying Greg and I, our names frequently teamed together. He had made it quite clear he would love to place our friendship on a more formal basis and I had told him the truth.

'In that case, I will have to wait for you to fall out of love with the guy and, in the meanwhile, we will go shopping and I will make myself indispensable until it's my face that fills your dreams.'

'And the script?'

He laughed, rolling his eyes. 'After my oh-so-gallant gesture, *that* stung.'

'You do remind me of Roland when you laugh.'

He yelped loudly. 'That's even worse. You certainly know how to put a man down. I have no desire to become my brother as you, I hope, have no plans to copy Grace.'

'You know I haven't. But I don't mind writing about her.'

He sighed. 'Another hint!' he said dolefully, only his eyes merrily disputing his words. 'In that case did you know the studio is hosting a party New Year's Night and you are my partner?'

'I am?'

'Doesn't Grace tell you these things?' He joined in my laughter as I shook my head. 'Come on, let's go shopping and you can tell me all about the girl next door.'

At the studio, our constantly being together sparked rumours and inuendo and although there was nothing romantic in those meetings, I grew to appreciate spending time with him, despite working sessions that ended in argument, especially when Greg applied a stopwatch to sentences he decreed as boring or verbose. 'If our heroine says that line, half the people in the audience won't understand it, the rest will walk out of the cinema and demand their money back.'

For me, used to a diet of leisurely prose, the requirements of a script to convey its meaning in as few words as possible proved a difficult concept to grasp. Yet, as much as I hated Greg's constant demands for a re-write, a juggling of the phrases I'd so painstakingly created the night before, he knew his business and slowly the script under his tutelage began to take shape.

Gradually, as the birth of the baby grew closer, it ushered in a happier time for us all, the reminiscences between Hans and Ruth replaced by a discussion of the future and the many changes having a child would bring. Those were conversations I was happy to participate in, amused by the sparring between Hans and Ruth about names and sex, with Hans insisting it would be a girl because Berthe had had a second boy.

'How on earth is that remotely scientific?' I enquired, smiling. Ruth had sided with me on that occasion, so that for an instant it really was like old times, rather than the boring facsimile of the previous months churned out night after night; something new we all wanted to pursue.

Except for the ballet.

Planning it as a surprise, when Hans sprang it on Ruth, she grabbed the tickets out of his hand, and tore them to pieces.

'How could you! Your old girlfriend?' She stormed. 'And old is the right word. Why would I want to see some pensioner creep around the stage.'

'Because the whole of Paris is talking about it.' His tone remained level, despite his clenched fists. 'Life doesn't begin and end with the movies, Ruth.'

Was that the moment?

I know I held my breath. Never once in my hearing had he called her Ruth. Silently I urged him on, my loyalties all with Justine, and I was disappointed when he said nothing further.

In the end, he and I went together, fortunate enough to get two returns in the top circle. Did he tell Ruth? I didn't ask and he didn't say.

It was a new production of Giselle although Justine hadn't been their first-choice. The ballerina chosen for the part had broken her arm, and Justine had been awarded the prize because she was familiar with the role, having danced it before her marriage. That much I knew, keeping silent about the occasional letter she and I exchanged. She only ever wrote a few lines, her handwriting as eloquent as her presence, with an unusual choice of words that set the page alight, equally as her dancing did the theatre – its audience reduced to awed silence. I'm not certain if Hans breathed at all while she was on stage, her portrayal of the young innocent girl quite sublime, her movements as lithe as any teenager's. At that moment, if a window had opened at the back of the stage, she would have floated through. Hans had bought a pair of opera glasses, handing me coins for the pair fitted to the seat in front – neither of us wanting to miss a single movement whether the slow adagio with her partner or the exquisite high-reaching *jettés* that formed part of her solo, or even the final scene where Giselle, betrayed on all sides, goes mad.

I know I wept and Hans was reduced to silence, turning to me after the final curtain when Justine, her arms full of flowers had taken her last bow. 'I was a damn fool, wasn't I?'

I wanted to shout, yes. Instead, I asked, 'what about the baby?'

It was his shrug that told me his decision. The relationship between Justine and Hans was no longer any different from the ballet performance we had just witnessed: splendid maybe but not real life.

Filming was finished by the end of February and, by then, although she refused to admit it, Ruth was thankful, at least on the surface. The studio had appointed a body-double for distance shots a few weeks previously and she so resented the substitution, religiously attending the studio every working day in case she was called for a re-shoot, the limousine diligently driving us – maybe two hours later, at seven rather than five – and avidly watching scenes in which her character was involved, smiling to cue and hating every minute. A 'that's great,' from the director to her stand-in or a scattering of applause from the crew reduced her to tears. Tears only I got to witness, wiping them hurriedly away if anyone knocked on her dressing room door.

'For pity's sake, Ruth. Stay at home,' Hans pleaded. 'Make time for the baby and for yourself.'

'You don't understand,' she complained. 'If you were an actor, you'd know how it feels to see someone else wearing your clothes and stealing your scene.'

He didn't argue, and he didn't add the words, *then stay at home for me* because he was never there either. In the weeks before the birth, even on mornings when, reluctantly, Ruth was too tired to get up, he went out, despite Ruth's tears at his selfishness, taking his work satchel with him. Driven out for a walk by a lack of air in the apartment, I couldn't apportion blame. I too found the wintry skies fascinating, watching an endless coverlet of winter grey crack open to reveal a trace of blue, before the clouds jealously darkened again and released cold rain onto the already saturated fields.

At that moment I, too, would have loved to have been an artist able to bring such scenes to life as Hans did.

Except he wasn't doing that.

'What are those?' I pointed to his portfolio, a Japanese symbol on its cover revealing the name of the manufacturer. An expensive brand, too expensive for our small shop – even though Hans insisted we call it an emporium, 'because it's better than a shop' – each of the heavy sheets protected by a layer of transparent vellum.

He blushed, like a kid caught with its fingers in the toffee jar, saying offhandedly, 'It's just something I wanted to do for the baby.'

They were water colours, a medium Hans rarely used, the first pages of winter grasses revealing a delicacy I never imagined existed in that clumsy youth who stumbled on the stairs when he had drunk too much the night before and overslept. Reluctant to remove my gaze from one image in order to see the next, I slowly turned the pages, wishing I might possess the multi-facetted eyes of a fly, able to view them all together, dazzled by the breadth and depth of his talent. Using the finest of brushes, the drawings presented a glimpse of winter before spring tiptoes over the threshold: snowdrops half-hidden by a fall of snow, a single flower, bolder than all the rest, flaunting its green inner skirt to any insect made reckless by a glimpse of sunlight. Then marching in a parade of military magic came regiments of soldiers shouldering green pikes, and wearing silly white helmets with green frills on their heads. A cascade of early flowers followed, celandines with their florets of gold floating on a pool of green leaves and the timid cowslip, a ball of flowers like yellow toffee-apples on a stick.

On the next page, shy violets blushed and hid behind their leaves, while catkins dancing on the breeze flaunted their frilly skirts. Birds featured too, blackbirds with glossy feathers scavenged among dead leaves, a robin with a grub in its beak, and an earwig sheltered from the rain under a rotting piece of wood.

They were so delicate yet so precise, I wished Pappy could have seen them. He would have been overjoyed to discover all the arguments and disputes had not been in vain and his most irascible pupil had finally acquired the skills he had so longed to teach him.

'Hans, they're exquisite. The brushwork – the delicacy reminds me of Grandfather's paintings,' I complimented.

He blushed with pleasure. 'Brushwork?' he teased. 'How come you're suddenly an expert on brushwork?'

'Justine was a good teacher,' I reminded.

24

Beth was born on March 31, the weather worse than inclement, floods and gales surging across the borders of several countries, although in Ruth's room there was only sunlight, her many admirers turning it into a spring bower of flowers and cards.

'Will you write and tell Papa in America? He'll be so thrilled and don't forget to tell him that she has been called Elizabeth after Mama. Is she pretty? Hans says so.'

'Haven't you seen her?'

'Of course, only she was red and crying then and I'm not allowed out of bed for a week.' She picked up a large envelope and waved it at me. 'The studio forwarded me a script, the film in Hollywood I told you about. That will keep me amused until I get out of here.'

Hans visited daily and, discovering her room full of visitors, tight-lipped he vanished off to see the baby. 'Beth,' he insisted, 'her name is Beth,' standing with his nose pressed to the nursery window until some kindly nurse took pity on him and allowed him inside.

I'd never seen Ruth look more beautiful. Roland obviously thought so too because he haunted her room, persuading her into doing a series of photographs and an article for a top magazine.

'It's not my fault,' she flushed when I complained how unfair she was being. 'Visitors always ask for Grace Manning.'

'Grace Manning possibly; not Roland de Courcy. What is he doing here? You left his bed a long time ago.' I commented, as startled by my vulgarity as Ruth obviously was.

Justine's influence, of course. She'd always complained I was too mealy-mouthed. 'There's fire somewhere,' she had rebuked. 'Find it.'

And I had found it, although I wasn't exactly sure who I was angry with: Ruth or Grace?

'He's starting his own production company,' Ruth defended Roland.

'And that's more important than your future with Hans?'

'Oh, grow up, Magrit, and stop trying to put me down. Look at that business with the script. This has nothing to do with Hans, Roland and I are business partners – that's all.'

'Can't you see how it hurts him when Roland takes pride of place in the publicity shots?'

'Oh, that's nothing.' Irritably she flicked over the pages of the magazine she was reading, the impatient gesture dismissing my words. 'They were taken for the fan magazines. You know how they are. Besides, Hans knows I love only him.'

Frustrated by her blinkered arrogance, I pounced on Greg when he passed on the story of the magazine article that showed Beth in her mother's arms. 'For goodness sake, remind Roland he's not the father, and to keep away.'

'Provided you explain to Hans that in the eyes of the law, he is.'

'That can't possibly be right,' I exclaimed, shocked but frightened too. 'Ruth – I mean Grace wouldn't do that to him, would she?'

'For pity's sake, Maidy, do yourself a favour and strip off the blindfold.'

Earlier we'd been working on the script and he snatched off his spectacles, using them as a pointer. 'I warned you about the Ten Commandments. They should be printed and distributed to would-be starlets and hangers on, except no doubt they'd be obsolete before the ink even dries. Here's another you can add to the list: If the truth can't advance your career and a lie can – use the lie.'

The pages of the script stung my hand and I hastily flung it down. 'That's what this is. This polite, emotionally-deficient script is almost pure fiction.'

He bent down and, plucking it up off the floor, pressed the thick wedge of typescript back into my hands. 'Okay you win. You want the truth.' He tapped the pages. 'Grace is more than capable of doing just that to Hans, particularly if it bought her the front page in a prominent fan magazine.' He took a breath. 'I don't know about Ruth. When we reach that section in the script, perhaps you will reveal, in confidence of course...' His tone was still ridged with irritation. 'How many people she hurt to get to Hollywood and I will respond and tell you about those my brother stepped on.

'Maidy, believe me,' his tone had quieted, 'if you get to tell the story you want, all that will happen is that I, in all seriousness will lose my job and never work in films again: Grace definitely and Roland, possibly, will lose the ear of powerful producers and be consigned to B movies, while two people, equally as ruthless as they are, maybe worse, will step up and take their place.'

I knew what he told me to be the truth, as loath as I was to accept it.

When Ruth returned from hospital, she brought not only the flowers, also the people who had sent them – men who flew in from New York or California, the salon bristling with cigar smoke and conversation.

'If Roland's production company gets off the ground, I will be executive producer.' Greg was exultant.

'And what do you have to do for that?' I teased, well acquainted with the term, after hearing it touted so often between the movie magnates who visited Ruth.

'Search out film scripts for Roland and Grace.' He waved the finished script at me.

'Isn't that what you do now?' I said naively.

He laughed. 'Okay! How about an office with my name on the door?'

I smiled. 'Is that it?'

'Pretty much. By the way, you should do that more often.'

'What?'

'Smile… laugh… throw your hat into the air. You take life way too seriously. And, yes, unless this script sells and sells big, my name on a brass plate will be all I get. But this script will get us there, I'd bet my last dollar on it.'

'Even Ruth can't play herself,' I objected.

He grinned at me. 'You'd be surprised. If we dress it up, change the country, add a few brothers and sisters, change her hair colour, and I bribe the producer to withhold the script and feed it to her page by page, she won't guess until right at the end and by then it will be too late. Remember the night of that dress?'

I laughed. 'It has a title now?'

Of course, I remembered. Giving into Greg's nagging, I had bought the identical outfit in green, wearing it for the Christmas party.

'The other day, Roland told me I had to persuade you to do a screen test.'

Seeing my mouth open ready to object, he grinned at me. 'You can't blame the man for keeping an eye out for likely talent. You know, unknown actress…' He held up his hands, his fingers angled against an imaginary line of credits. 'I quite like the name Magrit,' he teased, 'it's different.'

'And I like nothing at all.' I frowned my refusal.

'Would you really say no, if Roland offered you good money?'

I faked a shudder.

His carefree expression vanished. 'Then if you don't go back to the States with Grace, once all this is done and dusted, what are you going to do? You need a job. Of course, you could always marry me,' he added, his affable tone unchanged.

Smiling, I shook my head.

'Why not?'

'Because you aren't in love with me.'

I kept my tone light-hearted, pretending that's how I viewed his proposal – as an altruistic offer made on the spur of the moment.

'If I'm not in love with you,' he raised his voice, 'why the heck do I keep wanting to pick you up and put you in my pocket – that must mean something.' He sounded indignant.

We were in the studio and instantly a chorus of 'Quiet' rang out.

Grabbing my arm, he opened the door into the corridor. 'Well?'

'Because you're kind and very nice – and actually it's you who should be in films. You have a natural talent for drama.'

He had recovered his composure. I was glad, I valued his friendship too much to hurt him. He smiled. 'One ego in the family is quite sufficient,' he added in a normal tone of voice. He stared around. 'No chairs. Sorry, you'll have to make do with a wall while I finish my proposal.'

'I thought you had finished it. I'm sorry but the answer will still be no.'

'Hear me out,' he retorted indignantly. 'I was actually being serious about our marrying. In Hollywood, people marry for the craziest of reasons, most of which have nothing to do with being in love and everything to do with looking for a leg up. No marriage can survive that sort of selfishness. You stand a better chance if you marry someone you like and get on with, rather than someone you feel passionate about. Passion doesn't stand a cat in hell's chance of surviving the strains Hollywood life puts on it. And if you really enjoy someone's company and never find them boring – as I do with you – then you should definitely consider marrying them.'

'I'm sorry, Greg.' I reached out and took his hand. 'I think I'm the sort that needs to be in love.'

'You mean that guy, the one you refused to tell me about? Did he ever get in touch?'

'No. He's waiting for me.'

'To do what?'

'To make up my mind.'

He shrugged and rummaged up a grin. He was hurt, I could see that, but hopefully not too badly. 'Admit it though, Maidy. Because of me, you've learned one hell of a lot about the movie business.' His irrepressible grin burst out again. 'Just think how useful that will be when you write your first novel.'

'That's why I'm staying in Europe.' I couldn't say France because in truth, once Grace and Hans left for America I wasn't sure where I'd end up.

'That's definite. You're not returning to the States with Grace?'

'Not with Grace, no.'

How could I when the man I loved was here?

'Pity,' he sighed. 'It's a good script.'

It wasn't, it was a terrible script. Barely scraping the surface of her life, there was a flood of poignancy that would have the audience reaching for their handkerchiefs and Ruth's popularity would soar.

She still bothered me. The contract from Hollywood had, with the arrival of a telegram, become the *cancelled* contract. It obviously weighed on her mind and she had taken to nervously glancing in the hallway mirror every time she passed it, as if expecting her beauty, like the contract, also to have vanished. Yet quite the reverse was happening. The men that visited the apartment, who discussed deals and counter deals between puffing their cigars, had shown their willingness to open any doors not yet open, hanging on to her every word. And despite not being aware, once again Ruth was Queen Bee, although it was no longer naive college boys who circled around her, they had been replaced by middle-aged men for whom a crisp banknote smoothed away any and all difficulties. Now, most days the air in the living room was thick with voices talking box office. Good box office, the mecca of all their hopes, the pinnacle of acceptance and achievement – something they believed Ruth could give them.

'So, what *are* you going to do?' Greg added.

I didn't know – that was the trouble; the argument between

Hans and Ruth about the gallery was still not settled. 'If you want, you can have New York,' he had eventually conceded. 'It means I'll have to close Flambeau – it would prove quite impractical to supply both galleries, besides being too costly. But I get to choose where in the city. This is my field. I don't interfere in your life.'

He didn't, ignoring the comings and goings and the meetings that kept the maid and butler busy serving coffee and wine, as new arrivals at the airport found their way to the apartment.

If I had once naively imagined the arrival of Beth would bring forth a great deal of billing and cooing between Ruth and Hans, I no longer did, for neither had the time. Yet, they seemed happy enough, at least Hans did; quite content with his family and wanting nothing apart from days without interruption in which he could apply his mind to the real love of his life – capturing the various textures of light and shade with his paint brush and replicating them on canvas.

Ruth, I wasn't sure about. To the untutored eye, the image she and Hans projected was one of total devotion; the smiles, the rapture, endlessly talking to one another, it all looked perfectly genuine. But the talking was just that, on Ruth's part anyway, talking without listening. And it was not until Greg announced they were leaving for America the following day that I understood its cause. With Roland in the one continent that mattered, Ruth would lag behind in the popularity stakes.

'It's so important, Maidy,' she complained when I asked, wasn't that the role of an agent to keep a client in the public eye? 'Being away from Hollywood last year; how many new faces will there be, just waiting for me to slip up.'

By the end of May, with the days counting down until their departure and with nothing settled, I tackled Hans. The nurse had left two days before and Ruth, blithely saying it wasn't worth engaging anyone else, asked me to take over her duties. 'Only temporary, the moment we reach New York, I will engage someone,' she promised.

I looked back at the long line of promises, with endearments paraded as evidence of friendship.

'Hans, will you tell me something?'

I had Beth in my arms, her arms as always reaching out to Hans, one of his fingers clutched in her tiny fist.

'What?' he said, barely listening, his attention fastened on his daughter.

'Do you really want to go to America?'

He had obviously never asked himself that question and he stared at me blankly.

'It won't be for ever,' he declaimed. 'We're bound to be back in a year or two.'

'But your work is here, Hans,' I reminded. 'Don't you remember – oh, how long ago it was – telling me you wanted to paint the sun-kissed shores of the Mediterranean.'

Uncomfortable under my scrutiny, he mumbled, 'I can't leave Beth. No need for you to come, I told Ruthy last night. She and I will care for Beth until we get to New York.'

'In that case,' I said sternly, ignoring his reassurance. 'Re-open the shop in Flambeau.'

'It's not ...' he began.

'Practical especially with you in New York. Yes, I understand that. But you said yourself it may only be for a year or so and it doesn't make sense to close it. We've built up a good trade in art materials certainly enough to keep the shop running and we can sell framed prints rather than originals. Do say yes, Hans. And as I need a job let me run it for you. Tell Ruth you're doing it out of brotherly love, because you'd hate to see me living on the streets.' I smiled the last words, well aware the rebuke I wanted to make would fall on stony ground.

My words were unexpected, both shocking and surprising. His head came up, his glance meeting mine, the relief very evident. He hugged me to him; I had offered a way out. A breathing space.

'Yes, I'll tell Ruth.'

'Tell me what?' Ruth came out into the hall where we were chatting, 'I'm off out – I have a meeting.'

The bell rang.

With so many people in and out of the apartment all day, the doorman at the main entrance had given up announcing visitors and without thinking Ruth opened the door.

Her face changed, the alteration both so instantaneous and so shocking she might well have been punched in the solar plexus. She stumbled back, grasping the wall behind her for support. I didn't move, watching the beautiful profile soften until she looked little older than a schoolgirl – the brittle sophistication gone. Standing there now was a girl, the love for the boy who had rung the bell totally genuine and all-consuming.

Zande!

As movement came back into my body, I took a step forward, already conjuring up excuses for Ruth's reaction. *It's acting … that's all it is. It can't be anything else, it's all she knows. After so long playing her games, Ruth isn't capable of genuine emotion.*

Except it wasn't acting. I was wrong. *So wrong, it hurt.*

'Ruth!' The tone of Zande's voice was the one that called to me in my dreams. 'I must have made a mistake; I was told Magrit Bader lived here.'

Almost absentmindedly, his gaze leapfrogged straight to where I was standing with Hans, his arm around me, Beth cuddled into my shoulder.

I saw his face change, disbelief sweeping in, and then he turned away.

'Zande, wait,' Ruth called, and she ran after him, the entrance door swinging shut, leaving only silence behind.

I couldn't speak, stunned to silence by the brevity of the vision although even a fleeting glance sufficient to pick up on the shock that swept over Zande at seeing me in the hallway. Hans didn't break the painful silence either, comprehension slowly and painfully penetrating his bemused expression.

'Who was that?' his voice rasped, edgy with tension.

'His name is Zande,' I said. 'Four years ago, he was a college student in Herrendorp.'

'And Ruth has been in love with him all this time.'

It wasn't a question; it was simple confirmation that his reasoning had not misinterpreted the situation. How silly and naïve I'd been to imagine Ruth might ever find contentment, not while she still hankered after Zande.

'Yes.'

I couldn't let this farce run on, not this time; too many lives had already been damaged. I added Hans to the list, his skin pale and sweating, his daughter's tiny fist keeping him upright.

'He was the reason Ruth broke her engagement to Pieter.'

I kept my part out of it. Last time I'd attempted an explanation, I wasn't believed. Now I no longer needed to protest my innocence.

He reached out to take Beth, the ashen colour of his face slowly absorbing warmth from her tiny frame. 'Will she be back?'

'I don't know.' I said miserably.

'Then I'll care for Beth.'

He straightened up, already older than he had been thirty minutes ago but once again firm on his feet. 'Go back to Flambeau. I will send the paintings I'd planned for New York to the printers by carrier. He'll arrange their delivery to the shop.' Attempting a smile, a muscle twitched painfully. 'Your customers will have missed you.'

How strange. It had occurred to neither of us that I should go home.

I didn't bother going to bed, and after I had packed my suitcase, I sat by the open window waiting for the headlights of the limousine or even a taxi to enter the driveway. Nothing disturbed the blackness apart from the occasional star shooting across the heavens, bringing hope to others watching for just such a phenomenon. But not to me. As a glimmer of light entered the sky, I pulled a card from my bag, carelessly dialling the number on it. The phone rang twice and a man's voice answered, 'Hello.'

Expecting it to be Justine, I wasn't quite sure how to respond, and catching sight of the bedside clock, mumbled an apology. 'I'm sorry to have woken you. I must have the wrong number.'

'Maidy. Is that you? And, no, you didn't wake me.'

'Yöst?' I recognised his warm tones.

I stared down at the card puzzled, quickly searching for the card Justine had given me with her Paris phone number on it, the two bits of cardboard almost identical. In my confusion, I had mixed them up. 'Yes, it is me. I'm sorry, I meant to phone Justine.'

'No one phones anyone at five unless there's a problem. Is there?'

The block of ice in my chest shifted. 'I'm not sure,' quickly adding, 'I was waiting to find out.'

'Find out? That sounds ominous.' His tone changed. 'Where are you?'

'In Paris.'

'In that case, take the train to Bordeaux and we'll find out together. I'll meet you at the station.'

I glanced down at my hands; they had stopped shaking. 'I'm not sure about train times.'

'Not to worry. I'll take a book and read. I'll be there, I promise.'

Showering, I changed my clothes, and fastening my case called out a goodbye to the room before closing the door behind me.

Hans was in the kitchen feeding Beth and glanced up as I pushed open the door. The staff didn't arrive until seven and it was quiet, the only sound the baby's contented sucking.

'I thought you were Ruth.'

'She didn't return?'

He inclined his head, not removing his gaze from the child's face, his lifeline in the present crisis. 'No.'

'Do you mind if I leave?'

I guessed like me he hadn't slept. And with greater reason. I wondered if he was still battling the dark, wandering helplessly, or had already decided on a plan of action. Watching his gentle manner with Beth, I hoped it would be the latter. It would break his heart to give her up; even life with someone who had betrayed you, might be better than that.

'Coffee?'

'I'll get some at the station.'

It was fully light now and, aware there would be a taxi at the gatehouse, I kissed Beth on the forehead and, placing the card with Yöst's address on the table, closed the apartment door after me and set out along the path.

Overnight, wanting to escape from yet another tragedy instigated by Ruth, scenario after scenario had been rehashed, with perhaps as many different versions as the stars that had drifted past my window. Now, in the light of day, my thoughts had calmed. This wasn't my tragedy. I could pick up my suitcase and walk away as I was now doing. This tragedy had been waiting in the wings for its cue for more years than I could remember ... ever since Hans first fell in love with her.

25

'No, I haven't been waiting long,' Yöst greeted me as I emerged from the station. 'Katarina looked up the time of the train from Paris.'

'She's staying with you?'

'No, Rico and the other dancers are. Emilee and Katarina are staying up at the big house with Berte.'

Kissing me briefly on the cheek, he took a step back. 'Breakfast, I think, at my favourite café. This way.' Pointing to a sports car, its top already down in acknowledgement of the temperature, he took my suitcase. 'Your carriage awaits.'

I nearly burst into tears then at the kindness in his voice and hastily sniffed them away.

Expecting to stop off at a café close by, I was astonished when Yöst swung the car away from the city centre with its bustling shops and crossed the stone bridge onto the far bank of the Garonne; the arches of the Pont de Pierre as busy a thoroughfare for boats as the roads were, carrying traffic in and out of the city. He was a capable driver, diligently observing the rules despite the vehicle's obvious liking for speed, very different from Hans who preferred to gaze at girls and buildings, and within a few minutes the city's imposing skyline of historical buildings had vanished, replaced by fields almost exclusively devoted to wine production. There must have been a shower of rain earlier, moisture still coating the bushes planted closest to the road.

Neither of us spoke, and discovering the soft purr of the engine to be almost soporific, the tumultuous emotions that had pummelled me into submission throughout the long hours of the night gradually began to recede, until eventually I was able to enjoy the view, and feel the warm breeze ruffling my hair, everyday sensations for those whose lives were less convoluted than my own. And, although we weren't chatting, our silence held none of that awkwardness that so often takes place when virtual strangers meet up again. And Yöst was a stranger. After all, we had met only briefly and exchanged two letters since, yet with him I experienced the naturalness of old friends who have no need to fill the silence with words. Aware of his relationship to Zande I wasn't surprised, even so it was an amazing gift.

After a while, the gentle slopes forested by young vines lapsed into ragged hillsides both stony and barren, as if the rain even now glazing the vine leaves had long been denied to them, their downslopes a hopscotch pattern of stunted bushes and withered grass where anaemic-looking cattle were grazing.

The road flattened again, the rise and fall of the land gentling into yet another wine-producing area, with bare ridges of earth between fields rather than hedges and sunlight glinting off the metal of the Appellation notices. Between the lines of dense greenery both men and women were working, all of them wearing straw bonnets to protect them from the sun. On seeing the car, they snatched these off, waving and Yöst tooted the horn. He didn't wave back, keeping both hands firmly on the wheel.

'They know you?'

'Reflected glory, I'm afraid.' He slanted his eyes at me but didn't turn, keeping them on the road. 'It's Rico's car and everybody knows him.'

A subtle change in the landscape brought woods into view and with them a river, sunlight glinting off its surface like expensive jewels. The reverse of the housing that bordered it. Shuttered against both heat and sunlight they looked deserted, although the scrawny goats and chickens aimlessly milling around their wire-netting enclosure inferred something different, as did a group of bare-footed children on the riverbank fishing.

For a few minutes more the road and river ran together before the road broke away and entered an avenue bordered by trees, the ground rising sharply towards a church which crowned the summit of a hill, an unbroken line of rooftops like disciples flocking up the hillside towards it.

'Is *this* where you live?' I asked as we drove down the village street, the lines of housing on either side painting patches of light and shade on the road ahead.

'No. This is where we have coffee.' He half-turned, smiling. 'I promised you my favourite restaurant. This is it. It just happens to be near where I live. And then you can talk if you're ready to do so. As I said, no one phones at five unless there's a crisis.'

Strangely, it no longer felt like a crisis, Yöst's easy manner taking the sting out of events the previous night.

'This is Adelita's place.' He pulled to a halt outside a corner property, its terraced forecourt shaded from the sun by a wide trellis of purple bougainvillea. By contrast, the subdued colouring of the north that I had left that morning reminded me of a patient in extremis, from whom all colour has fled.

'Is she someone you know well?' I nodded my thanks to the waiter who on seeing us rushed to place a carafe of iced water on the table.

'Adelita? She was. You will often hear her spoken of, especially by Katarina…' He peered at me intently. 'Adelita taught her to dance.'

'Tell me about her,' I said as the coffee arrived, a plate of croissants fresh from the oven accompanying the brown coffee pot. All at once I was hungry, saliva flooding my mouth.

'She was the greatest dancer I have ever seen or will ever see, unless you decide to surprise us.' I laughed a negative and took a bite of croissant, the flaky pastry so light it broke into crumbs in my mouth. 'Ramon, Rico's father, would never have permitted his son to dance, he wanted him to become a farmer. But for Rico dancing was all he ever thought about. That and sleep,' Yöst recalled with a smile. 'And so Adelita and Rico entered into a secret pact. Neither ever said how it came about. Most likely it was Rico's fascination with her dancing, whenever she performed for the family after dinner, that gave him away. In any event, once or twice a week, on the pretext of going to confession, she'd ask Rico to drive her to church.'

He nodded uphill towards the church, its tall spire reminding me of a finger pointing the way to heaven.

'She used to tell people that she had committed so many sins in her life, she would never be able to confess them all. I'm not sure if the parish priest believed that but he did agree to the deception. Instead of reciting *Three Hail Marys*, Adelita dropped money into the poor box in exchange for the use of the vestry for an hour. Then sedately,' he chuckled, 'pure of thought and deed, after drinking wine, they drove back to the farm. It was their secret and the villagers kept it. Hence the name.'

'What happened to her?'

'She was shot not long after the war started, trying to protect what belonged to her.' His expression altered, all at once weary, and I realised even now his arm wasn't entirely pain free and the long drive from the station had tired him.

'I'm so sorry.'

'About what?' He looked at me astonished.

'Making you rescue me.'

'You aren't responsible for my arm. Ready to talk?'

I nodded. 'Although, it's not really my story, in a way I am just the narrator except for the bits that involve Zande.' Yöst raised an eyebrow but didn't interrupt the flow of words that made up my story, occasionally stumbling when they didn't fit, and on noticing his puzzled frown, repeating phrases that had been unclear. I understood them well enough because they'd been with me always. Even so, I carefully clarified their meaning, wanting the lives of everyone concerned to be laid out neatly like the pages of a book.

When eventually I ran out of words, he didn't respond, his gaze fastened on some children playing a game with a bat and ball. He sighed. 'Poor Ruth, what a weight of expectation she has placed upon herself.'

I went to voice an objection and remained silent. Pappy would undoubtedly have made a similar comment, placing the blame squarely on her childhood experiences.

'I knew a little of this. Naturally not Ruth's part although I'm not entirely sure your conclusions are justified.'

For a second hope flared. 'Has Zande been in touch?'

'Not since yesterday morning when he left for Paris. Still, that's not unusual. He's the sort to lick his wounds in private. I had given him your address in Paris. 'Maidy...'

He leaned forward over the table and took my hand. 'Zande went to Paris to let you know that Albert Meijer has died. It's a great loss; I've known him for twenty years and have so much to be grateful for. He'd been staying with me at the vineyard and before he became too ill, he filled in all those blank spaces in my head.' His voice dropped, sounding reflective, his easy smile lost among memories replanted by the generosity of his guardian. 'I lost a lot of years, Maidy. One of the tales he often told was about you; this little girl who had entertained him with her stories. And Zande, knowing how close you had become, offered to be the one to break the news to you.'

The tears I'd held back the previous night did flow then, dabbing at my eyes with my handkerchief; the waiter watching on concerned.

'Albert wouldn't have wanted you to cry.' Yöst offered me his own handkerchief. 'He'd had a good life. Come along, let's go home. Rico's waiting.'

'Home?' I echoed shakily.

'Yes, why not? Have you anywhere else you need to be?'

I recalled Justine saying, albeit quite loftily, 'I am between engagements.'

'No. I'd love that.'

Ignoring the paved road we had driven down, Yöst swung the

car into a narrow track which followed the line of the river, its potholes reducing the car's speed to a crawl. Intent on avoiding the worst of the ruts, he didn't speak concentrating on his driving, although I could see by the play of emotions across his face that he was deep into memories of the past.

'I grew up around here.' He offered an explanation.

Emerging onto a paved road, he stopped the car on the bridge over the river and pointed towards a lane, the outline of a barn visible through a grove of olive trees. 'The main house, what I've always called the beehive, is up there. It's not far from the winery – just across the river. Maestro is staying there. Says that's where all his memories are. Mine too. I was twelve when I first saw it.'

'Do you own the vineyard?'

'No. The land belonged to a Monsieur Benoit and had been in his family for generations. He had no family left – not once the war had run its course – and bequeathed the farm and orchards to Ramon, who had been his tenant, and the vineyard to Rico. He'd once seen Rico dance as a boy and never forgot it. Nor did I.' The final few words were spoken quietly, and meant for him alone. 'I'd always wanted to be a farmer. I can't now of course so I manage the place for him. And since there is absolutely nothing wrong with my legs, I march around putting the fear of god into the workers.' It was said with a rueful smile, and I recalled the men and women who had waved a friendly greeting, instantly rejecting the words, *fear of god*.

Accelerating up a steep hill, he swung the car into an elegant driveway bordered by shade trees, the woody stems of the wines with their green bonnets filling the ground in every direction. At the far end were a series of buildings; the foreground taken up by a Spanish-style hacienda, the red tiles of its roof almost gaudy against the sea of green.

'That tall building…' Slowing the car to a crawl, he pointed, 'is the original winery, complete with cellars where the bottled wine is stored before it is sold. If you go exploring, you'll find the original wooden vats where the grapes were trampled. We still do that, although we sold off all but the fields that produce the best vintage. Rico wanted a dance studio.' He smiled as if it was the most natural thing in the world to have a dance studio way out in the country. 'And the top floor has been converted into guest bedrooms.' He patted my hand. 'It's a bit of a madhouse when Rico is here.' But there was no apology in his words, only excitement.

'Oh, and I forgot to mention,' he accelerated. 'A friend of yours is staying. Jaan, is that right?'

'Jaan?' I echoed.

Momentarily, he looked anxious. 'You do know him. He promised you did.'

I laughed. 'Yes, very well. It will be wonderful to meet up. It's been four years.'

'That's what he said. He was planning to leave this morning but when he heard I was meeting you off the train, he changed his mind.'

I hadn't taken Yöst's warning about it being a madhouse seriously, believing it more along the lines of a housewife who hastily excuses the untidiness of her house to an unexpected guest. But it was. The moment Rico burst onto the scene, his sculptured silhouette elegant in a frilled white shirt and tight black trousers, I was lost in a maelstrom of names and faces that spun off at a tangent leaving me none the wiser.

To my utter bewilderment, I caught sight of Jaan and then not again until the following morning and it was Katarina who rescued me, showing me to my bedroom on the ground floor, with its double doors that opened onto a terrace ringed by bay trees.

It was an elegant house, with louvred doorways that matched the shutters on the windows, both bedrooms and living room with views down the steep incline to the river at the bottom. Equally the size of Ruth's apartment and glowing with colour, I recognised objects I had seen on sale in New York shops.

'That's Rico's doing.' Katarina picked up on my interest. 'He collects mementos from every city he has ever danced in and as you see he collects people too, although the people you met are mostly dancers who come here each summer for a rest and to discuss next season's programme. You and I, we will ignore them and be quiet together, which is essential, otherwise you will be constantly reaching for the aspirin bottle.' She laughed. 'Why do you think I stay with my niece, Berte, at the farm? The people here are wonderful and most have astonishing histories, which they will be eager to share with you, but there's no getting away from it, they are far too noisy.'

She dropped gracefully into a chair. I was reminded of Justine, both women having a natural elegance. When they walked into a room, you noticed. 'Tell me, are you here to learn to dance?'

'I don't know.'

'I'd be happy to teach you, if you are,' she ignored my reply. 'Naturally, neither Yöst nor Rico have said anything.' Noticing my concern, she smiled. 'No! No! That's quite normal, I assure you, something I'm quite used to. My brother-in-law, Ramon, he was the same. He collected up all the waifs and strays and took them home. And whereas his wife and I used to be in charge of feeding them, now we have a team of devoted helpers while I sit idly by.'

My first evening was taken up by an impromptu concert at which Maestro played and Rico danced and everyone, it would seem, from the entire district came to watch. Only the notables were given chairs, the rest, working men and their families, were seated on straw matting, but no one complained, not even the little children forced to be quiet and sit still while Maestro played. Even the moon obliged adding its own light to the sound show happening on stage.

'How are you getting on?' Jaan said the following morning, when we eventually did meet up at breakfast.

According to the maid who served us, Yöst had already left for the fields, while Rico and the others were still asleep. 'What can you expect,' she explained with a shrug of her shoulders, 'when they stay up talking and dancing all night.'

Surprisingly, Jaan had changed very little. Always serious, he was perhaps a little more so, and I ascribed the word *world weary* to him. It fitted. And maybe his hair was a darker blonde than my recollection, yet the misty blue of his eyes remained the same, as was the warm regard whenever he looked at me.

Conversation between us wasn't difficult, our views and interests so similar, although Jaan may well have found the opposite to be true. Conscious of my feelings for Zande, he had never once allowed his own interests to bypass his loyalty to his friend and may well have found that disquieting.

Then I asked the one question that needed asking, which only he would understand. 'Did you?'

Immediately he looked uncomfortable, fidgeting with the teaspoon he'd used to stir his coffee. It clattered against his cup, making me jump. 'No,' he shrugged. 'It would seem faithfulness to one's partner remains the only elixir on offer.'

'I'm sorry, Jaan.'

'Yes.' He gave a half smile. 'So am I. And no, if that's your next question. I haven't married.'

'Why not?'

'It gets to be a habit after a while.' He rummaged up a smile.

I didn't need to ask *what does*? He meant waiting.

'What happened to the others…?' I stopped remembering it was only Waldger and Zande, and I knew how Zande was.

'Waldger…' He hesitated. 'Waldger died, Maidy.' I understood then his disillusion with life. 'That's why I'm here. Zande wanted to mark his death with a gathering of friends. It's hardest for him because the two of them have been friends since their schooldays.'

The words *I'm so sorry* weren't applicable. As words of solace they barely scratched the surface, especially not for those who had grown up sharing everything, even the tragic circumstance of their life. And while there'd been many weaknesses in Waldger's character, now I could only remember how life had been the playground on which he had honed his wit.

'Was he ill?'

'No, he wasn't ill, Maidy.' He said the words reluctantly. 'He took his own life.'

'But why,' I gasped out. 'He loved life.'

'Yet more than any of us, he found the restrictions we are forced to place on it unbearable.' He hesitated a moment, 'I know you care for Zande.'

I felt my cheeks warm. 'I...'

He reached across the table taking my hand. 'It's all right, Maidy; I care for him too. I remember Waldger saying he was the best of fellows. He was ... he is,' Jaan hastily amended. 'He knew better than anyone that what we are doesn't fit this new world, that's why he pushed so hard to find a cure. And for those joining the clan who were younger, it was Zande who helped them find purpose in their lives. He encouraged me to study and not live an idle existence because it didn't suit me, and for that, I will always thank him.' Jaan hesitated and I guessed the next words were proving difficult to speak aloud. 'Something broke in Zande when he learned of Waldger's death. You may be able to help him. I can't.'

After Jaan had left to catch his train, promising we would meet again soon, I sought out Katarina, asking if it was too late for me to change my mind and learn to dance and would she teach me? Yöst may have warned about the mayhem created by Rico's presence but not that seeing Jaan again would bring to the surface all those destructive memories I hoped were gone for good.

It was the perfect antidote although if I had once believed Rico's assertion that I was a natural dancer, I was utterly misguided.

It was flattery nothing more, it had to be, my feet stubbornly refusing to obey either Katarina's exhortations or my wishes, and their obstinacy quickly became the cause of much merriment on her part and irritation on mine.

'Try again and remember your head; your eyes must be looking straight ahead. Toe heel, toe heel, toe heel ... Flat,' she chanted on and on until, finally, the rhythm came to me. Then increasing the tempo, we swirled round and round, our shoulders brushing as we passed, until my feet became burning coals and I flopped down on the ground exhausted.

'You are too nice, Maidy,' she confided, whilst I sipped a

much-needed glass of orange juice, my feet in a bucket of iced water. 'In Flamenco, it is important to remember the women always despise the men until they love them. You must be fierce, stamping down their forwardness with the flat of your foot, yet, at the same time, offering encouragement with your skirt and your eyes. Never forget the eyes.'

Nevertheless, it had done its job, my emotions replaced by aching muscles and I found myself sleeping well, my dreams vanishing with the dawn. By day five, deciding I knew the dance well enough, Katarina suggested I participate in their training session. 'And then tomorrow we will begin learning new steps.'

I had not seen Katarina dance, not really. Our training sessions didn't count, nor did New York. The proud tilt of her head and her imperious stance reminded me of the infantas I had read about in history books, whose cruelty was matched only by their beauty and, as the other women joined in, circling around her, so did I. Nervously, I arched my back, striking my feet cleanly, my one hand whipping the edges of my borrowed skirt to one side, rejecting the man who had dared to approach. Then Rico came along, flirting with the women equally until it was his hand encircling my waist, his feet perfectly in time with the chords the guitarist was strumming in this dance of passion, and using my shawl to rope me to him, before abruptly passing on to the next woman leaving me jealous and angry.

'It's like life,' I commented to Rico at the end of the training session when he strolled over to compliment me on an excellent performance.

'It was my life until Yöst came back to us,' and he smiled across the room at Yöst who had been watching the session. 'For me, dancing destroys the demons.'

But it was not until the following morning that Yöst and I had a chance to speak, when he joined me for breakfast. He'd been out already, and was carrying a punnet of early peaches.

'I went to the farm empty handed and came back with these. They're always the first to ripen. Have one.' He pulled out a chair and sat down. 'They taste delicious.'

He had an astonishing face, his deep-set eyes unable to make up their mind whether to be blue or grey, yet, whatever they were, able to see below the surface of someone else's thoughts.

'Katarina told me you are leaving. You've made your decision?' He reached for the coffee pot, declining my offer of sugar.

'You remember saying that?'

'Yes, it's one of my oddities.'

'You aren't...?'

'No! Physically, you might say I was cured, if that is how you view our state.' He spoke lightly yet with an undertone and I remembered Waldger. 'Although, my hearing and sight have remained faithful.'

'I also have oddities, as you call them.' My smile held no guile at his peculiar choice of word. 'I am pretty sure it was your idea to ask Rico to teach me to dance, rather than his. Why?'

'Because you were so unhappy.' He reached over the table and took my hand.

'Yes, I was.'

'And now?'

I gazed around at the peaceful countryside, the early morning sun adding a wash of blue to the fields, taking stock of everyone who had entered my life since and become a part of it. 'Rico was right. Dancing does burn away the demons.'

'And you have found yourself?'

I smiled. 'That may take a while longer. Still, I can't hide away here forever, Yöst.'

'Then I will leave the door open until you yourself decide to shut it.'

26

In six months, the once fresh paint on the shop sign had lost its sparkle, mired by rain and wind that battered the old city in winter. Even the shop window looked shabby and uncared for, with condensation fogging the edges of the glass. A spider had spun its web across one corner, a little pile of desiccated flies dropped down onto the notice I had left in the window, saying we would reopen next summer. And summer was here, and while hikers oiled and polished their boots, artists flicked over pages in an art magazine seeking an advertisement they recalled seeing months ago, promising amazing views and comfortable lodgings, the plans of those living in the north about where to spend their holiday already confirmed.

Unaware if Justine had returned from Paris, I left my suitcase with the landlord and walked up through the grounds. The bus had dropped me at the top of the high street, and it would have been a simple matter to step across the square, the soft grey-blue of the Mansard roof visible through the spiny top growth of the pines. I'm not sure why I didn't. Maybe I wanted to delay my feeling of disappointment if the house revealed only closed shutters. It wasn't much of a diversion, a few minutes walking between tall walls that edged the fringes of the old city before the cottages with their stylish gardens came into view. Unchanged as though in a time warp and as colourful as when I left, the downstairs window was propped open while Justine's tenant tended her window box. Recalling Justine's comment, 'Have you ever passed the stables without her peering from the window scissors in her hand,' I waved merrily, forgetting our previous acrimonious exchange.

The firs edging the narrow walk had bushed out over the winter, the tip of their soft fronds kissing the back of my neck as I wandered up the allée towards the chateau. The gardener had obviously worked hard over the winter, and the expansive trellis of cordoned trees was neatly pruned. Sadly, I had, once again, missed the blossom, and I made a promise if stayed next winter, I would also stay through the spring. Justine, after a glass of wine, used to refer to the coppiced fruit trees as drunken revellers, unable to stand up without support. 'In winter maybe,' Hans had argued. 'Once in their spring finery, they resemble a long line of elegantly dressed scarecrows.' No longer scarecrows, already their twiglets were overflowing with tiny fruits which in a few short weeks would ripen into peaches, pears, and apples.

The windows of the studio were open. 'Justine,' I called up.

Her face appeared. '*Chérie*, in the nick of time. I was about to take a lover I was so bored. Now we will sit and talk, and drink coffee and wine. Come, come in – the door is open.'

As I pushed open the door into the kitchen, I heard her bare feet pattering down the stairs, the voluminous sleeves of her kimono with its colourful magnolia flowers making an entrance almost before the rest of her. 'If you are here, does that mean...?'

I hesitated, not wanting to see her eager smile fade. 'No.'

Momentarily the thin line of her mouth tightened. 'Never mind, I received a telegram, we will make do with that.'

'What did it say?'

'New York off,' she recited poker-faced. 'Open the shop. Sending Stock. Hans.'

'Oh, Justine, I'm so sorry,' I cried out, scarcely know whether to laugh at the terse tone or cry.

'No, no, no! Rejoice. From Hans that was a love letter. Come. We will celebrate,' and she indicated the wine rack. I read the labels, recognising they were all from well-known vintners. Of course, she had earned good money over the winter. 'Your choice.'

'We saw you dance Giselle.' I slid a bottle out of the niche reserved for it, balancing it carefully on my open palm to expose the label. She nodded acceptance. 'You were wonderful.'

'Which night?' She reached for the kettle, filling it. 'Coffee, food?'

I nodded to both. 'The Monday.'

Standing the kettle on the hot plate to boil, she darted over to the larder and, opening the door to the refrigerator, peered inside. Without thinking, I sat down at the table, already feeling comfortably at home. Never once in the Paris apartment had I experienced this, its silent exclusivity something generally awarded either to the titled or to the very rich, and I was neither. Justine would have qualified because of her marriage, except she had chosen to join Hans in Bohemia.

'I will cook later but for now, we will drink copious amounts of wine and eat cheese and paté. Yes, I danced well that night. I remember the applause. You said we?' She picked up a baton of fresh bread.

'You've been out?' I indicated the bread.

'No, I have made an arrangement. Who did you mean by we?' she repeated.

'I went with Hans.'

'And?'

'He said he was a fool.'

She grabbed my arm and, brooking no resistance, danced me through the kitchen and out into the courtyard, the steely strength of her muscles dragging me along. 'This happened to me once before, in New York.' I panted, made breathless by the speed of her feet.

Releasing my arm, she continued to dance, creating a performance ... I am not sure who it was for, although I had a sneaky suspicion it was for Hans, her body so delicately balanced she might have been suspended above the ground, repeating the pirouettes and jumps I had seen her perform on stage, her arms soaring mimicking the wings of a bird.

'Come.' Catching me by the hand, she dragged me over to the archway separating the wing of the house from the main body and pushed open the door of the annexe. 'Voilà – Look!'

No longer buried under the weight of history, it was full of light, its wooden shelves loaded with pottery scrubbed as clean as the farmhouse table. A modern refrigerator peeked from behind the pantry door, showing off the glossy patina of the newly purchased, as did the wine rack, although its shelves were empty. Suspended over the table, a light wood frame held scarlet enamel cooking pots and pans, with bunches of dried herbs nestling among them, the matching red of a geranium plant peeking through the newly painted windows. Even the tiles covering the floor had been scrubbed until they shone. At that moment, a workman, his overalls covered in paint, came into the kitchen. 'You wish for something, Countess?' And on receiving no reply from Justine other than a vague shrug of her shoulders, wandered out again, wiping his brush on an edge of the paint tin as he vanished into the hallway.

'You did it?'

'Yes, and it is perfect. It seems I not only dance, I also design.' She was excited as a child. I didn't comment, happiness for Justine was a very precious commodity. Her mouth dropped into a pout. 'I would show you the rest.' She shrugged. 'Sadly, that man is very strict – he is also an artist.' She excused him. 'That I understand. And now I have succumbed to the disease you wished on me...' The gloomy expression vanished, a smile tilting her mouth upwards. 'I am also intending to renovate the servants' quarters; then I will have no need to earn my living and can remain here eating cheese and paté, and grow fat.'

'Justine, he may not return,' I cautioned, aware her comment referred to last year when Hans and Justine often reverted to insults to emphasise their pleasure in each other's company.

'Of course, he will.' She waved her hand. 'Hans cannot leave a picture unfinished. For him, that's like a slur on his masculinity.'

It was almost the end of August before we saw Hans again. Throughout the months of June and July, the old city had hummed with visitors especially at weekends, when I inveigled Justine into helping. While I dealt with the sale of brushes and paper, she chatted to those seeking information about the artist. Except with her it was never just chatting. Showing her immense knowledge of Hans' work, she had them queuing up to buy a print. Those who had money, although more rarely, she persuaded into buying the original which would, she assured them, most definitely increase in value. I teased her about it, asking if it was a memento of the countess or the *prima ballerina* they were buying that day. Back in the spring, an art magazine must have interviewed Hans. He hadn't mentioned it; most likely forgotten among the many requests for interviews Ruth received. Nevertheless, it had done its job, bringing increased numbers of artists and art lovers to Flambeau.

On seeing Hans, I didn't dare speak for a moment – the air about me laden with tension. 'Is Ruth with you?' I eventually managed.

He was carrying Beth in a rush basket, the little girl covered in a light blanket, asleep. She had grown.

'No.'

The word hit home, its implications so onerous, the shield I had placed around my most innermost thoughts cracked under the assault.

My first instinct was to run away, dreading his explanation that Ruth had never returned or perhaps, even worse, that they were reconciled and she had, maybe… I searched for something plausible. Perhaps she had strolled up into the town, or she was parking the car. Not the car Hans drove but something far more grandiose that suited Ruth's lavish lifestyle.

Instantly, I wanted to be gone – to not learn the truth. I took a step and stopped. Only I couldn't. There were customers waiting to be served. Metaphorically I pulled my face straight, as always relegating problems of the day to the privacy of my room at night.

Hans waited for a mother and two children, who both wanted a new box of paints, to finish making their choice, before replying, 'It's just Beth and me now.' With a smile, he closed the shop door behind them.

I felt dizzy and sick, and collapsed down onto a stool. 'I don't understand.'

What stupid words. On one hand they implied hope; on the other despair. Yet they actually made sense – if only to me.

Hans grinned at me. He looked different, not so devil-may-care, more serious somehow. 'Ruth granted me custody.'

'Not her husband?' I gasped, scarcely able to believe what he was saying. Ruth had done that – given up something valuable that belonged to her?

'No.' He glanced around the empty shop, his gaze landing on the window display. 'The window needs changing.'

'*You are quite unbelievable,*' I shouted momentarily oblivious of the sleeping baby. The explosion of noise eased the pressure in my chest, and I continued more quietly. 'You wander in after three months with not a word and your only concern is for the shop window. Yes, I am aware it needs changing. We've been busy.'

He ignored my rant. 'What do you want me to say? I'm no good with all this hearts and flowers stuff, you know that. Besides, I wanted to ask you about Justine. Do you think she'll take me back?'

My glare petered out. He hadn't changed, as infuriatingly self-centred as ever. 'Explain first and then, if I forgive you, I might answer your question.'

My words may have sounded casual, yet we were both very aware of what I was asking … for him to bare his soul. He didn't flinch the task and it hurt, the wound still fresh. 'Ruth didn't return that night to the apartment. Of course, you know that. It was two days later. She said she went to a hotel and I believe her.' He glared at me as if I was the Doubting Thomas, although I'd not spoken.

'And?'

The shop bell rang out.

'Close up, will you?' he snapped irritably. 'It's almost lunchtime, anyhow. I'd hoped to get here earlier. The traffic out of Paris was dreadful, and Beth needs a bottle. She'll be awake in a minute and customers won't want a crying baby.'

He wandered into the backroom and I heard him turn on the tap for water.

After serving the customer, who thankfully only wanted postcards, selecting standard views of the old town rather than Hans' painting of it, I flipped the sign on the door and hurried after him. Large enough for a bed, a small table and a couple of chairs, the landlord had provided cooking facilities housed in a wall-cupboard, with a tiny gas stove perched on a shelf above the gas-cylinder. And since washing was not considered an essential element while eating was, only a small sink to wash in with a cold tap. There was no refrigerator, and Hans had covered the shelves with wire mesh to stop the mice that lived in the building's foundations eating his food.

'Do you think Justine will take us in?' he said, as the little girl stirred. 'I can't let Beth live here.' At almost five months, with her features smoothed out, her resemblance to Ruth was startling, except for the shape of her eyes. Those she had inherited from Hans.

'Go on,' I repeated, 'you haven't finished your story yet.'

'You're enjoying this,' he glared.

'That's not true, Hans. I know how badly the breakup has hurt you. It hurt us all.' I could allow myself that. 'Particularly Justine and that's your fault. So, yes, I do want to know.'

'All of it. It goes back a long way.'

I nodded.

He swung away, measuring out the milk powder and adding boiled water. 'You can't possibly understand how exciting it was when she replied to my fan letter, even more unbelievable when she told me she loved me. I couldn't believe it then, I still don't.'

He hesitated and glanced at me, possibly expecting what? Words of solace? How could there be?

His voice sharpened. 'All right, no need to rub it in. She never loved me, only this Zande-person. I asked her, why him? Can you believe, she said he made her feel beautiful. That's so stupid...' Hans kept his voice low, despite the anger in it. 'She is beautiful.'

I understood because I had felt the same – that was just one of his many gifts.

He swung around pleading. 'Don't you remember how it was for me, growing up in Pieter's shadow? Always the perfect son, tall and handsome, kind to widows and orphans.' Hans made it sound like an insult. 'He was good at everything. Even Ruth, who I adored, liked him better than me. She used to sit on the stairs waiting for him to finish work.'

'I sat on the stairs.'

'Yes, for him to tell you a story. I didn't know any stories.' He blinked. 'Probably, I wouldn't have bothered, not then, if I had known any. All I wanted was to go to college and I didn't even get that.'

I was tempted to tell him about Pieter, trapped in an existence with no possibility of anything changing until his death. I calculated quickly. Nine years maybe less, unless I managed to solve the riddle of his birth. For Hans, there were no such strictures. At almost twenty-four, both a long life and a resplendent future lay in front of him.

Placing Beth on his knee, he upended the bottle into her mouth, her hand reaching up to grasp his.

'Ruth wrote you a letter.' Awkwardly fishing in his pocket, he handed over the crumpled envelope. 'I haven't read it, still, I pretty much know what it says. Go ahead,' he urged. 'Open it.'

'Dear Maidy, I don't know why I'm writing to you. Yes, I do. Zande said I had to.'

I took a breath, scarcely believing her words, almost too scared to read further.

I know I am selfish but you're the only real friend I have and I thought if I tell you, you would remain my friend and if I needed you – you would come.

I saw Zande. He took me to dinner and then he left. I'd have gone with him to the ends of the earth if he wanted but he didn't. He said some horrid things, that I am self-centred and use people. But I was always kind to you, Maidy, wasn't I? He didn't seem to care at all that I'd had everything taken away from me once already, my clothes, even my shoes and my hair. More than that, my chance of having a brother or sister. I couldn't let it happen again, you understand, don't you, Maidy?

I am going back to Roland. You were silly not to marry Greg, I know he wanted you to. He didn't much like me, but he liked you and then you and I could have been neighbours. Anyway, Roland telegraphed to say the film we'd been contracted for is now on again and it would begin shooting as soon as I returned. Beth is staying with Hans; I thought it only right because Roland and I will be busy making films and will have no time for anything else. I suppose I don't really want anything else. I wanted to give Hans some money, but Beth was all he wanted. I was sorry to let him down.

Oh, I nearly forgot. Zande made me promise to tell you he loved you not me. He always had, right from that time he saw you on the canal bank. I don't see why, because you weren't very pretty and he came to Paris to find you. Remember the stories you told about the little house on the canal? Well, you must do because that's where your prince lived. You obviously knew the owner, Albert Meijer, very well. You never said anything to me about it. Anyway, Zande said he had died and left you the house.

Now I've kept my promise and told you what Zande said, please stay my friend. Ruth.

I'm not sure who it was I was crying for: Meneer Meijer, Ruth, or Zande who had been so much maligned in my thoughts. I should never had doubted. Just as well, when I poured out the history of events in Paris to Justine, I had managed to refrain from mentioning him.

'Maidy?'

'I think I need a hug.' I wiped my eyes. 'I feel so sorry for Ruth.'

Nestling the baby in the crook of one arm, he wrapped his other arm around me. 'What about me?'

'No,' I retorted fiercely and pushed him away. 'You don't deserve sympathy; you won first prize.' I pointed to Beth, already tumbling back down into sleep again. 'I did try to warn you.'

He flinched. 'All right, I behaved like a cad and I'm sorry. Will Justine let me stay? Beth and I need a home. And I need to earn my living.'

At that precise moment, I seriously questioned the folly of asking her. But then he was my brother and I was furious with him – mostly because he was so totally self-centred, although was that even relevant any more? He had moved on, the centre of his concern was now his daughter.

Dear Justine. From the moment she caught sight of us walking through the courtyard, I guessed she wanted to both sing and dance. She did neither, carefully schooling her expression and greeting Hans quite formally, the *prima ballerina* very much in evidence, even granting Beth little more than the barest of audiences, and as casually offering Hans a glass of wine.

'If you want you can use the annexe.'

We were sitting out in the courtyard, Beth's basket set down in the shade with a piece of gauze over the lip to protect her from flies. Hans' chair was facing the door to the annexe and registering his complete shock, I'd knew Justine had placed it there on purpose. 'Justine,' he protested, 'no one could possibly live in it especially not with a baby; it's a complete shambles.'

She wasn't looking at him, staring down at her nails, gently pushing back the cuticles one by one. I hid a smile. 'Oh no,' her tone was airy, 'it's quite the opposite. Your sister gave me the idea to renovate the rooms and lease them out; they're quite lovely. Of course, I'll need to charge you a substantial rent. Unfortunately, I had to buy a new front door, the other was rotten.'

'How could you?' he bellowed, momentarily forgetting he was the supplicant, forced to crawl across the floor on bended knees. 'The glass in that door was worth a fortune.'

Her reply came almost sugary sweet. '*Chéri*, how do you think I paid for the renovations? I received a fortune for it. Come and see.'

Ten minutes later, Hans came back out into the courtyard where I was sitting, nonchalantly swinging Beth in her basket from one hand. He looked almost happy. 'I'm off to fetch our stuff. Justine says there's a key?'

I pointed to the set on the table, obviously new, the brass clean and shiny.

'She loves me really.'

I hugged him. 'You won't...'

'Play the fool again?' He looked rueful. 'Most likely but Justine knows that.'

'It'll take time,' I warned, metaphorically wagging my finger.

'Oh no, it won't.' He smiled, full of confidence now. He leaned back against the door frame. 'One good picture, that's all it'll take.'

I envied his confidence and his happy ending. He didn't deserve it. Even Ruth had in the end generously fallen on her sword and departed for America. I was overcome with sadness, at long last understanding what Pappy had once tried to share with me ... that the family's incarceration in the camp, short though it was, had left an indelible mark on her. Would she find her happy ending? I fingered the envelope in my pocket, Ruth's words resonating through my fingers. Maybe not, but perhaps the only one possible.

'You think I should forgive him?'

Justine wandered out from the annexe, carefully locking the door after her. Strangely, the new paint and paper had spread an air of gaiety over the entire house, so much so that I imagined the gargoyles smiling down from their rooftop perch. I checked the lightness of her stance, aware Hans was the cause, her feet almost gliding across the floor. 'For the sitting room.' She showed me a scrap of fabric. 'Tempi,' she swore, her warm tone sullied by impatience. 'It's Sunday tomorrow and the fabric shop in Flambeau will be shut. I wanted to buy some material for Beth's room.' She darted back into the kitchen and I heard the sound of the fridge door opening.

'Do you think I should forgive him?' she repeated as she emerged from the kitchen clutching a fresh bottle of white wine and two glasses.

'No.' I raised my eyebrows, displaying my astonishment. That was something else I had acquired living with Justine, her face and body frequently replacing the need for an explanation. Not the swearing. Maybe on occasions it proved appropriate, but I still politely declined.

'You're missing out on one of the greatest achievements of language,' she teased, when I told her.

'Forgive him? No, not yet.' I softened my refusal. 'I love Hans, he's my brother so of course I do, nevertheless, he treated you very shabbily.'

'Yes, and look what's come out of it, a repentant lover and a beautiful baby.' She skirted over the anger and sadness it had also brought. 'Although I doubt if Beth'll be a ballerina, not if she takes after Hans.' She raised her glass. 'How long should I make him suffer do you think, before I let him back into my bed?'

27

I waited for Hans to return, the Renault crammed with his belongings, then, muttering something about needing to cash up, ran back down to the shop and phoned Yöst.

I'm not sure anyone noticed my departure, Justine prattling on about the changes having a baby in the house would bring. That morning she had received a new contract and she waved the typed pages in the air, pinpointing phrases and reading them out aloud, wanting me to share in the compliments and plaudits she had received for her role in Giselle. I was so pleased for her. Even if Hans had failed to return, her future was settled, sprinkled with the starlight she had dreamed of throughout her childhood.

I didn't hurry, wandering through the courtyard idly plucking a leaf here or a flower there, thinking about the many stories I'd been party to despite not really taking part – always watching from the side lines. I had told Yöst before I left that my story was not yet begun; would it ever? Or was I to remain like the proverbial automobile that inexplicably refuses to start, despite numerous people peering under the bonnet, while the engine coughed and spluttered, easing into life just briefly before fading away again. Everyone needed a story to pass down to future generations. Meneer Meijer's story may have run its course, but his children would keep that alive, telling anecdotes from their childhood whenever they met up. As for the rest – Berthe and Pappy – their stories were still in the making, while Justine and Hans, theirs was at the very beginning, with everything to look forward to and to live for. And while fame and fortune were waiting up ahead in Ruth's story, I also hoped it would bring with it a measure of happiness, her letter to me generous. Only Pieter was still denied a story – the sunlight that had once enveloped him extinguished by the black hole into which he had fallen.

Yöst answered on the third ring. 'Is everything all right?'

'Yes, is Zande there? I need to speak to him. I had a letter from Ruth. She says Meneer Meijer has left me the house. It has to be a mistake? Why would he do that?'

I heard the sharp intake of breath. 'Zande's here. I'll give him a shout.'

A confused muttering came from the background. 'Zande says he has no need of it and, according to Uncle Albert, you do.'

Yöst's voice faded becoming muffled and I guessed his hand was blocking the receiver. I caught the word 'no' forcefully said and then, 'she made her position quite clear,' and recognised the old Zande, angry and full of pain. 'No!' he said again.

Another silence, followed by a string of gobbledygook, impossible to decipher.

Had the party line become crossed and I was listening to one of our landlord's children rowing with a friend, and not Zande and Yöst at all?

The voices continued reverberating back and forth and I heard Zande's troubled tones again. 'It won't change my decision, how can it?'

Then Yöst's voice, quieter now and quite clear. 'It's a week to the wedding. At least, do that for me, spend it with her. It might change things.'

The silence was deafening.

'How the hell can it?'

Another silence, then more confused muttering. 'All right,' Zande shouted, 'you win.'

I waited.

'Maidy.' The line cleared. 'No doubt you heard some of that. Yöst really can be a stubborn ass sometimes. My sister Tania is being married in a week's time and he was planning to invite you to go with him. He's changed his mind. Insists the journey will be too tiring. It won't of course – that's just his way of forcing my hand.' I heard the indrawn breath, his next words stilted. 'I know we broke up but… as I'm going, I'll take you if you want.' He still sounded angry.

I don't know where my reply came from, perhaps a stray memory of similar situations when Zande became insufferable if allowed his own way.

'No! You don't have to take me anywhere, if it's that much of a problem.'

'You don't want to go with me?' His voice held disbelief.

'I didn't say that.'

'You're angry.'

'So are you,' I shouted, furious with myself for being so very stupid. I should have left it. Never go back, I reminded myself.

'Only because Yöst is shouting at me.'

'I don't believe you. I can't imagine Yöst ever losing his temper.'

'He doesn't.' Laughter entered Zande's speech. 'I find it totally infuriating. He's no fun. Where are you living?' The light tone held but there was underlying strain there too.

'Flambeau.'

'I've got another week.' I heard the slight hesitation before the words, 'Can we meet up and spend it together?'

A storm of arguments and counter arguments started up. Hadn't I already wept an ocean of tears? Did I really want to put myself through it again? 'In Paris, you turned away; you didn't even acknowledge me.' I kept my tone level, attempting to ignore the rapid pounding of my heart.

'No, you're wrong. *I'd never turn away from you.* It was the shock of seeing Ruth. I can't explain it otherwise… Please believe me. Magrit.' My name sounded like a caress. 'I said I would return if you wanted me to. Do you? Please say yes.'

At that moment I understood what Yöst had meant when he told me I would have a decision to make. It was there waiting… a fifty-fifty choice. Except, if I said no, I would inherit a lifetime of bitterness and regret.

And if I said yes? Was I prepared to reap a whirlwind of joy and happiness that might last no more than a moment or two? My life flipped past dull and uneventful…

'Yes.'

A brief silence. I heard the intake of breath.

'All right then. How about tomorrow morning – at ten?' His voice had regained its control. 'Yöst will be pleased and most likely become quite insufferable as a result.' I imagined his eyes lighting up, laughing at me down the telephone. 'You know where.'

Justine was furious when I told her. 'And suddenly he's respectable?' she flung at me, when I mentioned we were going to a wedding together in Holland.

'I never said he wasn't respectable.' I refilled the ice tray, placing it back in the freezer.

'If you are going to quibble over semantics, the word you used was suitable. It amounts to the same thing.'

'And Hans is, I suppose?'

'In about twenty years – maybe.' Her glower was replaced by an ironic smile. 'Maidy, is it worth going back? Look how miserable you were first-time round.'

'So were you, when Hans left, and you're willing to chance it.'

We were in the kitchen preparing dinner, although I doubted any of us would bother over much; the heat and humidity of the previous days affecting everyone, tourists and residents alike, everyone lacklustre and wilting like flowers in their containers, desperate for a drink.

'Oh, Justine, please be happy for me. Even if it's only for a week, it will be my week.'

'*Chérie*, believe me I am happy for you.' Flashing her glorious smile, she pointed up at the skies; the fearsome heat trapped by heavy cloud stealing the daylight. 'In this heat, it's impossible to sound enthusiastic about anything.' She picked up the tray, meaning to carry it into the annexe where we were eating, Hans refusing to leave Beth alone. She hesitated. 'I warned you about beautiful men making rotten husbands.'

I blushed. 'He's not mentioned marriage.'

'No, but you've been thinking about it?'

'No... I... Why would you say that?'

'Because you're a girl and we are programmed to think that way.'

Yes, I had thought of marriage, feloniously skirting around the single impediment to any relationship between us. Sometimes, unable to sleep, I'd carry my dreaming with me to the window, where the stillness of the night was fragranced with music and laughter, and only happy endings were allowed.

Abruptly, there was a crack of thunder and the sky flashed with light, an entrée to a loss of power that sent us scrabbling around for candles, the promised rain unleashing its torrents on the hillside. After less than a minute, the gargoyles, silent since my return from Paris, added their voices to the cacophony of sound, gurgling and gasping in celebration as thunder rolled and roared.

There was little sleep for any of us apart from Beth while the storm raged. Not wanting to leave burning candles unattended, we gathered in the living room, Justine and Hans chatting amicably and no longer tip-toeing around one another. Perhaps that was the effect of the storm, a force far greater than all of us. Hopefully, both were having thoughts about a future together and for all the difficulties and impediments to be washed away down the drain with the storm water.

I was up early, chatting with Hans in his own kitchen while he gave Beth her bottle, amused to participate in a conversation that dwelt exclusively on the well-being of his small daughter, explaining carefully that he wasn't planning to ask Justine to care for her while he painted. 'I'll take her with me. To be honest…' He coloured, his cheeks flushing with embarrassment. 'I never thought I'd be saying these words but I can't bear Beth to be out of sight longer than a moment or two.'

Now, as I ran through the grounds, anxious not to be late, I wondered if either had given thought to the delicate question of where they were to live? I wasn't going to raise it, content with our freedom from stress and strain, the music from Justine's studio a stately gavotte.

That morning, afraid my happiness might incite the envy of one or other of the gods, I had put on a blouse and skirt, my usual attire for the shop. Now I wished I'd worn a dress – maybe the one sprinkled with gentian flowers that Zande insisted matched the colour of my eyes. He hadn't arrived, and after glancing at my watch for the hundredth time and telling myself perhaps he'd changed his mind, all at once I saw him, loping down the lane from the bus stop.

'You'd think by now I'd have learned not to argue with Yöst,' he greeted me.

Naturally, he had set the scene. It would have appealed to his Machiavellian sense of humour to duplicate the exact circumstance of our breakup. But the smile he gave me was neither triumphant nor exultant. Instead, it was that tiny uncertain softening of his lips and I realised he was equally as unsure about the wisdom of our meeting up as Justine had been.

'Can you hang on?' he swung his bag, 'while I get rid of this. Have you had breakfast? I doubt it.' He didn't wait for my reply. 'I'll order us some.'

At his approach the concierge dropped her knitting in her lap and raised both hands in greeting. I heard her exclamation of joy, followed by a flood of words. Zande laughed and, wrapping an arm around her, kissed her on her cheek – not the traditional salute, a kiss on either side, this was a personal gift from him to a friend. I remember someone saying, maybe Meneer Meijer, that everyone loved Zande and flocked to him like a moth to a flame. For the elderly woman, it was a very kindly flame. No doubt, that day she would return home and smile at her husband.

'What were you and Yöst arguing about?' I said as he reappeared.

'You.' He led the way into the garden, where a rattle of crockery indicated the presence of other guests. 'I left because we had reached an impasse. Yöst said I had been born with a yellow streak, after all.'

'Did he?' I sat down at the table he indicated, a waiter bustling up and pouring us both a coffee. How sensible of Zande to get the difficulties out of the way in public, so neither of us could stamp our feet or scream. 'What about?'

He glanced back over his shoulder at the people breakfasting, an amused smile on his face.

'You can read my mind now,' I shot at him.

'It was a guess. I hate people listening to my secrets.' He reached across the table taking my hand. 'Yöst says, I'm scared of finding happiness. But, if we want to be together, we shouldn't let pride stop us.' His eyes laughed at me from across the table. 'Naturally, he was talking about me. He had once faced the same dilemma, and that took years to resolve.'

Silence fell.

His expression changed, pain taking over. 'Magrit, we've never really talked about what I am. Not really, yet it's what makes me.' I leaned forward wanting to object to his use of the term what. 'No,' he placed his fingers on my lips. 'Let me finish. This unbelievable wondrous event that still happens to a few of us…' His mouth twisted. 'You might well say lucky few because our heritage is still considered wondrous by the older generation; yet because of it we are forced to hide away in the shadows. And because of it, there is a wall between us.'

A momentary silence fell. I sensed him struggling with something and waited.

'You heard about Waldger?' He raised his head, and I was surprised to see anger rather than grief.

I nodded. 'Yes, I'm so sorry.'

'That's why Waldger took his life. He wanted to walk in the sunlight and I failed him.'

Remembering Jaan's words about Zande pushing him to find a cure, I thought back to the day Tristan died, and Zande's anger and grief on that occasion. I understood, of course I did. This was Zande; his friends were his responsibility.

'What happens to us in the future has to be your decision.' He kissed my hand. 'Because it's your brick wall. This week, though, can we at least pretend it doesn't exist and not let it come between us?'

Only spits and spots of conversation from the next few days were memorable, at least for me, because for the very first time in my life, I was doing the talking, using words formerly spoken only to my bedroom walls. Were any worth remembering? That no longer mattered only his reaction to them.

Sometimes, most of the time, we were so close in our thoughts, we might have been cloned from a single element. Yet, rarely his mind wandered away into some other place, like the moon orbiting Earth, where I couldn't follow, as if trying to reach a decision about something. Then gathering himself together, he would kiss me, wanting to make up for his momentary lapse in concentration and embark on a story about his childhood and a glade in the woods which his sister insisted belonged to the fairies, and only they had permission to use it.

We didn't go far not like before, and once the grass by the river had dried, that's mostly where we spent our days, sitting side by side while families with children played on the bank, and I told him about growing up in that large house riddled with staircases that became the focus of our childish games. Pieter was there, of course he was, he had formed the largest part of my childhood and I wouldn't hide it, not from Zande. His eagerness for every detail never wavered, he reminded me of a squirrel hoarding great quantities of nuts for the winter. 'If I tell you everything now,' I protested, 'what will we talk about over the years.'

'There aren't sufficient days left in the world for that to happen,' he replied and kissed me.

Then as the sun sloped down towards the horizon and the slate blue of the evening sky replaced it, our conversation lapsed into nonsensical murmurings in which our thoughts at ease with one another wandered down pathways of little interest to anyone apart from ourselves.

Certainly not Justine and Hans. Their relationship that had gone through so much was gently searching out a new path and each day, from a starting point of anger, hurt and shame, it was achieving solid ground. Beth of course was responsible for that and with her as the fulcrum, I knew they would stay together. I felt the same about Zande and me, the mistakes of the past too far distant to hurt either of us. And when Hans offered to run the shop for a morning, I introduced Zande to Justine. We had drunk coffee together, and Zande charmed her as he had first charmed me – talking knowledgably about the theatre.

'How do you know about theatres?' I said almost jealous of Justine's attention.

'Maestro and Rico. Once or twice when I took a holiday from my work, I travelled with them.'

And on the Thursday afternoon, with the sky once again overcast and threatening rain, and with our idyll fast drawing to a close, we danced. Justine was away in Bordeaux, her success in Paris prompting an invitation to dance at a gala.

'Show him the house by all means but please remind him, this is not a *carte blanche*. What am I saying? I'd better tell him that since your feet are no longer on the ground,' she exclaimed, with a wry smile in my direction.

I blushed. 'There's no need, he's a changed man.'

'*Mon Dieu!* What naivety. I shall instantly telegraph the theatre asking them to cancel the performance,' she teased. 'It's against the laws of nature for a man to become *a changed man*.'

But he was.

And so, leaving the grey clouds outside, we took the sunshine inside with us and playing the music that Justine danced to when she was happy, we also danced. And, of course, that too Zande did well.

'Is there nothing you can't do?' I asked laughing and almost out of breath.

He didn't reply. Reaching up, I brushed the corner of his

mouth with my fingers, smoothing the twist of pain away. Changing the record to a slower tempo, he took me in his arms again, closer this time, my face nestled against his shoulder, our bodies merging in the rhythm of the music, his hand clasping mine. I felt the melody vibrating inside me, the tension building between us, our bodies taut with longing.

Abruptly, he drew away. Walking over to the record player, he switched it off. 'Once again, we've come full circle.'

We had and I knew it. 'Yes,' I begged, 'but please don't ask that question again.'

He nodded and drew me to him. 'No, I won't ask, not again.'

28

The journey up north, long though it was, provided relief from feelings that had overwhelmed us both. It was then I understood the extent of Zande's forethought. Predicting this might happen, he had set out to create a cornucopia of memories so that now we could sit side by side and revisit those tales of friends and family so carefully crafted in the early part of the week. I was grateful to have them and whenever he thought me absorbed in the pages of a book, I was most likely retracing the steps we had taken together in the last few days and delighting in them.

Occasionally, the close attention of the men in our railway carriage provoked a jealous frown, especially when their gaze lingered longer than was strictly polite, and I teased about it, reminding him of his own inadequacies in that department, until he joined in my laughter, insisting that the leopard in him hadn't yet changed all its spots. Though not until we reached Paris did we become truly invisible, people there too preoccupied to care about anyone else. Then, once again, he took my hand guiding me through the crowds of people, the majority of whom were heading in the direction we wanted to go, towards the Gare du Nord. And shortly after, with its wheels clattering across the points, even the train spoke a different language, the language

I had grown up with and one he also knew well. It too brought back memories until, finally, we reached the outskirts of the city where it all began.

If I had expected to feel both sorrowful and awkward on entering the little house, with its turreted roof and pocket handkerchief of a garden, I was wrong. There was no discomfort, instead a feeling of homecoming, as if Meneer Meijer had called out to me from the kitchen or from upstairs: 'Come in, make yourself at home, I won't be a moment.'

'Tania promised me whatever happens in the future, you would be happy here.'

I paid little attention to the comment and in hindsight I should have – too busy exclaiming, 'This is perfect. This is where I will write my books,' immersed in a future with Zande in it. There was a wooden bench-seat tucked under the tiny balcony and, after supper, we sat there, my arm tucked through his, my head resting on his shoulder.

Lulled into a sense of false security, I found myself skipping forward a half century just to continue this on-going sense of peace, our thoughts as quiescent as the canal water that drifted languorously past. By then, we would have prevailed against the brick wall and done our raging and our shouting, and have lived our lives happy for the most part, courtesy of this tiny house, and reached some sort of harbour.

'It was always a happy place,' Zande commented, 'even with war raging across the continent. That was Tante Marie's doing – she reminded me of a mother duck fiercely protective of her brood. One thing, though, I do regret.'

'What?' I said, barely attending – happy, just happy.

'When we moved here from Herrendorp, we didn't change schools. Uncle Albert figured the upheaval too great. For all sorts of reasons, I wish we had. To think you were close by all that time and I never knew.'

I frowned. 'I'm glad.'

'Never!' He raised our joined hands, staring at them quizzically. 'Why?'

'You'd never have noticed me – especially after Ruth joined the school; all the boys were in love with her.'

'Probably,' I picked up on the teasing tone. 'But I have noticed you now. Yöst was right.'

He stretched his long legs, reminding me of a cat comfortable in this new environment, his body relaxed staring out into the darkness, only the gentle slap of the water against the bridge breaking the silence.

'About what?' Still not paying attention, adrift in my boat of dreams.

'The reason for our dispute.'

'You said…' I broke in.

'I say a lot of things.' The airy tone was back and I knew if I glanced up, he would be smiling. 'So does Yost. He's become a real nag,' he added mischievously. 'He told me, if anyone could alter my mind about the future, you could. When I asked him why, he said because you asked nothing of the people around you.'

'But I…'

He dropped a kiss on my nose. 'It's true. With you at my side, life may be worth living.' Getting to his feet, he pulled me up with him. 'Not quite how I imagined our first night together,' he murmured, sounding rueful. He took my hands, raising my eyes to his. 'Do you know how hard it is for a man to want something so badly and know he can't have it?'

'Zande, I…'

'No.' He grimaced, his eyes mocking the strictures he had placed on himself. 'It would be too easy, Magrit.'

'And if there was no brick wall between us?'

I didn't mean to say those words but suddenly there they were.

I saw the hope in his eyes. 'Are you sure?'

'I think I must be. We…'

'Then say it again tomorrow when you are certain.'

Next morning, we didn't sail, taking the ferry across the lake to Norland instead. It made sense, the crossing reduced to just over an hour. After that night three years ago, I had wished never to see Klüsta ever again, yet its menacing heights were impossible to ignore, cycling past it on my way to and from college, although I had kept my promise and never once looked directly at it. Now I was forced to, the steamer captain calling out the island's history over the megaphone, and hiding my disquiet by fixing my gaze on a skein of migrating geese flying south.

'Those rocks, they are not called the Devil's Hand for nothing,' he bellowed in both Dutch and English, to the fifty or so other passengers all, apart from us, visiting the cheese factory and village. 'That is where in the war, hundreds of prisoners died. The night it happened some believe an angel appeared.'

'The Headman, Meneer Fleurie, will greet us when we dock,' Zande took my hand as the steamer, after running up the west side of the lake, pulled into the dockside at Norland. 'It's traditional. He's not comfortable about opening the village to the world but puts up with it because it provides a good income.' He pointed along the street, where tables had been set up with pairs of decorative clogs stacked on them.

'Is that where Mevrouw Meijer's clogs came from.'

'Yes. Yöst spent one winter with the farmers learning how to make cheese, I did too but that was later. With his first wages he bought us each a pair of clogs. Mine had birds on them and…'

'Your aunt's,' I broke in, 'flowers. Forget-me-nots.'

He squeezed my hand.

Nevertheless, despite the numbers, the old man greeted everyone with a firm handshake, his wife standing by his side, bobbing a curtsey.

She was dressed in a black patterned blouse and matching dirndl skirt, as were the group of young girls whose job it was to give out leaflets about the history of the village. I had chosen the dress I wore to Ruth's wedding with a jacket over, for the early morning air was chill, a reminder that autumn would soon be returning to the northern skies. On the steamer, with everyone else in trousers or sweaters and skirts, I had felt overdressed. Now, I was glad.

'Remember I told you about Hörst? He's Yöst's best friend and I always hoped he would marry Tania. He took a long time about it,' Zande added with a grin, 'a bit like you. That was his home during the war.' He pointed to the windmill which dominated the village like some benevolent overlord.

Although I was familiar with its image, which was used on both their butter and cheese labels, neither had prepared me for the reality; its height and massive girth reducing the street of houses to Lilliputian size, cattle grazing the distant fields little bigger than a child's toy.

He took my hand, raising it to his lips, my pulse pounding away at his touch. 'Luckily, he saw sense just in time. As did I.'

Yes, I wanted to shout out, unbelieving of the change in him. Throughout our week of talking and love-making, the tension that had dominated his voice when arguing with Yöst had lessened but not gone away – not entirely. Once or twice, in the middle of telling me something, he would come to an abrupt halt, momentarily staring off into the distance, before picking up the thread where it had broken off. 'One day, Maidy, I will tell you, but not today,' he would reply when I asked.

Now that tension had gone.

Justine had once commented the age difference made him a man while I was still only a young girl. She was so wrong. He resembled a colt allowed out into the meadow for the first time; his eager glance taking in everything around us as if he had never seen them before. 'You look wonderful,' he had said, when with a teacloth tied around my waist, I prepared breakfast for us both. 'From now on breakfast will be my favourite meal but only if you are there.'

'And because Yöst couldn't make the wedding,' Zande was still talking. 'Tania and Hörst have decided to spend a part of their honeymoon with him.'

The little church was full, the regular congregation swollen by tourists standing at the back, wanting to add their best wishes to the couple. I recognised a family from the ferry, the men removing their hats as they entered the church. 'One of Hörst's many uncles. His family live on the mainland now and run the shop,' Zande whispered.

There was no organ, only an accordion, its rasping cadences too sour for the lovely vision that was the bride. A series of loud thumps with a gavel announced her appearance, escorted by the headman, Meneer Fleurie.

Even if I'd grown up disputing the existence of fairies, Tania would have convinced me, her ash-blonde hair scattered across her shoulders like a gossamer shawl, her profile delicate and smiling. Dressed in a cream blouse and long skirt embroidered with flowers, Meneer Fleurie proudly patted her hand all the way down the aisle, and seemed almost reluctant to relinquish it to Hörst.

The service, conducted in the ancient language, none of which I understood, was over in ten minutes. There was an exchange of rings and we came to the bit which I knew to be: now I pronounce you man and wife. At Berthe's wedding, the minister had said to Yoav, 'You may kiss the bride.' Even so, the congregation seemed surprised when the cleric officiating paused. 'For our many guests,' he addressed the congregation in English, 'we have reached the point in this celebration when I bless the couple, pronounce them man and wife and wish them much happiness and many children.'

Up until that moment Zande's expression had been light-hearted, eager even, sharing a smile when I whispered how lovely Tania was, and obviously looking forward to meeting up again with friends. As the words were repeated in formal Dutch, he rocked back on his heels. I watched the blinds come down, anger and something more … defeat … sweep over him.

'What is it?' I whispered as, wanting to display their approval, the congregation burst into both laughter and applause.

He squeezed my arm. 'Nothing.' He forced a wry smile. 'I need fresh air… And no doubt several glasses of wine. Come on, let's get out of here.'

Others had the same idea, and as the bride and groom slowly made their way back down the aisle, we followed. Among the many faces, I recognised Robert van Vliet, Zande's father, in one of the rows. He hadn't changed in four years, maybe the supercilious attitude that I'd already encountered more marked but no older.

Startled, I tugged at Zande's sleeve. 'Have the swans returned to Klüsta?'

'The swans! Why?'

'Your father.' I pointed. 'He's here.' As if he had heard my voice, Van Vliet's gaze immediately focused on me. 'Hadn't you better go over and speak to him?'

Zande didn't reply for a moment and I sensed him struggling to recover his equilibrium.

If so, he didn't succeed. The sneering tone I believed gone for good rang out, his expression bleak, shutting me out. 'Why would I do that; he has every right to be here. After all, he owns most of the land – at least the carinatae do. That's something else I hate about him; he always thinks of it as his land.'

I heard his words but paid them no attention, my own emotions more pressing, dithering between alarm at the thought of the swans return and dread at its implication. Did I even want them here? Yes, Pieter might well be among them… The thought of my brother being so near excited but it also scared me. His return to the city didn't necessarily indicate a change of heart … or that he would visit the family. And the city dwellers, the fishermen? They didn't want the swans; they had made that very clear.

Reduced to silence, we followed the line of people, all of them strolling in the direction of a wooden building, its open doors tied back with white bunting, where tables covered in snowy-white tablecloths laden with glasses of festive wine and cheese had been set up.

Offering me a glass and taking one for himself, Zande downed it in a single gulp. All around both guests and visitors were doing the same; the cheerful banter swelling as the wine took its hold, hands and arms reaching up into the air, to toast the bride and groom.

'Zande, please, talk to me.' I shouted over the press of people laughing and talking. 'What happened in the church?' I persisted.

He replaced the empty glass on the table and picked up another. 'You mean seeing my father isn't enough?'

I eyed him anxiously. 'No. Tell me. We promised no secrets.'

'This isn't a secret,' he retorted harshly, yet even I knew his anger wasn't aimed at me. 'How can it be a secret when an entire congregation heard what the cleric said. Nothing much, just the little matter of pronouncing Tania and Hörst man and wife...'

'There isn't...'

'Oh, but there is,' he anticipated my argument. His voice dropped and I bent forward to catch his words. 'It's the brick wall, that blasted brick wall we can neither climb nor go around. Yes, maybe we can climb over yours because you love me. Not mine.'

His words didn't make any sense and then he was gone, exerting his charm on friends who greeted him with affection, unaware he was deep inside a world only he knew about.

Apart from me.

He didn't return, leaving me to talk and laugh with strangers who had decided, as I had, that's what was expected on festive occasions, the room echoing with cheerful banter. And later in the afternoon, with the ferry sounding its horn, impatient to gather up its passengers and depart, it was Tania who made her way through the crowd to my side.

'I have so longed to meet you. You have brought my brother such happiness, something he has craved since losing Tante Marie. I wish we might have met years ago when we were supposed to, then none of today's difficulties would have existed. At least, now, you have a chance to be together.'

She was older than me, and taller, and up close quite lovely, yet, I found her gaze disconcerting, as if she could read what I was thinking – although at that precise moment, my thoughts were of Yöst and how much she resembled him.

'Do I? That's quite a compliment since Yöst is my favourite person in all the world.' Not waiting for a reply, she continued. 'Didn't Zande tell you the future also formed a part of my gifts.'

'No, he didn't.' I stared across the room, seeing him in conversation with one of the farmers. As if I had called out, he glanced up, his mouth softening in a smile meant only for me, and I felt my rigid fingers relax. Perhaps it would be all right, and I had imagined the air of despair that hung about him like a dark shadow? 'We spoke mainly about your adventures growing up. And how lovely you were. And you are,' I hurried into speech again. Hörst is a lucky man.'

Her laughter was like music. 'I'm the lucky one, he's the brave one.' I must have looked puzzled. 'Knowing who we are, it's not an easy decision to make, is it? Especially for someone like you.' All around us people were chatting, occasionally glancing over at the bride, perhaps thinking our conversation mirrored theirs – idle chitchat, perfect for happy occasions.

'Why me?' I said, alarmed by the direction our conversation was heading in.

She kissed me on the cheek. 'He won't bring a child into this world.'

Was that the wall he found impossible to climb over?

Shocked I took a step back.

Tania must have read my expression. 'You didn't know? Oh, my dear. That's what held Hörst back – the children. Now his siblings and their children will become my family.' Even as I went to question her statement, her expression changed, the gaze resting on my face unfocused – her eyes momentarily vacant. 'Oh no,' she cried out, and heads swung in our direction.

'What is it?'

'It's something else much worse.' Her sight cleared, and she changed the whispered words into laughter. 'The ferry is about to depart and you must leave. And I must find Hörst.'

A kiss as light as a butterfly's wing grazed my cheek and then she was across the room.

'He's over there,' I called after her. She didn't hear or if she did it wasn't Hörst she meant; it was Zande – tugging urgently at his arm.

Abruptly, the room quieted, maybe the tension between them had registered with other guests as it had with me, heads turning to follow their every move.

Were others thinking, as I was, how extraordinary they looked together – the light and the dark – each as beautiful as the other. Singly they might well have passed unnoticed. Together, they were beyond anything mere humanity might create. As the silence deepened, I overheard a scattering of words: *you promised* and *they'll be gone again in a day or so* and saw Zande's shrugged response.

Leaving Tania, he prowled across the room to my side, heads swinging back and forth as if loath to leave Tania behind and settle on something less entrancing.

'I can't bear that she always knows what I plan to do before I do it,' he growled at me. 'I thought she'd left all that nonsense behind.'

'And what are you planning to do?'

Had I expected a snarling response? Taking in the bleakness of his expression … perhaps. Even so, there was no smile when he glanced down at me, only anger and pain, but his voice remained gentle. 'I'm not sure – not yet.'

'Will you tell me when you have made up your mind?'

'You'd trust me to do that?'

'Always.'

For a moment I thought him about to break down, the corners of his eyes sparkling with tears, his body leaning in towards me. Then he swung away and headed for the door.

We left Norland together and yet apart, standing separately on the deck of the ferry, lost in our private world of grief, and not until we were walking back from the harbour with the little house in view, did he take my hand.

He raised it to his lips, and I saw tears on his cheeks. 'I am so sorry to spoil your day, Maidy. Believe me,' his voice cracked. 'I didn't plan it this way. Unfortunately, there's some business that needs attending to and I have to leave you.'

'Business with your father.' It wasn't a guess.

'Yes.'

I wanted to protest … to shout out, *No, you can't leave me or won't it wait until tomorrow? It's our last night together and you promised me a week – one whole week.*

But I had never whined or begged, how could I start now? *Not even when your life depends on it*, I heard my questioning inner voice. *No, not even then.*

I drummed up a smile. 'Our week's not quite up, not until tomorrow.'

'I know it's not.' Returning my smile, he drew me close. 'I was planning on our being together a lot longer than a week. Unfortunately, this business cannot wait.' I pulled my head back, reading the expression in his eyes. They looked despairing and again I wondered what Tania had said to create such agony. 'It concerns my sister and Waldger, and perhaps a few of the others. Oh yes, and Jaan. I forgot about Jaan. It's got to end; it's waited far too long already and only I can end it.' Raising my hand to his lips again, he held it there. 'Thank you, Magrit. Thank you for being you.'

And then he was gone.

I had to go after him. Whatever he was about to face, I would face it too. And afterwards if we couldn't become lovers, I'd take what he could offer and be glad. But not this. Not this.

Life came back into my legs and racing upstairs, I tossed off my beautiful dress, flinging it to the floor like yesterday's rubbish. Yesterday ... why hadn't I known our idyl was about to end so precipitately? Because yesterday I was so lost in love, I could see nothing. Grabbing a pair of flat shoes, I ran after him.

Using the same shortcuts Zande would have used a moment or two before, I cut through the narrow alleys to the inn at the old port, my running footsteps echoing across the paving stones of the courtyard.

To my astonishment, I saw Jaan on the quayside.

'Why didn't you stop him?' I shouted.

Yet not loud enough for him to hear. I called out again.

'Maidy.' He spun round. 'I was on my way to see you. Yöst told me you'd be here. Isn't that Zande?' He pointed to the dinghy with its red sail already rounding the island's southern tip. 'Where's he off to?'

'Klûsta.'

He blanched white. 'You sure he said Klûsta?'

'Yes. We attended Tania's wedding; his father was there. Something to do with all of you.' My words spun out faster and faster. 'He and Tania were quarrelling about it.'

Once before I had seen Jaan in a state of panic. It erupted again now. 'Tania? No, it can't be.'

He swung round, his hand shielding his eyes from sunlight to better follow the pinprick of red sail just disappearing out of sight. 'He promised Yöst.' He shouted the words.

'Jaan! What is it?' I grabbed his arm. 'What did he promise Yöst?'

'Here, take these.' He shoved a thick envelope into my hand and I saw my name, neatly printed on the front. 'I have to stop him. It's not worth it, not for any of us – no one could ask that.' Ignoring my question, he raced down the steps and onto the wooden landing stage, where a lone dinghy was tied up to one of the iron mooring rings on the wall.

A tidal wave of fear swept over me. Ripping open the package I pulled out the deeds to the canal house, the loose sheets a maelstrom of unpronounceable words and meanings. I didn't bother reading them; those pages were unimportant. Like a film contract, it was the few lines at the end that mattered – especially the signature.

The house had been bequeathed to Zande Meijer in its entirety by Albert Meijer. Below was a codicil; the formal words repeated, only the date and the name different – my name, Magrit Bader, staring back at me from the page.

That's why Yöst had sent Zande to me, convinced I could change his mind.

And I had … I had.

'I'm coming with you,' I shouted, racing down the steps. Tripping on the last one, I grabbed Jaan's arm to stop myself falling. 'When I asked you about the book before, you lied to me. You had already found it, hadn't you?'

Somehow, I was in the dinghy with Jaan already raising the mast. 'We'll have to sail.' He ignored my words. 'We daren't use the short crossing, the jetty was washed away in a storm.'

There was no storm – not like the night I searched for Ruth but everything else was the same, with its desperate need for resolution. 'Jaan,' I shouted. 'What did he promise Yöst? Tell me, please.'

He glanced up from fixing the pins in the base of the mast to keep it upright. 'I didn't lie.' He ignored my plea. 'It wasn't a book, only an account of the initiation ceremony of a new leader, the Black, written in ancient script. Yöst found it among Albert Meijer's possessions and gave it to me to translate. I doubt he'd ever once looked at it,' he excused the elderly man.

'And you told Zande.'

'No! We both know what he's like. I didn't even know he was in the house. He wasn't, not when I arrived, I'd swear it. I'd travelled down specially to talk with Yöst, to decide what we should do. He must have arrived soon after and you know how acute our hearing is.' He was shouting, not with anger – with despair. 'It could only end if the Black were to die and for there to be no heir. A single line of writing.' As he had always done in times of stress, Jaan whipped off his glasses. 'I should have burned it, not scrupulously translated each word, thinking how clever I was to have fathomed out the ancient language. It wasn't much, at most a paragraph and in it a few lines about primogeniture – the rights of the eldest to inherit all. The remainder was about the ceremony of the celeste and the rules and obligations of the newly fledged. Van Vliet, Zande's father, he must have known. Yes, of course he knew.' His words sounded despairing. 'Zande told me that was the first thing the Black always said when welcoming the new fledglings, for them to sire sons ... him too.'

I remembered the swans that flocked the shores; they too had once been human and most would have sired children.

'When Zande confronted Yöst, there was the most unholy row.' Jaan didn't look at me and I guessed the words he was about to speak hurt but that wouldn't stop him saying them. He had always believed in playing fair. 'That's why he sent Zande back to Flambeau. A few days ago, he rang. Said he was happy and promised not to argue anymore. Why would he change his mind?' Jaan continued his train of thought. 'And why today of all days, Tania's wedding day?'

I watched the main sail, a tight bundle of cloth first unravel and then rise slowly up the mast. I wanted to scream aloud my plea for him to hurry, every move reducing the time left for Zande and me.

Then we were moving, my thoughts stuck in a groove repeating the words *at last he was happy* over and over. Tania had known – that's what she had seen, disguising it with a laugh and some nonsense about the ferry.

It didn't make sense. None of it made sense. Why, if at last he was happy?

I heard the shouting as we reached the cove. Protected by raging currents, up close its looming cliffs denied the presence of a landing place, and I was astonished to see a wooden jetty with boats tied up, Zande's among them. He hadn't hurried, deliberately tying off the sail and coiling each of the ropes neatly on their cleats, and I prayed for the outcome still to be in doubt.

I didn't notice anything else, already chasing up the steep path towards the sound and I would have fallen had Jaan not taken my arm, the ground rough and broken.

'This whole area was destroyed in the war and we've been working on it.'

Stopping to catch my breath, I stared round seeing evidence of its dark history, boulders scattered like chess pieces, even lichen reluctant to set down roots in this hostile place.

Still holding my hand, Jaan guided me through a narrow cut in the side of the cliff. It wasn't dark, lanterns reflecting off the rock floor. Rounding a snag in the rock, we emerged into daylight again, my sight taking precious seconds to recover. Below was a great oval space, perhaps created aeons ago by a meteor strike, its ferocious heat leaving the rock surface smooth and unblemished. I saw people and a collection of gaily caparisoned huts, tiny against the bracelet of jagged peaks encircling them.

I wasn't interested in them, only in finding Zande. He had

to be here somewhere. Then I caught sight of Tania, Hörst's arm around her.

For a moment I thought myself mistaken. This was their wedding day, and by now she and Hörst would have departed for the mainland to catch their train.

She saw me in the same moment and ran over. 'Please, this is all my fault. I believed it settled between us. We returned as soon as I discovered differently but he refuses to listen. *Please*, help us.'

I didn't need to ask what was settled, nor why Zande refused to listen. I knew – perhaps I had always known.

Then I saw him, my line of sight following the cries of the villagers: men, women, a few children even – swans too, two dozen or more, adding their discordant hiss to the general melee. Echoing back from the rockface, the sound slowly grew into a vast chorus of noise, people, their faces tilted upwards, their outstretched arms imploring, pointing to the source of their alarm, the cliff top where two men were locked in an embrace. I recognised the distinctive fair colouring of Van Vliet, their leader, grappling his son and heir, Zande, his brown skin even from a distance visibly marked and bleeding.

It was useless to shout, any noise I made would be instantly swallowed up in the cacophony of outrage swelling up from the crowd. I couldn't run and stop them either, even if Jaan's arm around my shoulder hadn't been holding me back, the press of the crowd too great. Nevertheless, I couldn't understand why no one else was attempting to scale the heights and stop the fight. I know I screamed at Jaan to let me try. Yet, even standing next to me, he didn't hear.

The figures vanished – so suddenly, it was like a physical shock, the loud scream originating from the crowd slowly fading and dying away. At first, I believed them hidden behind a rock. Then I spotted the black feathers and vast wingspan of a pair of swans, their wings undulating as they did for battle, their long necks striking, entangled – disentangling only to make the next blow harder – striking again and again. How long were we watching: seconds, minutes, hours, days… The whole of my life? That's what it felt like.

Then suddenly, with a chorus of screaming to accompany them, the entwined mass was tumbling down the rock-strewn slope, swiftly gathering speed as it fell.

Did one attempt to get away and take to the air?

I couldn't tell, the sequence of images passing across my vision too fast for recognition. Flailing helplessly, the black-winged bodies remained locked together as their momentum thrust them out over the lip of the waterfall, tumbling in slow motion through the torrent of water. Wings caught on a jutting rock and I felt the shock strike deep within my own body, my arms ripped from their sockets, watching the man I loved and his father battle it out for supremacy. They struck the ground, crashing into the jagged edge of the rock basin.

Jaan and I were first to reach them, fear now paralysing the limbs and vocal cords of the onlookers, including their audience of swans – all of them silent. One of the fallen shapes was already changing, his humanity restored. I understood what that signified, I had seen it before. Slowly, the blond features of Robert van Vliet emerged.

I knelt by the second shape, my hand resting gently on the black feathers, the ability of those born carinatae to change their shape from human into a swan no longer a barrier to the love between us. Gasping for breath, the dark plumage was replaced by Zande's flesh, torn by the rocks, broken and bleeding.

'You can't die,' I stormed at him, as Jaan covered him with his jacket, 'I won't let you.'

The grip on my hand tightened, and light crept back into the dulling eyes, giving me hope.

He smiled. No longer mocking but gentle and full of love. 'I always said you weren't good for me, Maidy, because you made me want to be a better man.'

'But you were always a better man,' I gulped, trying to hide my tears. 'The only person who didn't know it was you – everyone…' I flung my arm out wildly, 'else did.'

Looking up at Jaan, Zande asked the question. No words – nevertheless, Jaan understood. 'Yes, Zande, it's happening. They're changing. See for yourself.' With his arms cradling Zande's body, Jaan raised him off the ground, the effort bathing Zande's face in sweat.

All about us, where once swans had gathered, the ground was covered in feathers like a sudden snow shower and men were standing up on legs they had almost forgotten how to use, hastily grabbing towels and pieces of clothing to cover themselves.

'Maidy, is Pieter among them, I can't see?'

On first noticing the bevy of swans, Pieter had been far from my mind, every emotion reserved for Zande. As a final act of love, I searched about recognising my brother, unchanged after all these years, a lock of fair hair falling across his eyes.

I knew then, why. 'Yes.'

'That's all right then.' Zande gave a sigh. 'I've paid my debt.'

'Zande, you didn't – you couldn't – not for me.'

I felt the pain of tears deep inside of me.

'No, Maidy. It was time for it to end. Too many have suffered because of who we are. And you wanted children.' He raised his hand as I tried to deny this, his voice gentling and weary. 'In Paris, I saw your face when you were holding the little girl. Besides, isn't that what the marriage service is all about?' A trace of his old arrogance sounded. 'And we are very good at begetting children.' His words faded and I held my breath, only releasing it as his voice gathered strength again. 'I loved you too much to let you live my life and so I gave you Pieter instead.'

It was so like Zande. The master of the unexpected and despite my tears, I smiled. 'That's not fair, I never gave you anything.'

He held my glance, his fingers tightening with the effort. 'Yes, you did. You gave me memories and those I am planning to take with me.'

He smiled and I kissed the corner of his mouth. It trembled under my lips and then lay still. I closed his eyes on the world and turned away, allowing Jaan and Hörst carry his broken body, like some fallen emperor, down to the cove where the boat he designed and built waited for his return.

Above the sun was setting into its colours of crimson and

pink heralding the end of yet another day. Tomorrow would mark the first dawning of a new world in which Zande played no part.

Epilogue

I wouldn't despair; Zande wouldn't have wanted that, reserving my tears for when I am alone in my bed. It could never have ended well, and not all the begging and pleading to the gods could ever have made it so. By winning the fight against his father, Zande had finally set to rights all the hurts and grievances that had blocked his desperate wish for a normal life.

I won't wither away either. Few people are loved as I have been – so deeply that he was willing to sacrifice his own life to give me back my brother. Now, at last, Pieter can go home. I looked about me at the milling figures, but saw no further sign of him. Perhaps he has already set out on his journey, safe in the knowledge that, finally, he might hold up his head again. And soon, once his hand and his eye have grown accustomed to handling tools, he will fulfil his dream of becoming a master craftsman, able to make beautiful mirrors exactly as Pappy has always done. And he will marry, of course he will. Maybe not for love, I doubt anyone can replace Ruth, and he and Berthe will fill the house with their children and Pappy will learn how to smile again and make jokes.

And me? I will go back to the vineyard and we will bury Zande there. With Meneer Meijer's death, Yöst has already assumed responsibility for the carinatae's affairs, and he will redistribute the land and bank accounts between the surviving men. And men will gather to pay their respects, as they did for Waldger. Jaan will be among them, and in the twilight, no longer able to rise up into the skies in tribute, they will reminisce about Zande, and Yöst will finally relinquish the epithet, *he was the best of us all* that had once applied to him. And on a day full of sunshine, Jaan and I will lay flowers on Zande's grave.

And then I will dance, because Rico once promised me dancing banishes the demons.

But not yet. For now, whenever I stamp my feet in their broad-heeled shoes and flick my skirt in derision, I want to recall the arms that were wrapped around me in a dance of love.

But one day, I will.

And then, with my grief all burned away, I will return home.

Not to the Bader house, except one time to collect my grandmother's shawl and to wrap my arms around Pappy's neck and kiss him goodbye. He will understand without asking my reasons for not returning – that I know too much of our history for the house ever to be comfortable again with me in it.

I won't go far and, wanting to smoke his pipe, when Pappy takes his daily walk along the canal, once in a while his feet will carry him along the little passageways in the direction of a tiny house that nestles into a bridge – both the smallest and the oldest in the city. And we will drink coffee together.

And one day Jaan and I will marry. Zande was right. That moment in Paris, he had seen in my face that I wanted children. And I will wrap my firstborn in my grandmother's shawl and when she is old enough to listen to my stories, I will tell her a fairy story about a man with golden wings – and she will know by the expression on my face that it is true.

The End

Sunset on Golden Wings is the sequel to *The Year the Swans Came*, and chronologically follows Book 3 in the Children of Zeus Series.

If you have enjoyed our story, discover how it all began with:
The Click of a Pebble, An Ocean of White Wings, The Drumming of Heels,
the prequel trilogy, Children of Zeus

Learn more about Barbara Spencer

Website: https://www.barbaraspencer.co.uk

WordPress: https://picturesfromthekitchen.wordpress.com/2021/02/25/the-making-of-a-legend/

Facebook: https://www.facebook.com/Barbaraspencerauthor

Twitter: https://twitter.com/BarbaraSpencerO

Lightning Source UK Ltd.
Milton Keynes UK
UKHW011252130521
383658UK00001B/31